FALLEN GODS

Quintin Jardine

headline

First published in 2003
by HEADLINE BOOK PUBLISHING

10 9 8 7 6 5 4 3 2 1

Cataloguing in Publication Data is available from the British Library

ISBN 0 7472 7448 7 (hardback)
ISBN 0 7553 0151 X (trade paperback)

Typeset in Times by Avon DataSet Ltd,
Bidford-on-Avon, Warwickshire

Printed and bound in Great Britain by
Mackays of Chatham plc, Chatham, Kent

HEADLINE BOOK PUBLISHING
A division of Hodder Headline
338 Euston Road
London NW1 3BH

www.headline.co.uk
www.hodderheadline.com

This book is dedicated to the memory of
the lovely Gretta Bell, my mother,
who died as it was being born.

Acknowledgements

My thanks go to:

Pat Holdgate, Church of Scotland (and my apologies, if required, to the real Principal Clerk to the General Assembly).

The late Robin C B Stirling, OBE, the last of a now extinct species of weekly newspaper editor, gone to the great caseroom in the sky. He really did write all his copy in green ink with a fountain pen.

Martin Fletcher, for doing his best to make me better.

1

Nobody could remember weather like it in June. 'A side-effect of El Niño,' the lovely weather woman on BBC Breakfast had described the phenomenon, on the third morning of the blizzards that swept the Scottish mountains, a savagely unprecedented sting in the tail of a winter which, after seeming for a while to be endless, had been interrupted by the wettest spring on record.

The hardy Highlanders had moaned their way through the dark months, counting at the same time the money as it flowed into the ski resorts, but even they found the summer snows too much to bear. On the second day, there was a report of a suicide on a remote farm, whose tenant had lost more than half of his sheep.

And then, on the fourth day, it was over, as dramatically as it had begun. The clouds disappeared, the temperatures rose overnight by as much as eighteen Celsius, and the snows melted in the course of half a day.

They poured into the mountain streams, which fed into the tributaries, which in their turn flowed into the River Tay, turning it into a sudden raging torrent.

The people on the North Inch of Perth knew what was coming; many of them had experienced it before, and had supposed that it could not happen again, even though in their heart of hearts they knew that it could.

A few piled sandbags in their doorways as high as they could, in the vain hope that they would prove an effective dam against the murky rushing water. The rest, those who had learned the hard lesson, moved as much of their furniture and as many of their valuables as they could into the upper floors of their terraced houses, and moved out to camp with relatives until the worst was over.

If they had stayed, they would have seen the river rise, little by little at first, then more swiftly, foot by foot, until finally it broke out, forming a new loch as it swept across the low-lying Inch, finding the streets and the waiting houses, making a mockery of the sandbags as it poured through them, finding the lower floors and cellars, and filling them to drowning depth.

Some had stayed, sitting safe upstairs, and even out on their roofs, in the blazing sunshine, watching the personal disasters unfold, and shaking their heads as they did. 'This will never be allowed to happen again,' the politicians had declared as the North Inch householders had cleared away the mud from the last inundation.

But all too often, the attention span of politicians lasts no longer than the next election, and so, inevitably, it had.

Meanwhile, three thousand miles to the west . . .

2

'It must have been a hell of a shock for you, with your husband just dropping in his tracks like that.'

'Have you been playing football for long without your helmet?' Sarah Grace Skinner asked, wryly, her voice suddenly brittle. 'Of course it was a hell of a shock. All I could do was scream.' Her mouth set tight for a few seconds. 'Bob collapsing at my feet, I'm a damn doctor, and all I could do was stand there and scream.'

Ron Neidholm's massive quarterback's hand enclosed hers. 'Hey there,' he murmured. His voice had always struck her as surprisingly gentle in such a big man; its contrast with the rest of his physical make-up had always amused her. Indeed it was that, rather than his rugged good looks, or the blueness of his eyes, which had caused the fluttering in her chest at their first meeting, thirteen years earlier. 'Don't go taking the guilt on yourself,' he told her, earnestly. 'This is your husband we're talking about, and at your parents' burial into the bargain. Goddamn right you screamed. In your shoes I'd have done the same thing.'

She glared at him across the small table, and then the moment passed, and her face creased into a smile. 'Oh no you wouldn't,' she retorted. 'You're a lawyer. First you'd have checked whether the ground was slippery, in case you could sue the funeral company, then you'd have gone straight home to look out the will.'

He laughed out loud. 'That's what you think of me, is it? I may have a law degree, but I've never practised, remember.'

She took her hand from beneath his and reached out to touch his face, her fingers tracing its scars, gently, on his nose and above his left eye; then she slippe it inside his open-necked shirt, feeling the lump on his collarbone, th relic of an old fracture. 'Maybe it's time you did,' she whispered.

3

'Maybe it is,' he admitted, with the awkward grin she remembered so well, 'but it's just I love football, Sarah. Even when I was at college, it was my whole life. Apart from you, that is,' he added, quickly.

It was her turn to laugh. 'I don't think so. That damn ball was always more important than me, when it came to the crunch. Pity help the woman who forced you to a choice.'

'That's never happened: not even with you, if you remember. When I told you I was going to Texas to turn professional, you just said "Fine. Good luck." You didn't give me any argument.'

She leaned forward and looked him in the eye. 'Would there have been any point?'

He shook his head. 'No. To be honest I was glad when you took it so well. I had this idea that I'd come back from the season, whenever it ended, and you'd be there, waiting for me. Was I ever wrong, huh? Like Babs Walker said, you got bored damn quick.'

Her eyes narrowed, and her mouth tightened once more. 'Yes, my dear friend Babs . . . devious little bitch that she is. I tell you, if she wasn't Ian Walker's wife I'd have knocked her head clean off her shoulders for what she did. I thought it was just going to be the three of us for supper, after Ian's evening church service. When I walked in there last night, and saw you . . .'

He grinned again. 'I could tell, don't worry. When I caught the look on your face, I thought *Oh shit!* and tried to remember what I'd done to make you hate me.'

'It wasn't you.'

'I know that now, otherwise I wouldn't have dared suggest we have dinner tonight.'

'In that case, I'm glad you understood: you never did a thing to make me hate you. No, it was Babs who got under my skin. I knew straight away it was all her idea; it's in her nature. She's supposed to be my best friend, yet she does things like that. She'll say she's only looking out for me, and I guess she thinks she is, but sometimes it's her motive I can't stand. She hated Bob from the start, you know.'

'I'd guessed as much,' he admitted. 'She . . .' He was stopped in mid-sentence by a tap on the shoulder; he looked up, into the eager face of a middle-aged man.

'Mr Neidholm,' the intruder burst out. He had fine features, lank brown hair and wore a formal black suit. He was holding a white card, and a pen. Oddly he was wearing white gloves, but Sarah noticed blotches on his wrists and realised that he suffered from a skin disease. 'I'm sorry to interrupt you and your companion, but I'm a shameless fan of yours,' he gushed. 'Would you be kind enough to sign this menu for me?'

The big, fair-haired footballer smiled across at Sarah apologetically, then shrugged his wide shoulders. 'Of course,' he said. 'Gimme it here.' He took the card and the man's Mont Blanc ballpoint and scrawled a signature.

'Thank you so much,' the man exclaimed. 'You've made my summer.' He turned to leave, then paused. 'May I just say that I desperately hope you play at least one more season. Will you?'

Ron reached up and patted him on the shoulder. 'We'll see,' he said. 'In a couple of months I'll know for sure.'

'That was really nice of you,' she said, as the fan made his way back to his table.

'Comes with the territory; football's about guys like him, about little men with physical limitations to the point of handicap, even more than it's about the fat guys with dreams who dress up in the colours and make jackasses of themselves every Sunday in the season. I'm always available to someone like him. Besides,' he added, with a grin, 'if I ever do practise law . . . not that I'll need to . . . he'll remember it, and so will everyone in this restaurant who saw us.'

'I don't believe you're that cynical,' she said. 'I know you, Mr Neidholm. You did it because you're nice, and for no other reason. Not everyone's as devious as our Babs.' She hesitated. 'You were going to say something about her when that man appeared. What was it?'

'Nothing. Or something that's probably best left unsaid.'

'Too late now, big boy. Go on.'

He sighed. 'If you insist. I was going to say that she made a point of showing me a photograph of you and a guy she said you had a thing with, when you and your husband had marriage problems a while back.'

'Cow!' she hissed. 'I told her to get rid of that.'

'So that was true?'

5

'Yes, it's true. Bob and I did break up at one point; I came back over here to the States and I did have a relationship with someone. But it's history, and so, very definitely, is he. God,' she gasped. 'Babs really does hate Bob, doesn't she? Even now, she won't let go.'

'Forget her,' he said, firmly. 'She was always like that, even years ago. You're right; for a minister's wife, she's something of a bitch.' He picked up the empty bottle of San Pellegrino that lay on the table and glanced idly at the label.

'Did they ever pin down what happened to him?' he asked.

She shuddered. 'His heart stopped, just like that. Makes you think, doesn't it. There is no Superman; there is no Planet Krypton. Not even the great Deputy Chief Constable Bob Skinner was invulnerable. Now let's talk about something else.'

'Okay, but why are you so bitter?'

'Because he's gone,' she snapped. 'That's why I'm bitter. I'm angry with him, and I'm angry with the whole fucking world. Ron, I'm trying to come to the terms with the fact that my peaceful, lovely parents have been robbed and murdered in their peaceful, lovely lakeside cabin. Even now, with them both in the ground, I can barely make myself believe it. I needed Bob beside me more than I ever did before, and yet he's gone, and left me here in Goddamned Buffalo New York, with my three children, and the aftermath of all that horror.'

'But come on, Sarah. It was hardly his choice.'

Tears welled in her eyes. 'Yes it was! He's gone because of his career, his fucking career!'

'Okay, okay, okay, calm down.'

She took a deep breath and dabbed her eyes, briefly, with her napkin. 'I will if we talk about something else.'

'Sure, let's do that. Do you still have much to do to get your parents' estate through probate?'

'Not about that either,' she said. 'Let's talk about you. Will you play another season, like that man asked you?'

Ron Neidholm, Sarah Grace's college lover, looked at her across the table, in an hotel dining room which seemed, suddenly, to be empty apart from them. 'Honey,' he said, in the soft drawl he had acquired in his Texas days, 'I have three Superbowl rings, and I have been All-American or Pro-bowl quarterback more times than I can even remember. That doesn't stop me wanting more glory, or more trophy jewellery, and the Nashville Cats are offering me an unbelievable amount of money to throw that damn ball for another season.

'If that guy had asked me a month ago whether I'd take it, I'd have said "Too damn right!" But now, I'm not quite so sure.'

She frowned; she had always showed her surprise that way. 'What's making you hesitate all of a sudden?'

'You are, Dr Sarah Grace Skinner. You are.'

3

Paula Viareggio looked to her left and saw herself in the big mirror that stretched across the width of the dressing table. She saw him too, although he was lost somewhere in a dream. She slid out from underneath his muscular arm, rolled out of the huge sleigh bed and stood up.

Still looking in the mirror, she touched herself between her breasts with a fingertip, then traced it slowly down to her navel. *Not bad*, she thought, appraising her body in the morning light. She did not think of herself as being vain; no, she was simply proud of her olive skin with its velvet feel, of her long supple limbs, and of her classic high-cheekboned face. Most of all she was proud of her long cascading hair, turned silver from black in her mid twenties, helped on its way, if truth be told, by some judicious colouring by Charlie Kettles, her hairdresser. 'Yes, not bad for thirty-something,' she murmured.

She heard a muffled grunt behind her, as Mario McGuire came back to wakefulness.

'Where you gone?' he whispered.

'Nowhere,' she answered.

'Come back in here then.'

'Let me guess,' she laughed. 'You're going to tell me you're at your best in the mornings.'

'Something like that,' he agreed, cheerfully.

'As if I didn't know that already.' She turned towards him, facing the bed. 'This can't go on, you know.'

He propped himself up on an elbow. 'Bloody hell,' he exclaimed. 'You spend all those years trying to get me into your bed, and now you're giving me a hard time over it.'

'You know what I mean, Mario,' she said, heavily. 'This situation can't go on. What did you tell your wife this time? Are you working late in Galashiels again?'

'I didn't tell her anything. Things are bad enough between Maggie and me, without burdening them with unnecessary lies.'

Her mouth dropped open for a second or two, until she loosed a short, sarcastic laugh. 'Hah! Are you going to tell her where you've been, then . . . presuming you deign to go home at some point today?'

'No. I'm not going to tell her anything, and she's not going to ask. I promise you that. She won't.'

'You're kidding yourself!'

'Maggie will not rock the boat.'

'If it was my bloody boat, I'd tip you over the side. In fact I think I'll do just that.' She reached out, grabbed a corner of the duvet and yanked it away, uncovering him. 'Go on,' she said. 'Get up, get dressed and go on home to your wife, and your new family, where you belong!'

He smiled up at her. 'If you really mean that, I will.' He rolled out of bed in a single easy movement and headed for the bathroom. Involuntarily, she reached out and caught his wrist, before he was halfway there; he turned and pulled her towards him, enveloping her in his arms, pressing her body against his, burying his face in her hair. 'No,' he whispered, 'I didn't think so.'

They moved back to the bed, leaving the duvet on the floor. 'Listen to me,' Mario said softly, stroking her belly with the flat of his right hand. 'A few months ago, on any given Saturday morning in Edinburgh, it would have been Maggie and me lying like this. I loved her, no mistake, and I wouldn't have looked at another woman. I still wouldn't, if it weren't for you. But that's all gone; Mags has changed, and changed for good.'

'But why?' she asked. 'And why so suddenly? That's what I don't understand.'

He kissed her on the forehead. 'I don't think I can find the words to tell you . . . no, not even you . . . exactly why, or how, it happened. Let's just say that all her life, she's been fighting this battle with herself, about how she relates to men; now, finally, she's lost it.' He hesitated. 'Paulie,' he asked, 'can I trust you to keep a secret?'

'Don't be daft. You know you can.'

'Okay.' He fixed her with his eyes. 'Maggie was raped,' he told her, firing the words at her, watching her hands go to her mouth in horror, waiting as she took it in. 'The man who did it killed himself,' he went on, when she was ready, 'and it was all covered up, but that's what her emotional breakdown, the one we pretended was flu, was about: not all, but that was a big part of it. Now, in the aftermath, even though she's back in control of herself, she just can't bear me to touch her. She can live with me around the house, okay. We're pleasant to each other. We still care for each other. But physically, our marriage is over.'

Paula looked up at him with doubt in her eyes. 'She'll get over it in time though, won't she?'

'No,' he replied. 'No, she won't, or at least it's very unlikely that she will. She's had counselling, we've both had counselling, and the top guy in the business has told us that in his opinion, nothing's likely to change.'

'But can't she be put on medication?'

He snorted. 'What? Love potion number nine, do you mean? No, Paulie, there is no medication that will counter what's wrong with Mags. She's lost the ability to love, and not just to make love, either. She's withdrawn herself from me.'

'Aren't you even going to try to draw her back?'

'Turn on the McGuire charm, you mean? No, I'm not.'

'But why not? The two of you had so much going for you.' She frowned. 'I know it's a hell of a thing for me to be saying, but surely, big boy, if you really gave it a go . . .'

'Yes, but that's the point. I loved her, and I still care for her, but I don't love the woman she's become. We sleep in separate bedrooms now, and one night I heard her locking her door. She doesn't need to, though. I've got no wish to open it.'

'But what about the wee boy you're adopting? The lad you took in after he was orphaned. I thought the idea was that you were going to raise him together.'

He drew in a deep breath. 'We are, and until Maggie says different, we will. I'll go home this morning and we'll take Rufus out. If it's as nice a day as yesterday, we might take him to the seaside.'

'Will you be allowed to adopt him, though? I thought you had to have social workers confirm that you have a stable marriage, and all that guff.'

Mario hesitated. 'What?' she asked, reading his indecision, as he pulled himself up to lean against the high, curved headboard of the bed.

'I didn't want to tell you this; I didn't want to tell anyone who doesn't have to know, but especially not you. So promise me again it stays our secret.' She nodded. 'The thing is,' he continued, 'we don't need the law to let us adopt Rufus. He's Maggie's half-brother.'

He looked at her as she worked through the implications of what he had told her. 'God!' she whispered at last.

'God had no hand in it,' he said, grimly. 'Mags's father, may he rot in peace, was a real bastard. Rufus's mother was barely more than a kid, but he liked them young . . . liked to hurt them too. Anyway, even if the relationship wasn't there, we wouldn't have a problem with the social workers. We're both detective superintendents of police, for fuck's sake.'

'How could I forget?' she muttered. 'Okay, so you've told me. That's how things are for you. So where does it leave you and me?'

He smiled at her. 'It leaves us, cousin, as joint trustees of the Viareggio family enterprises, with compelling business reasons to meet regularly . . . even if I have given a bright young corporate lawyer my power of attorney, because of my public position.' He looked down at her long body and grinned. 'It's perfect cover for having it off as well.' He paused. 'Talking about cover, you know my mum's moving to Tuscany pretty soon? I was thinking about going out to help her settle into her new place. Do you fancy coming?'

Paula managed to gasp and laugh at the same time. 'Are you crazy?' she exclaimed. 'I may have lusted after your body for most of my adult life, Mario, but the last thing I want is for my Auntie Christina to find out that I've finally got it. The same goes for any other member of our family, and maybe for anyone at all, if you value your job.'

'It's a big house that my mother's bought,' he pointed out. 'And don't forget; she's very clever and she's very, very shrewd. She knows about you and me, I'll bet, even though she hasn't said anything.'

'You serious?'

'Sure. I'm her only son; we don't need speech to communicate.'

11

'But what'll she be thinking about it?'

'Same as me . . . *Keep it to yourselves* . . . which is, I suppose the best advice we could have. I concede also that going to Italy together would be taking it too far, from the family's point of view. So we won't.' He paused. 'Not that the job is a consideration, though.'

She looked surprised once again. 'What? Is the police force not big enough for you and Maggie any more?'

He shook his head. 'No, that's not it. I'm not sure that I'm as committed to it as I need to be: not any more, at any rate. We're all still stunned by what happened to Bob Skinner; things just aren't what they were without him around.'

'Yes,' she agreed, 'that was a shocker. What his wife must be feeling; to have him collapse just like that in the middle of her parents' funeral.'

'Too right. As for me, well, Willie Haggerty, the assistant chief constable and Dan Pringle, the head of CID, may be good guys, but put together they don't make one of big Bob. I just can't get used to the idea of him not being around any more. With everything else that's going on in my life, the idea of turning it in and running the Trust full-time has its appeal.'

Paula drew herself up beside him. 'Do you mean that?'

'I'm not sure. How would you feel if I did?'

'Honestly? A bit scared. The way things are, I can handle it when you go home; but if we were working together through the day, it might be more difficult. Have you talked to Neil about this?'

'McIlhenney? About us? Not in so many words, but he's nearly as close to me as my mother. He knows too.'

'Not about us, you idiot, about leaving the force?'

'Yes. He says he feels much the same. He was the big fella's executive assistant, remember, as well as being one of his few real pals. But at least he can shut himself away in the Special Branch office, and go home to Louise and the kids every night.'

She turned her head and looked him in the eye. 'And you can't, can you, you poor love. All you can do is fit me in, whenever the opportunity arises.'

He slid his arm around her shoulders and pulled her down until they were lying side by side once again. 'It's a hard old life, Paulie,' he said, and then he grinned, the bright wicked smile she had known for so long, and wished for so long to have directed at her. 'All we can do is get on with it.' He rolled over, into her embrace. 'Hey,' he whispered in her ear.

'What?'

'I really am at my best in the mornings, you know.'

She beamed at him. 'Oh, I know, I know. I really do!'

4

Deputy Chief Constable Andrew Martin flexed his heavy shoulders as he walked into the big kitchen, feeling the muscles stretch his formal white shirt. Bob Skinner had always disliked wearing his uniform, and now that he had attained command rank, his closest friend had come to feel the same way.

However he was still new to the Tayside force, and understood that he had to be seen in it, if for no other reason than that the men under his command would know who he was. Happily, the day promised warmth, and he had been able to discard the heavy jacket for the white shirt, with shoulder-panels to denote his rank.

'Now there's a picture,' said Karen as she turned to look at him. 'You look just like Sir James Proud in that get-up.' He smiled, knowing that it was a copper compliment; nobody could wear a uniform like his former chief constable.

'Where are you going today?' his wife asked him; she had been up for two hours, since the baby had wakened her just after six a.m., demanding her first feed of the day. Danielle Martin was two weeks and two days old, and for all that he had had half a year to prepare for her arrival, her father was still slightly stunned by her very existence.

'Uhh?' he asked. His mind had been on other things.

'Are you awake yet?' she laughed. 'I asked where you were going this morning. Dundee is it? And why, on a Saturday? The football season's over, is it not?'

He blinked. 'Sorry, love; I was just thinking about Bob for a second or two.'

Karen patted his shoulder as he fed four slices of wholemeal bread into the toaster. 'I understand,' she said quietly. 'It still gets to you, I know; me too.'

His green eyes flashed as he smiled at her; there was a new warmth in them, a depth of feeling that had appeared at the moment of Danielle's birth, and had stayed there ever since. He nodded towards the infant, asleep in her carry-cot. 'At least we've got her to take our minds off it.'

He pushed down the lever to start the bread toasting. 'As it happens I'm not going to Dundee. No, I'm going down to the North Inch; the flood water's subsided, and it's just about dry enough for us to begin the clear-up operation. In theory it's down to the householders, but I've detailed fifty officers to help them. Community policing, remember; that's part of my remit now.'

Karen frowned. 'Is there anything that isn't part of your remit?' His duties were a sore point with her. An ex-detective sergeant herself, she knew how badly her husband had wanted a break from criminal investigation, yet during his first month on the Tayside force, he had come to realise that within the smaller force he had joined, there was nothing over which the DCC did not have a level of oversight.

'No,' he agreed, 'probably not. But I'm enjoying it, nonetheless; the chief and the senior officers are all first-class professionals and good to work with. And don't tell me you don't like living in Perth, either.'

'I don't know yet whether I do or not,' she replied. 'Fine, it's prosperous, the streets are clean, and we have this nice old house up on the hillside, but we're lucky. Suppose we'd bought that place we looked at in the town centre. We might have been flooded out with the rest of those poor sods.'

He laughed. 'But we didn't and we weren't, so don't damn the whole town because of something that didn't happen. Anyway, it was an absolute freak of nature. There were precautions taken after the last time, but nobody could have predicted last week's weather. If you didn't believe in global climatic change before, believe in it now.'

Karen Martin frowned. 'So that's what our daughter has to look forward to, is it?'

The toaster popped; he took out the first slice and began to spread it with honey. 'It won't be that dramatic all the time,' he replied; 'besides, it'll be her norm. We were brought up during the Cold War, remember; that was ours, frightening as it seems now. I was at a dinner last month and I met a guy who'd flown nuclear bombers. He told me that in 1962 the world was literally five minutes away from the edge. The crews were in their cockpits, with sealed envelopes containing the bits of Russia they would be expected to find and obliterate. You know what else? They didn't have enough fuel to get back . . . not that there would have been much to come back to. No, I'm glad she hasn't been born into a world like that.'

'She hasn't? What about September 11, and the aftermath . . .'

'Ah but . . .' He stopped. 'Let's change the subject. That wee girl over there represents the start of the finest years of our lives. She's a shining light in all the gloom we've had recently. Let's just focus on the good times and enjoy them.'

'That's a deal,' Karen agreed, pouring coffee into two mugs. 'We can start with our holiday this summer. Where are we going to take Danielle?'

Andy took his two slices of toast and honey, and his mug, and sat down at the kitchen table. 'Well,' he began, 'Broughty Ferry's quite nice.'

The baby was still asleep when he left the house fifteen minutes later, having agreed with his wife's proposal that they find a rental villa somewhere in France, in early September, and drive there. He climbed into his metallic blue Mondeo, reversed it carefully out of the driveway, and headed into the centre of Perth.

Even in the morning traffic, it took him less than ten minutes to reach his destination. He parked beside a row of five police transport vehicles, each one full of officers, and stepped out into the morning sunshine. He looked out over the flat plain of the North Inch; the sun of the previous few days had begun to dry it out, but it was still muddy and unsightly. He dreaded to think what the insides of the houses looked like.

He glanced around him as he walked towards the terrace that faced the River Tay, where, he knew, the worst of the flooding had happened. His eye fell on a uniformed inspector, in summer dress, as was he. 'Good morning, Harry,' he called out.

Inspector Sharp turned and made an involuntary move to attention as he recognised the newcomer. He was one of the two senior officers in charge of policing Perth and its surrounding area. In the larger Edinburgh force, which Martin had just left, his opposite number carried a much higher rank.

'Hello, sir,' the dark-haired, middle-aged policeman responded; he made to salute, but the deputy chief constable waved it away with a smile.

'Don't start that, for Christ's sake; on my first week in this job I started to get tennis elbow. How's it going?'

'It's not yet, sir, but then it's not quite time. As you ordered, we contacted all the householders who moved out and told them we'd pick them up from their temporary lodgings and get them here for nine.' He nodded towards two patrol cars that had just drawn up. 'That's them starting to arrive now. I've got our boys and girls waiting in the minibuses over there, ready to help with the really dirty stuff, and with the heavy lifting. Some of these people have lived here for years, and are quite old.'

'Fine. Have you got plenty of tools; shovels and stuff for shifting mud? I guess there'll be plenty of it down there.'

'There'll be all sorts of stuff down there in those cellars, sir. I was a young constable the last time something like this happened, and I was involved in an operation just like this one. There was fish, rats, condoms, you name it . . . and this flood's been a lot worse.' He frowned, briefly. 'Mind you, it's not quite right to call them cellars; with these houses they're more like basement floors, some of them with several rooms. Their gardens are well below street level, and they back on to the houses in the street behind; so they've filled up, and the water's come in from there as well as from the front door above.'

'How deep has it been?' Martin asked.

Sharp scratched his chin. 'The water was over four feet deep across the Inch,' he replied. 'That means it was above ground-floor level in the houses. So it must have been fifteen to eighteen feet inside them, anyway.'

'Bloody hell; I understand now what you mean about the mess. We'd better see for ourselves, then. Go on, Harry; get the show on the road.'

He stood back and watched as Inspector Sharp went about his business, speaking to each of the householders who had been brought to the scene, then waving the waiting constables and sergeants, some of them smiling, no doubt at the prospect of overtime, from the transport vehicles. They were all wearing overalls, and green rubber boots. Suddenly, Martin felt gripped by guilt; or perhaps it was only the eagerness of a new commander to set an example.

'Inspector,' he called again. Sharp turned back towards him. 'Do you have a spare set of waders, and boots, my size? Ten at a pinch, or bigger. Oh yes, and a shovel.'

'Probably, sir,' he shouted. 'Bobby,' he yelled across to a sergeant, who seemed to be supervising the helpers. 'See if you can sort out some gear for the DCC.' The officer nodded, and headed off towards the minibuses; Martin decided that he would be as well to follow, to simplify the process.

The waders and boots that were left in the limited carry space of the vehicles were, not unnaturally, the dirtiest and scruffiest in the police stockroom, fifty officers having had their pick of the rest. He grabbed a set that looked as if they would fit him adequately, and struggled into them, trying not to guess where and why they had last been used.

When he returned to the terrace, he found Inspector Sharp speaking earnestly to a second group of homeowners who had been brought to the scene. There were five of them, and from the way they stood together, he guessed that they were two couples and one single person, an old lady who looked at least seventy-five years old. She was white-faced, and her dull grey hair was tied back in a bun, from which a few wispy strands had escaped, to wave on the morning breeze. She was dressed in a long, shabby blue coat, even on a day that was already fulfilling its promise of warmth, but, like the other four, she had come prepared for her task, in that she wore a pair of black, ankle-length rubber boots over her thick brown stockings.

She looked apprehensive; Martin moved towards her, almost auto-matically. 'I was just suggesting to the people, sir,' said Sharp, as he approached, 'that they might like our officers to go in to their houses first, to do what we can to make sure that the stairways are safe, before they venture in.'

'That seems sensible to me,' the deputy chief constable agreed. He looked round the group. 'Is everyone happy with that?'

The male halves of the couples nodded, but the old lady pursed her lips and knitted her brow. 'Ah'll go in ma ain hoose, son,' she said.

'It might not be safe, Mrs . . .'

'Miss!' she snapped, cutting the inspector off short. 'Miss Bonney, Wilma Bonney. Ah've been through this before, and the last time your lot cleared up for me wi' their big feet they broke half my china. That'll no happen again. Ah'll be fine goin' in there. At my age, Ah've learned to watch my step.'

Martin was on the point of suggesting that it might have been the flood that had broken her china, when he thought better of it. 'In that case, Miss Bonney,' he suggested, 'maybe you'll let me come in with you . . . just in case some of your furniture's been moved about by the water, and has to be shifted.'

She stared at him, as if she was weighing up his sincerity or his trustworthiness. Whatever test she was applying, he passed. 'Och, all right,' she muttered. 'You'll be careful where you put your feet, though.'

'I promise.' He smiled at Sharp behind her back as he followed Wilma Bonney's brisk walk across the street. He kept close to her, for the mud on the roadway was still damp in places, and he was afraid that she might slip, but she was as surefooted as he was in his clumsy footwear.

'Number twelve,' she announced, leading him towards a blue doorway, on the far side of a broad flagstone landing, just a single step up from the pavement. Martin looked down and realised that it formed a bridge across a narrow basement yard, on to which three barred windows looked. The glass in each was broken.

Miss Bonney delved deep into her purse and produced a Yale key, which she used to open the door. Martin saw that the frame around the keeper of the lock had been repaired, and remembered being told by Sharp that he had sent carpenters to the scene when the flood had receded sufficiently, to secure several houses where the water had smashed its way in.

'Oh dear.' He heard the woman sigh as she looked into her home, and he sympathised at once. There was a watermark eighteen inches above the floor level; the carpet runner in the entry hall lay twisted and filthy, embedded in an undercoat of stones, mire, paper and other detritus. 'Ah couldna' have expected anything else, could Ah, son?'

'No', he agreed, solemnly. 'I suppose not.' He stepped into the hall and looked into the living room that opened from it. He was both surprised and pleased to see that it was empty of furniture, although its fitted carpet, whatever colour it had been originally, was now almost black.

'Ma nephew helped me move my stuff upstairs,' she said, reading his mind, 'or at least, as much as he could. He's a good boy. He'd have come wi' me this morning but he's at his work.'

'What about the basement?' asked Martin.

'He moved what he could, but there's some big kitchen furniture and wardrobes and the like that he couldna' shift up the stair. He moved ma good china . . . the stuff that your lot didna' break the last time . . . but all ma usin' stuff's still down there, and ma washing machine, and ma fridge.'

'Let's go and see it, then.'

'A'right.' She led him to a steep, narrow staircase behind a door at the back of the hall. She was about to lead the way down, until he stopped her. Every tread was covered with mud.

'Please, let me go first. I insist.'

She frowned at him, but let him go ahead of her. He took the stairway slowly, as carefully as he could, gripping the rails on either side as hard as he could, for they too were slippery. The walls on either side were sodden, and in places the plaster bulged outwards.

It was only when he got to the foot that he realised she had been following behind him. She stepped carefully off the last tread, and stood beside him, looking around the big room into which they had emerged. 'This is ma kitchen,' she announced; unnecessarily, for he could see, or at least make out the shapes of a cooker, and a tall fridge. He glanced down at his feet, and saw that he was standing in mud up to his ankles. The place was an almost indescribable mess; it was strewn with more stones, crockery . . . some of it broken, he noticed . . . and with tins and packets of food from storage cupboards and from the fridge. But it was more than just the mess; the place smelled terrible. For some reason, he remembered a holiday in Spain, when a truck had come to pump out a blockage in the sewer not far from Bob Skinner's villa.

He looked at Miss Bonney; she caught his glance and gave him a faint smile. There might have been a tear in her eye, but then again, there might not.

'I'm very sorry,' he said, sincerely.

'It's no' your fault, son,' she replied, quietly. 'It's God's; naebody else's but his.' He heard himself sigh.

'What else is there down here?' he asked.

She pointed to her right, to a door in the far corner. 'Ma laundry room's through there, wi' a toilet off it.' Then she nodded to her left. 'Through there, there's a big bedroom, a smaller one, and a cupboard. Ah'll just go and see whit they're like, and then, Ah suppose, Ah'll have to let your folk in after a', tae help me clear oot this mud.'

'Yes,' he murmured. 'It's best.'

He watched her as she squelched across the kitchen, towards the door on the far left. Her boots made a sucking noise with each step.

She reached the doorway, and turned, laboriously, to step through. Then, without warning, as he watched her, Martin saw her hand fly to her mouth. She gave a short gasping cry, and stumbled back until she lost her footing, and sat down with an audible splash on the muddy riverbed which had invaded her home.

He did his best to rush over to her, but his footwear made haste impossible. When he reached her, the old lady was trying to push herself up. He leaned over her, took her gently under the arms and raised her to her feet. 'There, now,' he said, hoping to soothe her. 'What happened?'

She neither answered him, nor looked at him. Instead she kept her eyes fixed on the doorway. He turned; when he saw what held her gaze, he almost stumbled himself.

In the short corridor that led through to the front rooms, there lay the body of a man. It was on its left side, half submerged in the mire. Looking at it, Martin knew at once why the smell had been so bad.

'Jesus!' he whispered. 'Is that your nephew? Could he have come back here and been caught in the flood?'

'No,' Miss Bonney whispered. 'Ma nephew's a great big lad. Ah've never seen thon before in ma life.'

The Deputy Chief Constable cursed himself for not having brought a two-way radio. Then he remembered the cellphone in his trouser pocket. He fished inside his waders until he found it. His white shirt was unimaginably muddy, but he gave it no thought as he dialled the headquarters number.

'This is Mr Martin,' he told the switchboard operator, as soon as he answered. 'Patch me through on the radio to Inspector Sharp.' The man obeyed, without a word.

'Yes, sir?' Sharp's voice was remarkably clear. 'Anything up?'

'Very much so,' he answered, tersely. 'Have we had any missing persons reports in the wake of this flood?'

'No, sir,' the inspector replied. 'None at all. We had an eye out for them too, don't worry.'

'Well, we've missed one. He's down here in Miss Bonney's basement. Get an ambulance along here will you, but tell them no lights and siren, I don't want any unnecessary fuss.'

He ended the call, and turned back to the old lady. 'Can you stand on your own for a bit?'

She gave him a withering look. 'Of course.'

In three long strides he stepped over to the door, then shuffled his way through, until he stood over the body. Years of experience had taught him to ignore, or at least tolerate, the smell. He crouched down and leaned over, to see better. It was in a filthy state, and there were early signs of decomposition, but it was still clearly the corpse of a middle-aged man. It was clad in what looked like a heavy shirt, rough jacket, and flannel trousers. He glanced along towards the feet and saw socks, but no shoes.

He leaned further across, meaning to use the opposite wall to lever himself upright again, then paused, unusually aware of his contact lenses as his eyes narrowed. The body was lying awkwardly, and its right arm seemed to have been twisted behind it by the water.

From this new angle he could see clearly a mark on the wrist; it was vivid, the kind of groove that could have been left by a ligature.

'Bloody hell,' he murmured, then pushed himself to his feet off the wall, fumbling for his cellphone once again.

Within a minute he had Sharp back on line.

'It's on the way, sir,' the inspector reported, briskly.

'That's fine. Now, still without causing any fuss, I want you to call the head of CID for me. Get him here, with whoever's on duty in the Western Division office, plus a full scene-of-crime team, including a medical examiner. And do not, repeat do not, let anyone into this house.'

5

'Busy Friday in the Borders, was it?' Maggie flashed a smile as she asked the question, but nothing but indifference showed in her eyes.

'You know what Fridays are like, Detective Superintendent Rose,' he answered; nothing had been asked directly, no lie had been told. 'What about yours?'

'My division's always quiet on a Friday. All my criminals are out getting drunk.'

She peered at him as he came to stand beside her, filling the kettle from the kitchen tap. 'You should keep an electric razor in that office of yours, McGuire. You need a shave.'

'It's my new weekend look.'

She sniffed. 'At least you don't need a wash. That's a very fetching shower gel you've been using.'

He ignored her jibe. 'Where's Rufus?' he asked.

She nodded towards the window. 'Outside, in his den.'

He looked out into the garden and saw that the door of the new summerhouse, where the toddler kept his larger toys, was open. 'He's happy, then. I thought we might take him down to North Berwick later on.'

'If you like,' his wife muttered.

As he put the kettle on its stand and switched it on, he saw the tension in her jawline. 'Mags, what's up?' he asked.

She turned and stared at him, incredulity in her eyes. 'Are you serious? You come swanning in here at going on eleven on a Saturday morning, and you ask me what's up?'

'Mags . . .'

'Don't.' She held up her hands as if to fend him off, although he had made no move towards her. 'Just don't. I know it's all my fault. I can't be a wife to you any more, so how can I expect you to be a husband to me? I'm sorry; I shouldn't have got sarky with you. Things being as they are I suppose I should be grateful that you come home at all.'

'I'll always come home, honey. You know that.'

'God knows why.'

'Yes, he does, because I stood before him and told him. I love you.'

'What's to love?' She slapped her abdomen, violently.

'There's more to you than that.'

'Just as well,' she retorted, 'for I was never very good at it anyway.'

He winced. 'You weren't . . .' he began, but she cut him off.

'Don't look at me like that, it's true. That particular part of marriage has always been an effort for me, especially since we found out that we couldn't have kids. It was difficult enough when there was some point to it. I tried, for your sake, but now I just can't, not any more.'

The sound of boiling water reached a crescendo, then subsided as the kettle switched itself off. 'Okay,' he said, reaching for two mugs. 'I've told you; I understand.'

'Yes, and I understand you too. Here, let me do that.' She brushed him aside and took the mugs from him, then spooned coffee granules into each one. 'I'm sorry for being such a bitch.'

He sighed. 'You're not. Shop; let's talk shop,' he exclaimed, suddenly.

'If you insist,' she agreed, brightly. 'I had a chat with our colleague Detective Superintendent Jay yesterday. He and I are thinking about having a joint raid on those saunas your cousin Paula owns. We have some in each of our divisions.'

He gasped. 'Don't you bloody dare!' he snapped. 'Those places are licensed and they're above reproach.'

Her laugh was filled with sarcasm. 'They're sex shops, Mario.'

'Maybe, but that's how we control the game in Edinburgh, and you and Greg Jay know it. Paula doesn't take a penny from the women who work there and she makes sure they're clean and drug-free.'

'I know, you've told me this before. She's really a social worker.'

'In her own way.' He looked at her, eyes narrowing. 'You're pulling my chain, aren't you?'

'Just a bit.'

He returned her faint smile. 'I've changed my mind; you are a bitch. Anyway, she's selling them.'

'She is? Why?'

'Because I asked her to.'

'Ah, you do find it embarrassing, then.'

'Just a touch, but that's not it. I don't believe that her ownership of those places is compatible with her position as a trustee of the Viareggio businesses. That is definitely not a business sector we want to get into, or even be associated with, by implication.'

'Her late father thought that too when he was a trustee, and she paid no attention to him.'

'Uncle Beppe wasn't thinking about taking the businesses public.'

'And you are?'

'It's an option.'

'Whose idea is it? Yours, or Alexis Skinner's.'

'It's Alex's, but I'll take a bit of the credit; I asked her to do a report for us on possible ways forward.'

'Very good.' She smiled again. 'You know, of course, that a lot of people are calling you an arse-kisser, for appointing the boss's daughter to look after your business affairs.'

'Give me their names,' he said, grimly, 'and I'll go and see them, one by one. Or are you one of them?'

'No, I'm not,' she retorted. 'Give me credit for knowing you better than that. Anyway, I know how good a lawyer she's become. You don't get to be an associate of her firm at her age if you're not. She must be costing you, though, and in travel too, with her being based in London.'

'It's worth it.'

'How's she taking what happened to her dad?'

'How do you think? She's in shock, like the rest of us.'

'No surprise.' Maggie picked up her coffee, walked over to the back door, opened it and stepped out into the garden. Mario slipped off his jacket, threw it across the kitchen table and followed. Hearing them, Rufus toddled out of his playhouse and waved.

'Does Alex's firm do family law?' she asked him, as she waved back at her tiny half-brother.

He blinked, caught by surprise. 'No,' he replied, feeling a sudden lurch in his stomach. 'Why do you ask? Do you want a divorce?'

It was her turn to be taken aback. 'What? No, don't be daft. There's no such thought in my mind, for all that I've been bitching. You asked me if there was something wrong earlier on, when I got tore into you. As usual, my dear, you read me right.' She reached into the back pocket of her jeans and took out a folded white envelope. 'This came in today's post.'

Mario took it from her. He looked at it and frowned when he saw that it was addressed to Mrs Margaret McGuire, a name his wife had never adopted. He flipped it open and took out the letter inside. The heading was the first thing that caught his eye.

'Redway Chatham, Solicitors, Guildford,' he read aloud. 'What the fuck's this?'

He looked at Maggie and saw that her earlier tension was back. 'It's all in legal language,' she said, 'and English law at that. I'll save you the trouble of wading through it. I've done that often enough now; I understand exactly what it says. Redway Chatham are acting for Rufus's great-uncle, Mr Franklin Chamberlain, of Alton, Hampshire, and his wife Lydia.

'They are asking us, very politely so far, to hand him over to them. If we refuse, they say they'll instruct solicitors up here, and counsel if necessary, to petition for custody in the Scottish court. They say that it will be up to me to defend that if I choose, and to prove my claim to a blood relationship with Rufus. If I do, it'll be for the court to decide between us, as potential parents.'

'Jesus!' Mario exclaimed. 'Who is this guy Chamberlain, do we know? What is he? His sister, Rufus's grandmother, has a shady background; that we do know. What if he's from the same school? No, no, bugger that for a game.'

'The man is Rufus's mother's godfather,' she told him, 'as well as being her uncle. And he's legit.; very much so. I've had him checked out already. He's forty years old, he's deputy chief executive of a major insurance company, and his wife is a county councillor. They have two children themselves, one only a year older than Rufus.'

'So what?' He waved the letter in the air in anger. 'Are we poor people? Are we, hell. Do they think we can't bring him up? Too bloody right we can. Who the fuck do they think they are? What makes them think the sheriff will find for them . . . or the Court of Session, if it goes that far? Like I said, Alex's firm don't handle this sort of stuff, but they'll recommend someone, the best. I'll call her now.'

He started for the house, but she caught his arm and held him back. 'Wait,' she said, softly. He looked at her and saw that she was on the edge of tears.

'I can't, Mario. I can't go to court over this. If I did, I'd have to prove that my father and his were one and the same man. DNA would do that beyond doubt, but what if Chamberlain's counsel wouldn't leave it at that? What if he asked me questions about our estrangement, about why he left and why I never tried to find him, even though I was better placed to than most, as a police officer? And I'd be under oath; I would have to tell the truth, the whole truth and nothing but the truth. Can you imagine the press coverage? I can, and I know that I could not take it. I'm having enough trouble holding myself together as it is. If we fought this, and if that happened, as it would . . .' She shook her head slowly, from side to side. 'Everything would be over; my career, me, everything. Love, if that can of worms gets open, there's no telling where they'll burrow.'

He stood there, white-faced where before he had been red with anger, knowing that everything she had said was true.

'The Chamberlains sound like responsible people,' she went on. 'They can only be doing this because they care about Rufus. We have to give him to them.'

Mario's shoulders slumped. 'And where does that leave us, Mags? What does it leave us?'

'It leaves us each other,' she answered. 'For as long as you want, that is.'

He pulled her to him and hugged her, but she stiffened in his embrace, and he released it, at once. They stood there, awkwardly, listening to Rufus chattering to his toys, in the playhouse they had built for him.

And then a phone rang; the song of a mobile. He strained to hear it. 'Yours or mine?' he asked.

'Mine.' She left him and trotted back into the kitchen.

27

She returned a minute later, her cellphone still in her hand. 'I've got to go. There's a fire in the Royal Scottish Academy in Princes Street, and they're saying it's arson.'

Maggie looked at her half-brother, who had emerged from his hut and was smiling up at them both. 'You take him to the seaside,' she told her husband. 'It'll probably be the last chance you get.'

6

The medical examiner was not best pleased; his putting stroke had never been better and he had been looking forward for weeks to the summer meeting at Rosemount Golf Club.

He looked up at the two men who stood in the doorway of Miss Bonney's kitchen. 'What can I tell you?' he exclaimed. 'I can tell you he's bloody dead. That's self-evident. Did you really have to drag me down to this morass to tell you that?'

'I'm sorry, Doctor Duck,' said Detective Chief Superintendent Rod Greatorix, the Tayside head of CID. 'You know it's the form in a situation like this.'

It was untypical for the even-tempered Andy Martin to be irked by the doctor's attitude, but he was. The man had moaned from the moment he had come splashing awkwardly down the stairs. 'I've got fifty officers in this street,' he snapped at him, suddenly, 'shovelling all sorts of shit. They're getting paid a hell of a lot less than you, so please, spare us your troubles.'

The doctor rose to his feet and turned belligerently towards him. 'And just who the hell are you, sir?' he demanded. 'And who do you think you're talking to?'

'My shoulder-flashes are covered by this scene-of-crime tunic,' Martin replied, 'but if you could see them you'd know that I'm the new deputy chief constable. Now I don't care, frankly, whether I get off to a good start with you, but you'd be well advised to start impressing me. I expect the highest standard of professionalism at crime scenes, and I will not tolerate anything less . . . from anyone.'

'Are you questioning my professional competence?' the man shot back.

Even in the murky cellar, Martin's green eyes seemed to flash, dangerously. 'No,' he said, evenly and quietly. 'I'm telling you to get on with your job.'

Dr Duck looked at him for a few seconds longer, as if he was weighing him up, then he squatted down beside the body once again. The deputy chief and DCS Greatorix backed off and left him to his work.

'Is his name really Duck?' Martin whispered.

'Yes; first name Howard.'

'Mmm. In that case I can see why he was golfing today, rather than shooting.'

'Gentlemen,' the doctor called from the corridor. 'I've done as much as I can here; it would be helpful if the body could be moved.'

The head of CID looked at Martin, as if for approval. 'I know I made the call that this is a suspicious death, but this is your show, Rod,' the DCC assured him, answering the unspoken question. 'It was wrong of me to go for the ME, but he got under my skin. I won't interfere again.'

Greatorix nodded, then spoke quietly to the police photographer, white-clothed like the rest of them. 'Okay, doc,' he answered, eventually. 'We'll lift him out for you.' He moved towards the hall, waving to a detective constable to join him.

'Careful,' the doctor warned.

'Why?' the DCS asked, warily. 'He's not going to fall apart, is he?'

'No, no; not yet, at any rate. But he's waterlogged and so are his clothes. He'll be heavy.'

'I'll help,' Martin volunteered. 'You two take a leg each, I'll manage his shoulders.' The detective constable looked at him, doubtfully. 'What's up?' he laughed. 'Have you never seen a chief officer lift anything heavier than a pen before?'

'I've never seen one offer to do it, sir,' the man replied.

'Well, you have now. I'll take the top end; you guys take the feet.' He considered the massive kitchen table, which looked as if it had been there since the house was built. 'We'll plonk him on that.'

The fact that the body was lying on its side in a confined space made their task all the more difficult. Martin had trouble easing his hands under its trunk, but eventually he managed, and pulled it clear of the mud. It came free with a great sucking sound; together, the three were able to turn it onto its back and lift it clear of the floor. Rigor mortis had come and gone, so the body was pliable, but the trickiness of their footing meant that they had to inch along, until finally they were able to lay the burden down on the table, face up.

'Thank you, gentlemen,' said Dr Duck. 'I wonder if I could have some water now?'

The detective constable, who, the DCC had been amused to learn, was named Martin Andrews, nodded, picked up a bowl from amid the shambles on the floor, filled it from the tap in the sink, and placed it on the table, beside the body's head. The medical examiner thanked him again, and took a box of tissues from his case. He soaked a handful in the bowl, and began to wipe the thick mud from the head and face.

The police officers watched him work in silence for several minutes, until finally he nodded and glanced up at them. 'Yes,' he murmured, 'I thought so.' He beckoned. 'See here.' The three moved in, their eyes following his pointing finger, which drew them to the body's right temple, between the right eye and the top of the right ear. The skin was broken and discoloured. They focused on it, each trying not to look at the rest of the grotesque, puffy, dead face.

Duck pressed the area firmly, his fingers feeling around. 'There's been a severe blow to the head; hard enough to cause a fracture, I'd say. What I can't say is whether it was sustained before or after the man went into the water. There's very little blood, but that doesn't mean anything. Only the pathologist will be able to tell you whether the injury was sustained pre- or post-mortem. It's over to him now, I'm afraid.'

'Take a look at the wrists,' Martin murmured. 'Could he have been tied up?'

The examiner frowned, but did as he had been asked. 'It's possible, I suppose,' he said.

'Time of death?' asked Greatorix.

The ME looked distastefully at the victim, and sniffed. 'Several days ago. That's another for the pathologist.'

'Okay, doc, fair enough; you can head off now. Give me your statement tomorrow.'

'I will.' Dr Duck glanced at his watch. 'If I'm lucky,' he grumbled, 'I might even find a partner for later in the day.'

31

They listened as he squelched his way back up the narrow staircase. The deputy chief patted the body on the shoulder with a gloved hand. 'Inconvenient of you to die,' he murmured.

'Identification,' said DCS Greatorix, abruptly. 'Andrews, don't remove any of his clothing . . . that'll be done at the mortuary . . . but go through his pockets.'

The young man, who was in his mid-twenties, grimaced. 'Could that not wait, boss?' he asked; it was almost a plea.

'No, it can't. Go on, lad; just think of the day when you'll be able to order people like you to do the really dirty work.' He turned to Martin. 'Fancy a breath of air, sir?'

'Do I ever.' They followed in the doctor's footsteps, up the steep stair and into Miss Bonney's hall. Martin stripped off the all-covering scene-of-crime tunic and threw it on the floor, beside the one that the doctor had discarded. 'I won't be going down there again,' he said. He looked down at his white shirt, then at his reflection in a mirror that hung on the wall, above the level of the flood.

'Your wife's going to be pleased when she sees that shirt, Andy,' Greatorix chuckled.

'What makes you think she's going to see it? This one's for the bin.' He frowned, suddenly and savagely. 'I hate it when they've been in the water, Rod. It doesn't happen very often with homicides . . . that's assuming this is . . . but I had one in Edinburgh a year or so back. What a fucking mess he was in; much worse than that guy.'

'It's never nice,' the DCS said. His new deputy chief glanced at him, privately feeling self-conscious about being higher in rank than such an experienced and clearly capable officer. The head of CID was somewhere in his fifties, and could have been up to twenty years older than him. Martin knew that he had been a candidate for his job, and guessed that it was only his age that had told against him. Graham Morton, the Chief Constable, had made a point of telling him how highly Greatorix was rated, but he had known that from the grapevine within the Superintendents' Association.

'I've had a few in my time too,' he continued. 'They're a bugger to begin with in terms of what you pull out, and they can get worse. I just hope young Martin comes up with a name and address, otherwise we could have a problem. That's quite a big river over there, especially when it floods, and without an ID we won't have a clue where our guy went in. The only thing I can say with any certainty is that he didn't drift upstream. Christ, he needn't necessarily have gone in in our area at all. I've got a bad feeling about it already, Andy. I know he was in a state, but even at that, he looked like a bum. He needed a shave, and his hair looked as if he'd cut it himself . . . and badly at that.'

'Let's wait for Andrews, then,' said the DCS. He led the way out of the front door and down on to the pavement. There was an ambulance parked nearby; its rear doors were open and the crew, a man and a woman, were sitting inside. Two cars were parked alongside; one belonged to the DCS and the other to the detective constable and his sergeant, a woman named Joan Dunn, who was sitting with Miss Bonney in what she called her sewing room, on the upper floor of her home.

Out on the Inch, he saw a television crew. 'Who are they?' he asked his colleague.

'Grampian, I think,' Greatorix replied. 'Yes, I recognise the girl who's talking to Harry Sharp; she's a reporter.'

'They can't know what we're up to here then.'

'Not yet; they're probably just filming the clear-up, and Harry won't make her any the wiser. But sooner or later she'll work out that the ambulance crew aren't here for a tea-break. Do you want to deal with her when she does?'

'No. Like I said, this is your show.'

'Excuse me, sirs.' DC Andrews' voice came from behind them, from the doorway. The head of CID waved to him to join them.

'I've been through all his pockets,' the young officer reported. 'There's not a clue to his identity. There was nothing there but three pounds seventy-four in his trouser pocket, and this, in the inside pocket of his jacket.' He handed something to Greatorix.

The object was encased in plastic. At first, Andy Martin thought it was a driving licence, but realised quickly that if it had been it would have borne a name. He looked closer, and saw that it was a photograph. 'Odd,' the chief superintendent muttered. He glanced at it idly for a few seconds, then handed it to the deputy chief. 'Maybe it's him, in his younger days.'

Martin looked at the plastic packet. As he did, some control mechanism within him made him stifle the gasp that sprang to his lips, and held him straight when he felt like wobbling. With its covering, the black-and-white photograph had survived the flood, and was clearly recognisable. It was that of a young man, dark-haired, tall and powerfully built, but no more, he guessed, than twenty-one or twenty-two years old. He was looking solemnly at the camera, and he wore a dark suit with broad lapels. Martin stared at it in silence, until he realised that the other two were staring at him.

The deputy chief constable tucked the likeness into the pocket of his shirt. 'I've been promising you all day that I won't interfere, Rod,' he said, 'and I still mean it. But I think I can help here. With your permission, I'd like to hold on to this for a day or so. I don't think this is the man inside, but it could help us find out exactly who he is.'

'If you can do that, sir . . .' said the chief superintendent.

'Thanks,' said Martin. He headed off towards his car. 'I'll be in touch,' he called back over his shoulder. 'As soon as I can.'

7

It takes very little to cause traffic congestion in the centre of Edinburgh. A major fire alert in the heart of Princes Street is a recipe for major-league chaos. Maggie Rose was stuck in it for a while, until she called HQ and had a motorcycle officer locate her and clear a way for her through the queues.

She had to concentrate as she followed his lead, but still thoughts of Rufus, and of Mario, forced their way into her mind. She knew that she had no choice but to give the boy up, and she knew that her husband realised that also. However, what he did not know was that even if she could have seen a way to keep him, she would probably still have opted to hand him over. He was, after all, her father's son; taking him in had been Mario's idea, not hers, and while she had gone along with it, it had taken a great effort on her part. The truth was she felt nothing for the boy.

As for Mario . . . the core of her feelings for him had not changed. She believed that she loved him, even if she could no longer force herself to do so physically, the act having become completely abhorrent to her. She had no illusions about the meaning of his overnight absences. At first he had been 'working late', but recently no excuse had been offered and no questions asked. Her outburst that morning had been a mistake that she regretted already. She could guess where he was spending those missing nights, and with whom, but if that was what it took to keep them together, she could handle it. She was confident that he was not going to leave her to move in with his cousin, and if Paula was prepared to feed his appetites on that basis, well, it was fair enough by her.

She pushed her musings away as her escort led her into Princes Street. It was closed off, from Waverley Bridge to the West End, and two uniformed constables were stationed at the Scott Monument, diverting traffic past Jenners and up towards St Andrews Square. Her motorcyclist, a sergeant, spoke to one of them and she was waved through without delay. She parked as close to the scene of the incident as she could, about one hundred yards away, and walked the rest.

As she approached, she counted four fire appliances parked in the roadway, outside the pillared entrance to the Royal Scottish Academy, with another three drawn up in the paved area to the right. At least two dozen firefighters were milling around, and beyond them a crowd of spectators were being marshalled by uniformed police. As Rose looked at the scene, she realised to her surprise that no ladders were deployed, and no hoses rolled out. She frowned, and looked for signs of smoke coming from the grey stone building, but she saw none.

She strode past the throng and trotted up the entrance steps. There, in the open doorway, the first person she saw was Chief Superintendent Manny English, the uniformed commander of her division. 'Where's the fire?' she asked him.

'Out,' he replied, curtly. 'The staff here fought it successfully with extinguishers.'

'All that lot outside are a bit of overkill, then,' said Rose.

'Perhaps that's true, but it's better to look over-cautious in hindsight than to look negligent.'

She made an effort to keep from smiling. Within the force, English had a reputation for over-caution that bordered on the legendary. 'It's your business,' she said, 'Manny, yours and the firemaster's, but what if there's another major incident this afternoon with most of the appliances here and doing nothing, and the traffic screwed up good and proper?'

'That's a damn good question, Maggie,' said a voice from the side. She turned to see Senior Fire Officer Matt Grogan, in his white helmet, bearing down on her and the divisional commander. 'Do you have the gift of second sight?' he continued. 'We've just had a call-out from the Exchange district, up Lothian Road. There's been a major outbreak in one of the new office blocks up there. It's just round the corner from the fire station, but of course all our bloody appliances are down here, aren't they! I need your people to clear the traffic for us, Manny, and I need them now!'

36

'Yes, yes, I'll deploy officers at once.' English stepped out into Princes Street, shouting orders to a nearby inspector. Grogan was about to follow him, when Rose caught his sleeve.

'Hold on a second, Matt,' she exclaimed. 'What about this incident?'

'It was deliberate, Maggie; no doubt about it. But my boys have searched the whole place, and found no other surprises. Your man Steele's through there. He'll bring you up to speed on it. Now I must go. From the sound of things we've got a real fire up there, unlike this one.'

'Thanks. Good luck.' Grogan shouldered his way through the door and broke into a run; Rose turned and headed up the stairs that led into the main hall of the Academy.

The big room was split into a number of alcoves, but she had no trouble locating the scene of the fire; a crowd of people, one or two in uniform, the rest informally dressed, stood directly ahead of her, all staring into a booth on the left of the gallery. She could not see what they were looking at, since a wall blocked her view, but she could read the shock and distress on their faces.

'Ma'am.' She turned, to see Detective Inspector Stevie Steele, as he stepped out of an alcove on her right. He was tall and good-looking, in his early thirties, single and something of a heart-throb, she had heard, although he tended to keep his private life to himself. She knew that he was a former boyfriend of Paula Viareggio, and there had been one other dark rumour about an attraction, but Rose had always thought that he was too smart to risk that.

'Less of the formality, Stevie,' she said. 'There are no other ranks around, are there?'

'No. I was in on my own when the shout came in.'

'Has there been an arrest?'

'No. It looks as if someone planted an incendiary device on a timer.'

'We'll need back-up then.'

'I've got technicians on the way; we're going to need them. I'm expecting a couple of DCs as well to start taking statements.'

'Why, exactly . . . just what is this?'

'Didn't you see the signs outside?'

'No. I saw Manny English; that was enough.'

Steele laughed. 'Yes, I decided to keep well out of his way, otherwise I might have found myself on points duty too. Actually,' he said, 'what we have here is an exhibition of religious art. Do you know anything about the subject?'

'I wouldn't know a Botticelli from a Beryl Cook,' she answered, truthfully.

'You'll find him here,' the inspector told her, 'but not her. You'll also find Titian, and El Greco, and even Dali's *Cubist Christ*. This is the RSA's big summer attraction; it pulls together great works, from various schools, and it's scheduled to run all the way into September. It's being sponsored by the solicitors, Candela and Finch, to mark their bicentenary, and also the refurbishment of the Academy building itself; the opening ceremony was just getting under way when the brown stuff hit the fan. The people you probably saw outside in the piazza are their guests.

'The problem is that someone's torched one of the prize exhibits. That's what they're all staring at over there; I've got the Academy's security staff standing guard over it, to make sure no one touches it before Arthur Dorward's lot get here.'

'Bloody hell!' Rose exclaimed. 'What is it? Not the Botti-what's-it, I hope.'

'No. It's a work called *The Holy Trinity*, by a modern Chilean artist called Isobel Vargas. It's what you would call controversial, although some people have gone further and called it blasphemous.'

'Why so?'

'Because the Blessed Trinity are all depicted as female.'

'What, you mean Mother, Daughter and Holy Ghostess?'

'You got it in three. At least that's what it did look like; it's a bit changed now. Come and see for yourself.'

He led her over, excusing them quietly past the silent onlookers, and into the alcove in which the exhibit had been placed. It was still hanging there, still perfectly lit from above, but no longer in the form of the artist's vision. The gold frame . . . about five feet deep by four feet wide, Rose estimated . . . was largely undamaged, although foam from a fire extinguisher still dripped from it in places, forming puddles on the floor below, but the painting itself had been virtually destroyed. It was a mass of blackened, hanging threads with a gaping hole in the centre through which the scorched wall behind could be seen. Three of its corners retained colour and shape, but even they were badly blistered.

'Pretty comprehensive,' the detective superintendent muttered.

'Oh yes,' Steele agreed. 'I haven't touched it, and neither did the fire boys, but Grogan said he thought that an incendiary device had been placed behind it, in the bottom left corner. You'll see that's been completely destroyed. As I said, he thinks we'll find the remains of a timing device when the technicians look behind it.'

'When did it happen?'

'I can tell you that,' a dry, cultured voice interrupted. Rose turned to look up at a tall, grey-haired man in a dark business suit, with flecks of dandruff about its shoulders and lapels.

'This is Mr David Candela, the senior partner of Candela and Finch,' Steele explained.

'I thought this was your bicentenary,' she said to the man.

He nodded, taking her meaning at once. 'It is, but there's been a Candela in the firm since its foundation. We're very proud of the family connection. It's unique in its longevity, I believe.'

'Congratulations,' said the detective. 'Now tell me about the present.'

'Certainly. I was right in the middle of my opening speech, standing just there . . .' he pointed to a spot in below the Botticelli which hung on the far wall '. . . when there was a damn great whoosh to my right, and the damn thing went up in flames.

'I got quite a shock, I can tell you. All hell broke loose, of course; the curator, who was standing beside me, went into a blue funk and ran off to call 999. A couple of the security Johnnies, they grabbed fire extinguishers and started to go at the fire. It was going like . . .' he gave a short braying laugh at an impending joke '. . . like blazes, I suppose, but they got it out eventually. By the time they did, though, it looked like that. It's a bit of a bugger, really; we're underwriting the insurance costs of this show.'

'Has your firm upset anyone lately, Mr Candela?' Rose asked.

'My dear lady,' the man replied, affably, 'my firm has been upsetting people for two hundred years now. We have developed a style over that time which tends to get right up the noses of the people on the opposite side of disputes in which we become involved. Kick 'em bloody hard in the thingamajigs; it's the only way in litigation, and we're bloody good at it, I can tell you.'

Smiling in spite of her dislike of being taken for a dear lady, Rose nodded towards the wrecked painting. 'Can you think of anyone you might have upset enough for them to do that to you?'

Mr Candela drew himself up, seeming to find another couple of inches in height in the process. 'Dear lady . . .' he began.

'Superintendent,' said Maggie, affably.

'Superintendent then,' he continued, unruffled, 'the people against whom we litigate tend not to be, shall I say, at that end of the market. They went to different schools. Some of them may be arseholes, I'll admit, but I do not believe that any of them are arsonists. Go down that road if you choose; I'll co-operate, if only to annoy some of the buggers even more, but you won't find your man among them.'

Rose sighed. 'I'm sure you're right, Mr Candela, but I can't take that as read. It's a line of enquiry I'll have to follow.' She turned to Steele. 'Stevie, a word.'

They walked back to the alcove from which they had come, in time to see the red-haired Inspector Arthur Dorward, the head of the scene-of-crime team, slouch glumly into the hall. 'Another unhappy copper,' said Rose, in greeting. 'It's over there. We think you'll find the remains of a firebomb behind it. As usual, we'd like to know everything about it, and we'd like to know yesterday. If that's not possible, later on today will do.

'While you're at that, Stevie and I will start to go through the basics.' She pointed up into a corner of the gallery towards a video camera. 'That has to be connected to a tape. Maybe we'll get lucky and it'll give us a result.'

Steele looked at her with something approaching disdain. 'Sure, Maggie, sure, and maybe God really is a woman.'

8

Sarah stood on the porch of the cabin. The sun was rising in the sky, its light glistening and dancing on the waters of the lake, and the day was becoming hot, yet she clutched herself as if she was shivering.

'It's taken a hell of an effort for you to come here, hasn't it?' Ron Neidholm murmured from behind her.

She glanced at him over her shoulder as he leaned against the frame of the open door. He was one of the biggest quarterbacks in football history, six feet five and two hundred and forty-five pounds according to the official website, and he seemed to fill it.

'Oh it has,' she agreed. 'At first, you know, I decided that I never wanted to see this place, the house where my parents were murdered. Then gradually, I realised that I had to, if I was ever going to come to terms with it. It was really nice of you to offer to bring me up here; I could never have come on my own.

'Even with you alongside me, it wasn't easy; you probably didn't notice, but the closer we got along the road, the more I was trembling.'

He reached out and touched her shoulder, then slipped his fingers through her auburn hair, and rubbed her neck gently, feeling her tension. 'I noticed all right,' he said, as he moved close behind her. She leaned against him; her eyes closed as her head fell back against his chest. 'How do you feel now?' he asked.

'I don't know,' she whispered. 'I feel that I should cry, but I can't. At one point I thought I'd drench the place in gasoline and burn it to the ground, in a grand gesture, but now that I've seen it, I can't do that either. It's just so beautiful here.'

'Beautiful, and isolated; and vulnerable.'

'You don't need to remind me.'

Feeling a small shudder run through her, he slid his arms around her and held her tight. 'I'm sorry. It was stupid of me to say that . . . but then I never did have a way with words.'

She turned in his embrace, and looked up at him. 'You didn't need it,' she said, with a smile in her eyes, if not on her lips. 'You had other ways.'

'I still have, honey: I still have.'

'I'll bet you do. And plenty of opportunity to use them too, I'll bet. In Britain or America, you footballers are all the same.'

His face took on a mock frown. 'Hey, I'm a national figure; I can't get up to stuff like that. Besides, when you get past the thirty mark, the groupies tend to pass you by.'

'More fools them, I'm sure.'

'Nah, they just assume there's a little wife at home, that's all. Most times they're right, too; most of my contemporaries have families.'

'Have you ever been married, Ron?'

'No. Not even close.'

'Why not?'

'Football.'

'That can't go on for ever.'

'I know.'

'What you said the other night, about maybe giving up . . . were you serious?'

'I'm always serious, Sarah, especially about you.'

Sarah took a deep breath and looked up at him. 'Ron, things have changed since we had our thing at college; apart from everything else, I have three kids.'

'Yeah, and great kids they are; I hope I can spend a little more time with them when I take you back.' He glanced around the surrounding woods and out across the water. 'Now you've finally seen this place, do you think you might keep it for them to enjoy?'

She gave a soft whistle, and smiled. 'They might enjoy it, but it would be a nightmare for me. Mark isn't exactly an outdoor boy; he's a mathematician and a computer buff, and he's happy anywhere with a telephone line. But James Andrew is action boy personified. As soon as I turned my back on him he'd be halfway up a tree. As for Seonaid, it's early days yet, but she's showing signs of turning out the same way. No,

I haven't decided what to do with it yet. I have been toying with an idea, though, of giving it, or at least making it available to, an outfit that works with deprived inner-city kids. What do you think?'

'I think that would be very noble.' He looked at the heavy logs that formed the walls. 'The structure would make it pretty difficult to spray-paint, and they'd probably take their knives away before they brought them up here, so you wouldn't have gang symbols carved anywhere.'

'Cynic,' she laughed. She stepped back from him, holding on to his left hand. 'Speaking of getting back to Buffalo,' she said, 'as we were, how long have we got here? When should we be thinking about heading back to the airfield? I know you've been flying for a few years now, but we don't want to take any chance of doing it after dark. Your plane isn't that big.'

His face creased into a broad grin. 'You know what the private pilot's greatest enemy is? Fog, that's what. Why, you can have what looks like a perfect day, just like this, yet the temperature can change just a degree or two and great banks of the damn stuff can appear out of nowhere. And when they do, only the big aircraft can fly.'

Without warning he gazed out over the lake then pointed, with his free hand. 'Hey, over there; I'm sure I can see a fog bank, can't you?'

She looked out over the shining water. 'No', she replied. 'I don't believe I can.'

'What the hell,' he chuckled. 'It was worth a try. The stuff is so damned unpredictable after all.'

'Yes, I've heard that. And you know what? I can be pretty damned unpredictable too.' She held his hand against her face, and kissed it. 'If we'd been somewhere else, and the moment had been right, I might just have seen that fog bank. But not here, Ron; not here.'

9

Afternoon was turning into evening as Martin rang the doorbell, and waited. He was no longer in uniform, but dressed in jeans, a white tee-shirt and a black bomber jacket that he had owned for years. Its leather was creased and softened with wear, and it was the most comfortable garment he had ever known.

The day had gone from warm to hot, but the air conditioning in his new Mondeo was efficient, and so he was comfortable despite the seventy-five-mile drive.

Rather than the few moments he had expected, his wait turned into minutes. He rang the bell again, frowning. Finally, the heavy front door opened.

The man who stood there was wearing only shorts and trainers, and was glistening with sweat. He was taller than Martin at around six feet two, and looked at least ten years older. His face was lined, with a deep scar above the nose, and his gun-grey hair was sticking to his temples and standing up in spikes on top. But his body was that of a much younger man, wide-shouldered, narrow-waisted, with long muscles on his arms and legs and a six-pack that looked rock hard.

He swung the door open wider and smiled, that warm, endearing grin that Andy knew so well. 'I'm sorry, son,' he said, then stopped. 'Listen to me, calling you son. I should probably call you "sir", since you're a serving deputy chief constable and they've got me destined for the scrapheap.

'Come on in, anyway. I was working out in my gym upstairs. I thought I'd have plenty of time before you got here. Either you've come down that road like a bat out of hell or I'm slowing up.'

'Jesus, man,' said Martin as he stepped into the house. 'You were out running earlier when I called you on the mobile. You shouldn't be going at it this hard.'

Bob Skinner's smile disappeared. 'Too fucking right I should,' he snapped. 'I'm going to show a few people just how stupid they are.'

'You are taking this too personally,' his friend replied, allowing himself to be led into the kitchen. 'They're just being cautious, that's all. Remember when Jimmy had his heart attack? It was a while before they'd let him back to work.'

The bigger man sighed, as if he was making an effort to be patient. 'Listen, Andy, for the umpteenth time, I did not have a heart attack. I had an incident that turned out to be something called sick sinus syndrome, a condition in which your heart rate drops without warning and you pass out. They put me on a treadmill in hospital in the States, once I'd recovered, with all sorts of monitors attached to me. You're supposed to walk steadily on it; I ran nearly two miles in the ten minutes of the test.

'The bloody thing's hereditary; my mother had it when she was in middle age, and so did my Uncle George. It passed off with them as they grew older. They didn't know what caused it then and they still don't.'

He reached up and touched his chest, about four inches above the left nipple. 'If these things had been around then they'd probably have had them fitted as a precaution, just as the Americans insisted on doing with me.'

Martin looked at the area where the pacemaker had been inserted. The scar was still fresh, but it had begun to fade and had been overgrown already by chest hair. The flat lump that he had seen before, where the device lay on top of the ribcage, had almost disappeared, enveloped by renewed muscle.

'I tell you, Andy,' Skinner insisted, 'I am as fit as I have ever been and, probably as a result of this thing, fitter than I've been for years. I went round Gullane One in seventy-three yesterday, and I've never hit the bloody ball as far.'

'Doesn't the pacemaker affect you at all?'

'No. It's set to kick in if my pulse rate drops below fifty-five, or if it rises to one-seventy-five. Even when I'm running flat out it never gets that high.'

'Nonetheless,' said the other man, 'you have to ally a bit of patience to this physical work you're doing. Rules is rules, like they say, even for Deputy Chief Constable Bob Skinner. When are you due for your next medical?'

'Not for another month, on the present timetable . . . but I'm going to do something about that.'

'Why, for fuck's sake? You haven't had a sabbatical in years. Play bloody golf, enjoy yourself, go back to Sarah in the States; stop doing your head in, and everyone else's.'

'Don't mention Sarah to me, please. She actually wants me to chuck the police. Can you believe that? And why the hell should I go to her? Okay, there's legal work to be done tidying up her parents' estate, but there is such a thing as airmail. Anything she has to sign could be sent over here and notarised here.'

'It's a lot of money, Bob.'

'So? It's her money. And how does that affect my career?'

'Significantly, if you choose to look at it that way.'

'Which I do not!' Skinner opened the big larder fridge in a corner of his kitchen and took out two cans of Seven-Up. He popped them both and handed one to his friend. 'You, at least, know how I feel about my job,' he said, more quietly. 'Sarah seems to have gone native back in Buffalo; she's moved Trish, the nanny, over there, and she's settled herself and the kids comfortably into her parents' home. She's even sending Mark to school over there.'

'But she says it's temporary, doesn't she?'

'She says so, but I don't think I believe her, Andy. She's turning back into a Yank and she wants me, and my kids, to become Yanks too. It may be her world over there, but it is not mine. There's no logic to her, anyway. Her parents died over there, tragically, and some stuff happened in the aftermath that I can't tell even you about. You'd have thought she couldn't wait to get back here, to our life, after all that.'

'Maybe that's why she's reluctant to come back right now,' Martin suggested. 'Maybe she still has some getting over to do.'

'And maybe that's why she wants to turn me into a kept man?' Skinner shot back at him.

'Don't be daft; it's not that and you know it. Whatever you call it, you dropped like a stone at her feet and she thought you were dead. That's how she put it to me; she's a doctor, and she thought that. It might have turned out to be a freak condition, but your heart stopped, man. For ten to fifteen seconds, so she told me. Of course she's worried about you . . . and she does want you around, for all that you say.'

'Is that so? Well, last time I spoke to her, she told me that if I was so devoted to Scotland I could and I quote, "fucking well stay here". She told me in a loud voice too.'

'When was that?'

'Last night. I called her again at lunchtime and she wasn't even there. Trish said she's gone off on some sort of trip, but she wasn't sure where.'

'Call her on her mobile.'

'She's left it behind. She's probably got herself sorted out with a man over there.'

'Bob!'

Skinner glanced at him, defensively. 'Why not?' he muttered. 'It wouldn't be the first time.'

'All the more reason to go back over there then, is it not, if that's what you're thinking?'

'Ah man, I'm not. She's just playing me along, that's all. She thinks I'm being unreasonable; I fucking know that she is.' He paused, to take a swig from his can. 'Look, I've been obsessive in the past, I admit that. But this is different. I have enemies on the joint Police Board, as you well know. Councillor Agnes Maley and her friends have always been afraid of me, and they haven't gone away; Jimmy Proud's squashed them in the past, but he could never get rid of them. Forget their politics, that doesn't have much to do with it. There are a couple of them who are friends of, or friends of friends of, people with whom you and I have had professional dealings in the past. That's to say, we've banged them up.

'These characters, led by Agnes, have wanted me out for years. They tried once before, remember, without success; now they've plucked up the courage to have another go. Even as I speak, there's a group of them on the manpower sub-committee who are trying to change the rules, so that people who've had a range of specified complaints and incidents, including the minor heart procedure that I've had, must be retired on grounds of ill health. They're saying, for example, that the chief should have been retired automatically after he had his wobbler. It's not just about me, you see, although I'm the prime target. These people want all the power over the police that they can get. They're not an isolated group either; that sort of thinking runs pretty high up in the current regime. Look at these civilian patrols they've got in some places now. Fucking crap.' He paused.

'Jimmy Proud's fighting it, of course, but if they bring a positive recommendation to the full committee and put a three-liner on, it could go through. Once I'm back on duty, though, they're stuffed. They can't do it retrospectively, because I'd sue them and win, and they know it. That's why they've told me I have to have another month's recuperation before I have my medical.' He smiled, wickedly.

'So on Monday, I'm going to demand a definitive medical, now. If the force examiners, who report to . . . and take their orders from . . . this wee sub-committee, try to stick to their timetable, I'll go to court and interdict them. Mitchell Laidlaw has the petition ready to roll. He's acting for me, by the way. I need the best there is, in the circumstances.'

'What if you lose?'

'I won't. Mitch never loses.'

'But if he breaks his duck this time, and you don't succeed; will it be the end of your life, Bob? No, it won't.'

'That is unthinkable, pal. It's not going to happen. I won't have my career end just because of a temporary electrical malfunction in my ticker. I've got places to go yet, as you know.'

'That wouldn't scupper your plans though, would it?'

'If I wasn't a serving officer, yes it would.'

Martin frowned; he was silent for a few seconds as he considered what his friend had said. 'I see,' he murmured at last. 'Bob, I'm sorry. I've been so wrapped up in my new job that I didn't realise things were so serious for you. I understand now.'

'I'm glad you do. There are four people in the world I need to have on my side over this; Neil McIlhenney, you, my Alex, and Sarah. You make it three for; it's the one against that's tearing me apart.'

'Would you like me to call her, Bob, to put your case, so to speak?'

Skinner smiled, gratefully. 'It's nice of you to offer, son, but she has to work it out for herself.' He drained the can. 'But listen, when you said that there was something you wanted to talk to me about, I didn't get the impression that it was my bother with the Maley tendency on the Board.'

'No, it isn't.'

'Fine, but give me a minute, will you. I'm fucking honking; I must have a shower, or I will start to rot. Once I've done that, we'll go for a walk on Gullane beach and enjoy this fine day, and you can tell me what the problem is.' He left the kitchen.

On his own, Andy wandered through to the living area. He knew the house well: the Skinners had built it after their split, and reconciliation, when they decided to sell both their weekend house and their Edinburgh bungalow, and bring up their family full-time in the East Lothian village of Gullane. He looked at the photograph of Sarah, in its usual spot on the sideboard, and began to worry. He was slavishly devoted to her, remarkably so, for she might have become his mother-in-law. He had been engaged for a while to Alexis, Bob's daughter from his first marriage; the engagement had ended acrimoniously, but both he and Sarah had made sure that it did not affect their friendship. He thought about what Bob had said. He gave no credence to his suggestion that she might have found someone else, but he knew that she was as stubborn as her husband; if she had taken up a position, she would not give it up easily.

The living room opened into a big conservatory; he wandered through the glass doors and gazed out across Gullane Bents and over the Firth of Forth to Fife. He saw three tankers moored in the wide estuary, riding high in the water as they waited their turn to take on a cargo of oil at Hound Point.

'Okay, then?' Bob's voice snapped him back to the present. His hair was still damp from the shower, but he was ready to go, having changed into light cotton trousers, a pale blue polo shirt, and Timberland sandals.

They left the house, Skinner setting the alarm with quick, nimble fingers, and headed out into the village street. One left turn took them down on to the Bents, down the road that led to the car park, thronged as always on a June Saturday afternoon. 'Where'll we go?' Bob asked, then said, 'tide's on the way out; the Nature Reserve.' Decision made. He led the way, half running, half walking, down the narrow path that led to the sands. Jumping down from a dune onto the beach, he started to head westward, then stopped.

'What's up?' asked Andy.

Skinner pointed, with his right index finger. His friend followed its direction until he saw, near the water's edge, a big, dark-haired man, muscular in a shortsleeved shirt and denim cut-offs, knocking a brightly coloured ball towards a toddler.

'That's McGuire, isn't it?' Skinner muttered.

'Yes. That must be the kid I heard he and Maggie are adopting.'

'Let's go the other way then. Mario's a good guy, but I'm not in the mood for any more chat about my career prospects.' Without waiting for an answer he turned on his heel and headed off towards the rocks and dunes at the eastward end of the big bay.

'I didn't see Maggie there,' said Martin, 'but I've heard the talk. How are things with him and Detective Superintendent Rose?'

'Officially, fine. But in reality, from what Neil tells me, they're rocky. I didn't press him about it, for in truth it's none of my business, but I think it's to do with Mario becoming a trustee of the family interests, along with his cousin. You know his cousin, do you?'

'Paula Viareggio? Stevie Steele's ex? Oh yes, I know her all right.'

Skinner laughed. 'Christ, not her too! Is there a woman in Edinburgh you didn't shag when you were single?'

'Plenty, and I didn't know Paula in that way. I just met her a couple of times. She's a deep one; she had a way of letting you know right from the off where you stood with her, and the answer I got was always "No way". Her and Mario? Is that what they're saying? No, they're cousins, remember.'

'They're also Italian.' Skinner laughed. 'But Mario doesn't run the trust on a day-to-day basis. He's appointed a lawyer to do most of the work for him, so that he's hands-off. He only takes decisions on her advice.'

'Her?'

'Alex. My kid's getting on in the world.'

'Glad to hear it. How is she?'

'Very well, and before you ask, she isn't behind McGuire's problem with Maggie either. She's still based in London; there's an actor bloke in tow, I believe, but I've still to meet him. Anyway, enough of all that. How about you? How's Karen? How's the baby?'

'Lovely, both of them. Bob, I wish I could ask you and Sarah to be godparents, but I think you have to be Catholics.'

'Don't worry about it. I'm the wrong guy to ask anyway; God and I are barely on speaking terms most of the time. There's not much point asking Sarah and me to do something together either, but let's not get into that again. Tell me about the job, how are you liking Tayside?'

Martin smiled. 'It's excellent, Bob, it really is. Sure, compared to ours . . . yours, I should say . . . it's a pocket-sized force, but I'm coming to think of that as an advantage. The clear-up rates are about as good as they could get, for a start. Graham Morton's a first class chief constable, and so are all his officers. I can say honestly that since I've been there, I haven't come across a single piece of dead wood.'

'No Greg Jays, then?'

'None at all,' he replied, then realised he had been tricked into a comment. 'Greg isn't all that bad, though,' he added, quickly. 'He's a divisional CID commander after all.'

'Aye, but he's past his sell-by date for the job. He's lost his spark, and the new blood, like Rose and McGuire, are showing him up. He's still well short of compulsory retirement though, and unless he chooses to go that gives me a problem. I think I've solved it, though. Willie Haggerty was all for giving Maggie Manny English's job when he goes next winter, but I'm planning to put Greg in there. It's uniform, it's a nominal promotion and it needs a good book operator, which he is.' He paused, and his face darkened. 'Mind you, before I can do that, I need to get myself back on the job.'

They walked on in silence for a while, until they had left the big bay behind, passed Freshwater Haven and come to another beach, this one deserted, without a soul on its pale golden sands. Skinner pointed to a path that led off inland. 'We can take that and get back round the edge of Muirfield,' he said, 'or we can go on and have ourselves a real walk.'

Andy Martin frowned. 'The short route will do me fine,' he replied, firmly, 'but before we go any further in any direction, I want to get down to the thing that brought me here.'

'Do that, by all means. I'm intrigued.'

The younger man stopped, beside the ruins of an old stone cottage, and took a seat on what was left of a wall. Skinner followed his lead and perched alongside him, on his right.

'You'll have heard about the flood we had up in Perth,' he began, 'after all that freak snow melted.'

'The El Niño thing? Sure, I heard. I still find time to watch the telly, son.'

'In that case you can imagine what the place looks like now that the water's gone down.'

'A quagmire, I'd guess.'

'Right. This morning we began the clear-up operation in the houses that were flooded out. I was warned to expect all sorts in there; cats, dogs, fish and frogs, sheep and even a few deer. I was not warned to expect what we did find. I went with an old lady into her basement, where she came upon the body of a man.'

'Shit. Washed away by the flood?'

'Aye, with a mark on his wrist that could have been left by a rope, and a mark on the side of his head that could have been put there before he went in the river. There was enough about it for us to be treating it as a suspicious death.'

'Dramatic. You sure he wasn't the old lady's bidey-in?'

'Miss Bonney wouldn't know what a bidey-in is, Bob. She's sweet seventy-six and probably never been kissed.'

'Lucky for her. So what do you want from me? If it's advice on the flood patterns of the silvery Tay, I know fuck all about them. If it's the loan of some people to help with your investigation, you'd better talk to Haggerty rather than me.'

'That's a "No" to the first. As for the second, we're not at that stage yet, and when we are it'll be my head of CID who does the asking of Dan Pringle.'

Martin reached for the back pocket of his jeans, then paused. 'Once the photographer and the doc were finished, we went through the man's pockets.'

'We?'

He grinned, fleetingly. 'Okay, our young DC did. There was no wallet, no driving licence, no old envelope with his name on it.' Finally, his hand completed its journey to his pocket. 'Only this,' he said, drawing out the monochrome photograph, still in its plastic container, and handed it over.

Skinner took it from him; as he looked at it, Martin watched him intently. He had never seen a reaction remotely like it, not from Bob Skinner, at any rate. His eyes widened, his mouth fell open, he seemed to slip, for a moment, on his stony seat, and he gulped.

His friend sat, listening to the gulls as they broke the silence, waiting as he stared at the photograph. Finally he was able to form a long slow whisper. 'Oh my God.'

'You see?' said Andy. 'That's you as a young man, isn't it?'

It was his turn to be astonished, as Skinner shook his head slowly. 'You can be forgiven for thinking it, my friend; yes, even you. But this is not me. No, this is a photograph of my father.'

'Your father?'

'Sure as God made wee green apples.' He looked to his left into Martin's green eyes. 'The man in the river: how old was he?'

'Bob, he'd been down there for a week and more, first in water, then half buried in mud.'

'I don't want his date of birth, son. Roughly, how old was he?'

Andy frowned, and looked out to sea. 'If I have to guess, I'd say he was mid to late fifties.'

Skinner stood up, rising off the wall in a single movement. 'Come on.' He was heading up the path towards Muirfield Golf Course even as he spoke.

Taken by surprise, Martin had to break into a trot to catch up. 'Do you think you know who he is?' he asked.

'I'm coming back up to Perth with you,' his long-striding friend announced.

'Fine, but do you think you can identify him?'

'I'm bloody certain of it.'

'So?'

'Let me see him first, Andy, and before the pathologist starts to hack him about, too. After that, I'll tell you all about him.'

10

Rufus was asleep when Mario carried him into the house, through the kitchen door. Maggie was waiting there; she looked him up and down. 'Couldn't you have rubbed some of that sand off at the beach,' she complained, 'instead of bringing it in here?'

He gave her a broad, innocent smile, straight from the Irish side of his ancestry. 'You should see the car,' he replied cheerfully. 'Don't worry, love. I'll hoover it all up later.'

'It'll be well into the carpets by then,' she grumbled. 'Go on, get him ready for bed and yourself cleaned up. I'll get the vacuum out. Has Rufus eaten?'

'Yes, we stopped in the Burger King at that Big W place.'

'How about you?'

'No.'

'That's good. I've got a sitter coming at seven . . . unless you've got other things to do, that is.' She snorted, almost to herself. 'Even if you have, I fancy a Saturday night out. If it comes to it I'll go on my own.'

She took him by surprise, but he said nothing as he carried Rufus off. The boy was coming back to a complaining wakefulness as he climbed the stairs. 'Come on, chum,' he whispered in his ear, 'let's get tidied up. Then you can dream about more sandcastles and your sister and I can go out to play . . . or eat, at least.'

He turned straight into the bathroom, stood Rufus on the floor, and took off his clothes, then stripped off his own shirt and shorts and stepped out of his sandals. He turned on the shower above the bath and lifted the boy in. They stood together under the warm power spray, Rufus squealing with renewed pleasure, for he loved the water, as the last of the sand washed off them and swirled away down the drain.

Finished, he took his towelling robe from behind the door and put it on. Then he took a big bath towel and rubbed the child gently dry. 'Okay, pal,' he said, straightfaced. 'Bedtime?' Heavy-eyed, Rufus smiled and nodded.

'Good boy.' The child ran through to his bedroom; when Mario stepped in afterwards he saw him taking his pyjamas from under the pillow where they were always kept. As the big detective helped him put them on, he felt a lump rise suddenly in his throat.

'This isn't forever, wee man,' he said, quietly, as much to himself as to Rufus. 'You'll have to go and live with someone else soon.' The boy's face fell; Mario hugged him. 'Don't worry, wee fella, you'll love it; you'll have even more toys, and other kids to play with, too. But when you do go, you'll come back and visit us every so often, won't you?' Reassured, he smiled and nodded.

He was asleep seconds after his blond head hit the pillow. Mario looked at him for a while, and then went through to his own room. He selected clothes for the evening . . . brown slacks, white shirt, and a lightly checked Daks jacket with brown leather patches at the elbow . . . but before dressing he picked up his mobile, which he had retrieved, with his wallet and his keys, from his shorts, and called Paula.

'Hi,' she answered warmly, knowing from her telephone read-out who was calling. 'Had a nice day?'

'Been to the beach.'

'*En famille?*'

'No, just me and Rufus. Maggie had to work. How about you? You had a good one?'

He saw her smile, in his mind's eye. 'The morning was best,' she replied, 'but the rest's been okay. I went to the shops and spent lots of nice money. Here, there was something going on in Princes Street. It was blocked.'

'A fire,' he told her, 'in an art exhibition. That's where Maggie had to go.'

'Which one?'

'The RSA, I think.'

'Oh no, I was going to take you there.'

'You probably still can. I don't know how bad it was. What you doing tonight?'

'Taking my mum to the pictures. Why? Do you want to come?'

'She'd love that. Anyway, I can't.'

'Mmm.' Paula was silent for a second. 'What's up, love?' she asked, eventually. 'You're not having a guilt trip, are you?'

'No, I'm having none of that. It's Rufus; I think we're going to lose him.'

'Oh no,' she said. 'How? Why?'

'I'll tell you when I see you. What are you doing on Monday evening?'

'From the sound of things I'm having a visitor.'

'Is that okay?'

'Of course; if you'd made it any later you'd have been in trouble. Will you want to eat?'

'That too,' he replied. 'See you then.'

The sitter arrived just as he was slipping on his jacket, freshly shaved and with his thick black hair as carefully brushed as he could manage. Maggie was finishing her own preparations in what had been their bedroom once upon a time, and so he went downstairs to let her in.

She turned out to be a couple; PC Harold 'Sauce' Haddock, a probationer from Maggie's division, and his girlfriend, Imelda. He wondered about the name; the girl looked pure Scottish. He guessed that either her parents must have had an interest in Filipino politics or her mother must have had an interest in collecting shoes.

They had sat for them before, but he still showed them into the living room. As his did so, his wife appeared behind him, in the doorway. 'Hi, Sauce,' she said brightly. He turned to look at her, and felt the flutter that came to him occasionally when she caught him off guard. Her red hair was shining and she was dressed in a sheath-like green dress and a short, matching jacket. Her eyes seemed to shine too, as she took his arm.

'You remember how everything works from the last time, don't you: telly, DVD, music, all that stuff?'

'Yes, ma'am,' the young PC nodded, holding up a slim carton. 'We've brought a film, *Con Air*; we'll leave it for you to watch if you like.' Imelda stayed mute; she was even more shy than her boyfriend.

'Thanks, but we've seen it. Look, Rufus is asleep upstairs, you won't have any trouble with him, because he's been at the seaside this afternoon and he's bushed. There's drinks in the fridge and sandwiches in clingfilm on the work surface. Help yourselves. We won't be late, but you've got my mobile number if you need us.'

She took Mario's arm. 'Bye,' she called, as she walked him to the door. He said nothing, just gave an easy smile that he hoped would confirm the appearance of a normal couple. He was a shade nervous about Maggie's choice of a serving copper as a sitter, but she liked the lad and trusted him.

She released his arm as soon as the front door closed behind them. 'Where are we going?' he asked, as they climbed into her car, which was parked in the road, rather than in their driveway.

'I've booked a table in Kublai Khan,' she replied. 'I fancy something exotic, and I reckoned Mongolian was about as way out as we could get.'

'That's okay by me.' He smiled, easily, to cover the fact that he was lying. Her CD player came on with the engine as she turned the key in the ignition. Maggie was a major fan of Mary Chapin Carpenter; 'State of the Heart' was playing, loud. A good choice, he thought; it was more upbeat and less sorrowful than some of her more recent stuff, although it did include a track called 'Never Had it So Good', with a lyric that he found rather pointed in their situation. Fortunately, he thought, they reached the restaurant just before Mary came to 'Quittin' Time'.

His private worry was eased as soon as they walked into the Leith restaurant. The big detective had been there before, a week earlier, with Paula: it was one of her favourites. Fortunately the maître d' was indeed masterful; if he recognised his guest . . . and Mario was aware that he was not someone who was forgotten easily . . . he gave no sign as he greeted them and showed them to their table.

He selected a bottle of an unusual Canadian red from the wine list, and a bottle of still water, then glanced at the menu. 'Your choice,' he said to Maggie, 'so you pick for us both.'

'Let's just go for the banquet, then,' she said, as the wine waiter returned, then sat in silence as her husband approved the wine.

Once they were alone again, he looked across the table at her. The smile had gone, and he saw that her underlying tension was working its way back to the surface. 'How was Rufus?' she asked. 'Did he enjoy the beach?'

'Does Santa Claus have a beard?' he answered. 'Of course he did.'

'And have you thought about it, about the situation, and that letter?'

'Of course.'

'And do you agree with me, about what we have to do?'

'He's your brother. It's your decision.'

'There's no decision,' she retorted, plaintively. 'I've got no choice.'

His eyes dropped from hers. 'I know,' he murmured; he looked up again. 'Do a deal with the Chamberlains. Tell them we won't contest if they give us visiting rights. I reckon they'll accept that, rather than risk a court action that they could well lose.'

She looked at him, gratefully . . . for reasons which he did not grasp entirely. 'I'll try.'

'Good. I'll speak to Alex about finding an appropriate lawyer to act for us.'

'There may be no need,' she said. 'I may have met one.'

She told him about her business at the Royal Scottish Academy, and her meeting with David Candela. 'His firm has a two-hundred-year-old letterhead, and he has a simple approach to what he does. He's a dry old stick, and I don't suppose he'll act himself, but I'm sure he'll take us on. I'm also pretty confident he'll get the result you want.'

'*We* want, Mags,' he interrupted. 'The result *we* want.'

'Of course,' she agreed quickly, but not quite in the right tone.

'You want rid of him, don't you: you want him to go.'

'No.'

'Mags, love, be honest.'

She shook her head. 'I just can't, Mario. I'm sorry. I've tried, but it's too difficult for me. If I'm being really honest, when I got that letter this morning, I said to myself "Thank God". He may be my brother, and he may be just a child, but I can't love him. It's too much to ask.'

He looked away, across the room, and gave a huge sigh. 'Of course it is,' he exclaimed, so firmly that at first she thought he was angry. 'I really am a stupid, selfish, insensitive bastard. I never asked you, did I? I just told you that this was what we were going to do. I never asked myself either, how you would feel bringing up your father's son. I am so sorry, Mags,' he told her. 'I had it in my head that Rufus would be the cord that would tie us together. Now I look at it through your eyes, I agree with you. Thank God that these people exist, and that they appear to care for him as they do.'

His eyes came back to her. 'So where will it leave us, when he goes?'

'Where do you want it to leave us?' She hesitated, then leaned forward. 'I'll ask you this straight out, just this one time. Do you want to leave me and go and live with Paula?'

'No, I want to live with you.'

'Even though I can't bear you to touch me?'

'Maybe that'll change.'

'Mario, all our married life, and before, I've been as good an actress as Louise McIlhenney used to be. Maybe in the future, every so often, I could get drunk enough to let you get your end away. But would you want that?'

'I don't have to answer that, do I?'

'I hope not. So what's to keep us together?'

'I love your soul, Mags, as much as I love your body. If you had motor neurone disease, or MS, or some other crippling thing, I wouldn't leave you, and I wouldn't force myself on you, either. So why's this any different?' He dazzled her with his sudden smile. 'Let's give it a name. Let's say you're suffering from chronic post-traumatic paralysis of the pussy, and leave it at that. If there's a miracle cure, great; if not, no matter.'

Her face stayed straight, but she flashed him a quick grin with her eyes. 'Do you really mean that?'

'I really do.'

'What about Paula? Let's take it as read that I know you're sleeping with her, and I don't mind. I know what a horny bugger you are, and in truth I'd rather you were going to her than to one of her saunas. But does she want you to move in with her?'

'No.'

'What if she did?'

'She won't, and you can take that as read too; Paulie is a truly independent girl. Nobody could live with her, and she knows it.'

'Do you love her?'

'I love her body, although not as much as yours. As for her soul, it's too like mine for me ever to love.' He glanced over her shoulder. 'Here comes the waiter. Get ready to order.'

59

She gave him their simple order. The young man wrote, nodded and left. As he did, she took Mario's hand in hers, if only for a second. 'Okay?' she asked.

'Okay,' he replied. 'Just try to believe in miracles, that's all I ask. Do that and you never know.'

'I'll try, but I do know.'

'We'll see. Let's talk shop. I heard a radio report about what happened at the RSA. You got a result yet?'

She shook her head. 'No. We let all the guests back into the building and we took a lot of statements but they all say the same thing; the painting just went up in flames . . . whoosh! Stevie and I looked at the security videos, but there wasn't a single lead on them that we could see. Arthur Dorward's got the debris in the lab; I'm waiting for him to report.'

'What do you reckon?'

'We have Christian fundamentalists too; from the reproduction of the ruined picture that I saw in the exhibition catalogue, that's what I reckon.'

'And you're probably right.' He paused, as the first of their dishes was brought to their table. 'Here,' he continued, 'I almost forgot. I took Rufus to Gullane today, instead of North Berwick, and guess who I saw on the beach? Bob Skinner and Andy Martin, that's who. They gave me a body-swerve too; thought I didn't notice them, but I did. They were doing some serious talking. I wonder what it was about?'

'Big Bob's predicament, probably. How was he looking?'

'From what I saw at a distance, he was looking very fit. Do you think he'll get back? Or do you think Councillor Maley's lot have got him this time?'

'They see the chance,' Maggie answered. 'What they're lacking are brains, resources and courage. He'll get back all right.'

'I'm glad you think so. I don't know about you, but with him gone, I find Dan Pringle becoming more and more unbearable as head of CID.' Then he smiled, as if he was anticipating something pleasant. 'Here, it strikes me that those characters are lacking something else too.'

'What's that?'

'Foresight. They can't imagine what's going to happen after he does get back.'

11

Essentially, mortuaries are the same in every town, every city, every First World country. Bob Skinner had been in a few, including, recently, one in the USA, where he had identified the bodies of Sarah's parents; he knew that if there was a qualitative difference, it sprang from the thoughtfulness of the staff, in the way they prepared what the viewer was going to see, and in the way they prepared him to see it.

The mortuary at Perth Royal Infirmary was one of the better ones. There was a private viewing room, and the senior attendant took pains to explain to Skinner that the body was still subject to post-mortem examination, and therefore it had not been possible to prepare it cosmetically for inspection.

'What I see is what I get,' the big policeman said, tersely. 'Is that what you're trying to tell me?'

The attendant hesitated. 'Well . . .' he began.

Skinner put aside his loathing of the aftermath of death, and smiled, making a conscious effort to respond to what he knew was kindly meant. 'It's all right, I understand. And I appreciate it. It's okay; I'm ready. As a matter of fact, now that I think about it, I realise that I've been expecting a moment like this for years.' Behind him, Andy Martin frowned, but said nothing. 'So just wheel him in and let me have a look.'

'Certainly.' The attendant nodded and left the room through big double doors, rubber-trimmed to cut down the noise of their crashing together. A minute or so later the doors swung open, seemingly of their own volition at first, but pushed by the attendant as he backed through them, pulling a trolley, with a younger assistant on the other end.

Until that moment, Bob Skinner had not been aware of the whirring of the fan, but he noticed it at the same moment that he smelled what was under the white sheet, and he was grateful for it.

'Will I turn back the sheet now, sir?' the attendant asked.

'No, I'll do it,' Skinner replied. 'But I'd appreciate it if you all left me alone for a minute or two.'

'Whatever you wish.' The man pointed to a button on the wall. 'Just push that bell when you're finished. You don't need to wait for us.'

'Fine.'

The two staff members left by the double doors, while Martin withdrew through the door at the other end of what was in effect a corridor.

Left alone, Skinner took a deep breath and composed himself, gathering together thoughts and memories that he had buried for years. Finally, he took a deep breath and drew back the sheet that covered the bulky shape on the trolley.

He had been expecting to see what he did, and he had known who the dead man was from the moment Andy had shown him the photograph, yet it still made him wince, and give a small gasp. The body had been stripped, and washed clean of mud; he pulled the sheet back to the waist and looked down at it from the side. The skin was pale and flaccid. The hair on its head was still thick, and grey, although it too had been carefully washed, and the dampness made it look darker, he guessed, than it had been in life. The arms were folded across the belly and he could see, on the left wrist, the mark that Martin had mentioned, the one that had aroused his suspicions. He leaned down and peered at it closely, then smiled, faintly.

He walked round to the other side of the trolley and looked at the broken skin on the side of the head. 'Where are you when I need you, Doctor Sarah?' he whispered. 'What would you be telling me now?' He laughed. 'Not to touch him for a start, but what would you be looking for?'

He pulled the sheet back completely and examined the body carefully. There were several bruises on the arms, legs and chest. He had learned enough about pathology from his wife to know what, normally, that would mean. He checked for lividity patches, but found none. Finally, he took another long look at the dead man's face. It had changed, in the many years since last he had seen it, but not beyond recognition, not even in death.

'So long,' he whispered, and covered the body once more. Then he turned, pushed the button on the wall and walked out of the viewing room, to rejoin his friend.

'Well?' Andy asked.

'There are no signs of blood settlement,' Skinner replied; he kept moving, leading the way out of the mortuary wing and into the hospital itself. 'He wasn't left lying anywhere for any significant time after death. That probably means that he died just before he was put in the water, or was hit over the head, chucked in and left to drown. You'll need to wait for the pathologist to tell you that.

'Did you look at the other wrist, when you found him?'

'No.'

Skinner shook his head and made a tutting sound. 'You'd kick a DC for missing the obvious, Mr Martin,' he said. 'There was no mark on the right wrist; the one on the left goes all the way round. So?'

His friend looked at him, sheepishly. 'Wristwatch,' he murmured. 'The man was wearing a watch with a leather strap. Immersion in water made the body swell, until eventually, it burst.'

'Exactly. If you go back and have another look in the old lady's basement . . .' he said, then stopped and moved on.

'As for the rest, there appear to be superficial marks to the face and hands, sustained after death, in the water, I'd say, and there's significant bruising all over the body. All the damage may have been done after death, but it's also possible that someone gave him a good going over with some sort of a club: a clawhammer, maybe.'

He strode on, briskly, until finally they emerged from the infirmary building into the late mid-summer evening, and stopped in the car park.

'That's all very useful, Bob,' said Andy. 'I'll pass it on to Rod Greatorix. If you've got any idea where the hammer was bought that would be good too.'

Skinner grinned. 'Command rank has changed you, pal; clearly you've taken the senior officers' sarcasm course.'

'Maybe so, but I'm still waiting for the thing that no one else can tell me. Who is, or who was that back there?'

'In time,' his friend replied. 'I'm still digesting it, and I really don't want to go into it here. Now if you're going to keep your promise and introduce me to your new daughter, we'd better get going or Karen'll have put her down to sleep for the night.' He opened the door of his BMW and nodded towards Martin's car. 'Lead on, I'll follow.'

While Perth likes to think of itself as a city, even in Scottish terms it is no more than a medium-sized town. They arrived at the Martins' house on the hill in a little under ten minutes. Karen looked Skinner up and down as he stepped into the hall. The last of the detective sergeant's deference had gone from her; now she was every inch the deputy chief's wife. 'You're supposed to be ill,' she exclaimed; 'unfit for duty. You look like you're in training for the Olympics.'

'I am, in a way,' Bob replied, with a grin. 'I go for my gold medal next week.'

'I hope you make it.'

'I will, don't you worry.'

'Be sure you do. More people than you can imagine are missing you.'

'Not for much longer. Come on, where's this wee lass of yours?'

She led him into the living room, where Danielle lay in the modern equivalent of a carry-cot. She was awake and restless, aware somewhere that her last feed of the day was due. 'Hey, you little beauty,' said Skinner, 'may you have your mother's looks and your mother's brains, as someone once said.' He reached into his jacket pocket and took out a small package, which he handed to Karen. 'Teething ring and a dummy,' he muttered. 'Don't fall for that crap about dummies being bad for them. They're not, and they're great for parents; essential, we've found.'

Then he reached into another pocket and produced an envelope. 'That's for her too, from us.' He passed it to Andy, then dropped into an armchair.

'What is it?' his friend asked.

'It's a bond, for three grand. It'll mature in eighteen years, when Danielle's university age, and there should be enough there by then to keep her out of too much debt.'

'Bob!' Karen exclaimed.

'Shush. I've done as much and more for my kids and I'll do it for yours; it's all the more appropriate that I do now.' He grinned. 'Just don't have too many, that's all!'

'Thanks, Bob,' Andy said, 'from all of us. But what did you mean by appropriate?'

Skinner sighed. 'Sit down and I'll tell you.'

'This sounds serious,' Karen murmured, picking up the carry-basket. 'So while you do, I'm going to feed the baby and put her down for the night. Then I'll feed us. Bob, are you staying?'

'If I'm invited. I've brought some kit.'

'Good.' She left the room, carrying her daughter.

'Well?' asked Andy, sitting in the spare armchair.

Skinner looked his friend in the eye, holding his gaze steady. 'Remember, when once I said to you that you were like the brother I never had?'

Martin nodded.

'Well, that wasn't quite true.' He paused, opened his mouth to speak again, only to let out another deeper sigh. He sat there staring straight ahead for countless seconds. A CD had been playing in the background, unnoticed; now Eddi Reader's crystal voice, singing of perfection, seemed to fill the room. Finally, he blinked and went on. 'That man,' he said. 'That man you met in Miss Bonney's basement today: he was my brother too.'

And then something happened: something that at first amazed Andy, then filled him with a sudden, scary panic; something that he had never seen before, nor ever imagined he would see.

Bob Skinner, his mighty, impregnable friend, buried his face in his hands and began to cry, his chest and shoulders heaving in great, wracking, uncontrollable sobs.

12

'You sure about this?' The upstairs room was light and airy; the window was open and sunshine poured in. They had made good time on the flight back from the lakeside cabin; it was still afternoon in Buffalo, New York.

Sarah lifted the light duvet and looked down at him. 'At this moment, you are asking me that? It's pretty obvious that you're sure.'

'Ah, but he's got a mind of his own, and no conscience; I have both.'

She moved her hands down and took hold of him, gently. 'If we're clear that, for now, all I'm doing is renewing an acquaintance with an old friend, then yes, I'm certain. And believe me, if you look closely enough in the right places, you'll find visible evidence of that too. So shut up; don't try and find the way you never had with words, not now.'

'Nuh,' he grinned, then rolled over, covering her and letting her guide him, in a single movement. She cried out as she felt all of his great length slide slowly and rock hard into her, then thrust herself upward, forcefully, as if she wanted even more. He felt her squeeze him inside and almost came, but he hung on as she did so, keeping perfectly still against the clenching and unclenching of her buttocks as she drove at him, feeling her fingers digging into his back as her frenzy grew.

Finally, her frantic movement slowed, and she began to relax; she felt the moistness, but realised that it was hers. He began his own thrusts then, short and slow, taking his time, keeping his weight off her, keeping most of himself out of her, concentrating on her pleasure point, until she began to come again. When she did, he was ready for her; she swung up her strong legs, gripping him as he rode all the way back into her, as they climaxed together, heaving, gasping, crying, until at last, they were both spent.

Afterwards, they lay there, side by side once more while their breathing softened, and their hearts slowed. 'Wow,' she whispered. 'Did you rob a sperm bank? I thought you were never going to stop.'

'Nah,' he chuckled. 'I've just been saving it for a special occasion.'

'That sure of yourself, uh?'

'I wouldn't say that, but ever since I saw you at the Walkers' last weekend, and after I heard how things were with you and your husband, I've just had a feeling that this was going to happen. Don't tell me that you haven't.'

She touched his face. 'No, I won't. It was no more than a twitch in my pants at first, but after our date alone on Monday, I knew it too. And today, after we got back from the cabin, I didn't want to, I couldn't, wait any longer.'

'For which I am eternally thankful.'

They lay in silence, for a while, until eventually a great hand slid up and cupped a heavy breast.

'I won't ask you whether you'll go back,' he said softly. ' But what if he comes for you? Am I going to have to fight him for you, d' you reckon?'

'No way,' she answered. 'Even if I decided that I wanted to be with you for good, I wouldn't let you anywhere near him.'

He grinned. 'Of course you wouldn't. I forgot; that was a damn silly thing to ask, him with heart trouble and all, not to mention me having ten years and more on him, and a great chunk of weight. I promise, even if he comes at me, I won't hurt him.'

Sarah propped herself up on an elbow, and looked down at him, unsmiling. 'You don't get it, do you? For a start, Bob doesn't have heart trouble, not as you mean it. He has an inherited condition which would probably have passed over in time, but which has been treated, as a precaution, by the fitting of a pacemaker. Physically, there's nothing else wrong with him; as a matter of fact, for his age, he's fitter than anyone I've ever seen. All else aside, he's at least as fit as you.

'No, my darling, I won't tell Bob about you, even if I decide that he and I are split for good, not for his safety, but for yours.'

'Uhh?' Incredulous, he looked at her, and then he laughed. She put a finger to his lips, silencing him.

'Ron,' she said, 'you may be a professional athlete, and you may be as big as you are, but my husband could take you apart, piece by piece.'

Hurt pride showed on his face. 'You what? You think I can't look after myself?'

'I know you can, on the football field, but this is not a game, and Bob does not play. He is trained, and he's trained himself, to fight for his life, if necessary. There was a time, a few years ago, when he had to, against a real killer, a monster, a man who was far bigger even than you. When the cavalry got there, the guy was unconscious; he didn't come round until he was in Edinburgh Royal Infirmary. Believe me, taking Bob on would be a career-ending move. Your only chance would be to hit him on the pacemaker, but I don't think you'd get near it.'

He raised an eyebrow. 'So by getting into the sack with me, you're putting my life at risk?'

She smiled, and shook her head. 'No, because he's not going to find out. The only person who would tell him would be you, and I hope I've persuaded you not to be that stupid.'

'What about Babs Walker?'

'She's certainly not going to find out.'

'She put us back together, remember.'

'Then I'll make sure that she and Bob never meet again.'

'What if he asks you straight out if you've been a good girl?'

'That presupposes I'm going back to him, which is far from certain. But even if I do, he won't. Bob and I have been married for a while, but he doesn't really know anything about my sexual feelings. Even when we had our first split, he accepted that I had my fling to get even for his . . . because that's what I told him. It wasn't entirely true; maybe about ten per cent, but that's all. It happened because I met someone who turned me on, just as you do, lover.'

'And have there been others?' he asked, huskily.

She slapped him lightly on the chest. 'No, there have not!' She smiled. 'Do you think I'm that easy?

'Sure, between you and me ending, and my meeting Bob, I had relationships. I was even engaged, briefly, in New York. Ron, I enjoy sex. It's always been a part of my adult life and it always will be. I try to be good at it too.'

'You succeed.'

'I wasn't fishing for that, but thank you anyway, kind sir. No, I've always taken the view that if you ain't both getting the most from it, you might as well both be doing it alone.' She grinned again. 'I have to say that this is not a unanimous view among men . . . present company and my husband excepted, of course. My first fiancé, gorgeous boy though he was, was a sad example of horizontal single-mindedness.

'Anyway, to answer the question I think you asked, since I've been married, my infidelities have been limited to you and the other guy I mentioned. But even if there had been others . . . and I'll admit that there's one guy in Bob's force with whom I came close. He still starts my juices flowing whenever I look at him . . .' She paused. 'Why is it only married men,' she asked, 'that society allows to put themselves about? Why should their infidelities be taken as excusable, while a woman is seen as a whore for following the same urges? I wanted to have great sex with you, Ron; that's why I called Trish tonight and spun her a story. And great sex we have had.'

His face seemed to darken. 'So love doesn't come into it,' he murmured.

'Oh, don't take it that way; it does in your case. I loved you in our college days, and even now there are things about you that I love. I couldn't sleep with you if there weren't. I really am not like that.'

'And Bob?'

'Oh yes, I love him; don't think otherwise, not for a second, even though I'm here with you now. He has his imperfections. He's been unfaithful too, a couple of times; he's a driven man, and he's got a hell of a temper. He has something else though, something I can't put into words, that transcends all that, and it's what's tied me to him through everything. From the moment I met him he pushed all my buttons at once, without even knowing it.

'But now, he's putting his career before me and before his family. That's something I could never do, and that's what I'm having big trouble dealing with. I'm angry, I feel alienated, and that in part . . . although I doubt it would have happened with anyone else but you . . . is what's brought me into your bed, in your house.

'Bob could retire now, justifiably and honourably, given all the things he's done. Financially, he and I, and our children, are well fixed for life after my inheritance, and even in his own right he's comfortably off. I wanted him to quit; maybe, just maybe, without this trouble he's had I might have persuaded him. But the fact that he's been told that he may have to retire . . . that's what's made him explode. That's why he's gone back to Scotland. He's gone to confront the people who think they can tell Bob Skinner what he can and can't do. I feel sorry for them; they don't know what they've turned loose.'

'What do you mean?'

Sarah frowned. 'There's a dark side to him. I've told you how tough he is, but it's more than that. If he's under threat, or if those close to him are, then God help the people who are doing the threatening.'

'Are you afraid of him?'

'No.'

'Not even if he found out about you and me?'

'No.'

'But you're afraid for me?'

'I'm afraid he'd beat the crap out of you. Look, if the roles were reversed, if you and I were married and I was sleeping with Bob and you found out, wouldn't you react like that?'

'I suppose,' Ron conceded. 'Standard caveman behaviour.'

'Well, he's better at it than you, that's all.'

He grinned, then moved a hand towards her. 'And are there things I'm better at than him?' he asked.

Sarah looked him in the eye, and patted his approach to one side. 'That is an area,' she said, her voice becoming muffled as she slid below the cover, then finally, as she found what she was seeking, inaudible, 'where I never make compari . . .'

13

Andy Martin looked into the future and saw a quandary. In the fifteen minutes since he had recovered from his breakdown in the armchair, Skinner had said not another word, other than to apologise, repeatedly, for his weakness.

But he was a witness. He had information crucial to the progress of a murder investigation and he had to be interviewed, regardless of his emotional state.

Andy went through to the kitchen and returned with two bottles of Rolling Rock beer. As he returned, the Fairground Attraction CD came to an end, and the changer replaced it with a new Peter Green blues album. Normally, Bob would have reacted. Typically he would have asked him if it was Eric Clapton . . . on first hearing, he thought that all blues guitarists were Eric Clapton . . . but as he sat there, all he did was nod his thanks as he took his uncapped beer.

He stared at the carpet as the first two tracks on the album played themselves out; then as the horns came in, upbeat, at the start of track three, he put the bottle to his lips and took a long draining swallow.

When he was finished, he laid the empty bottle on the occasional table beside his chair, and looked across at his friend.

'Right,' he said, abruptly. 'Now that I've finished making an arse of myself, do you want to take my statement yourself, or do you want to get a couple of your guys up here?'

A smile of undisguised relief seemed to flood Martin's face. 'I reckon you're worth the head of CID. I'll call him now and ask him to come up.'

Skinner frowned. 'No, wait; that's not fair on Karen. We'll go to him.' He reached out a hand. 'Here; don't you drink that beer. Give it to me.'

Andy grinned and handed it over. 'Fine, but Karen's making dinner.'

'Then tell your guy to have his as well and we'll see him afterwards.'

'Man, we're still in the early hours of the investigation; you know how important the first stages are.'

'How long was he in the water?'

'About a week.'

'Where did he go in?'

'We haven't a clue.'

'Then let's not risk your happiness and my digestion by spoiling Karen's excellent dinner. I'm not going to be able to lead you straight to whoever it is you're after.' His forehead creased and his eyes turned hard and cold. 'Even if I could, I don't know that I would. I might be inclined to pay a call on him myself.'

Martin felt himself shiver. 'For Christ's sake, Bob, don't even think that.'

'Ah, but I do, son. Because I'm human and because it's in my nature.'

'Then suppress it, please.' Andy looked at him, with pure concern. 'Man, you shouldn't be handling this alone. Let me call Sarah in the States and tell her what's happened.'

Skinner looked at him as if he was a stranger. 'You do that and I'll make you eat your silver-braided hat, Deputy Chief.'

'Well let me call Alex, then.'

'Nor her either; she doesn't know she ever had an uncle, nor Sarah a brother-in-law. I'll handle this, Andy. I promise you I'll behave myself and tell you everything I know; but not here, or now. I'll do it in a formal situation, because for my own sake, I need to make sure I stay dispassionate about it. Now, are we about ready to eat? I'm fucking starving.'

Martin smiled and shrugged his shoulders. 'We should be just about there. You finish that beer, and I'll call Rod Greatorix to set up a meeting.'

He was heading towards the phone in the hall, when Skinner called him back. 'Hey,' he said, pointing towards the CD player with the Rolling Rock in his hand. 'If I didn't know that was Eric Clapton, I'd say it was the guy who used to be in Fleetwood Mac.'

14

They were halfway though the Mongolian meal when Maggie's cellphone played its distinctive tune. She looked at Mario, awkwardly, apologetically; he grinned and shrugged his shoulders. 'Could just as easily have been mine,' he said. 'Go on.'

She flipped the phone open, pressed the 'yes' button, and answered, 'Rose'.

'Sorry, Maggie,' said Stevie Steele. 'I hope it isn't a bad time, but you did say to keep you informed.'

'I know I did; it's not a problem. Are you still at it?'

'Afraid so.'

'I thought you'd have had it wrapped up by now, at least as far as you could. What's up? Have you been watching more video tapes?'

'I have, but it was a waste of time,' said the inspector. 'I went back far enough to watch the picture being hung on the wall. It wasn't tampered with at that point, and from the tapes we saw earlier on, there's no sign of anyone interfering with it after that.'

'So it must have been rigged to go before it was delivered to the gallery?'

'Not necessarily; the exhibits came from all over the place. The curator waited until he had them all on the premises before he hung them. They were kept in a storage area below the main hall; it isn't covered by video cameras so in theory the device could have been planted there.'

Steele hesitated. 'Tell me, Maggie,' he went on eventually. 'Did anything strike you as wrong about the notion that it was set off by a timer?'

As her husband looked on, Rose frowned. 'You could ask why it was, I suppose. And I guess the answer could be either to give the arsonist time to get well clear, or, to have the painting go up before an audience, as a sort of a statement.'

'If that was the case, he got it right, didn't he, our fire-raiser. Bang in the middle of old Candela's speech.'

'True. So unless that was pure coincidence, whoever set it must have known the timings and running order of the opening ceremony.'

'So you'd think,' Steele agreed, 'except . . .' He stopped in mid-sentence.

'What?'

'Except for the fact that there was no timer.'

Maggie's eyes widened. 'Come again?'

'The technicians have finished with the picture. They found the remains of a device, sure enough. It had been laid against the frame and conductors had been attached to the back of the canvas, to make sure that it went up fast, from the centre. Then the back of the painting had been covered over with heavy brown paper, sealed with gaffer tape. There's nothing unusual about that, and none of the gallery staff thought twice about it.

'The bomb, if you want to call it that, was primed and hung on the wall, ready to be detonated. But when it was, there was no ticking clock involved. It was set off remotely, triggered by a radio signal.'

'Bloody hell! From how far away? Can they tell?'

'Up to four hundred yards, according to Tony Davidson, the telecommunications guy. It could have been blown from anywhere in Princes Street, or from the top of the Mound, even. But was it? After all, it did happen right in the middle of the speech. What does that suggest?'

'That whoever did it was actually there, in the hall.'

'Exactly. "Light the blue touch paper and withdraw", I reckon. And just to put the tin lid on it, at five this evening, the Press Association had an anonymous call from a guy claiming responsibility for, I quote, "an act of retribution against blasphemy". He didn't name any organisation; he just said that much and hung up. All the PA reporter was able to say was that he sounded like a teuchter.'

'The Presbyterian militant wing, in other words.'

'Aye, or just as likely a nutter, who had nothing to do with it. The story was on the radio and television bulletins by the time the call was made. Oh yes, and the call came from a phone box.'

'Like as not a fruitcake, then, I agree. Do we have a list of everyone who was there?' asked Rose.

'We have the complete invitation list,' Steele replied. 'It includes clients, other lawyers and professionals, the Lord and Lady Provost, the Chief Constable and Lady Proud . . . who declined, by the way . . . a couple of Supreme Court judges, and the media. We have a list of all the people who were signed in and given lapel badges with their names on them. We have a list of all those guests whose badges were not picked up. We have a list of all of the staff on duty. But we do not have a list of those people, guests or otherwise, who simply wandered in and past the registration desk without picking up their badges . . . as some people do at these bashes.'

'Weren't there invitation cards?'

'Yes, but they were taken at the reception desk, not at the door. There were a couple of security people on the steps who were supposed to look at the invitations, but they've admitted already that it was quite possible for someone to have got past them. There were full taxi-loads of people arriving, five, ten at a time. No way did they check everyone.'

'No. Listen, Stevie, where are you?'

'In the office.'

'I'd better get along there then.'

'Why, Mags? To do what, exactly?'

Rose frowned. 'The video tapes from the security cameras. We'll need to check every face against those lists, looking for someone who isn't on any of them. And we should take that phone call seriously. This is borderline terrorism, so we should get Neil McIlhenney and Special Branch involved. We should tell Dan Pringle as well.'

'I've done some of that already, Mags; I've told Neil. I agree there's a chance we'll come up with a face that's on his files. I'll leave it to you to break into the head of CID's Saturday night. But there's something else we have to face up to as well, and this is why I think we should sleep on it . . . apart from the fact that I'm knackered and cross-eyed from looking at tapes. If we don't find that face in the crowd, and it's long odds against that we will, then what we have on our hands is a gathering of Edinburgh's great and good, their spouses, partners and the rest, every one of whom is a suspected arsonist.'

Maggie Rose let out a whistle loud enough to turn heads at the next table. 'You are right,' she conceded. 'I must have had too much to drink already. Get on home, Stevie . . . or off to wherever you're expected. I'll see you in the office tomorrow, nine a.m. sharp. We've got a minefield to find our way through here, and no mistake.'

15

The car park in front of the Perth divisional office was busier than might have been expected, even on a Saturday night. A row of lights blazed in an office suite on the first floor.

'CID,' Martin explained. 'We didn't see any point in setting up a mobile enquiry headquarters, just round the corner, especially since it's no more than a suspicious death, and highly unlikely that it happened where the body was found, so Rod Greatorix is running the thing from here.'

'I'm impressed,' said Bob Skinner. 'You've got an unidentified victim, a bum for all they know, yet you're still pulling out all the stops. You're making your presence felt already, Andy.'

'No, I'm not. This is not the homicide capital of Scotland, but Rod knows how to go about setting up an investigation as well as if not better than I do.'

The older man grunted. 'I suppose he does. Sorry, Andy, that was pure bloody arrogance on my part. I know about Greatorix; he was head of CID here when I had the job in Edinburgh. He's sound, all right. I'll make all the right noises when I meet him, don't worry. How much did you tell him, by the way?'

'Only that I had a positive ID on the victim, and that he should meet me here at ten. I didn't see the point in saying anything about you till we got there.'

He saw Skinner's grim smile in the dashboard light. 'That'll be a nice surprise for him, then,' his friend murmured. 'Let's go and see him.'

Martin gripped the door handle, then hesitated. 'Okay, but before that, will you do something for me, as my closest friend?'

'Maybe. What?'

'Will you phone Sarah?'

'Pass.'

'Bob, please. You've got a hold of yourself now, but I've never seen you like you were before. I'm worried about you.'

'You think I'm going to keel over again? Don't worry, I won't.'

'I know that, but it just seems to me that you've got stress coming at you from all angles just now. If you talk to Sarah and get everything on an even keel with her, it's got to help.'

Skinner gave a small growl in the darkness. 'Martin, sometimes you are just full of the naivety of youth. But if it'll keep you happy . . .'

'It will. Here, you can use my phone.'

'Don't be daft, I've got my own. Now step outside, will you. So far tonight you've seen me cry like a baby. I don't want you to see me crawl as well.'

Andy laughed as he stepped out of the Mondeo and closed the door behind him. Inside the car, Skinner took out his cellphone and scrolled through the phonebook until he found the number of the Buffalo house. He pressed the green button and waited; the call was answered on the third ring, by a Scots voice, that of Trish the nanny.

'I'm sorry, Bob,' she said. 'Sarah isn't back from her trip yet; she called me to say not to expect her until later on.'

'Do you know where she is?'

'No. She said it was to do with the estate, that's all.'

'Okay, thanks.'

He closed the line and was about to put the phone back in his pocket when he saw Andy standing expectantly in the car park. 'Shit,' he muttered and scrolled through the stored numbers once more until he found Sarah's cellphone, and dialled it.

Three thousand miles away Sarah swung her legs out of Ron Neidholm's bed and picked up her Nokia. She looked at the incoming number, and for a second her thumb hovered over the red off-switch until, with a sigh, she took the call.

'Yes, Bob,' she said, loud enough for Ron to hear her and firmly enough for him to know to keep quiet.

'Where are you?' her husband asked. 'What's this trip Trish told me about?'

'I've been to the cabin.'

'What! You told me you never wanted to see it.'

'I know, but I changed my mind. I felt that I had to visit it.'

'Are you still there?'

'No,' she said, truthfully. 'I'm on my way back,' she lied.

'How did you get there?'

She thought, quickly; at the same time picking her shirt from the floor with her free hand and covering her lap with it, in an automatic gesture, as if he had found them and was standing in the doorway. 'One of the lawyers took me,' she said, 'in a private plane, then in a hire car. Now why the interrogation?'

'I'm sorry,' Bob replied, at once. 'You took me by surprise, that's all.'

'So we're both good at that. Now what is it?'

'Need it be anything? Can't I just be calling you?'

'If you're calling to say you're catching the first flight over, yes you can. If not, then what I said yesterday still counts.'

'Sarah, I can't do that.'

'Okay, have your damn medical next week. Once you're cleared for duty, take some family time and come across.'

'I can't do that either, love. Something's come up, apart from the job.'

'What? Have you had another incident?' For the first time she sounded anxious.

'No, I'm fine.'

'Is it Alex? Is something wrong with her? Or Andy, or his baby?'

'No, none of that. I'm in Perth now; wee Danielle's magic, really, and Karen's doing great. No, it's something else, a personal thing, a long, involved story that I should have told you a long time ago. I can't now, though, not over the phone. Sarah, I really would like it if you'd come home. Just for a week or so, even. I need your support.'

'Hah!' Her laugh was harsh and brittle. 'Those words sound familiar. Last time they were used between us, I was saying them to you. I needed you, Bob, to help me cope with my parents' death, to be there when I went through my mother's belongings, to help me with questions about the estate and to advise me about things in which you've got much more experience than I have. I needed your support then, and I begged you for it. And what did you do? You caught the first fucking plane out of here, that's what you did. Well that is exactly what I'm not going to do.

79

Something's come up for me too, and I'm staying right here.'

She could almost hear him struggle to keep his voice even. 'Sarah, I need you with me.'

'So? You'll just have to do what I did, and tough it out. Maybe then you'll find out what I did, all of a sudden. I don't fucking need you . . . for anything!'

She jumped up, ripped the battery from her cellphone, and threw the separate pieces, tangled in her shirt, across Ron Neidholm's bedroom. When she turned back towards him he was there, by her side, to wrap her in his arms, as she exploded into tears.

Back in Perth, Bob Skinner stared at his dead phone, his face twisted with anger. He realised that he was breathing hard, and forced himself to bring it back to normal. When he was back in control, he closed his eyes. 'What do you want, man?' he asked himself aloud. 'Maybe she's right, maybe you did let her down. Maybe we're both right. What the fuck, someone's got to give. So let's just do what she says. Have the medical, see Maley's lot off, then go over there like she wants.'

He found Sarah's number again and called it, but it came up unobtainable. 'Playing that game, eh,' he muttered, his anger flaring once again. 'You can bloody well stay in the States, then, but not with my kids.'

He shoved the phone roughly back into his pocket and stepped out of the car. Andy Martin looked at him, hopefully. 'Bad idea, Andy,' Skinner snapped.

'Do you want me to talk to her?'

'Like I said earlier, don't you fucking dare. Now let's see your colleagues.'

He strode off, ahead of his friend, towards the police building. DCS Rod Greatorix was standing in the entrance hallway, beside the public reception desk. A bewildered look spread across his great gruff face as Skinner burst through the entrance door. He looked at the newcomer, and then at Martin, behind him.

'Andy?' he began.

'Let's go somewhere private, Rod,' his deputy chief replied.

'By all means. Through here.' He led them up a flight of stairs, then along a corridor to a small office, glass-panelled like the rest of the suite. Several detectives were working in other rooms; one or two glanced at them, briefly, as they passed.

'Would anybody like coffee, or tea . . . or something stronger?' the head of CID asked, as the others took seats, facing the small desk that was the room's only furniture.

'I'm fine, thanks,' said Skinner curtly.

Martin shook his head. 'I didn't want to get into this over the phone, Rod,' he began, 'and neither did Bob . . . whom you know, of course.'

'Of course I do.' Greatorix nodded and smiled. 'It's been a year or two, sir; that course at Tulliallan, wasn't it. That was the last time we met.'

'Yup. We were both lecturing, as I recall. A distinguished class; one of our students is a chief constable now, and another's in the police inspectorate. I'm not here to lecture now, though.'

'Then what is it?'

'I'm here to help you with your enquiries.'

Greatorix gave him a look of pure incredulity, then he leaned back in his chair and smiled. 'Is that right? Are you going to tell me that it was you who banged that bloke on the head and chucked him in the Tay?'

Skinner looked him in the eye, unsmiling. 'There was a time, Rod, when I wanted to do just that, but it's long gone. No, I'm just going to tell you who he is. You'd better tape it, for the record.'

The Tayside detective had switched into serious mode. 'Just a minute then,' he said. 'I'll find a recorder from somewhere. Will we need a second officer present?'

'Andy's the second officer.'

'Of course.' Greatorix left the room.

Skinner turned to Martin. 'I've never told you much about my father, have I?'

His friend shook his head. 'No, but I don't suppose I've ever told you much about mine.'

'I've met your father, for Christ's sake. But no, it's true, I haven't. I'm not a demonstrative guy, Andy. Quick-tempered, yes, but on a personal level I'm not good at discussing my feelings. That's why, in my past, I've been able to bury things so deep. Maybe that's why Sarah and I are in trouble now. I'm not the sort of person who can just laugh and kiss it off, and she isn't either. There were all sorts of things I never knew about Leo and Susannah Grace, until after I'd seen them stretched out on mortuary tables. And when I think about it, there are all sorts of things I don't know about Sarah herself. When I went to Buffalo for the first time without her and met her friends, it was like they were talking about someone I hadn't met. And now she's back over there, with her own agenda, it's as if the part of her I don't know has come to the surface and taken over. She went on about needing me, but I can't see for what.

'None of us ever think of ourselves as bad communicators, until we realise how little we know ourselves.' He caught Martin's eye. 'How about you and Karen? Do you talk to each other, about each other?'

Andy laughed, softly. 'Bob, before Karen and I got together, each of us lived our private lives so openly that there was hardly anything about either of us that was news to the other. But yes, we do; we share things. I hardly go to church any more, but Karen's my confessional, and I'm hers. I wouldn't like to think that I'd any secrets from her.'

'That's good. Sarah and I should learn from you . . . but then again, she may have secrets that I wouldn't want to know about, and I don't know if I could bring myself to tell her all of mine.'

'That's for you both to judge; but at the very least, talking about the problem has to help. Anyway, you started to talk about your father. What was he like?'

'William Reid Skinner? He was a hell of a man. All of my life I've tried to live up to him, and all of my life I've fallen short.'

'Most of us think of our fathers that way, Bob.'

'Maybe, but that's how mine was. He was a lawyer, like Sarah's dad, and as successful in his own way, by Scottish standards. He was a quiet man, very dignified and very controlled. You couldn't make him lose his temper even if you tried. He never raised a hand to me in my childhood; indeed I don't remember him ever raising his voice.

'I asked him once how he could be like that. He told me that he left that part of himself in the war. When I asked him what he did, he looked away from me, and he said, "I killed people, Robert". When I asked him where he fought, he wouldn't tell me at first, but I pressed him. Eventually he said that he'd been in France in 1942, and later in Yugoslavia and Greece. You know what that meant.'

He frowned. 'When I got involved with MI5 and such, I asked our friend Adam Arrow in the Ministry of Defence to find out if there was a file on him anywhere. There is; it's among a batch that are still sealed, but Adam told me roughly what was in it. D'you know, he won the George fucking Cross, Andy, but he never told me. He must have thrown it away, because there was no sign of it among his effects after he died, nor any reference to it.

'You know what Adam's like, and some of the things he's done. Well, when he told me about my father . . . Man, there was respect in his voice, bordering on . . .'

The door opened, interrupting him. 'Sorry to have taken so long,' said Rod Greatorix. 'Come Monday morning, the buggers in this office are going to get a message about keeping a stock of tapes at all times.' He laid a big black twin-deck tape recorder on the desk and stretched its lead across to a plug in the wall. Finally, he stripped the clear wrapping from two tapes and inserted them into the waiting slots.

'Okay,' he announced, 'we're ready to go ahead. I am Detective Chief Superintendent Roderick Greatorix, Tayside Police; also present is Deputy Chief Constable Andrew Martin of this force, and Deputy Chief Constable Robert Skinner, from Edinburgh. Mr Skinner is here to volunteer evidence of . . .' He stopped in mid-sentence and glanced at Martin.

'Identification.'

'Thanks . . . of identification, in respect of the current murder enquiry. Mr Skinner?'

'Thank you, chief superintendent. I have to tell you that I have seen the body that was found today in Myrtle Terrace, Perth, and can identify it as that of Michael Niven Skinner, aged fifty-six years.'

Greatorix stared at him in surprise. 'What was your relationship to the dead man?' he asked, at last, remembering that he was taking a formal statement.

'He was my older brother.'

'What do you know of his whereabouts in the period leading up to his death?'

'Nothing.'

'When did you last see him?'

'Approximately thirty years ago.'

'But you are certain of your identification?'

'Absolutely.'

'Do you know of any associates he may have had in the period prior to his death?'

'No. I have had no contact with my brother throughout my adult life.'

'Was he married?'

'Not that I know of. A GRO check will tell you, for sure.'

'What happened to alienate you for so long?'

'I tried to kill him.'

Andy Martin reached across and switched off the recorder. 'For Christ's sake, Bob,' he exclaimed.

'It's true,' Skinner retorted. 'I've lived with it ever since. Now switch that thing back on.'

Martin restarted the recorder. 'Interview temporarily interrupted,' he said, 'but now restarted; same three people present.'

'Thank you. As I was saying, the last time I saw Michael there was a violent dispute between us. I was sixteen years old, and at home. I heard my brother shouting, at the top of his voice, screaming obscenities. I found him in the kitchen, and I also found my mother. Her nose was bleeding. Michael had demanded money from her, and when she had refused him, he had punched her and tried to take it from her purse.

'I wasn't full-grown, but I was a big lad nonetheless. I went straight for him. As I've said, there was about ten years between us in age, and my brother had been taught how to look after himself in the army, but he wasn't in the best of shape, not any more. I remember he threw a couple of punches at me, but I just walked straight through them and nutted him. He didn't shift off his feet, though, so I hit him. I remember it clear as day, straight fingers in the gut, and a punch to the left temple that almost broke one of my knuckles. He went down then, all right. He was spark out, and I wanted him to stay that way. My brother had thumped, abused and threatened me for much of my young life, but he had run out of time. I had outgrown him. Still, I knew what he was capable of if I gave him half a chance. So I grabbed him by the tie as he lay there, and I hit him again, and again, and again.

'I reckon I'd have finished him, if it hadn't been for my father. He was a very strong man, and big as I was, he got behind me, put a full nelson on me, and lifted me clean off Michael. I struggled for a while, but I couldn't move; he could have broken my neck with that hold if he'd liked.

'Eventually, when he thought I'd calmed down, he let me go. But the thing was, I'd never lost it. I'd known what I was doing all the time. The bastard had hit my mother and I was going to kill him. At the time I was angry with my father because he didn't react just like I had, but later I came to realise that he couldn't let himself feel that way. I thought I was a hard boy then, but I found out later that I was nothing compared to what he had been.

'I was still ready to do for Michael, though, and my father knew it. So he called the police, as well as a doctor. Michael was taken to Law Hospital; he was still unconscious when he left the house, but I heard that he came round in the ambulance. They kept him in for a couple of days, and then he was charged with assaulting my mother.

'My father got one of his partners to represent him. It was carved up between him and the fiscal that Michael would plead guilty and be remanded for psychiatric reports. They showed that he was legally sane, but had a serious personality disorder. He was also a chronic alcoholic. The sheriff read the reports and put him on probation, on condition that he enter a psychiatric hospital as a voluntary patient.

'He was in there for six months. I don't know what they did to him, but I'm told that it calmed him. They couldn't keep him off the drink, though. I don't think they even tried, since that kept him on an even keel too. My father found him somewhere to stay, a hostel in Gourock, well away from the family home, and well away from me. The only order he ever gave me in my life was never to see my brother again. He told me that he was afraid, for both of us, of what might happen if I did. Michael was looked after, financially, to a modest extent. He was unemployable, so my father set up a trust fund for him, to keep a roof over his head, to feed and clothe him, and to keep him in a certain amount of drink . . . enough, but not enough to let him drink himself to death.

'And that is how my brother lived out his life for the last thirty years; until he fell in the Tay and drowned, or just maybe, until someone hit him over the head and chucked him in the river to die. It's ironic, isn't it, that the last two times I saw my brother he was laid out on a stretcher.'

Bob Skinner looked at Martin and Greatorix, then nodded at the tape recorder. 'You can switch that fucking thing off now,' he said. Neither of the other men moved, so he reached across himself and pressed the twin 'stop' buttons. The head of CID took the tapes from their slots. 'I'll go and brief the team,' he murmured, and left the room.

The silence he left behind was unbroken for around half a minute. 'Why did he turn out that way, Bob?' Martin asked, eventually.

'As I said earlier, son, he was a flawed personality; he was weak and he was jealous. I've only ever tried to live up to my father, but I think that Michael had to out-do him. Mum and Dad wanted him to go to university . . . he was bright, he'd have made it no problem . . . but he insisted on joining the army, straight from school. I don't know if any strings were pulled, but he got into Sandhurst.

'He got his commission in the Royal Engineers when he was twenty. He served in Germany at first without incident, but then he was posted to Honduras, in support of some counter-terrorist operation out there, and the trouble began. He was drinking pretty heavily by then; he had done since he was about sixteen in fact. He used to keep a stash of booze in a cupboard in his bedroom. I found it one day and he walloped me. I was seven at the time, but he slapped me cross-eyed and broke one of my fingers.'

'He did what?' Martin exclaimed.

'You heard. He took it and snapped it just like that, and he told me that if I didn't keep my mouth shut about it and about his bevvy, he'd break the fucking lot. I believed him. I told my mum I'd slammed it in a door.'

'Bloody hell!'

'It was the first of many. He used to beat me up regularly; I'd just take it and keep it all to myself, waiting for the day. When Michael went to the army I started karate classes, and I did a bit of boxing too, until I gave that up.'

'What made you chuck it?'

'I hurt a kid one day. I was fifteen; for a minute I imagined the boy was Michael, and I just hit him too hard. I detached the retina of his right eye. That was enough for me; I was a boxer, not a man-hunter. I wanted to be Ali, not Marciano. There was only one guy I really wanted to damage. The fact is, if the thing with my mother hadn't happened, I'd have done him anyway, probably with no one around to stop me.'

Skinner paused. 'Anyway, back to the army thing; like I said, he was in Honduras, a section commander or something. His CO carpeted him for being unfit for duty once; he was given a reprimand, a stiff warning with a threat of demotion, but from what I gather that just made him sneakier. Finally, there was an incident on a jungle patrol. The platoon Michael was with was attacked by insurgents; there was a fire-fight, and the guerrillas got wasted, but two of our guys were killed. The trouble was that when they dug the bullets out of them, they were found to have come from Michael's gun.'

'Jesus. Was he charged?'

'No, no, no; that would have caused a scandal and it wouldn't have done. No, they gave the dead boys medals and buried them with full military honours, and they gave Lieutenant Skinner an immediate discharge.'

'Did your father know?' asked Andy.

'It was my father who told me about it, years afterwards. One of his old service buddies was in the Advocate General's office; he called him and tipped him off on the quiet. When Michael turned up back in Motherwell, he spun everyone a tale about being invalided out, but it didn't wash. He had no pension for a start, no discharge money, and what little he had saved went on drink, damn quick. He was twenty-four when he came home. Within six months he was the town drunk. He broke my mother's heart long before he broke her nose. At first my father tried to keep him in check by refusing him money, but he just stole stuff from the house. The bastard even stole from me.

'So, against that history, will you tell me, Andy, now that he's dead, after thirty years of being cut out of my life, at my father's behest at first, but eventually of my own choosing, why do I feel so fucking guilty about him? And why do I want so badly to avenge his death, if it wasn't accidental, when back then I wanted to kill him myself?'

'Because he's your brother, I guess. It's only natural.'

'But I never thought of him as a brother, only as a thug about the house. No, I feel guilty because I'm grateful. We did have the same mother, same father, and we both swam out of the same gene pool. Yet it was Michael Niven Skinner got the bad seed, and Robert Morgan Skinner who grew into the straight arrow. And it was a pure fucking accident; it could as easily have been the other way round.

'My father never stopped loving him, you know. I think what he had to do hastened his death. But I found no forgiveness. I let him rot away in Gourock, when I could have reached out to him. And I did worse than that; I kept his existence a secret from his niece, and later from his sister-in-law.'

'Your first wife must have known about him, though. She was around then, wasn't she?'

'Sure, Myra did, but she was warned never to mention his name in our house. Anyway, she died before Alex was old enough to understand, even if she had let anything slip to her about him.'

Skinner knitted his forehead until his eyebrows came together. 'I may not have killed him physically, Andy, but I did in every other way. Whatever there had been between us, he was my only brother, yet I let him live like a dog and die like one. Ah, man, the secrets that we keep.'

16

Sarah Grace Skinner looked out of the window as she buttoned her shirt. Her hair was still damp from the shower, and stuck to the collar, but she ignored the small inconvenience. She was still brooding over the fury of her argument with her husband.

She and Ron had gone back to bed afterwards, but the mood had been more than broken, it had been shattered like a smashed windscreen. So while he had gone downstairs to dig out his rarely used coffee percolator, she had set about dressing, and restoring herself to a state in which she could face Trish, and Mark, if he was still up and about.

She looked out over Ron Neidholm's front lawn; the sounds of the street drifted through the open window. A car drove by sedately. The kid across the way kicked a soccer ball against his parents' garage door. The deep voice of Celeste Polanski sounded from next door as she bellowed the latest in a lifetime of instructions to her meek husband Mort. The Polanskis had lived there for even longer than the Neidholms. Celeste missed nothing; Ron had always called her the Sheriff of Sullivan Street.

The house was modest for a sporting icon, much smaller than the mansion she had inherited from her parents, but then, Ron was a modest guy. Also, she knew that it was not his only home; he had shown her a photograph of his farm in Tennessee, where he had spent the last seven years of his football career, and of his condominium in Maui, where he passed much of his vacation time, and in which he had installed his mother.

Ron and his younger brother Jake had been raised in a single-parent household, after their father's departure with a travelling saleslady from Tulsa, a year after Jake's birth. Crystal Neidholm had devoted her life after that to raising her boys, and to her job as a teacher in the local elementary school. She smiled up from a photograph on the dressing table, alongside a more serious study of Jake, in air force uniform.

Sarah winced as she looked at the younger Neidholm. She and he had been classmates in high school, and had even had a few tentative, feely-fumbling dates, but Jake's overwhelming focus had been on his worship of his older brother and on the real love of his life, aeroplanes. He had gone straight from school to the US air force, and had won himself a pilot's seat in a fighter squadron. His career and his life had come to a blazing end five years earlier, when a prototype bomber had gone out of control over the New Mexican desert during a test flight.

Ron had been no more than a name to her until her college days; she had seen him around, but Jake had never introduced them, and being in different grades in a large school their paths had never crossed. It had taken Ian Walker to bring them together, at a party in his apartment towards the end of Sarah's freshman year, and after she and Ian had moved on from each other. The attraction was instant, and it had taken no more than a couple of hours for it to translate to action.

They were at different colleges, since Ron was a law major and she was in med school, but that was no barrier to their relationship, which had all the intensity and vigour of youth. She had taken him home at an early stage, and in turn she had met Crystal. All round, assumptions had been made.

And then the moment of choice had come; Ron's graduation, and with it, the prospect of a pro football career. Under a selection system that would have been illegal in Europe and in most other first world countries, he had been a first-round draft pick of the Seattle Seahawks, who had traded him at once to Dallas. The process had come as a bombshell to Sarah who, innocently, had believed that he would be able simply to sign up with his home town team, the Bills.

She had been two years short of graduation when it had happened; he had asked her to switch colleges and come with him, and she had countered by suggesting that he have himself traded again to a New York team, or forget football and practise law. She had given him no outright ultimatum, but when he left she had made a choice, nonetheless; she would not be anyone's camp follower.

When he returned in triumph at the end of his first pro season, she had told him that she was too involved with her studies to become involved in anything else, although in truth she had had two relationships over the winter, one of which was still active. A year after that, she had graduated herself and had moved to New York City as an intern, and to begin post-graduate study in forensic pathology.

She had followed Ron's career with more than a touch of pride, but as her own life had developed, professionally and personally, she had felt no longing for him. Nor, after her marriage, had she ever felt the need or the inclination to discuss him with her husband. Over the years she had come to see him as no more than the prize name on her sexual cv, not imagining that they would ever meet again, especially when her mother had told her that Crystal had left Buffalo for Hawaii.

And then Barbara Walker, her dear, devious friend Babs, had thrown them back together, in the very moment of Sarah's vulnerability. She had known damn well what would happen, and as usual she had been right; for sure, an interrogation would follow. Unconsciously, Sarah's mouth tightened as she thought about it.

'How you doing?' Ron called upstairs.

She slipped her feet into her shoes, and walked to the door. 'Just about there,' she replied. 'Crystal didn't leave a hair drier here, did she?'

'Not that I know of; sorry.'

'That's okay. I guess it's still warm outside; it'll be dry by the time I get home.' She picked up her bag and her reassembled but inactive cellphone, checked that she had left nothing else behind and walked downstairs, feeling a tenderness as she moved that took her back to her college days. People had often wondered how a quarterback had come to be nicknamed 'Rhino'.

The percolator had run its cycle as she walked into the kitchen; she sniffed. 'Brazilian?'

'Colombian.'

'I'll take that.'

'Black?'

'No, with a little milk.'

He chuckled. 'You've been in England too long.'

'Scotland, as my older son would be quick to tell you.'

'Sorry, Mark; Scotland then.'

'Maybe I have.'

He handed her a mug. 'From what I heard upstairs, you ain't going back, though.'

'Don't make assumptions,' she snapped.

'Hey, I wasn't; but you sure put the shoe leather to old Bob there. You didn't leave much room for doubt.'

'Maybe not, but there are other things to think of; my career for a start.'

'What career?'

'Are you kidding? My medical career, that's what. I'm a practising consultant pathologist, with a reputation as one of the best in the business. I have a personal investment in Scotland that's quite distinct from my marriage.'

'Yeah,' he said quietly, 'but they do pathology in the States, don't they? And a hell of a lot more of it, I'd guess.'

'But why should I come back to the States?'

He bowed his head and looked at her, from under his heavy eyebrows.

'Are you asking me something here, Ron?' she challenged.

'Maybe I am.'

'Aren't you a couple of assumptions ahead of yourself?'

'Am I? After this afternoon?'

She sighed, loudly. 'Ron, we just made love, that was all. I was horny, so were you; I wanted you, you wanted me. So we had each other. But that doesn't wipe out the last dozen years of my life.'

'That's in the past.'

'Not in mine it isn't; it's a current issue.' She stared at him. 'Ron, why did you come back to Buffalo?'

'To attend your parents' funeral.'

Sarah was taken by surprise. 'You did?'

'Yes. I was there, among the crowd. It was hardly surprising that you didn't see me given what happened.'

'How did you find out about it?'

'I read about it in a newspaper in Maui, but Babs Walker called to tell me too.'

'Ah,' she murmured. 'And what made you decide to stick around afterwards?'

He shrugged his shoulders. 'After what happened with Bob, I just thought you might need support.'

'You just thought?'

He took a sip of coffee. 'Yeah. Babs suggested it, and when she did, I agreed.'

'Good old Babs. Ron, do you think we might have been manipulated just a little?'

'Eh?' He gasped in surprise. 'How can that be?'

She laughed. 'For such a smart guy you can be so innocent.'

'Are you trying to say Babs set us up to get back together?'

'I'm saying that she's playing games with us, and that so far things have gone in line with her plan.'

'Why the hell would she do that?'

'I've told you why. She detests Bob. She's had a down on him since our first separation, but it goes deeper than that. He terrifies her because of everything he is, and isn't. Babs was brought up to believe in the all-American hero. When we were kids you and I were the ideal couple, in the world as she sees it. Bob, on the other hand, is as far from the Pro-Bowl as you can get. He's from another planet as far as she's concerned. He shares our values, but he plays by a completely different set of rules. On top of all that, he has this . . . charisma, let's call it. It can radiate from him, and to Babs it expresses itself as pure danger.'

'And what is it to you?' Ron asked quietly.

'Excitement. There's something about him that's thrilled me, from the moment I met him. I could say the same about you. With you it's sheer sexual attraction, allied to your sheer unadulterated niceness. With him it's . . . everything.'

'So why . . .?'

'Because,' she said, cutting him off, 'there's a singlemindedness about him that can turn into remoteness, and that cannot be deflected. Bob's about control, not simply over me, but over his whole life. He can't even stand to be a passenger in an automobile. Anyone who threatens that control, or tries to interfere with his life, is in for huge trouble. It's

93

happened now, and it's pushed even me and the kids into second place. I don't know if I can ever get over that.'

'Don't I give you a reason not to want to?'

Sarah sighed then smiled at him. 'I want you to pick up that knife over there,' she said, 'and make a cut in your left thumb.'

'Uhh. Why?'

'Because if you're even going to start giving me that reason, it'll be by putting me first. I want you to give me a written declaration that you will not leave me behind to go off and play just one more season for the Nashville Cats. And to make me believe it, I'm going to want it signed in your own blood.'

She walked over to the counter beside the sink, picked up the knife by the handle and offered it to him. 'Go on,' she said. 'But only if, in your heart, you really mean it, and you know for certain that never in your life will you blame me for making you miss out on the chance of that one last great moment.'

Ron took the knife from her and held it to his thumb. For a moment she though that he really was going to cut himself open, but just as she gasped, he laid it back down.

'No,' he murmured. 'I can't promise you all of that. Some of it, maybe, but not the last part.'

She patted his chest. 'See? You guys, you're both the devils I know, and you both say you want me, on your terms. So the way I see it, I've got to figure out which devil I'm better off with, or whether I should leave you both in your different underworlds.'

The giant smiled down at her, gently. 'While you're doing that, are you going to carry on seeing this horny devil?'

'I don't know whether I should. I doubt if it would help me think objectively.'

'I tell you what,' he said. 'Mom wants me to sell this house for her, so I'm going to stick around for a while.' He reached into his pocket, and brought something out. 'I don't think it would be right for me to be around your kids too much, so here's a key to the front door. If you feel you want to be with me, don't even call; just come. If I'm not here, the alarm code's eleven ninety-one. Deal?'

She took the key from his hand. 'No promises, but okay. If I find I

94

can't resist you any longer, I'll come. But that won't necessarily imply anything, understood? It might just mean that . . . Hell, you know what it might just mean.'

He chuckled. 'Sure. Understood.'

'Right. Now get me back to my kids.'

17

Skinner and Martin were heading for the stairs when Rod Greatorix stuck his head out of the door of the main CID office. 'Mr Skinner,' he called. 'Can I have a word before you go?'

The two stopped and went back to join him in the private room. 'There's a couple of things I need to deal with,' he began. 'First and foremost we'll need to announce the identification. As soon as we've got the post-mortem findings I want to issue a public appeal for information about your brother's movements in the period leading up to his death. We need to get a handle on where he was when he went into the river, or we can't even start a proper investigation.'

'Of course,' Skinner agreed.

'How do you want us to handle it? I mean I don't have to say that Michael was your brother.'

'You don't, Rod, that's true. But it'll get out, as sure as God made wee sour apples. You need the press working for you on this. If they start to dig into the story of the black sheep of my family, they might come up with useful information faster than you. By and large, journalists are better than detectives at asking questions. I'll talk to them about my estrangement from my brother if they want.' He frowned. 'There's just one thing, though. I want to speak to a couple of people before this hits the press. There's my daughter, for one; she has to hear it from me. Then there's Neil McIlhenney; after Andy here, he's my closest friend.'

'How much time do you need?'

'If you brief the press at midday tomorrow, that'll be okay. Alex is flying up from London tomorrow morning for a business meeting on Monday. I'm picking her up at the airport at eleven-thirty. I'll see Neil before that; there's something else I want to talk to him about, anyway.'

'Okay, sir. You've got that; the press won't be awake much before noon on a Sunday anyway.'

'Thanks. Now what else did you want?'

'I'd like the name and address of the hostel where your brother lived, and the name of the manager. He'll have to be interviewed, and possibly some of the other residents as well.'

'It's called Oak Lodge, it's in Gourock like I said, and it's run by the Jesuits. That's as much as I can tell you. I'm going to want to talk to them myself, though.'

'Bob . . .' Martin began.

'It's for my own peace of mind, Andy. I have to find out how he was.'

'You won't go running your own investigation now, will you?'

Skinner looked at him, wide-eyed. 'Who? Me? Listen, a complaint from your chief constable to my police authority about my conduct is just what I don't need right now.'

18

Maggie Rose found the divisional CID office in Torphichen Place depressing at the best of times; on a Sunday morning, with the normal buzz of the rest of the building reduced to a murmur, it seemed to drop to a new level of drabness.

The faces around her were keen, though, and in the main, fresh. Stevie Steele, on her right, was as sharp as the razor that had shaved him. Opposite her across the table, Detective Constable Alice Cowan sat straight-backed, disturbingly young, but in no way overawed. On either side of her, Ray Wilding and George Regan, detective sergeants both, leaned back in their chairs, exchanging glances behind the girl's back. And in the doorway, carrying a tray with six mugs, PC Sauce Haddock looked at least three years older in plain clothes than he did in his baggy uniform.

'Okay,' the detective superintendent began, as Haddock found a place on the table, and began handing round mugs, 'let's get on with it. I'm sorry to pull everyone in on a Sunday, but this one can't wait till tomorrow. It's already taken on a high profile, and we can't be seen to be holding back on it.

'I'm giving it priority, and so, I have to tell you is the head of CID. Mr Pringle would have taken this meeting himself, but he had an engagement last night, so he's sent Ray Wilding, his exec., both as a member of the team and to report back to him.' The irreverent George Regan, who had served directly under Dan Pringle in the past and knew his Saturday night habits, grinned broadly, but she let it pass.

'There's another in-house consideration we'd all do well to remember,' she continued. 'The chief constable was on the invitation list for yesterday's event; as it happened, he couldn't go, but that doesn't mean that he won't be taking a keener interest than usual in our progress.

'Right; you all know the gist of what happened yesterday, but the forensic people, ours and the fire specialists, have taken it a bit further. Detective Inspector Steele will bring you up to date.'

She leaned back from the table and picked up her mug, looking sidelong at Steele. Since his promotion he seemed to have grown in authority every day; she knew that Bob Skinner had marked him out, and that the DCC was rarely wrong . . . on a professional level at any rate. Quickly, but comprehensively, the DI set out the results of the forensic investigation. He explained that while there was a possibility of the device having been triggered from outside the gallery, the thickness of the Royal Scottish Academy's walls and the timing of the detonation made it, in his view, unlikely.

'Too risky; the device was an expert job, and I don't believe that whoever planted it would have taken any chance that it might not have gone off. So, what we're left with, potentially,' he concluded, 'is a room full of blue chip suspects. But before we get there, before we start digging into everyone's background and interviewing people who might try to make very big waves about it, we have to make sure that the perpetrator isn't right before our eyes, thanks to the Academy's security cameras.

'So all of us,' he glanced at Haddock, 'and that means you too, young Sauce . . . you're not just here as the gopher . . . are in for the job we love to hate, identifying people from poor quality security videos, and looking for someone who shouldn't be there.'

Steele paused and smiled. 'I know, I know. You're going to tell me that you don't know everybody there, so how can you identify them. But we do know everyone who's signed in, and thanks to the very discreet co-operation of DI McIlhenney's friend, the *Scotsman* picture editor, who's in charge of the biggest photo library in town, George and I have come up with a list of mug-shots to match most of the people on the guest list . . . not just the signed-in list, because we have to allow for the possibility of people just walking past the reception table. There are those who expect everyone to know them, and who won't wear badges for that very reason.

'Those whose photos we don't have will be mostly the partners of guests, but quite a few of them are on that list as well.' He stopped as DS Wilding raised a hand. 'Ray; question?'

'Yes, Stevie; why don't we bring in the organisers to help us spot all the legit. guests?'

'I'll bring in David Candela if and when we have to, but I don't want to trouble him at this stage. And anyway, there's no guarantee that he'll know every spouse of every business associate. We do have one secret weapon, though.'

'Who's that?'

'My mother-in-law,' Maggie Rose answered with a smile. 'Mrs Christina McGuire. She was on the guest list, and although she didn't attend, she knows just about everybody who's anybody in Edinburgh on a business or social footing. She's agreed to look at all the faces we can't identify. There won't be many left after that, I can promise you.'

'In an ideal world,' Steele went on, 'we'll be left with just one unidentified face. Correction, in a truly ideal world we'll spot someone who isn't on the list but who is on a Special Branch file . . . that's why Alice Cowan is here, by the way . . . and we'll have our prime suspect.'

He leaned forward on the table, showing Maggie his clean, sharp profile, and making her think, unexpectedly, of Paula Viareggio. 'The tapes we're really interested in,' he said, 'run for about an hour and a half, from the arrival of the first guest, through the incident, and thereafter. They come from four different cameras. I've had them copied, and enhanced as far as is possible . . . which isn't very much . . . and I've split them into six lots. We'll each have a video player, we'll each have a different section of tape and we'll each have a complete set of mug-shots, with a name along side it. With all of us working at it, Ms Rose and me included, it's shouldn't take too long.

'So let's get at it, and see if we get lucky.'

19

Bob Skinner felt his spirits rise as he saw his daughter walk through the domestic arrivals gateway of the Edinburgh Airport terminal building, towing her cabin luggage behind her on its small wheels. She had that effect on him every time he saw her; she was a beacon of light within him, and had been since the moment of her birth, around a quarter of a century before.

Every time they were reunited after a separation, he saw something new about her; on this occasion he thought of the movie *Lord of the Rings*, and of Liv Tyler. Yes, put some bounce into the actress's hair and she definitely had a look of his Alexis. Maybe that was why he had seen the film three times. Quickly he wondered whether that made him look like Ms Tyler's father, but decided that there was no way he would pass for a seventies rock star.

Alex ran up to him and hugged him, letting the small suitcase find its feet beside her. 'Oh, I am so glad to see you,' she exclaimed. 'I know we had that net meeting chat from the States, but I still didn't know how you'd be.' She stood back and gave him an appraising, up-and-down look. 'And you're great. Is this pacemaker nuclear-powered or what?'

He laughed. 'If it is, it's like your tongue. Shut up, girl and let me look at you.'

'But I mean it,' she insisted. 'You're glowing with health.'

'I've been working on it,' he admitted. 'I'd been getting sloppy before the incident, but I'm back in top shape now.'

'So what do these idiots mean, saying that you can't go back to work?'

'That's what your boss is going to ask the court, if they persist in it.'

'They'd better not then; Councillor Maley and her pals don't want to mess with the might of Curle, Anthony and Jarvis, and especially not with Mr Laidlaw.'

'They especially don't want to mess with me, but that's tomorrow's agenda. In the meantime, let's go over there and have a coffee. There's something I have to talk to you about. Have you got any other luggage?'

Alex shook her head, making her shoulder-length hair ripple and shimmer in the neon light of the arrivals hall. 'No. I've got the power suit packed in here. I'm only up for a couple of days, remember.'

'Yeah. Sorry it's so brief. How are you liking London anyway?' He picked up her bag by its handle and walked her towards the escalator. The cafeteria space on the first floor was always less crowded, even on a Sunday morning.

'I like the professional atmosphere, and the people I'm with, but I'm not so keen on the city. You spoiled me, Pops, bringing me up in the country. How's Andy?' she asked, abruptly. 'And the baby?'

'And Karen,' he reminded her. 'They're tip-top, all three of them. Andy's looking at home in Tayside already, and Karen's enjoying being a mum. You know, I still don't think you were very clever the way you went about it, but I reckon that breaking off your engagement has turned out to be the best thing you could have done for him.'

'I think I should be offended by that,' said his daughter they walked towards a table by the window.

'Don't be. It was the making of you too. It was all fine at the time, but really, you were infatuated, and long-term, Andy was looking for something you weren't ready to give him.'

She reached up and patted his cheek as he laid down her bag. 'You're a fine one to be lecturing me about relationships, Pops.'

He gave a half-snort, half-laugh. 'You could be right. Cappuccino?'

'No, latte.'

'Okay.' He wandered off to the coffee booth and returned with a café latte and a tall beaker of Coke for himself.

'So,' said Alex heavily. 'What gives with you and my stepmother? I called her last night, you know, to ask after my various small siblings. She sounded strange, and awkward in a way that I've never known Sarah to be before. She and I have always really been two girls together; we've got on like a house on fire. Whatever you've done, you've really upset her, Pops.'

'Did she say anything to you, about us?'

'Not really. I had a feeling that there were things she wanted to say, but stopped herself short. Maybe she thought I'd automatically take your side.'

'And would you?'

'Yes, of course. But I'd try not to let Sarah know that. Come on, tell me; what's up?'

'Simple. She thinks I should be there supporting her, I think she should be here supporting me.'

'Against the powers of darkness, in the shape of Councillor Maley and her faction?'

'That's part of it, yes.'

'Then it's rubbish. You've never needed anyone's support against the likes of her. You're just putting it that way to cover your guilt over leaving Sarah with the kids in the States and charging back over here like a mad bull.'

'Did Sarah suggest that to you?'

'No. She didn't have to. I know you even better than she does, Father. I know exactly how you feel and how you think. But I'm a woman too, so I know what Sarah's feeling.'

'Listen, girl,' he retorted, 'my job's under threat. These people are trying to use my condition to get rid of me. What else could I have done but come home to deal with them?'

'If you want my legal opinion, it'll cost you dinner tonight, in the Roseberry.'

In spite of his indignation, Bob grinned. 'Deal.'

'First, you could have sought two objective medical opinions in the USA, ideally from practitioners who are consultants to the county or state police. Assuming they certified you fit, you could have instructed Mitch Laidlaw to present them to the police authority and to demand that you be returned to the duty list immediately, with a Supreme Court interdict in his hand if necessary. That done you could have phoned Uncle Jimmy and asked him to put you on compassionate leave.'

'Mmm. And you think that would have worked, do you?'

'You could have instructed me, never mind Mr Laidlaw, and it would have worked. If you'd passed the medical, under the present rules the Court would have given you the interdict and Maley's lot would have been held in contempt if they'd gone against it.

'It's still not too late to change your tactics though,' she pointed out. 'Why not set up a full medical examination by two independent cardiologists up at the Murrayfield? If they clear you, my boss can go to Maley and demand your reinstatement, or by-pass her even and go straight to the chair of the Police Authority.' Alex smiled, and put her hand over his. 'That would be the sensible way of doing it. But you are you, Pops, and when it blew up I'd never have expected you to react in any other way than you did.'

'So Sarah's right?'

'I won't say that, because I don't know the whole story. Didn't she suggest what I just did?'

'No. She told me I should let them get on with it. She told me I should take my collapse as a sign from God and give up my job.'

'Oh dear,' Alex whispered. 'Mistake. Then again,' she continued, firmly, 'I thought exactly the same thing when she called to tell me you'd had an incident. And that coming, as it did, right on top of what happened to your poor friend Joe Doherty dying so suddenly as well. I'd have thought twice about saying it to your face, though.'

'And you'd have been right. What happened to Joe and what happened to me are in no way related.' He looked out of the cafeteria window, across the airport car park. 'Still, I will do what you suggest. I'll line up a couple of specialists to give me a going over, tomorrow, if possible, and we'll take it from there.

'But that is tomorrow; all that apart, the God that Sarah mentioned does indeed work in mysterious ways, and because I did come back, I was on the spot to become involved in something very important, and very, very personal. It's really what I have to talk to you about, before you hear it on the telly.'

Alex raised her eyebrows. 'Sounds intriguing; I'm glad I came.'

'So am I. Let me ask you a strange question. Does the name Michael Niven Skinner mean anything to you?'

In an instant, all of the mischief went from her expression; looking at her, Bob imagined he saw her lawyer's face. 'Ah,' she exclaimed. 'So that's it. Yes, it does. He's my uncle, isn't he?'

Very few people had the capacity to take Skinner completely by surprise, but Alex had always been one. 'How did you . . . When did you . . .?' At the third attempt, he found words. 'How long have you known about him?' he gasped.

'Since I was sixteen; we did a genealogical study at school, as part of Modern Studies. Some of us were taken up to the General Records Office and shown how to go about constructing our family trees. I knew about you and me, so I started with Grandpa and Grandma Skinner. I fed in their names to the computer. Maybe you can imagine how surprised I was when I found our tree had an extra branch, and that according to the records, it was still alive, although not bearing fruit.'

'Bloody hell,' he whispered. 'Why didn't you ask me about him?'

'Pops, I've always trusted you; always. I knew that if you had kept his existence a secret from me for sixteen years, you must have had a bloody good reason, and that you would tell me if and when you were good and ready. Now you have done, there's something I have to ask you straight out, something that's been on my mind, given what my mum was . . .' She hesitated, as if she was afraid to utter the words on the tip of her tongue. '. . . Given that we know she had affairs,' she exclaimed, at last. 'He isn't my real father, is he?'

It was one of those times: Bob Skinner was taken aback, completely. 'God, no. Not a chance. You can rest easy on that score; you are my daughter. You were conceived on holiday in a cottage on Mull; even if Myra had been that way inclined at the time, she'd have had to walk a bloody long way to find anyone else to do the deed. Besides, every time I look in the mirror I see in me your eyes, your mouth, and your chin; a bit careworn perhaps, but yours for sure.'

For a second Alex's own chin trembled, but she held herself together. 'Thanks, Pops; silly or not, that's been my private nightmare, for a while now. So tell me, how did my uncle Michael become a non-person?'

And so he told her, the same story he had told Andy, and more. He confessed that after Michael's expulsion his mother had had a breakdown, and that she had become an alcoholic herself, neglecting him, becoming more and more remote from his father, and drinking herself inexorably to an early death.

'I'm sorry, Alex,' he said when he had finished. 'These are all things you've had a right to know; I shouldn't have kept them from you.'

'Yes you should, if that's the way you saw it,' she retorted. 'It hasn't exactly made my morning now you have told me. I know that every family has a closet with skeletons in it, and I also know that sometimes the best thing to do is to leave the door closed.'

She sipped her latte. 'So what's made you open it? Was it your near-death experience in America?'

'Hell no! When I came to in that ambulance all I thought about was Sarah, you and the kids. No, it's because of Michael's real-death experience in Perthshire; that's the reason. It's going to be all over the news bulletins in an hour or so.'

He told her of the discovery in Miss Bonney's basement, and of the photograph in her uncle's pocket. When he was finished she shivered, for all the warmth of the morning. 'The poor man,' she whispered. 'For all he did, that he should die like that. Or did he have it coming to him?' she asked. 'Maybe he never changed. Maybe he never stopped behaving like an animal, until finally . . .'

'No,' Bob said. 'I may have respected my father's wish that I never see Michael again, but that didn't stop me from keeping an eye on him from a distance. For the last few years, until he moved to Edinburgh, Willie Haggerty's been giving me reports about him. More recently, someone else I trust on the Strathclyde force has been keeping a discreet eye on him for me. He's never been in any trouble all the time he's been living through there.'

'Then there's the Jesuit.'

'Who?'

'Brother Aidan, the superintendent of Oak Lodge, the hostel where your uncle lived. Once a year, he makes a report to the trustee who looks after Michael's money, letting the family know about his general health and his lifestyle. Originally, the trustee was your grandpa; since he died, it's been me. The reports have come through the solicitors who set up the trust.

'Andy's detectives will start their investigation with him, but they've agreed to let me talk to him first, to explain what's happened. He's an old man, and he might need advance warning so he can think about the last time he saw Michael, and what he was doing around then. So what I plan to do is put you in a taxi and send you home to Gullane, then, after I've paid a call on Neil McIlhenney, get through to Gourock.'

'Hmmph!' Alex snorted. 'You can forget that for a start. If you think you can drop this bombshell on me then leave me behind as you go off to open a can of God knows how many worms . . . well, you can think again, Pops. If you're going to Gourock, then so am I.'

He looked at her and grinned. 'Would it work if I ordered you to get in a taxi?'

'It never has before. Why should it now?'

'True.'

'Besides, if this story is going to hit the press soon, I'd rather not be in Gullane when the phone starts ringing.'

'That shouldn't happen. I've told Andy to say to the press that I've been estranged from Michael for the last thirty years, and that any enquiries about him should be addressed to my family solicitors. But I don't suppose it'll hold them all at bay. You're right; there are bound to be a few calls. So you can come with me, if for no other reason than that.'

'Very graciously conceded,' said Alex. 'By the way, why do you want to see Neil?'

'To give him advance warning of what's going to hit the press.'

'Couldn't you phone him?'

Alex's father gave her a look full of intrigue. 'Ah, but that's not all I want to see him about. I've had a thorn in my side for too long. It's time I got rid of it.'

20

Sarah struggled towards wakefulness, wondering where the sound was coming from. When it dawned on her that it was the phone, ringing beside her bed, she mumbled and threw out an arm, hoping to prod someone into answering it. She was caught in the confused tail of a departing dream; she might have been reaching out to Bob, or possibly to Ron, but she could not be sure which it was she imagined was lying beside her.

But the tone trilled on, until she came fully to her senses and realised that she was alone. She glanced at the time; it was eight-fifteen. Since Trish was not answering, she guessed that she was either in the shower, or busy changing Seonaid. Grumbling silently, she threw herself across the bed and grabbed the handset.

'Hi there,' came a silvery morning voice. 'Don't tell me your household was still asleep. With three kids, how do you do that?'

Sarah often thought that when Babs Walker was called to the Master her husband served, it would be because of a terminal case of cheerfulness.

'Easy,' she answered, stifling a half yawn. 'I don't waken the poor little things at seven o'clock on a Sunday morning. It might be a working day for you, but it's rest time for most of us.'

'The Devil finds work, Sarah,' Babs chirped. 'Got to keep those hands busy. Speaking of which, where were you when I called you yesterday? Your nanny was rather vague on the subject. Wherever it was, you were behaving yourself, I hope.'

'You hope no such thing, and you damn well know it.'

'Hey, come on, of course I do; I'm a minister's wife, after all. It just so happens that Alice Bierhoff saw you and a certain large and rugged pro footballer getting out of a car in his mom's driveway yesterday afternoon, and standing, shall we say, rather close together. I just hope we didn't break any commandments, that all.'

She felt her lips purse. Babs, in spite of herself, was her closest girlfriend, and they had been sharing most of their secrets since they were twelve. *But not this one*, Sarah thought, *or it might go straight to Bob at the first opportunity.*

'Alice Bierhoff is cross-eyed and can't see much further than the hood of her Cadillac,' she retorted. 'It was probably Ron's mother that she saw.'

'Alice wears contacts now. And what was Ron's mother doing putting on her bra in Ron's bedroom, with the shades up, when she drove past again a couple of hours later?'

If her friend had been with her, she would have seen Sarah's face redden. 'Barbara,' she said, 'it's too late to tell you to mind your Goddamned business, but please, just for once, will you go against your nature and keep your mouth shut about this. And tell dear Alice that if she doesn't want to have an emergency appendectomy, without anaesthetic, she'd better do the same.'

Babs laughed. 'I can deliver on the first of those, and I will, but I'm not so sure about the second.'

'Make yourself sure. Now what can I do for you? Surely you didn't call me at this hour just to quiz me about my sex life? For all you know you might have been interrupting it.'

Her friend chuckled. 'That would have been fun, but no, I didn't. I was wondering whether we'll be seeing you in church today?'

'Why, are the Lutherans starting a confessional?'

A peal of laughter rang down the line. 'Maybe we should, maybe we should. No, I was wondering whether you and the children might like to join us for lunch afterwards. It would give your girl Trish some time off.'

'She's having today off anyway; I was planning to take the kids to the lake this afternoon.'

'Were you now? Does Ron still have his boat there?'

'I have no idea. He wasn't included on the trip.'

'Well, whatever; what do you say?'

'Have you invited anyone else?' Sarah asked.

'I could do, if you'd like.'

'I wouldn't like, and with that understood, yes thanks, we'll be there. We'll be at Ian's service too; Seonaid's old enough to behave herself now, and James Andrew needs a little discipline in his life. Besides, I might see Alice Bierhoff. If I do, don't be surprised if I punch her contacts right out of her head.'

21

'I'd have come to you, you know,' Christina McGuire assured her daughter-in-law, as she opened the door of the Northumberland Street flat which she was soon to leave behind her, along with the rest of her Edinburgh life.

'Not at all,' said Maggie, 'you've got enough on your plate, packing up for the move to Italy. No second thoughts about giving up the recruitment business?'

Christina laughed. She was a tall, imposing woman; she looked to be in her early fifties, although she was in truth a few years older. 'My son wouldn't allow it, even if I did show any signs of changing my mind. I shocked him at first when I told him what I was planning, but now he's really taken to the idea of me living in Tuscany.

'He came to see me earlier on,' she said, leading the way into a big rectangular drawing room. 'He just happened to drop in around lunch-time, with Rufus, and with a damn great pizza. I don't know why he's so keen on the things. They were never on my table when he was a child.'

She frowned for a second. 'He told me what's happened about the wee boy. I'm really sorry, Maggie.'

'Thanks, but it's for the best. He'll be very well looked after, and he'll be among other children too. I'm reconciled to it; in fact, Mario's taking it worse than I am.'

'Is it for the best, though? What about you two? Will you be all right?'

'We'll be fine. When you leave everything else aside, Mario and I are the best of friends. There's no one I'd rather live with, and I know he feels the same way.' She was not sure that her mother-in-law understood completely what she meant; if she did, Christina gave no sign.

'That's good,' she murmured. 'As you know I've never been an interferer, but I'll leave happier for hearing you say that.'

Suddenly her expression became businesslike. 'Now,' she exclaimed. 'What, or who, do you have for me?'

Maggie sat down on a big soft couch in the middle of the room, took a file from her document case, which she dropped on the floor at her feet. Her mother-in-law sat beside her as she opened the brown folder.

'Not too much,' she said. 'There are only five faces on the video we're stuck with. I've had them transferred to photo-files and printed out.'

Christina reached out and drew a heavy coffee table across the carpet towards them. 'Spread them out there and I'll have a look.'

Maggie did as she was told. The faces of three women and two men looked up from the table. One was smiling, but the others looked as if they had been taken off guard . . . as indeed they had, for none had been aware that they were being filmed. One of the men looked particularly fierce. Christina picked up the A4 likeness, peered at it, and then laughed. 'That is undoubtedly the worst photograph I have ever seen,' she said, 'but maybe he looks like that on the Bench. That's Henry Corrigan QC; Lord Corrigan, the Court of Session judge.'

'Is it?' Maggie exclaimed, taking the sheet and peering at it. 'God, you're right. I've given evidence in his court, too, but I'd never have known him from that. Mind you,' she added, 'he was in his robes in the mug-shot the *Scotsman* gave us. I've never seen him without his wig. He's an ugly bugger, isn't he?'

'In every way. Not a nice man.' Christina picked up another photograph, one of the three women. 'This is his unfortunate wife, Madeline, or Maidie, Lady Corrigan.'

She laid it aside and picked up the other man's likeness. 'Now this is . . .' She stopped, thinking. 'James Woodstein,' she exclaimed with satisfaction. 'He's a marketing consultant, with a smallish client list. As I remember it includes David Candela's firm. We did a headhunting job for him once. We found him two excellent candidates, but he turned them both down, saying they were too expensive, and then he refused to pay us. Twerp.'

She picked up the photo on the left of the five. 'Sadie Grierson,' she announced. 'She's a relatively rare bird, a female corporate accountant. She was with one of the big players in London, until she was moved to Edinburgh to head up their Scottish office. She's so new in town that she's obviously not in the *Scotsman* photo library yet, but she's a client of my firm. I met her at a reception they had to announce her appointment.'

Maggie picked up the last of the five head shots. It showed a woman, not old, of indeterminate age, with a severe hair arrangement, sharp eyes and an even sharper frown. 'What about her?' she asked.

'One doesn't like to be unkind, but what about her, indeed. Who stole her scone, do you think?'

'I don't know,' Maggie muttered. 'But I wouldn't like to be him when she finds him. Do you know her?'

'Would her own mother know her from that likeness? No, I don't think I can help you with her.' She laid the photograph back on the table, and looked at it again. 'And yet . . .' She took a pen from the pocket of her cardigan and laid it across the woman's eyes. 'There's a girl about the town, an odd lass. They say she's very bright; to my knowledge she has a first in chemistry. She did a teacher training course, but that ended when she assaulted a girl who was rude to her. After that, she worked for a while for one of the children's charities, as a clerk, until they got rid of her for sending an offensive letter to one of the patrons. Then she went to work in the office of a New Town hotel, but she was moved on from that; a resident swore in her hearing and she emptied a vase of flowers over his head. After that her father brought her to me, in the vain hope that I could find her a job. That could be her, only . . .'

She picked up the photograph again, took the pen and drew a pair of spectacles, roughly over the eyes. 'Only when I met her she was wearing big thick glasses. That's the girl; I'm sure of it. Her name's Andrea Strachan, and her father's a lecturer in religious studies at Napier.'

'Where can we find her?'

'If I hadn't seen that photograph, I'd have said you could have found her in the Royal Edinburgh Hospital. Last I heard, she was sectioned after she tried to set fire to a church.'

22

Pops said he was old, Alex thought, as she looked across the coffee table in the sparsely furnished room, *but that was an understatement*.

Brother Aidan, the superintendent of Oak Lodge, was an ancient, twinkling, nutmeg of a man, a tiny figure with skin like well worn leather, sharp features and sparse, wispy, flyaway hair. Looking at him Skinner's daughter was struck by his resemblance to a character in the *Star Wars* series . . . a character depicted by a puppet.

'Did it strike you as odd that I offered you a drink,' he asked her father, in vibrant Irish tones, 'here of all places, where it's a problem to so many?'

The big detective grinned. 'Now that you mention it, I suppose it did.'

'Nothing odd about it at all. My friends who live here don't do so on the basis that they keep off the drink. Some of them just can't, poor souls, or they wouldn't be here in the first place.'

'How many people do you have here?' Alex asked him.

'Up to twenty-five, my dear. God knows there's a need for more places, but we have to strike a balance with the feelings of our neighbours.' The hostel was situated in a residential suburb on the western side of the Clyde coast town, on a hillside looking across the Firth to Dunoon. 'They're good folks in the main,' Brother Aidan went on, 'but if we tried to expand this place, one or two of them might object. And I'd understand why, too. My friends here are all good people too, at heart, but some of them can get a bit obstreperous from time to time.'

'What's the mix among the, um, residents?' asked Skinner.

The little priest scratched his chin. 'The mix? They're just men, all of them, people who would like to live in normal society, in a normal home, but with problems that make it difficult, nay, impossible, for them to do that. With some it's mental illness. With a few, it's personality disorders.

With others, it's just the drink. With one or two, like your poor brother Michael, it's both.'

He rocked back in his chair, and took a long look at his visitors, his sharp gaze finally coming to rest on Bob. 'So he's dead, then, my old friend.'

'I'm afraid so.'

'He was here the longest, you know. I came myself thirty-two years ago, and Michael joined us a couple of years after that.'

'How was he, all that time?'

'Sure, and how do I answer that? Sad, I suppose; yes, whatever else he was, he was always sad. At first, when he came here from the hospital, he was very disturbed. He was medicated, but there was still a great anger in him.'

'What did he have to be angry about?' Skinner blurted out, before he could stop himself.

'A great deal,' Brother Aidan replied, 'but it was all directed at himself. In those early years, I had a fear that it might drive him to take his life. But gradually, that anger faded, until only the sadness remained. He became, I'd have to say, a nice man, quiet, but popular within our community here. Eventually, if my friends here can be said to have a leader among them, that's what he became. He had been thrust out of his own family, but he had the good fortune to find another here. He was a great asset to us as well. He had all sorts of skills with his hands, from his army days; just about all of the maintenance around here, he did.'

The priest held up a hand. 'You mustn't take that as criticism, my son. I understand why your father did what he did. It hurt him very deeply, but as he saw it, he had no choice. Truth be told, that's how I saw it too.'

'You met my father?'

'Of course. He came to inspect Oak Lodge while Michael was still in the hospital. He was a substantial man, right enough, with an air about him that I saw in you the moment you walked through the door.' He smiled at Alex. 'And in you too, my dear, if I may say so. Michael would have been very proud of his niece, had he known of you.' Brother Aidan sighed. 'But he never did, of course; he never once asked me about his family. I think he knew that he wouldn't have been able to bear having a running commentary on their lives.'

'You told him when my parents died, though?'

'Of course. When he learned about your poor mother, I thought he really would end himself. He locked himself away and cried for a whole day. Eventually I had to have his door broken in. When I told him about your father, though, I have to say that his reaction was very strange. He was every bit as broken-hearted, but there was something else too. He was afraid for the security of his life here. He was convinced that you would wind up his trust and cut off his money.'

'God, I'd never have done that.'

'I knew you wouldn't, and eventually I was able to persuade Michael of that. Still and all, though, his view of life did change after your father's death. There was always that edge of fear in him.'

'Fear?'

'Yes, my son; he always had a fear of you. Michael told me about the terrible things he did to you, when you were a child. He told me what he did to your mother, and about what happened after that. I am not condemning you here, because I know what you saw. You were no more than a boy defending his mother; the most natural thing in the world. But your brother's last memory of you was of you beating him unconscious, telling him all the time in a quiet voice that you were going to kill him. He came to realise that among his many sins, possibly the greatest was to have put such hatred in the heart of one so young. He couldn't believe that it could ever leave you, and when the years went by without a visit from you, or cards on his birthday or at Christmas, his sadness and his guilt went all the deeper.'

Bob Skinner stared out of the window of the old priest's office. 'I'm carrying my own guilt now, Brother. Michael's dead, and I wish that at the very least I'd written to him, or called him, if only to wipe away his memory of that hatred, and to cleanse him of his guilt. It came to me, when I looked at him in the mortuary, that in my life as a police officer I've dealt with many people who were a hell of a lot worse human beings than my brother ever was, and yet I've shown most of them more mercy than I ever showed him.' He winced, as if his pain was physical.

'I can make the age-old excuse, of course; in not contacting him I was obeying my father's order. I worshipped my dad . . . as did Michael in his own very different way. It would have been a betrayal for me to have gone against him; for me, the ultimate disloyalty. But now, I'll go through my life believing that if I had reached out to him, maybe he wouldn't have wound up in that fucking river.'

Brother Aidan nodded. 'You may do so,' he conceded. 'But even if you had reached out, as you put it, I doubt very much whether Michael would have given up his life here. Your father put him here because he had a personality disorder and he was alcoholic. A Christmas card from you might have been nice, but it wouldn't have changed that. Be hard on yourself if you like . . . wearing a hair shirt on occasion is good for any man . . . but don't be too hard. Bury him where he belongs, beside his parents, then try to move on.'

Alex reached across and took his hand. 'Yes, Dad, please.'

Skinner let out a low growling sound. 'Mmmm. Time will tell if I can; my life seems to be full of guilt and anger just now. Maybe the best thing I could do is take over Michael's bed here.'

'You don't qualify,' said Brother Aidan, brusquely. 'There's a queue from here to Glasgow of people who need help, before we get round to those who just feel sorry for themselves.'

Reproved, the policeman smiled. 'True.'

'You mentioned a river,' the little priest continued. 'You've never told me how Michael died. Was that it?'

'Part of it, at least. Tell me, Brother, did Michael leave here often?'

'He'd go down the shops like everyone else, but if you mean did he take a trip somewhere, that happened only rarely. In fact, two weeks ago was the first time he ever went away for any length of time without me. Michael and I used to go on holiday together,' he explained. 'I have a nephew in a village near Cork, and we would visit him every year or two.'

'So what happened two weeks ago? Where did he go?'

'Glasgow, I was told.'

'On his own?'

'Oh no. He couldn't have done that. Not that there'd have been anything to stop him, mind, other than himself. My friends here are all free men; they can come and go any time they please. But many, Michael among them, choose to remain.

'What happened was this. A few months ago, your brother had a letter, out of the blue. He said it was from a man called Skipper, someone he'd known a long time ago, when he was young. Skipper said that he'd been abroad for many years, and that he'd only just come back to Scotland. He'd asked around about Michael and had been told by a friend of a friend back in Motherwell that he'd gone to live in Oak Lodge.'

'Did my uncle write back to him?' asked Alex.

'There was no return address, my dear. However a couple of weeks later, there was a telephone call for Michael, from the man. I didn't think he was going to take it at first. Apart from once when my nephew called from Ireland and he said a quick hello, he hadn't spoken on the telephone for thirty years. But he plucked up his courage and he did. The outcome was that Skipper came to visit him, shortly afterwards. They had a chat, then they went out for a drink together.'

'Did this guy have another name?' Skinner asked.

'That's the only one I know. I don't know whether it's a surname, nickname or whatever. In any event, he came another couple of times, and eventually, it was arranged between them that Michael would go to stay with him for a couple of weeks.'

The old man sighed. 'The truth be told, when you called to say you wanted to see me, I thought you were going to tell me that Michael wasn't going to be coming back. That's just what you did tell me, but not in the way I expected.'

'Sadly not. Brother Aidan, can you tell me what this man Skipper looked like?'

The Jesuit ran his fingers through his sparse hair. 'He'd have been about Michael's age, I suppose. In height, he'd have been around the same, but he was fairly thin; much more lightly built. He wore spectacles with blue lenses; sunglasses I suppose they were.'

'Hair?'

'Grey, like yours. A bit greyer, maybe. Does that ring any bells?'

'None. I'll maybe talk to a couple of people in Motherwell, who might have known my brother back in the old days. They'll probably be rogues or policemen, but some of them will still be around.'

'Why do you need to trace this man, Robert?' Brother Aidan asked.

'Because Michael's death may have been either suicide, or an accident, or something else. There's considerable doubt about it.' He told the priest the rest of the story, explaining where and how he had been found. As he spoke, the old man's mouth formed into a perfect O of horror.

He crossed himself. 'How terrible,' he whispered. 'My poor old friend, that he should die like that. But tell me, how did the police make the connection to you?'

'The only thing they found on his body was a photograph of my father. Someone who knew me saw it, spotted the likeness between us, and came to me.'

'Ahh,' Brother Aidan exclaimed. 'That would be it. It was all he had with him when they brought him here. And it was all he took with him just over two weeks ago, when he went away with Skipper, for the last time.'

23

'What do we know about this fire-raising thing?' asked Stevie Steele.

'It's in our records, right enough,' DS George Regan replied. 'And so is the girl's photograph, full face and profile, Strachan, Andrea. I pulled it, and it pretty much matches the face on the video. Her address is listed as 1f4, 43 Albany Terrace; I checked with the probation service. She's still there.'

'So what happened? What did she do? How come it means nothing to me?'

'It wasn't in our division, Stevie. It happened down in Joppa, at the back end of last October. They called it a church, but it was more of a gospel hall, one of these Baptist hand-clapping, hallelujah places; it was near the offices of the charity where she worked, and it got to her then. The Strachan girl seems to be a bit of a Christian fundamentalist; to her it was Sodom and Gomorrah all rolled into one big party. Eventually, God talked to her, didn't he, and he told her that he had chosen her to destroy it.'

'Schizophrenic?' asked Alice Cowan.

'That's what they said afterwards. As far as she was concerned, though, it was the Man Upstairs all the way, giving her His battle orders. So, her with a chemistry degree and all, she made up what would have been a pretty effective incendiary bomb, went to one of their services, and tried to tape it under one of the pews at the back.'

Steele held up a hand. 'Did it have a timer?'

'Aye, a wee alarm clock thing. It would have worked too.'

'Why didn't it?'

'She might be a clever girl, but she's still not all that bright. Somebody came into the church behind her as she was planting it, and

120

saw her. She ran for it, but they caught her just down the road, and called the police.'

'Court?'

'Nah. The fiscal was persuaded not to proceed on the basis that the lass was clearly disturbed, and she hadn't done any damage. So she was sectioned for six months under the Mental Health Act, and went into the Royal Edinburgh. Her probation officer says that she's still going back as an out-patient.'

'Have you spoken to anyone there?' asked Maggie Rose.

Regan shook his head. 'Not yet, ma'am. I thought I'd speak to you and Inspector Steele before I did that.'

'Just as well; we'll need to play it carefully there. The girl may have been committed, but she's as entitled to medical confidentiality as the rest of us.'

'What else did the probation officer tell you?'

'That she's responding to her treatment; the medication's continuing and there have been no signs of a relapse, so far. She's doing her best to change, the woman said. She's wearing contacts now, and her wardrobe's a lot less like a nun on a weekend pass.'

'Has she got a job?'

'Aye she has, ma'am. The probation service found her a placement with the Church of Scotland, in George Street. They had hoped she might have another go at teaching eventually, but the medical advice was against that.'

'The Church of Scotland, eh. The Moderator and his wife were guests yesterday, weren't they?'

'Aye, and the new archbishop, but I don't think that any of them are in the frame, eh?'

Steele frowned. 'Let's stay serious. George, okay?'

'Right, inspector, I'll get serious. Why are we sitting about here? Why don't we just pick her up, then?'

'What for?' asked Rose. 'The girl might have a genuine interest in religious art. It isn't an offence to gatecrash a private function. No, George; since you're so keen for action, you can get back into those tapes. Forget everyone else, just concentrate on Andrea Strachan. Let's see whether we can catch her in the vicinity of the Vargas *Trinity* at any

121

time. Then let's see if we have a shot of her at the moment of the detonation of the device. You never know; we might get lucky and find a shot of her pulling the trigger.'

'And if we don't?' the sergeant countered.

'Then we, that's to say you and DI Steele, will make further enquiries tomorrow, at the Church of Scotland, to see if the girl might have been there legitimately, through them, and at Candela and Finch, to check whether they issued informal invitations to anyone else.

'We'll keep her under surveillance, but I'm only going to move against this girl when all these avenues have been explored. She's a schizophrenic arsonist, George. If they hadn't done the probation deal over the church thing, she'd probably have gone to the state mental hospital at Carstairs. If she did torch that painting, that's where she's bound this time, for sure. She could wind up there for a good chunk of the rest of her life, so we cannot afford to make any mistakes.'

24

As it happened, Alice Bierhoff was in church, on the other side of the central aisle, but not too far away for Sarah to catch her eye and throw her a look that was meant to say, *Spread gossip about me, lady, and you'll wish you'd never been born.*

But Alice, a short dumpy woman . . . *She probably can't remember the last time she had any excitement in her life*, thought Sarah as she looked at her . . . was either tougher than she looked, or had forgotten to put in her contacts, for she replied with a small wave and a sweet, knowing smile.

Sarah let it go at that, for she had enough on her hands with Seonaid and a restless, fidgety James Andrew. Jazz had not been best pleased when his mother had told him that the trip to the lake had been postponed, and he spent much of the service determinedly punching the thigh of his adopted brother, Mark, who had been given the task of trying to keep him under control.

Once or twice, as they rose for hymns, Sarah glanced around her, looking for a familiar face, but there was no sign of him . . . and he was way too big to be concealing himself among the congregation. Finally they reached the business end of the hour, Ian Walker's sermon. It took Sarah a while to take a grip of what he was saying, but finally she understood; his message was that while society had evolved in ways that only God could have imagined during the two thousand years of Christianity, the ten commandments still stood at the centre of the faith, and still encapsulated the values by which Christians should live their lives.

Sarah sat poker-faced when Babs caught her eye; she wondered whether the preacher's wife had suggested the theme, or even if she had let him in on Alice Bierhoff's chance discovery, and if this was his discreet way of registering disapproval.

If it was, she found it more than a little rich; she remembered, among other things, smoking a little grass with Ian in her freshman college year. While there might not have been a commandment that referred to that specifically, she was pretty sure that it was covered somewhere.

It was on the tip of her tongue to remind him of the occasion as he bade his congregation farewell outside the church, but she decided to keep it in reserve. By that time Jazz was virtually uncontrollable, Mark was complaining that his leg was numb and even the obedient infant Seonaid was becoming restless.

'Are you going to behave?' she hissed at her younger son, as Babs Walker came towards them.

'Want to go to the lake,' James Andrew muttered.

'I have told you; Auntie Babs has invited us all for lunch.'

'Want to go to the lake.'

'Maybe later, then; maybe we'll go for a little while. Will that make you happy?'

The child's expression softened, but only a little. He whispered something that she could not hear. Gratefully she handed Seonaid over to Babs, as she arrived beside her and crouched down beside him. 'What did you say?' she asked him, quietly. Still his whispered reply was inaudible. 'What?' she asked again.

'I want Dad,' Jazz muttered, plaintively, on the edge of tears. 'I want my dad.'

Sarah felt her heart melt inside her. 'So did I, son,' she said, ruffling his hair as she stood. 'So did I. But he's had to go away.'

'Hi, guys,' said Babs, brightly, holding Seonaid up in the sunshine. 'My, but you're a little beauty.' The blonde-haired child gurgled and smiled at the attention. 'You ready for lunch?' she asked Sarah. 'My boys are looking forward to playing soccer in the yard with your boys.'

'Sure, but Mark might opt out of the soccer; the only kind he plays is on a computer screen. As for James Andrew, Matthew might be able to handle him, since he's seven, but Daniel might find him a little rough.'

'Rough? At soccer?'

'They play a slightly different game in Scotland; and James Andrew's learned from his father. Speaking of whom . . .'

'It's all right,' Babs broke in, forestalling her. 'Like I promised, there will be no extra lunch guest. I did call Ron, though. On reflection I thought I'd better tell him about Alice . . . before he heard from someone else, you understand.'

Sarah understood very clearly. 'What did he say?'

'My dear, he used language quite inappropriate for the wife of a Lutheran clergyman to repeat, and certainly not in front of the children. Let's just say that his view of Alice is in line with your own. Now come on; let's be going. Ian will be a little while, but the rest of us can head on back to the house now.'

Lunch at the Walkers proved to be a pleasant experience, even if the soccer game did come to an abrupt end with Jazz, still dour and fractious, punching Matthew, the older of his hosts' sons. 'I'm sorry, Babs,' said Sarah, as her friend wiped the tears from his face and the blood from his nose. 'This one,' she threw James Andrew a thunderous look, 'who will, incidentally, be lucky to get within a hundred miles of the lake after that, has been impossible lately.'

'He's missing his dad,' Mark explained, coming to his brother's defence in a way that touched Sarah, even through her anger.

'Be that as it may,' she said, trying to stay severe, 'he has to learn.'

'He kicked me,' Jazz muttered.

Once the peace treaty between the boys had been signed, they settled down to a chicken lunch, American style, although Sarah kept tight rein on the size of her children's portions.

'I enjoyed your sermon, Ian,' Sarah ventured, finally, once the four oldest children had been released to watch television.

The preacher smiled. 'I give them traditional values every so often,' he said. 'Babs suggested it was time for another round.'

'Indeed? What will it be next week? Keeping God with us on the campus? Finding Him through a haze of marijuana smoke like we used to do?'

Babs's jaw dropped. 'Why Ian!' she exclaimed. 'You never did, did you?'

'It's all right,' Sarah laughed. 'He didn't inhale either.'

Her friend read the sign correctly and kept the conversation on safe ground, from then on, until Sarah announced that it was time to go.

'Mum,' Jazz called from the back seat as they pulled out of the Walkers' driveway.

She knew what was coming. 'Okay,' she answered. 'Since you said you were sorry, we'll go to the lake. We'll need to go back to the house first, though. We're all still in our church clothes, and Seonaid needs changing.'

They were almost home when she saw him, driving towards her in his Camaro. She had teased him about it, asking if he had a Burt Reynolds fixation, but he had pointed out that he had trouble fitting into a Porsche. He did not slow down, nor did he seem to notice her, until the cars had almost reached each other. Then a broad easy smile crossed his face; as they passed he took his left hand from the wheel and waved. She thought that she caught a flash of something white on his thumb.

'That was the man who picked you up yesterday, wasn't it?' said Mark. 'The man who was going to fly you to the cabin.'

'That's right. He's Mr Neidholm; an old college friend and a very famous footballer.'

'Rangers,' Jazz announced.

'No,' said Mark, severely. 'American. He's too big to be one of our footballers.'

Sarah smiled and wondered whether Ron would take that as a compliment. Then she wondered why he had been there, and, if he had called to see her, why he had driven away.

One more turn and they had reached the Grace mansion. She slid the Jaguar into the long driveway, and, on impulse, stopped at her mailbox. She stepped out of the car and swung it open. There was a white envelope inside. She took it out, slipped it into the pocket of her jacket, and got back into the car.

'Okay, boys,' she exclaimed as she cancelled the alarm and let them into the house. 'Lakeside clothes, please. Shorts, shirts and sandals. I'll take care of us girls and see you down here in ten minutes.'

She carried Seonaid upstairs into her own bedroom and laid her on the bed, then took the envelope from her pocket and ripped it open. It contained a single white A4 sheet, a printed letter.

She whispered the words as she read it.

My darling Sarah

I'm not going to be a fool again. You mean more to me than all the Superbowl rings in the world, and all the nonsense that goes with them.

This is my pledge. If you will have me, I will finish with the game, in every aspect, here and now. I will practice law, as you practice your pathology, until it's time for us to sail off into the sunset together.

I love you. Will you marry me?

She looked at the signature. 'Ron.' It was scrawled, roughly, in a colour unlike any ink she had ever seen. She knew what it was, all right; she'd have known even without seeing the white flash of surgical tape on his left thumb.

'Oh damn,' she whispered, feeling her knees go weak as a sudden wave of panic surged through her. 'Sarah, it's choosing time.'

25

Of all the excellent restaurants in which she ate regularly, Alex had to admit that the Roseberry was her favourite. It was an emotional as much as a culinary thing. She had studied in Glasgow. Her professional life had begun in Edinburgh and had then taken her to London, for a period yet to be determined. For all that, there was something about the bay-windowed bistro on Gullane's main street that reminded her where her home really was.

She still owned her flat in Leith, although it was rented to a Curle, Anthony and Jarvis colleague during her London secondment. There, she had been found a very pleasant apartment in bustling Spitalfields. Yet she knew within herself that one day she would return to the village in which she had been raised. She even knew the house that she would like to buy, should the opportunity arise.

'Will you be selecting the wine tonight, Mr Skinner?' asked Ronald, the Roseberry's front-of-house partner.

'Not a chance,' Alex answered him cheerfully. 'I will, and we'll have a bottle of that nice Chablis, thanks.' She looked at her father as the waiter headed off towards the kitchen. 'You'd better not have anything too heavy tonight, if you're having your big medical tomorrow. Did you get it set up?'

'Yup. I called a cardiologist Sarah knows and told him the story. He and another consultant are going to give me a total going-over at the Murrayfield Hospital at five tomorrow evening. I've told Mitch what I'm doing; he agrees it's sensible. We'd probably have had to do it anyway, if the committee's doctors had refused to examine me.'

'How do the family solicitors feel about you using our firm for this one?'

'I haven't even told them; it's none of their business. If your firm had a private client department, I'd probably be on its books by now, given your connection. You don't, but this is a litigation matter. It's like golf. Who would you choose to hole a ten-foot putt to save your life?'

'Not you,' Alex laughed, 'that's for sure.'

'Right. You'd go for Tiger Woods. In a sense my life's at stake, but the game here is litigation. So by the same token, I'm going for Mitchell Laidlaw.'

'Then you'll win. You're The Man, Mitch,' she exclaimed, gallery-style, then paused. 'But Pops, just suppose the consultants find an underlying abnormality. Suppose they decide they can't pass you fit to go back to work. What would you do?'

'That's not going to happen.'

'Answer the question.'

Bob looked down at the menu on the table, as if he was studying it. 'I don't know,' he murmured. 'I've never contemplated retirement; I've never imagined a life outside the police. I've got a professional future that's mapped out for, oh, the next fifteen years anyway, and I've never given any thought to the idea of it being taken away.'

'Come on, Pops. You must plan on living beyond sixty-five. What will you do then?'

He looked up and shrugged. 'I dunno. Maybe I'll write. Maybe I'll just join the seniors' section and play golf every day, till eventually they carry me off the course.' He frowned. 'Or maybe . . . and this is something that has floated through my mind on occasion . . . I could find a visiting chair in criminology at some university or other.'

'Pops, you could do that now, without any difficulty, in Britain, and probably in the States as well. And maybe, just maybe, you understand, you should think about it. You've given more to the police service in little over half a career than almost any other man has in a whole lifetime. But it's taken you over. Nothing and no one gets in its way, not even your marriage. I want to see you fulfilled and happy as you grow older, not lonely, bitter and driven.'

'You're telling me to chuck it too?'

'No, I'm telling you to be broadminded enough to embrace the possibility.'

129

'Alex, I've got things to do yet.'

'Like being chief constable, you mean? Pops, you couldn't sit in Uncle Jimmy's chair for more than six months, and you know it.'

'Yes, I do, but there are other things, other avenues.'

'You mean like the Inspectorate?'

'Maybe.'

'I don't know if I can imagine you as Her Majesty's Inspector of Constabulary.'

'Fortunately, my darling, you're not the Queen.' He laughed. 'Not yet, at any rate.'

He made to go on, but Ronald arrived with a bottle of Chablis; he opened it and poured a little for Bob to taste. He nodded, and the waiter filled both glasses. 'Ready to order?' he asked.

'Another five minutes?'

'Sure.'

'What were you going to say?' Alex asked, as he left.

'That I'll make you a deal. I'll retire in twelve years, maximum; sooner if I feel that I'm burned out. And I will think more about the university idea, I promise. But first, I have to get through this medical and I have to crush these bastards who are trying to get me out of my job. Now let's eat.'

He nodded to the hovering Ronald, who made a smooth landing at their table. They ordered starters of haggis parcels, then baked sea bass.

'You realise,' said Bob as he left, 'that we've talked about nothing but me . . . and my poor, dead, disowned brother . . . since you got off that plane this morning. What about you? What about this actor?'

'Another time,' Alex answered, abruptly. 'We'll keep on talking about you for now.'

'Why? Have you got something to hide? Is this guy someone I'd know? Or is he someone I'd disapprove of?'

She picked up her napkin and bunched it as if she was going to throw it at him. 'Pops, there is no actor; there is no one. That was just a story I made up to stop being endlessly quizzed about my sex life.'

'Who's been quizzing you? Not me.'

'Sarah for a start, and various friends; I got fed up with it after a while, so I came up with an imaginary lover, just to keep them at bay.

I'm trying celibacy for a while, as a way of life; it's fun too. There's something nice about being unattainable. You can really get involved in the conversation at dinner parties for a start without smouldering across the table at some bloke. Been there, done that, thrown away the tee-shirt.' She spread her napkin on her lap and leaned back as Ronald served the starter.

'So,' she went on, as she picked up her first knife and fork, 'to get back to this afternoon, are you still planning to go through to Motherwell tomorrow?'

'Yup.'

'Should you be doing that?'

'What harm am I doing? I called Rod Greatorix before we came out and told him everything we learned from Brother Aidan this afternoon, and I'll do the same if I get anything tomorrow. I'm not keeping anyone out of the loop. If any formal statements need to be taken, the Tayside boys can follow up and take care of it. I haven't heard any howls of protest so far. This is shaping up to be a complex investigation, and they don't have the biggest CID in Scotland.'

'Lucky Tayside, eh. Having Bob Skinner helping them out? How does it feel to be reporting to Andy?'

'I'm not, exactly. But listen, kid, just about everybody'll be reporting to Andy one day.'

He was into the second of his haggis parcels when his cellphone rang. An elderly diner frowned at him across the restaurant; he shrugged a half-apology and took the call. 'Bob.' Sarah's voice was so clear that she could have been calling from the phone in the Roseberry's cloakroom.

'Hi,' he said, cautiously, even a little curtly, remembering their last conversation. 'How are you?'

'Fine,' she replied. He focused on her tone; there was no trace of anger there, but there was something, nonetheless, a distance between them that had nothing to do with geography. 'We're going to the lake for a while, but Jazz wanted to say hello first. Here he is.'

There was a pause, a couple of seconds no more, before a young, bright and heart-breakingly familiar voice came on line. 'Dad!' James Andrew shouted. 'Hello, Dad.'

'Hello, son,' Bob said, grinning inanely as Alex looked at him across the table. 'Are you still enjoying America?'

'I'm going to the lake.'

'So your mum told me. Have you been behaving yourself?'

'No,' said Jazz, cheerfully.

'What?'

'Punched Matthew Walker; made his nose bleed. He kicked me first, though.'

Bob stifled a laugh. 'Still, son, that's no excuse. Christ, he's the minister's son. Did you say sorry?'

'Yes. Mom made me.' The Americanism registered with Skinner, disturbing him.

'Well, don't do it again or you'll have me to deal with. You be a good boy from now on. Now put your mother back on.'

'He's just made it to the lake by the skin of his teeth,' said Sarah as she reclaimed the phone. 'Mark says hello too; he'll send you an e-mail.' He heard her take a breath. 'Bob, we need to talk.'

'Yes,' he agreed, 'we do. There's something I have to tell you.'

'Yeah, I have something to say to you too. Without shouting at each other, yes?'

'That would be nice, for a change.'

'Where are you?' He told her. 'That won't do,' she said.

'No, hardly. I'll call you from home, when I can.'

'Soon?'

'It can't be before tomorrow night. I have things to do tomorrow, through till seven.'

'Okay. Call me when you're ready; I'll make sure I'm here all afternoon.'

'Fine.'

He was about to end the call when he heard her speak again. 'Sorry?' he said, putting the phone back to his ear.

'I asked how your pacemaker's doing, that was all.'

'Fine. The wound itches every so often, but otherwise I don't know it's there.'

'That's good. That's the way it should be. When do you see the doctors?'

'Tomorrow.'

'You'll sail through, I know you will.'

'So do I.'

'Bob,' she asked, 'do you miss me even a little?'

Her tone was even, matter-of-fact. Suddenly, he felt as if the glass wall between them had become steel. 'Honey,' he replied, 'that's a question I force myself not to dwell on. If I did, there's no telling where it would end. Let's speak tomorrow.'

As he put the phone back in his pocket, he became aware of his daughter frowning at him across the table. 'What was wrong with that conversation?' she asked.

'I don't know. What do you mean?'

'I mean three words I didn't hear. I. Love. You.'

26

If pressed, Neil McIlhenney would admit that he had preferred his former job as Bob Skinner's executive assistant to his new role in Special Branch. But he knew that nothing was forever and so when the move had come about, following Mario McGuire's promotion to head the Borders CID division, he had taken it in his stride.

The death of Olive, his first wife, still hung over him like a black cloud. It was his constant companion, and he knew he would never shake it off, but to offset it he had his totally unexpected romance, and his second marriage, still new, fresh, and, to him, astonishing.

He knew from personal experience, bitter and sweet, that nothing in life was to be taken for granted, and when he thought about it he realised that he was better at his job as a result.

Alice Cowan was behind her desk as usual when he swept into his office suite. She was a keen one, that girl; however early Neil came to work, he never seemed to beat her to the punch. 'Morning, constable,' he said, brightly.

'Morning, inspector,' she replied, returning his friendly smile.

'How did your wee bit of overtime go yesterday, then?'

'Money for old rope, boss. We found a face, we got a name, and she's got nothing to do with us.'

'No? But is she someone we should have known about?'

'I wouldn't say so. She seems to be a sad lass, with a screw loose when it comes to religion, but not someone who represents any threat to the fabric of the state.'

'Is that right?' he exclaimed, with raised eyebrows. 'Does the name al-Qaeda mean anything to you?'

Cowan smiled. 'This girl's strictly a lone operator, sir.'

'If she has the skill to make and plant a device like the one that torched the Vargas painting, she could manage to stuff her trainers with explosives and get on a jet.'

'Not at Edinburgh she couldn't. Not since we started them examining the soles of their shoes at the barrier check.'

'Maybe not, Alice, but just as all knowledge is power, every small gap in knowledge is a potential weakness. Just you keep an eye on the progress of Ms Rose's investigation, and if this woman turns out to be the one, let's have a file on her. In fact . . . does she have form for this sort of thing?'

'Attempted, yes.'

'Then open a file anyway.'

'Very good, sir.'

He walked over to the coffee machine, which, like Alice, was always fired up and waiting whenever he came into the office, and poured himself a mug. 'Before you do that, though,' he said, 'grab yourself a coffee and come into my room.'

The strapping young woman declined the coffee and followed him through into his private office, taking her usual seat beside his desk.

'I've got a job for you,' he told her. He reached into his jacket, drew out a sheet of paper, laid it face up on his desk and slid it across to her. 'I want you to dig out the files we hold on all of these people.'

Cowan picked up the paper, and saw a list of eight names. She looked at the first and gasped, then scanned her way down the rest. 'Councillor Maley,' she began. 'Boss, these people are all on the joint police authority. Should we be doing this?'

McIlhenney smiled at her again, but this time there was no humour in it. 'We're Special Branch, kid. We can do what we bloody well like.'

'But these are politicians, and I'm not stupid. I know what they're about right now. Wouldn't we be abusing our position?'

'That's just what I suspect these people have been doing. If they have, I'm going to find out. When I do, I'm going to rein them in.'

27

Not being an adherent of any faith, Stevie Steele had admired the grey sandstone building that housed the Church of Scotland headquarters, but he had never before thought of stepping inside.

Much of the ground floor was actually retail space selling a fairly broad range of products, appropriate to the nature of the Church. Walking past, Steele saw Cliff Richard's face smiling up at him from a rack of CDs.

He found the reception desk and announced himself and the sergeant, using names rather than ranks. When he had made the appointment it had been agreed that its nature should be kept off the office grapevine if possible.

Steele's police training had taught him to avoid preconceptions, and so he was less surprised than he might have been by the appearance of the Principal Clerk to the Moderator of Scotland's established church, or indeed by his name. The Reverend Cahal O'Reilly, an ordained minister of the Church of Scotland, looked to be in his early forties, or perhaps even a few years younger. He greeted the detectives at the door of his panelled office, dressed in tight black trousers and a short-sleeved Ralph Lauren polo shirt, open at the neck and tie-less.

'Morning, chaps,' he said. Steele tried to detect an accent, but could hear none.

'Good morning, Mr O'Reilly. I'm Steven Steele; we spoke earlier. This is my colleague George Regan.'

The Principal Clerk stood aside to usher them into his room. 'Grab a seat,' he told them, pointing towards a meeting table. 'I'm afraid this is a smoke- and coffee-free zone, but I can offer you chilled water, still or sparkling.'

'I'm fine, thanks,' the inspector replied. 'You, George?' Regan who had a major caffeine habit, shook his head.

'So,' said O'Reilly, as he sat in a high-backed chair at the head of the table, 'what have we been up to? Which one of the fathers and brethren have strayed from the straight and narrow and how far is the stuff going to spread off the fan?'

The sergeant's eyes widened slightly, but he held his poker-faced expression. In contrast, a broad grin spread across Stevie Steele's face. 'Which of the shepherds has been getting among the sheep, do you mean?' he replied. 'You can relax. It's nothing like that. Are you aware of the exhibition of religious art, which opened on Saturday?'

'In a blaze, you might say? Sure, I know about it. I helped organise the damn thing.'

'You did?'

'Yes. I wasn't alone, you understand; my opposite numbers in other Christian churches and in other faiths were involved too.'

'You don't make it sound like a labour of love.'

'Pain in the arse would be a better description,' O'Reilly said, with a rueful frown. 'And it's a particularly sore point with me. Actually, I'd assumed that's what you wanted to see me about, all joking apart. I'm just not clear why you wanted to keep your visit hush-hush, given the publicity the thing's had.'

'We'll get to that, Mr O'Reilly.'

'Cahal, please.'

'Fine, Cahal. But can you fill us in on the background to the event?'

'Sure, it started off as a glory trip. Some bright boy in the Scottish Arts Council dreamed up the idea. He thought it would be a good lead-in to the Papal visit, and sold the sponsorship to Candela and Finch. Then they discovered they didn't really know how to go about organising it. All that C and F know about art is that you can write it off against tax, and the SAC boy found that it wasn't as easy as he'd thought to persuade galleries around the world to part with their priceless works. So, Nike baseball cap in hand, he had to come to me, to the Roman Catholic Church and to various others, to ask for our support. We wound up making a joint pitch for most of the major works on show over there. In one or two cases we had to visit curators to win them over.'

'What about the Vargas?'

O'Reilly grimaced. 'That's my sore point; it's cost me a lot of grief on the telephone this weekend. That was my baby. The Catholics didn't veto it, but given its, let's say, controversial nature, they didn't want to be seen to be involved in negotiations. So I got to go by myself to the Guggenheim in Bilbao, which owns it, to secure the piece. Some building, I tell you. You think our parliament's something? It's a Wendy house compared to that. Seeing it was the only saving grace of the whole show as far as I was concerned.

'We had to make all sorts of promises, of course. Among them we had to take personal responsibility for the reception and storage of each piece, and we had to be present when they were hung, to ensure that the positioning and lighting matched the specification of the owner gallery.'

'So you were there when the Vargas arrived?'

'I saw it unpacked.'

'How did it look when it came out of the crate?'

'Perfect. In perfect condition, that is. Personally I thought it was a load of crap, but everyone to their own taste and all that. I'm no art critic.'

'Did you see the back of the picture?' George Regan asked

'I suppose I did. Why?'

'Can you describe it?'

O'Reilly frowned. 'How do you describe the back of a picture? Frame, canvas, that's it; it looked like a sack stretched tight. Will that do?'

'Very well indeed,' said Steele. 'When it was hung on the wall the back was covered over with brown paper. While it was in storage downstairs, between the arrival and the hanging, someone placed an incendiary device inside the frame and then taped paper over to cover it.'

'That's what happened, was it? I read someone had claimed responsibility.'

'Someone usually does, Cahal. We don't always believe them, though. I have to ask you something; when you went to the Academy to receive the picture, did you go alone?'

The principal clerk leaned against the high back of his chair. 'No, I thought there was an outside chance that the couriers would actually expect us to remove the thing physically, so I took Jan Laing, my secretary . . . you spoke to her earlier . . . and Andrea, our clerk, with me.'

'Andrea?'

'Andrea Strachan; she asked if she could come with us for a sneak preview of the pictures. She's with us on a sort of temporary basis. We pay her a little, but she's more or less a volunteer. Jerome Strachan, her father, even if he is a bit right-wing in Presbyterian terms, is a friend of mine; he lectures in religion up at Napier. The girl's had emotional problems, and he asked if I could fit her in somewhere as a sort of therapy. She's a nice lass; pretty serious, but very helpful and keen, almost over-keen at times.'

'Do you know the nature of those emotional problems?'

'Jerome told me she's been treated for schizophrenia, if that's what you mean.'

'That's all he said?'

'Yes, and I didn't press him. Should I have?'

'Not the way I see it. He's your friend, so why should you?' Steele glanced across at a fridge in a corner of the big office. 'Do you think I could have some of that water you were offering earlier?' he asked.

'Sure.' O'Reilly rose to his feet. 'Still or fizzy?'

'Still; and don't bother with a glass. By the neck will be fine.'

The Principal Clerk took three bottles of mineral water from the fridge and brought them back to the table. He opened one himself and handed the others to Steele and Regan. As he took his, the sergeant smiled, for the first time. 'Why were you guys not on the list for the opening, since you did so much work?' he asked.

'If I was interested, George, that would be another sore point with me. All us organisers were thanked very effusively, by the boy at the Arts Council, and were told very apologetically that space at the opening bash would be limited and that only the Moderator and the archbishop would be invited; no one else from any of the executives.

'The Mod did his nut, I have to tell you; he was going to decline, but I persuaded him that my Saturday would be more ruined if he did that, than if I missed out. I was sorry Jan and Andrea didn't get in on the act, but as far as I was concerned, he'd drawn the short straw. I'd seen the exhibition and I don't like champagne, even when it's free.'

'What about the boy with the Nike baseball cap?' asked Regan, casually.

Cahal O'Reilly frowned, then his face split into a grin. 'Oh, he was there all right, don't you worry!'

28

'You've fair taken my breath away, Robert, I don't mind telling you.' The old man beamed as he handed a cup of tea to his visitor. 'When you called it was like hearing a voice from the past.'

'I'm just glad you remember me,' said Bob Skinner.

'Remember you? Remember you?' Pale blue eyes twinkled in a bald wrinkled head. 'I remember you all right, and even if I didn't I only have to look at you to know who you are. You're William Skinner's son, and no mistake. I remember him well, and your grandfather, Mr Michael Skinner, before him.'

The old man lowered himself gently into an armchair. 'I'm just astonished that you remember me.'

'Don't be daft, man, the whole bloody town remembers you. Nicol Falkirk, CBE, the editor of the *Motherwell Times* for the best part of the last century.'

'Not quite the best part,' his host corrected him, 'but a good bit of it nonetheless.'

'How old are you now, if you don't mind my asking?'

'Eighty-four, and starting to feel it.'

'But not look it,' said Skinner, deferentially. 'I passed by Hope Street when I was driving round town. I guess the paper isn't printed there any more.'

'Nor has it been for a long time. They turn it out on a big web offset press somewhere well out of the town. I'm glad I'm not part of it any more. I was an old school editor; I wrote my copy in fountain ink, and it was set in hot lead by craftsmen, then made up into page form by hand, by people who, in the main, lived in the town which they were serving. That's what a local newspaper should be, Robert; truly local. That's what it was like when you worked there as a young man in your holidays, remember; just before it was sold, and everything changed.'

'Worked is maybe an exaggeration, Nicol. Copy-boy, they called me.'

'Not a bit of it. You did your share in the months you were there. You could write better than some of my regular reporters, I'll tell you. They were always trying to copy the tabloid style, so they could move on to bigger jobs in Glasgow. More than a few of them did, of course; most of my trainees wound up with their own by-lines on the *Herald*, the *Scotsman*, the *Mail* and so on.'

The venerable editor laughed. 'I always liked the football reports you wrote, Robert. They were as partisan as anything,' he wheezed. 'You understood without being told that being unbiased is not the business of a local reporter. The readers expect you to be on the side of the home team.'

'They needed all the help they could get,' Bob muttered. 'They still do.'

'Ach, that's changed too. I was never a football man myself, but I don't approve of all these damn foreigners we have these days. This County of Lanark produced the likes of Matt Busby, Jimmy Johnstone and Ian St John. What chance does a boy have today?'

'Come on, Nicol; times change.'

'Maybe, but your father would have agreed with me. He usually did, apart from one time.'

'When was that?'

'When I told him that I had hopes you might become a journalist after you left university. He said to me that if I put that idea in your head, he'd hang me up by the thumbs until the rest of me dropped off them.'

Bob looked astonished. 'My father said something like that?'

'He certainly did; those were his exact words, at a civic centre reception too. And do you know what? I think he meant them. Your father was dead set on you going on to do law after you finished your arts degree, and following him into the firm. He wasn't best pleased at first, when you went into the police. He did his best not to show it, but I remembered that brush that we had, and I knew.'

'So did I,' Skinner murmured, 'but he got over it, eventually.'

'I was sorry to hear about your wife, Robert,' the old man said quietly. 'I remember young Myra very well; it was just too bad that she should die so young . . . the motor car's a blessing, but a curse too. That's why I've never had one. Aye, a girl of spirit, she was.'

'Sure, and then some. That was a long time ago, though.'

'I suppose it was,' he mused. 'That's the thing about getting old; your time-frame gets jumbled up.' He smiled. 'And how's your daughter?' he asked. 'How's she getting on?'

'My older daughter, you mean. Very well, I'm glad to say. Now, Alexis would have made her grandfather happy. She is a lawyer, and showing promise at it too.'

'You have another daughter?'

'Yes, wee Seonaid; she's coming up for a year. Then there's James Andrew, who's four and a handful, and Mark, who's going on nine.'

'My, my, you have been busy.'

'Not that busy. Mark's adopted.'

'Busy enough.' Mr Falkirk picked up his neglected tea, took a sip, screwed up his face and put it down. 'Now, Robert,' he said. 'Charmed as I am to see you, I know that you haven't come all this way to pay me a casual visit. What can I do for you?'

'You can write an obituary for me, and persuade your successors to run it in the *Motherwell Times*.'

'Oh, surely not. Whose?'

'You haven't seen a paper today?'

The old journalist shook his head. 'I don't bother with them any more. They're full of nonsense.'

'True. I have to read them though, today especially. The obituary's for my brother Michael; he was found dead at the weekend. There's no one but you that I'd trust to do it.'

The twinkle had gone from Nicol Falkirk's eyes. 'Oh dear me,' he sighed. 'I wrote your father's, I wrote your mother's, and long before that, I wrote your grandfather's. When a journalist comes round to writing three generations of obituaries, he knows he's lived too long. Of course I'll do it, and I'll make sure it gets a good show in the paper. I have emeritus status, you know.'

'Do you remember Michael?'

143

'Most certainly; and before you ask, I know the story, Robert. Your father told me what had happened. He wanted to make sure that nothing appeared in the paper. He was the company's solicitor, and so he had influence with the proprietors, but if he'd been any man off the street I'd have done as he asked. It is not the function of a newspaper to pry into the private grief of any family.'

He pushed himself up slowly from his chair, and walked over to a bureau beside the bay window of his bungalow. Skinner looked out through the lace curtains; the day had begun brightly in the east, but now the sky was overcast by grey cloud. It was Motherwell as he remembered it.

Mr Falkirk fumbled around in his desk, until he found a thick, well-thumbed reporter's notebook, and a fountain pen. A flash of memory came back to Bob from his copy-boy days as he watched the old editor resume his seat; he always wrote in green ink. 'Just give me the basics,' Mr Falkirk instructed; suddenly there was a professional tone in his voice. 'I know your family background well enough. What was your brother's full name?'

'Michael Niven Skinner; after my grandfather.'

'Age?'

'Fifty-six.'

'He'd have been educated at Knowetop Primary and Dalziel High, wouldn't he?'

'Yes. He played rugby for the school, and he won the English prize in his sixth year.'

'Thank you, I'll mention both of those. He wouldn't have had far to walk to Dalziel,' Mr Falkirk grunted as he made the notes, 'since your house was just across the road, in Crawford Street.

'And after that,' he continued, 'he was awarded a place at Sandhurst; that's right, isn't it?'

'Yes. He went straight from school. I was only about eight then,' Skinner mused. 'I remember him coming home on leave, with this wee swagger stick.' He winced inwardly, but declined to mention that he had often been beaten with the same stick.

'Where did he serve, after he was commissioned?'

'At home, initially, then Germany, and finally Honduras; he saw action there.'

'Yes. I remember your father telling me that it had a telling effect on him. He resigned his commission after that, didn't he, and came home?'

'Yes.'

'But he couldn't settle down, could he?' the old man probed, gently.

'No. He was a lost and troubled soul.'

'I know. I used to see him hanging around Motherwell Cross with his cronies, going in and out of the Horseshoe Bar, or into the bookmakers' across from my office, and I used to grieve for your poor parents. I'll gloss over that part of his life, don't worry. I'll just say that he moved to . . . Where was it again? I only knew from your father that he was committed for a while.'

'Gourock. He spent the last thirty years of his life in a Jesuit hostel in Gourock, overlooking the Clyde.' Bob felt the great sadness grip him again.

'And how did he die?'

'We don't know for sure yet. His body was found in Perth on Saturday; he had been in the river. The police there are treating his death as suspicious, for the moment, pending post-mortem findings. He managed to find some sort of peace in Gourock, he managed to find true friends, and he lived there in what passed with him for happiness, until someone from his past turned up and lured him away.'

'My, but that's awful. Do they know who this person was, the one he went away with?'

'No they do not, Nicol; or, rather, we do not. But you can be damned sure we're going to find out.' Skinner looked across at the veteran. 'Those cronies you mentioned; can you put names to them?'

'I'm sure I can. Let me see, there was Cammy Winters and Willie Day, our printing press men, and wee Benny Crainey, and Waggy Roughhead . . . they called him that because of the way his head bobbed when he walked. Then there was Jim Fletcher, the ex-policeman, and Pat Smith, the bookie's son.'

'Are they still about the town?'

Mr Falkirk scratched his chin. 'Let's see. Cammy and Willie are dead; I know that. So is Fletcher. Benny and Waggy are still around, but they're old men now and no threat, I'd say to anyone. Pat Smith sold his betting shop as soon as his father died and went off to Canada with the girl who used to work behind the counter. He left his wife more or less penniless. If he ever comes back her brothers will do for him; a rough lot they were.'

'Does the name Skipper mean anything to you?'

The old man frowned with the effort of recollection. 'Skipper? Skipper? Yes, of course,' he exclaimed. 'There was Skipper Williamson. Do you not remember him? He was a footballer; played for Motherwell, in the reserves mostly, unless they had a lot of injuries.'

Skinner sent his mind scanning through the line-ups of early nineteen-seventies football teams. 'Centre-half?' he asked. 'Good in the air, but not too great on the ground?'

'That's him. I think his real name was Cecil; but everyone called him Skipper after they made him captain of the reserves. He liked a drink too, but not in the pubs. The footballers used to go to the Ex-Servicemen's Club. They thought it was more discreet. And come to think of it, that was another of your brother's hang-outs.'

'Is he still around?'

'Very much so; but he's not in Motherwell any more, other than at home games, in the hospitality box he keeps at Fir Park. He was a part-timer, and had a good job in the steelworks, so he was able to save up all his football money. Like a lot of players in those days, when he retired he bought a pub, the old Gaslight Bar in Windmillhill Street. He refitted it, changed the name to the Bluenose Lounge, and attracted all the Rangers fans in the town. Since there are far more of them than there are Motherwell supporters, he made a fortune. So he bought another old pub, in Wishaw this time, and did the same again. Eventually, about fifteen years ago, he sold both places to one of the big brewers, and bought a hotel. He's done very well in that too, I hear.'

'Do you know where?'

'Pitlochry.'

Skinner felt a tiny chill ripple down his spine. 'He won't find many bluenoses up there,' he murmured.

'Oh, he isn't after that crowd any more. He's gone up-market. These days his clients are fishermen.'

29

'As I see it, Maggie, we don't have anywhere else to go after this,' said Stevie Steele, keeping his voice low, even though he and the detective superintendent were alone in the small waiting room.

'The girl was there when the picture was unpacked. She was there when the device was ignited, even though she hadn't been invited to the ceremony, as George Regan has just confirmed with the practice manager at Candela and Finch. Okay, we don't actually have her on camera pushing the button on the remote, but we've got solid grounds for bringing her in, regardless of what this guy's going to say to us.'

'Maybe so. No, certainly, you're right,' she answered, 'but for safety's sake I still want to speak to him. The girl's still an outpatient in terms of the Mental Health Act. If this thing ever does wind up in court, I want to make sure there's no chance of our being accused of ignoring her rights as such. And there's something else too.'

'What's that?'

'I'm not a one-hundred-per-cent book operator, Stevie. I have instincts and I pay heed to them until they prove unfounded. My instinct here is that this solution is too bloody easy. I cannot shake the feeling that there's a bigger picture . . . excuse the bad analogy . . . and that we're not seeing it. Now tell me honestly; don't you feel that too?'

The young inspector flicked a white flake of dandruff from the lapel of his blazer. 'Show me an angle we haven't covered, ma'am,' he challenged. 'Did she have an opportunity to plant the device? Yes, she did. Once Cahal O'Reilly had verified its arrival in safe condition, he and his secretary had to hurry back to George Street from the RSA for an evening committee meeting. They left Andrea there. No one at the gallery can remember her leaving, or can say for sure that she didn't have access to the picture alone. That part of the building isn't covered by cameras either. As for the device, it wasn't large; she could have had it in her handbag. And to top it all, she asked if she could go to the arrival of the container from Bilbao.'

'I know all that; now answer the question.'

Steele gave her a sidelong, killer grin. 'Yeah, okay. It's on a bloody plate and I'm like you. I get more satisfaction out of working for a living, which is what you're really saying. But consider this; I haven't even met this girl, yet I feel sorry for her. I don't want her to be the one who puts her away, maybe for good. Don't you think that could be true with you as well?'

'Maybe,' she conceded, as the door opened and a tall man in his late twenties, dressed in a white coat, bustled into the waiting room.

'Sorry to keep you,' he exclaimed extending a hand to Rose in greeting as the detectives stood. 'I'm Adam Broadley, Andrea's mentor.' He grinned. 'Okay, I'm her shrink, but I prefer to think of myself that way. We'll talk here, if it's all right with you; we'll get more privacy here.'

'Fine,' said the superintendent. 'I'm Maggie Rose, and this is my colleague Steven Steele. Has the probation officer explained to you what it is we want to talk about?'

'Not in detail, but enough.'

'And you're okay about this, from an ethical viewpoint?'

'Sure. You're police officers so you know Andrea's history already, and you know the circumstances of her sectioning. Where I'm slightly uneasy is in talking to you without her being aware of the fact, but I'll reserve the right to stop if I feel that I'm going too far.'

'That's agreed,' said Rose, 'so let's get straight to it. Do you know where Andrea is working?'

'With the Church of Scotland? Yes.'

'And you approve of that, given her history?'

'I don't see anything wrong with it,' Broadley answered. 'In fact it's probably a positive element in her treatment. She's schizophrenic, as you know; split personality in old-fashioned terms, but it's a bloody awful description. This illness can manifest itself in many ways, but in this case the patient hears voices. More and more these days, people think that their computers are talking to them. I call it the software syndrome. Andrea's experience is more of the traditional type. Her father's profession may have something to do with it, for she gets the word straight from God. A bit like Joan of Arc without the armour.'

'But with twenty-first-century weaponry instead,' Steele pointed out.

The young man laughed. 'True. If St Joan had had nuclear capability . . . it would have shortened the Hundred Years War, that's for sure. But Andrea Strachan, fortunately, is not a very determined warrior. If God was choosing someone for a mission, he'd look for someone more physically adept than her. Anyway, to answer your question, the fact that she is actually working in the HQ of an established religion is on balance good for her, in that it takes God out of her fantasy world, and puts him into her everyday life.'

'What put the voice in her head in the first place?' Rose asked. 'What made her attack that church?'

'Again I think her father's profession may have something to do with it. Mr Strachan is a very conservative Christian. He does not approve of unorthodoxy, in any form. It's obvious to me that Andrea's picked that up from him and that in her mind it's taken wings.'

'I understand.' The detective paused. 'At this stage, Adam, I think it would be best if I stopped asking questions and told you something. When *The Holy Trinity* by Isobel Vargas went up in flames in the Royal Scottish Academy on Saturday, Andrea was right there in the room.'

Adam Broadley looked up at the ceiling, almost theatrically. 'Ohhh dear!' he said, slowly.

'You think it's possible then?'

'I don't know for sure. She responded very well to her early treatment, and she's having no problems with her medication, but that sort of experience, or confrontation, would still be pretty dangerous for her. Did it happen through her work?' Rose nodded; he frowned. 'What sort of people is she working with, in that case? Didn't they know of her psychiatric history?'

'Not in that amount of detail.'

'You mean her father didn't tell them when he arranged the placement?'

'No. He told them in broad terms what her illness was, but he didn't tell them about the way in which it manifested itself. And of course since the case was dealt with summarily in court, and was barely reported, there was no way in which they could reasonably have known about it, other than from him.'

'Bloody families!' Broadley exclaimed. 'No matter how enlightened or intelligent they are, some of them still treat this illness like it was fucking . . . excuse my French . . . leprosy. It makes me so angry.'

He smacked a big fist into the palm of his other hand, then grinned. 'I'm still relatively new in my profession,' he exclaimed. 'I still have normal emotional reactions; I haven't become infected by my patients yet. Listen, I think I know what you want to ask me, so I'll save you the trouble. Yes, I think you should interview Andrea as soon as possible, but with one proviso; that I can be there.'

Maggie Rose smiled. 'That was going to be my next question,' she said. 'Thanks for volunteering.'

30

'That's fine, Mr Skinner, you can ease down and stop now.'

Bob ignored the consultant's call; wearing only shorts and trainers, he continued to pound along on the treadmill, running on the spot, but at five-minute-mile pace.

'I said you can stop now,' Peter Patience repeated, louder this time, over the noise of the treadmill.

'I'm enjoying this,' Skinner replied, sounding barely out of breath. 'I do at least four miles every day.'

'Good for you, but can you please do the rest later. My colleague and I need to look at the print-outs from the various monitors you have attached to you, and to do that we'd like to switch the bloody things off.'

'Okay.' Dripping with sweat, the patient nodded, and reached out to touch a button on the control panel of the apparatus, to ease down its speed. He slowed it gradually, until, after around a minute, he came to walking pace, then stopped. He stepped off the track and allowed Hugh Hurley, the second consultant, to strip the monitor pads from his bare torso.

'Is that us, then?' he asked.

'Just about,' said Patience. He pointed to Skinner's back. 'That scar; is that where you were stabbed?'

'Yes.'

'What about the two on your thigh, front and back?'

'They're where I was shot; entry and exit wounds.'

'That's not on your medical history,' Hurley exclaimed, with a hint of suspicion.

'No. It's not.'

'Want to tell us about it?'

'No I do not. If there were any after-effects I wouldn't be able to run freely, would I?'

'I suppose not. Okay, we'll keep it off our report.'

'You do that. Now; what sort of shape am I in?'

The two consultants exchanged glances, then smiles. 'Mr Skinner,' Patience began, 'as you know very well, you are in remarkable condition for a man in his thirties, let alone one who's nearer fifty than forty. You could and should have been returned to duty on the basis of the medical report which you brought back from America, and we are prepared to confirm without reservation that you are fit to resume active duty immediately. We'd be saying that if you were a soldier, never mind a senior police officer whose duties are assumed to be, in the main, sedentary.'

'They're bloody not,' Skinner grinned. 'What else will your report say?'

'It will note that you were diagnosed, after your incident in the US, as suffering from what is commonly known as sick sinus syndrome, in which the sinus node, the heart's natural pacemaker, malfunctions, leading in your case to bradycardia . . . slow heartbeat . . . and loss of consciousness. This condition may recur, but it is quite possible that, even without intervention, you would never have had another episode. We find no sign of it today. In any event, that eventuality has been rendered irrelevant by the fitting of a dual chamber pacemaker, which is set to maintain your heartrate at a minimum level of fifty-five beats per minute, operating on demand; that is only if and when your rate drops to that level. You'll get around ten years' use out of it; when the battery runs down, a new one will be fitted. Maybe by then the batteries will last longer, and that one will see you through to your eighties.

'As for the rest of you, your vision is virtually perfect, with maybe a slight touch of astigmatism in your right eye, your ears are prone to deposits of wax, but otherwise your hearing is normal, your urine is free of any diabetic indications, your liver function is healthy and your prostate is not enlarged.'

The consultant smiled. 'The bottom line on this is that although we're very happy to collect our fee, this examination has been entirely

152

unnecessary, and demonstrates a significant degree of stupidity on the part of the police authority.'

Skinner shook his head. 'Not stupidity. Malice.'

'I don't think we'll go that far in our report.'

'It's okay, I wouldn't want you to; or even to include the stupidity line. On the face of it, I just want to appear grateful for being returned to duty, but at the same time pleased that the manpower committee were so concerned about my welfare. Once I'm back on the prowl, they'll find out how I really feel about it.' He looked at the two cardiologists. 'You'll put all that in writing?'

'This evening,' said Hurley.

'And deliver it to Mr Laidlaw at Curle, Anthony and Jarvis?'

'First thing in the morning.'

'That's fine. There's a timetable in place. The chief constable has called in the authority chair and the chair of human resources to a meeting in his office at twelve noon. When they get there, they'll find that I'm the agenda.'

'In that case,' Patience declared, 'you'll be back in your office by one p.m.'

Skinner grinned, as he picked up a towel and headed for the changing room. 'Only I won't be. I've got other plans.'

31

She had fought against it all day. She had found distractions; insisting on taking Mark to school herself, to let Trish have an easy start to her day; taking Jazz to the playground for an hour longer than she would normally have allowed him, joining vigorously in his games until they were both too tired for more.

In the afternoon she had gone to collect Mark, and had spent time helping him with his homework, although the reality was that her older son never needed anyone's help. He had covered in Scotland some of the work he was doing at his American school, and the rest came easily to him.

In the evening, she had stood down Trish for cooking duties, even though it was her turn, under their informal agreement, and had made spaghetti bolognese, 'Mafia-style' as she called it, as she remembered seeing it done in the *Godfather* trilogy.

Finally, she ran out of excuses. There was nothing else in her mind except Ron, and her need to see him. It was so strong that she could actually feel it within her as an amputee will feel a phantom limb.

She waited until the children were asleep, and until Trish, who had developed an unexpected interest in baseball, had settled to watch an evening telecast of the Yankees on the road at Boston. Only then did she slip into her bathroom, shower, and make herself ready. She chose a black thong, a close-fitting brown dress, and the high-heeled shoes that she had bought to match it; that was all. She didn't expect that she would need anything else.

She applied only light make-up and a coating of hairspray, then slipped downstairs and out of the house. Both of her cars were standing in the driveway; she would have taken her father's beloved Jaguar, but she had the keys of the Ford Explorer in her bag and so she climbed in behind its steering wheel.

Ron's house was only ten minutes' drive away from hers, through the suburban streets of Buffalo. The daylight was fading, and the traffic was light; she saw few other vehicles along her route, until she turned into Sullivan Street and saw the modest house, just where the road curved.

It was a pleasant street, ordinary in a comforting way, the sort of vision that came to her mind in Scotland, when she allowed herself the luxury of thinking of home. The homes were all built on generous, but not huge, plots of land; they belonged to middle managers and professional people, to teachers and public service administrators. It was multi-racial, with blacks, Caucasians and Hispanics living happily and harmoniously together. She looked around as she drove slowly along, past an elderly man walking his dog. The movement of a car refocused her. It was picking up a child from a house almost opposite Ron's; balloons tied to a tree on its sloping lawn signified a party. Even in the dying light, other children were playing on the grass, and a woman was filming them with what she guessed was a camcorder. She smiled as she flicked her indicator; for all the War on Terror, her native land could still be a comforting place.

His flashy Camaro was in the driveway; at the sight of it, she felt a surge of anticipation deep within her. She parked the Explorer behind it, switched off the engine and took a deep breath. As she put the car keys in her purse, she saw his letter. She took it out, opened it and read it again. It was barely light enough for her to see the page, but she knew it off by heart.

'God, Ron,' she whispered to herself, 'if you had written this all those years ago, where would we be now?'

She frowned. 'Divorced, probably.' His drawing a line under a career of success was one thing, but she knew that giving it up would have been quite another. There would have been another pressure too. She would have had to compromise with her own career, to limit her horizons to wherever he had practised law, and perhaps to general medicine, rather than her chosen specialty, an ambition which had driven her all the way through med school.

155

Within herself, she knew that it would have been a disaster; Ron had been right to go to Texas. She had been right to chalk him up to experience and head for New York, and then to her appointment with fate, in the hypnotic shape of Bob Skinner, in Scotland. When she had gone there, she had only meant to stay for a couple of years. But she had not counted on him; no, not at all.

She closed her eyes, and for the first time that day, Bob's face appeared before her. Yet she could only see him angry, as he was when he had left, in spite of her pleas that he should stay with her, in spite of her threats about the potential consequences of charging back to Edinburgh in defence of a job which had almost killed him on more than one occasion.

Where's the difference? she thought. He had done what Ron had done, back in the eighties: chosen career over everything else. Wasn't it logical that she should do now as she had done then, and let him get on with it? And now Ron was back; back for good, he had promised, his life fulfilled, and hers if she wanted him. Where there had been bitterness in her parting with Bob, there had been nothing but tenderness, emotional and physical, in her reunion with her second lover. Where Bob had been adamant and uncompromising, he had been flexible, ready to see things her way, and make a commitment to her alone.

And yet that was her husband as he had always been: singleminded, determined, courageous, professionally outstanding, and at the same time, on more than one important, crucial occasion, emotionally blind. There was nothing different about him. The angry face in her mind's eye was that of the man she had married, and had been, all along. Would his life ever be fulfilled?

She thought of Ron. In their first relationship it had been all excitement; now it was all tenderness. She thought of the years that would stretch ahead with him; peaceful and content, with not a ripple on the surface of their smooth waters. Then she thought of Bob, and saw towering white-topped waves.

Sarah stepped out of the Explorer and walked up to Ron Neidholm's front door. She felt herself shaking in anticipation as she pressed the bell, as nervous as she had been on their first encounter in college, when she had wanted him with an urgency she had never suspected had lain within her.

There was no answer. Evening had given way almost entirely to darkness, but she realised that there were no lights within the house. Ron was either in his den, maybe with his headphones on, or possibly he had gone for an evening run. She peered into her bag once again, and found the key he had given her.

She unlocked the door, and opened it. 'Eleven ninety-one,' she said aloud, recalling the code he had given her in the expectation that the alarm would need to be deactivated. But there was no warning buzz; it had not been set.

'Ron,' she called, as she stepped inside. She listened for his feet on the stairs, from above or from the cellar, as he rushed to greet her, but there was no sound, no shouted reply. The door to his den lay directly in front of her, across the hall. She opened it, but saw at once that it was in darkness. She looked into his living room, in case he was asleep in his chair, but it was empty. She ran upstairs to his bedroom, in case he was in the shower, but it was neat, with no discarded clothes on the floor, and no discordant country song coming from the bathroom.

With more than a touch of frustration, she went back downstairs, to await his return; on impulse she stepped into the kitchen to make herself a coffee, throwing open the door and switching on the light in a single movement.

Ron was there.

He was lying on his back, his head almost at her feet. He was stretched out, massively, on the kitchen floor, staring sightlessly up at the ceiling. The hilt of a knife protruded from his chest; all of its blade was embedded in him, and most of the front of his yellow polo shirt had been dyed dark red by his blood.

Sarah had seen countless dead people . . . inside and out . . . through her career. As had been the case when Bob had collapsed, none of that counted for anything. She threw her hands to her face and screamed, as she had in the cemetery. There, she had been surrounded by friends; there had been people to come to her aid. Here, she had nobody to turn to. She was gripped by hysteria; she screamed again and again, until she felt her stomach begin to heave. Instinct alone made her run to the back door. She threw it open and vomited out into the garden.

From somewhere in the distance she seemed to hear a man's voice. 'Hey lady, is everything all right over there?' it asked, nervously.

'The hell it is!' came a loud reply; a woman this time. 'Move your ass, Mort. Call the friggin' police.'

32

'Have your guys taken a formal statement from Brother Aidan?' Skinner asked.

'Yes,' Andy Martin replied. 'Rod went to see him himself, yesterday afternoon.'

'Did he sharpen up on his description of the guy Skipper I told you about?'

'No. If anything he was probably vaguer than when you saw him. He couldn't swear to a thing about the man, other than his age bracket, around the same as your brother's.'

'Have you picked up any other leads up there?'

'None. The whole thing's a mass of uncertainties. We can't even be certain that Michael went into the Tay. There are various tributaries flowing into it; there's the Tummel, for example, that flows through Pitlochry. When the snows melted and the flood began, the whole river system was in spate.'

'So he could have been dumped in the water in Pitlochry and wound up in Perth?'

'In theory, yes,' Martin admitted. 'Not above the hydro dam though, he wouldn't have got past that. They did open the sluice to increase the flow of water out of the reservoir, but a body would have been trapped.'

'So what have you got that you're phoning me first thing in the morning? If it was just to say hello you'd have done it by now.'

'I've got the post-mortem report. The pathologist was a bit slower than I'd have liked, but . . .'

'I agree. We'll have thoroughness before speed, every time. So what's the verdict?'

'You want all of it?'

'Of course.'

'We don't have a homicide investigation, of any sort.'

Skinner whistled. 'I don't know whether to be happy or sad about that,' he said, eventually. 'He drowned, then?'

'No.'

'What was the cause of death?'

'Michael died of a heart attack; all his main arteries were clogged up to hell, and he had a failing valve. His liver was also in the sort of condition you'd expect from someone who'd had an alcohol dependency for at least forty years. The pathologist said that he could have died at any moment, but that he did just over a week before discovery. The condition of the body shows that he was put into the river shortly after death. No doubt about that.'

'The marks on the body? What about them?'

'Professor Hutchison agrees with you about the mark on the wrist; that he was probably wearing a leather watch strap and bloating of the body resulting from immersion could have stretched it to breaking point. We didn't find a watch at Miss Bonney's but it could have come off anywhere.'

'What about the head wound? What about the bruising to the body?'

'They were all pre mortem, apart from the head wound. That was inflicted after death, possibly by something he hit in the river. The other bruising was largely superficial. Analysis showed a significant amount of alcohol in the bloodstream. Joe Hutchison says that the bruising could have been caused by him falling while drunk, and rolling downhill. I asked him about your claw hammer scenario. All he would say was, maybe.'

'Stomach contents?'

'Jesus, Bob,' Martin exclaimed, 'do you want to go that far?'

'Yes, Andy, I want to know everything.'

'If you insist. He ate poached wild salmon, haunch of venison, well hung, mashed potatoes and turnip, and rum baba, shortly before he died, washed down with a significant amount of pretty good claret. The prof said that meal alone could have been enough to kill a man in his condition.'

'Sexual activity?'

'Are you serious?'

'Yes.'

'Bob, surely . . .'

'My brother was homosexual, Andy. What if the man who took him away from Oak Lodge was someone from that area of his past?'

'Man, you were sixteen when he left and you never saw him again. How do you know that?'

'I just do. Okay?'

'Okay. There is no mention in the report of any signs of sexual activity, or of any sexually transmitted disease or infestation. Maybe he did go off to live happily every after, but there's no evidence of it.'

Skinner sighed. 'So what have we got?'

'Not a murder, certainly,' said Martin. 'Nor is there any physical evidence that might support a charge of culpable homicide; in theory those bruises could have been a beating and he could have had his coronary as a result, but the prof said that they were a couple of days old at the time of death.'

'Could he have fallen in the drink and had his attack as a result? Did you ask that?'

'Yes, and Joe discounted it. He said that there would have been some ingestion or inhalation of river water even with that scenario, but there wasn't any.'

'Yeah, okay.' Skinner's disappointment was clear in his voice.

'He didn't put himself in the river,' Martin continued. 'We've established that. But even then, all I've got as a potential charge is concealing a death, which ranks pretty low on the priority list of CID in a small police force.'

'Meaning you're scaling down your investigation?' Skinner asked, quietly.

'As you would do in the same circumstances.'

'True.'

'So you won't mind if I go looking for this Skipper bloke on my own?'

It was Martin's turn to heave a sigh. 'And I could stop you, could I?' he exclaimed.

33

Adam Broadley was in a consulting room, rather than a waiting room, when Rose and Steele returned to the Royal Edinburgh Hospital on Tuesday morning. They had accepted the clinician's suggestion that rather than risk terrifying his sensitive patient by arriving at her home unannounced, he should ask her to come to see him, so that he could explain what was going to happen.

Andrea Strachan was seated behind a table when Broadley led them in to see her. She wore a dark twin-set, and her shoulders were hunched. Her eyes had a glassy look as she peered up at them. She had been with the police before, and when he introduced them, she was frightened.

Maggie Rose tried at once to put her at her ease. 'This is a routine interview, Miss Strachan,' she began, 'but given your recent illness, Adam thought that it would be best if it took place in his presence. We had no problem agreeing to that. Normally a discussion like this would be recorded these days, but this morning Inspector Steele will just take notes. So, if I can explain what it's about . . .'

'You don't have to!' the woman exclaimed in a shrill voice that fell not far short of a screech. 'I'm mentally ill, not mentally deficient. I know what this is. It has to do with that ridiculous painting going up in smoke. This is haul in the loony and pin it on her.'

Steele leaned forward and looked her in the eye, kindly, he hoped. 'No it's not, Andrea,' he said. 'We don't have a remit to find a scapegoat here. If we did, you'd be in a smelly room in Torphichen Place, not here in Adam's office.'

She seemed to soften, very slightly. 'Go on then,' she muttered, 'what is it about then?' The inspector looked to Rose, seated on his right. Recognising that their subject seemed to respond better to a man, she nodded and leaned back in her chair.

162

'First of all,' he resumed, 'I want to get some things clear, so that you can understand at least what's brought us here. Is that fair?'

'I suppose.'

'Good. First and foremost then, you were there when the picture was burned, weren't you?'

'Yes.'

'And you'd seen it before when you went with Mr O'Reilly and Mrs Laing to take delivery at the Academy?'

'Yes.'

'Fine; that's established. Next I want to tell you something, and then I want to ask you something. But I want to make it clear that I am making no accusation, just establishing facts. What I have to tell you is that the painting was ignited by an incendiary device, triggered remotely.'

'That's what you would say,' Andrea retorted. 'Some of us would say that it was God's punishment.'

Steele and Rose saw Adam Broadley's forehead clench in an involuntary frown at her comment, but it went unnoticed by the girl, who was seated beside him. 'If it was,' said the inspector, with a soft smile, 'He still used an incendiary. We found pieces of its casing afterwards.' For a second, he thought that Andrea smiled back at him, but if she did it was so fleeting that it was gone in less than a second. 'Now,' he continued, 'to what I want to ask you. You have an honours in chemistry, I know. Would you have the capability of making such a device?'

'In the event that God told me to do it? Is that what you mean?'

'No, it was a straight question; but you can frame it any way you like.'

She made a small, exasperated sound. 'You know I could, because I did it before, when I tried to burn that holy roller place last year. But let me save you a question. I didn't.'

'I wasn't necessarily going there, Andrea.'

'Not much.'

Steele grinned, in part at the girl, but mainly to preserve their fragile rapport. 'Well, maybe I was. But first I was going to ask you what you thought of the Vargas *Trinity*. Some people thought it was blasphemous. Did you?'

'Funnily enough I didn't; I saw it as a feminist joke, that's all. God doesn't actually have a sex; mankind was made in God's image, not just

163

a man. Yet he's been depicted as male; that's more of a blasphemy in a way. He's referred to in male terms, but that's purely a convenience. What Vargas was saying was that if you see God as a woman then since Christ was made in Her image too, then all three, the Holy Spirit included, had to be women. A joke, you see; a bad joke, I admit, expressed in an execrably bad painting, but not something that would move God to destroy it.'

This time she looked Steele in the eye, and held his gaze. 'I see,' he said, slowly. 'But what about those holy rollers? This is a genuine question, by the way, Andrea, no tricks. I'm interested. What made them blasphemous in your eyes?'

She seemed to bridle and he thought for a moment that the thread tying them together had snapped. 'The way they carry on, of course,' she answered, her voice rising. 'Have you seen the pagan way in which these people purport to worship God? All that hand-clapping and wailing and yelling, all that calling attention to themselves. They are approaching God without any humility, as if He was a celebrity of some sort, rather than the Lord of Creation before Whom we should all bow down our heads. Their practices bring Him into disrepute, and that's why He called me to destroy their temple.'

Broadley laid a hand softly on her arm. She shook it off. 'Oh all right, Adam,' she said, crossly. 'I accept that I was ill; I accept that I still am. But you have to accept that God's call was real to me at the time, and that it still is. Just as it was real when He spoke to me again on Friday. Yes, I know it's part of my illness, but it still has reality for me, and it is natural for me to obey Him.'

The physician looked at the detectives. For a second Steele thought he was about to intervene, and silenced him with a quick chilling glare. 'Let's get this straight, Andrea,' he continued, quietly. 'God spoke to you again on Friday, you say?'

She looked at him with a calmness that was almost serene, a total contrast to her attitude fifteen minutes earlier. 'Yes.'

'How?'

'This time it was on the telephone,' she told him.

'How did He speak to you before?'

'Last time it was through the television, when it was switched off.

Other times it's been through the speakers of my stereo. There's nothing odd about Him using the phone.'

'Will you tell me what happened?'

'Of course. I was at home, alone as usual, when the phone rang, or seemed to. I picked it up and He was on the other end.'

'How did you know it was Him?'

She smiled at him, and for the first time he noticed that behind all that severity, she was actually very pretty. 'Do you mean did He say, "Hello, Andrea, this is God"? No, of course not. He doesn't need to. He's in my head. I know that now, so when it happens I just accept it.'

'Okay. So what did He say?'

'He said that He had a task for me. He said that He wanted me to go to the opening of the exhibition on Saturday. There would be a purpose to it, He said. I would be His witness.'

'What did you say?'

'Don't be daft, inspector. You listen to God, you don't talk to Him.'

'Sorry. So you went to the opening ceremony?'

'Of course.'

'How did you get in without a ticket?'

'I'd been there before. The security people all knew me. I just waved and went in.'

'We saw you on the videotapes. You looked apprehensive.'

'I was. For all I knew, we were all going to be smitten with thunderbolts.'

'When it happened, when the picture went up, were you surprised?'

She gave him that smile again, this time with her eyes as well as her mouth. 'Inspector Steele, I suppose I was the only person in that room who wasn't.'

'But you did not do anything to set off that device and you did not create and plant it?'

'No, I did not. As I told you, this time I was only a witness. I suppose I was such an awful instrument against the Baptists that God felt He couldn't trust me again.'

Steele grinned back at her; for a few seconds they simply looked at each other, saying nothing.

'Is that it?' asked Broadley, eventually. 'Because if it is . . .'

Andrea Strachan turned to look at him. Steele thought of a butterfly, emerged from its chrysalis. 'I know, Adam,' she said. 'You don't have to say it. You'd like me to stay with you for a few more weeks.'

The young clinician looked almost grateful. 'I'd hope it won't be weeks, but yes, I would like you to spend some time with me.'

'If you wish. I know better than to argue anyway. You're as persuasive as the inspector here. Can you fetch my medication and some clothes from my place?'

'We've got medication here, but I'll have a nurse get some clothes for you. Come on, I'll find you a room.'

She stood, and the detectives followed suit. Just as she was leaving the room, Steele called out to her. 'Andrea, just one more thing.' She stopped and looked back. 'After God had finished speaking to you last Friday, what happened?'

'What do you mean?'

'How did the call end?'

'He said what He had to say, and then He was gone.'

'What did you hear after that?'

'A dialling tone, that was all.'

'Mmm,' Steele mused. 'In that case didn't it strike you as odd that God should hang up His phone?'

She left them with a shade of doubt in her eyes, for the first time since they had met.

'Stevie,' Maggie Rose exclaimed as the door closed, 'that was most impressive; a master class in interviewing. Well done.'

He blinked and looked at her as if he had heard not a word she had said. 'Sorry?'

'Ah, never mind. What do you think?'

'You're the boss. What's your take?'

'She probably did it, but we have no witnesses to her planting the device or igniting it. We could maybe search her home under warrant and find something that could have been the triggering device, but we'd still be a mile short of making a case. As it is she's under psychiatric care again, so she's no risk. Do you agree?'

Steele scratched his chin. 'Remember what we were saying yesterday about things being too easy?' he asked her. 'Well this is. I'm sorry but I just don't think she did it. I am quite sure she had a phone call on Friday, and I'm even more certain that it wasn't from God. Andrea's been handed to us on a plate by some clever bastard who doesn't want us to take this investigation any further. If you want me to buy that, you're going to have to order me. But even then, I don't think I can.'

Rose smiled. 'Are you sure you haven't just fallen in love?'

'Maybe I have, but that's got nothing to do with it. I can still spot a set-up when I see one.'

34

The pervasive example of Bob Skinner, who often said that the uniform was the last thing that had made him join the police service, may have made him less of a stickler, but Sir James Proud still enjoyed wearing his. He felt that it was part of his rank, and also that it let the people under his command know that he had respect for his job, and, through it, for them.

He prepared himself for his scheduled meeting, as always, in the private bathroom of his office suite. He ran a comb through his crinkly, silver hair, checked that his tie was straight, and finally turned to his uniform jacket. He held it up for inspection, then, spotting a flaw, brushed a few specks from the shoulders. Finally, when he was ready, he slipped it on.

He looked in the mirror as he fastened the heavy silver buttons, one by one. There was a time when he had had to strain to fasten the middle one, but the warning shot that nature had fired across his bows a year or two earlier had changed all that. Now the jacket was too slack, if anything; he might have to think about having it taken in, or maybe even order a new one. He would have enough time left in post to get the wear out of it; just as well, for he wouldn't be handing it on. The man who would be his successor was wider in the shoulders than him.

Sir James gave himself one last appraising look; although he intended that it would be brief, this was a meeting for which he wanted to be at his most impressive. 'Yes, Jimmy,' he said, satisfied at last, 'you are the very model of an old-fashioned chief constable.'

Turning sharply on his heel, he strode out of his sanctuary and into his office. The two lawyers were waiting for him, seated at his meeting table; Mitchell Laidlaw, representing Bob Skinner, and Tom Hogg, a respected solicitor from a small Glasgow firm from which he sought independent legal advice on behalf of the force, when the need arose. He looked from one to the other as he took his seat behind his desk, at Hogg, small, sharp-faced, sharp-eyed, sharp-witted, then at Laidlaw, the physical opposite, bulky . . . although it occurred to Sir James that he had seen him look more portly . . . round face, dark-haired, with eyes that seemed never to blink, and a gaze which gave the clear message that here was a mind which never worked at less than maximum capacity.

'Good morning, gentlemen,' the chief constable greeted his visitors. 'Sorry to keep you waiting; I was just fixing my make-up. Are the trains running all right this morning, Tom?' he asked the Glaswegian.

'I gave up on them long ago,' the solicitor replied. 'I use the M8. For all its uncertainties, it's still a better bet if you have an appointment to keep.'

'Sad but true, eh. How about you, Mitch? Traffic moving smoothly in Edinburgh, was it?'

'I took a taxi, Jimmy, just to be sure; no way did I want to be late for this one.'

'Your implied criticism is noted.' He glanced at his watch. 'Is your client ready to join us? I suppose he's paying his respects to Miss McConnell, or checking up on DS McGurk.'

Laidlaw pursed his lips. 'My client will not be joining us, Jimmy. We discussed the matter of his attendance; on balance he agreed with my view that it might be better if he did not come face to face with Councillor Maley. I'm here to present his position, and also to do any barking that might be necessary. If Bob was present himself, it might prove hard to restrain him from joining in, should there be any resistance to our proposition. Mind you, he was easier to persuade than he might have been, had he not been preoccupied with the death of his brother.'

'Yes, that came out of the blue. It must be disturbing for Bob, in all sorts of ways. There's this local problem, his . . .' Sir James hesitated as he searched for a suitable word '. . . difficulties in the States, and then all the old family skeletons this has brought out of the cupboard.'

'I never knew Bob had a brother,' Laidlaw confessed. 'My firm's never handled his family business, or I might have. Alexis did, though, although not from her father. She found out by accident, she told me yesterday, when I commiserated with her over it.'

'He didn't tell Sarah: I know that,' said the chief constable. 'As a matter of fact, I was one of the few people who knew about him, outside the community in which the Skinner family lived. Since Michael disappeared from there thirty years ago, his existence will have come as a surprise to just about everyone. Bob chose to tell me when I made him head of CID. He said that he felt that as such he could not have any secrets from his chief constable.' Proud Jimmy sighed. 'He could from his wife and daughter, though, which tells you rather a lot about his attitude to his job, and the lengths to which he'll go to defend it. At least we can try to resolve that matter for him today.' He glanced at his watch. 'Let's see if the ladies are here.'

He picked up one of his phones, pressed a button and spoke to his civilian secretary, Gerry Crossley. 'Are we ready?' he asked.

'Yes, sir,' the young man replied. 'The councillors are waiting in reception.'

'Thanks. Ask them to join us please, and send in the tea.' Since his health scare Sir James had given up coffee; it was no longer served in his office, and if he had had his way it would have been banned from the senior officers' dining room also.

Less than a minute later, the door at the far end of the room opened. The three men stood as Councillors Marcia Topham and Agnes Maley entered. The contrast between the two women was so marked that it was hard to imagine them as political colleagues. Councillor Topham was middle-aged, but managed to maintain her elegance in the face of the bulk that Proud had watched grow over the years. Councillor Maley was short and squat with short dark hair and distinctly unfeminine eyebrows, below a low forehead. Where the former's manner bordered on diffidence, the latter's was full of undisguised aggression. Agnes Maley had been a councillor for many years, and for most of them she had served on the Police Authority. For a brief dark period in the days of the old regional councils, she had been its chair. Although she had once been famous as a left-wing firebrand, she had somehow moved with the times, and had held on to her city-centre power-base despite the revolution within her party. Proud had succeeded once in having her removed from the Authority, but after the last round of elections she had engineered a comeback, and had infuriated the chief by seizing the chair of the human resources committee by a mix of trickery and intimidation within the majority group. The grapevine had it that, after the next council polls, she would replace the moderate Mrs Topham as chair of the Authority itself.

She bridled when she saw the two lawyers, and would have tackled the chief constable head on, had not Maisie, the dining room waitress, forestalled her by rolling in a trolley loaded with cups, a big steel teapot, and plates of plain biscuits.

It took only a few minutes for the tea to be poured and distributed, and for the biscuits to be passed round. As soon as Maisie had left the room, Councillor Maley opened fire. 'Right, chief,' she demanded brusquely, ignoring Topham completely. 'What's this about?'

'And a good day to you also, Ms Maley,' said Sir James, with glacial courtesy. 'And to you, Marcia.' He softened visibly as he nodded to the Authority chair. 'Thank you for coming, on short notice. This meeting has been called at the request of Mr Mitchell Laidlaw, of Curle, Anthony and Jarvis, who is acting for Deputy Chief Constable Skinner. Tom Hogg's here to advise me, and you ladies, if necessary, on the Authority's legal position.'

Maley twitched with inner fury at the gender reference. 'Councillors, please,' she muttered. 'Why wasn't I given notice of the agenda?'

'Because I chose not to give you any. Mitchell, do you want to open?'

Laidlaw nodded. 'Thank you, Sir James,' he said, noticeably more formal than before. He took five documents from his briefcase and gave one to each person at the table. 'I'd like to begin by asking you to read that report, carefully. It's an exhaustive report on the present physical condition of Deputy Chief Constable Skinner, prepared by Mr Peter Patience and Mr Hugh Hurley, consultant cardiologists at Edinburgh Royal Infirmary, following an examination which took place yesterday evening at the Murrayfield Hospital.'

'Mmm,' Marcia Topham murmured, nervously.

The chief gave the lead, picking up his copy and beginning to read, but Maley left hers on the table. 'This isn't relevant,' she protested. 'The deputy chief constable has to be examined by the force's official medical officer. He's said that he's going to give him a month more to recover before he looks at him.'

'That is not strictly true, councillor,' Proud intervened. 'It was your subcommittee that instructed the MO to wait for a month. Your minutes may not be publicly accessible, but I can see them at any time.'

'Thank you, chief,' Laidlaw said. 'That was my understanding also, from my client. It is his position that a delay is unnecessary and unreasonable. Further, it is his belief that it has been imposed to give your subcommittee time to rush through changes to local standing orders which would ban arbitrarily any officer who underwent the procedure that he experienced recently from ever returning to work, regardless of their physical condition, or prognosis.'

He fixed Maley with a piercing stare. 'I'll be blunt with you. If you refuse to read that report, I'm going to ask Councillor Topham, as chair of the Authority, to assume executive responsibility for this matter, and to exclude you from this meeting. If she refuses, I will be in the Court of Session at two p.m., where I will be granted, I promise you, an interdict compelling the Authority to deal with this matter now.'

'You can't do that,' the dark-haired councillor shouted. 'This is a committee matter.'

'Nonsense,' said the chief constable, sharply. 'This is not an appointment; it's an administrative matter, and either of you have executive power.' He turned to the other solicitor. 'Tom. What's your advice on the matter at issue? Do you think Mitch is bluffing when he assures us he'll get his interdict?'

Hogg picked up the report. 'If this says what I assume it does, I think it's ninety-five per cent certain that interdict would be granted ordering you to deal with this now. I think it is one-hundred-and-ten-per cent certain that the court would forbid you from making any changes in your regulations that might affect Mr Skinner, in advance of receiving a report on his medical condition. My advice is, read the report now, and deal with it now. To do otherwise would be seen as perverse and might even lay individuals open to a civil action raised by DCC Skinner.'

Proud looked directly at Councillor Topham, ignoring Agnes Maley completely. 'Marcia,' he said, 'you've had independent legal advice. Now, I'm not asking you to get into the issue of whether the subcommittee's decision to defer Bob Skinner's medical might have been motivated by antipathy towards him by certain members. We don't really want to go there. I am asking you, as chair, to consider the reputation of the Authority, and your own position should you find its actions condemned by the Supreme Court. Are we going to deal with this matter now?'

Mrs Topham glanced to her left. 'No, councillor,' the chief exclaimed, firmly. 'I'm asking you alone. Will you read that report?'

She looked at the document, then up at Sir James once more. 'I suppose,' she murmured. 'I suppose we must.'

Agnes Maley slapped the table. 'Ah, bugger the report,' she snapped. 'We all know it's a whitewash without even reading it. Okay, councillor, okay Sir James, you reinstate the man. But just you remember this; my time's coming, and it won't be in the chair of the Police Authority either. There's a by-election for one of the Edinburgh seats in the Scottish Parliament due next month, and guess who's going to be nominated as the Labour candidate as soon as it's called? Once I'm an MSP, I'll sort you buggers out.' She glared at Laidlaw. 'And your client will be top of my list: I promise you that!' She threw the report back across the table and stalked from the room.

In the echo of the slamming door, the chief constable looked at Mrs Topham. 'Is that true, Marcia?' he asked. 'Is that woman really going to the parliament? Surely to God your party organisation can't let that happen?'

The councillor was trembling slightly, as she replied. 'I don't think it can prevent it, James. Agnes Maley has a pretty effective power base in Edinburgh; none of the new brooms in our headquarters, or even in London, have been able to sweep her away. In theory her selection for the vacancy could be vetoed, but it won't be. There aren't the grounds.'

She pursed her lips. 'Agnes is a dangerous woman, all right, and she'll be even more so, when she gets to Holyrood.'

35

'Stevie, are you sure about this?' asked George Regan. 'I mean it's so bloody obvious that the Strachan girl's the one for this job. She had the opportunity, she's a nutter with a religious kink, she's got a track record for fire-raising, and she was there when it happened, with a personal invite, she says, from God. But, no, you don't think she did it. Are you kidding me, or what?'

Steele had had enough; Regan had been complaining for half an hour, since they had begun to review all the notes made and interviews transcribed after the Royal Scottish Academy fire. 'No sergeant,' he said, heavily, 'I'm ordering you to shut the hell up and get on with it. If you can't do that, feel free to go and see Detective Superintendent Rose and take it up with her. She'll probably arrange for you to swap jobs with young Sauce. That would suit me, for frankly, probationer or not, he'd be more use to me in here right now, and you'd be more use to the force in uniform, and out on the reception desk.'

Regan threw him a dagger-filled look, but Steele stared him down. 'What are we looking for, then?' he asked, grudgingly, and still grumpily.

'We're after anything that interviewees saw that was odd. We were so hot after the girl when we spotted her there that we didn't give these statements any more than a cursory glance.'

'I'm not surprised. God talks to the girl, Stevie.'

Steele grinned at his persistence. 'George, enough.'

'Aye, okay.' He picked up a folder.

'We are looking into that, by the way,' the inspector added.

'What?'

'God's phone call; Maggie's checking it out.'

'She's got His number has she? Or does her old man? They tell me he's got plenty of numbers in his book.'

Steele caught a flicker in Regan's eye. 'If you mean what I think you do, George, you should make a point of forgetting any rumours you've heard. You don't want to mess with Mario; no way, not at all.'

'He doesn't bother me.'

'Don't get in his way or he will. And don't let the boss hear you talk about him either, in case she takes it personally. One of those two's going to be the next head of CID when Dan Pringle goes; you want to remember that.'

'So what?'

Steele was about to tell him when his phone rang. He picked it up, with a touch of relief that the conversation had been brought to an end before Regan could say any more. 'Stevie?' said a familiar voice. 'It's Jack.' Detective Sergeant Jack McGurk had recently been appointed as Bob Skinner's executive assistant, during the DCC's absence in the US. He sounded excited, and Steele hoped that he could guess the reason.

'He's back,' McGurk exclaimed. 'It's official. The Big Man is back in post. The chief's just had me in and told me; he was reinstated by the chair of the Police Authority, after a private meeting this morning. He saw the buggers off, Stevie. I had a feeling something was going to happen today. Neil McIlhenney called into my office this morning, and warned me to stay close.'

'Did the chief say anything else?'

'No, but he had to stop himself from grinning all over his face.'

'Is he back in the office now?'

'Not yet. It might be a few days before he is, given what happened to his brother, and everything else.'

Steele wondered what 'everything else' might be, but he knew better than to ask with George Regan within earshot. The sergeant looked across at him and raised an eyebrow. Steele nodded, hung up and went through to Maggie Rose's office. He knocked on the door and walked in.

Before he could open his mouth, she smiled at him. 'I know,' she said. 'Mario just called me; he had it from Neil five minutes ago. Batman is back in action. Which means . . . that very soon we are going to have an anxious Dan Pringle, and maybe even ACC Haggerty, wondering what's going on with the Academy investigation.'

'Good point. I'd better get back and crack the whip even harder over George.'

Rose looked up at him from behind her desk; she was still smiling. 'Do that anyway, but I've got some more good news for you. I've just had the result of the check I told you I was going to run with BT. I've also had Adam Broadley confirm with Andrea that she didn't have any other calls on Friday . . . apart from the one from God, that is. It seems that as the ads used to say, He's every one-to-one you've ever had. When He called Andrea, He used His mobile. And guess what else? When He's not presiding over all of creation, He's a trainee solicitor with Candela and Finch.'

36

Although he lived by the sea, and owned a villa in Spain where people cast lines into any stretch of running water, Bob Skinner had never been a fisherman. Standing thigh-deep in water, waiting for hours for a short-sighted salmon to make a fatal mistake, may have been fine for the Queen Mother, but it had never held any attraction for him. His sporting tastes were all much more physical.

Nevertheless, he knew how serious a business salmon fishing was in Scotland, and, with the royal connections, how powerful a lobby its enthusiasts could be.

Skipper Williamson was doing well out of them, that was for sure. His fishing hotel, called Fir Park Lodge . . . a nod, Skinner knew, to the football club that had started him on the road . . . was situated not far north of Perth, near the town of Birnam.

Skinner had found it without difficulty on several of the many websites that attract anglers from around the world to Perthshire throughout the salmon season. He had driven north in Sarah's Freelander rather that his own BMW, in case there was a need for four-wheel-drive capability, but the hotel was easily accessible.

He had found it without difficulty; now, sat in a lay-by on the A9, he could see it clearly as he looked down through a gap in the trees. He trained his binoculars on its main entrance, then used their zoom to pan out. Fir Park Lodge stood in several acres of ground. It was a nineteenth-century, grey stone country house, with a turret on each of its four corners. There was a wide lawn in front, and to the left a car park, in which stood two big Toyota off-roaders and a minibus. Beyond them Skinner saw a Rolls Royce and a small white Mercedes A-class. He zoomed in again, and saw the house in miniature, on a corporate crest on the Merc's front door panel.

From the vehicles he guessed that Skipper Williamson had guests, and that they were probably at lunch, before heading back to the river. Behind the Lodge, he could see it sparkle; his web research had told him that Williamson owned rights on that stretch of the Tay, but that his visitors, placed with him by a variety of tour companies, were ferried around to other beats and other rivers.

He sat in the Freelander and waited. The call from Mitch Laidlaw had come through on his cellphone an hour earlier, but he had forgotten it already. Now that his job was secure, it was no longer his top priority.

Skinner had done some research on Cecil 'Skipper' Williamson. Through a contact in the General Register Office, introduced to him by his friend Jim Glossop, before his retirement, he had learned that he was fifty-nine years old, and that he had been married briefly in his late thirties and early forties. That marriage had ended on grounds of irretrievable breakdown. The big detective found himself wondering why.

He sat in Sarah's car with only a very rough plan of action. He had thought of simply walking into the hotel and introducing himself to Williamson, to see if that would trigger a panic in the man, but had discarded that. If the man had been responsible for his brother's death, or even if he had simply disposed of his body for some bizarre reason, it was likely that he would be expecting a visit from someone, sooner or later.

He had thought also of interviewing a member of the hotel staff. He had run a check that morning through a private contact in the Department of Social Security, and knew that Fir Park Lodge had five full-time employees, a resident housekeeper, two kitchen-maids, a waitress and a handyman. His name was Angus d'Abo, and a few years before he had done time in Perth Prison for housebreaking. He wondered whether Skipper would know that.

Before he braced d'Abo, though, if he did, there was something he wanted to do first. He had visited the *Motherwell Times*, where the helpful editor had found a photograph of Skipper Williamson from his archives, the only one the paper held. It was thirty-three years old, and it had been on newsprint, one of a sea of faces in a pre-season team picture. The journalist had photocopied it, extracted Williamson, and blown up his image as far as possible, but it was still grey and barely recognisable even to someone who had known him in those days.

He had visited Motherwell Football Club itself, but had found a modern business whose records did not stretch to reserve sides from the sixties. Other than in the passport office . . . and it would raise too many questions if he asked there . . . as far as Skinner could ascertain there was no up-to-date photograph of the man anywhere on the public record. Before he did anything else, he planned to take one, and to show it to Brother Aidan. If the old cleric identified him as Michael's visitor, then he would pick up d'Abo and put the thumbscrews on him.

He started the Freelander and pulled out on to the A9. A hundred yards along he made a left turn on to a minor road winding downhill, away from Birnam. A small, plain signpost marked the entrance to the Lodge grounds. He pulled up on the verge and leaned over to recover his camera bag from the back seat. He was fairly certain that Williamson was at home. The Rolls was his; he had been driving it when he had picked up a fixed penalty six months earlier.

Skinner fitted a telephoto lens to his Nikon; his plan was to hide in the woods that surrounded the hotel and its lawn, and to snatch photographs of every man who showed his face outside. Hopefully, Williamson would wave his guests off after lunch, and would be easy to spot . . . unless of course, he was fishing with them himself, which would be, the big detective conceded, a bit of a bugger.

He locked the car and slipped into the grounds of Fir Park Lodge, past the plain wooden sign. He left the drive at once and made his way through the thick, untended woodland towards the big house.

He was almost there when his cellphone rang in his trouser pocket. 'Shit,' he whispered, thankful that its sound was muffled. Because of his pacemaker, he no longer carried it in the breast pocket of his shirt, where it would have been all too audible.

He took it out quickly, and was about to switch it off when he remembered that he was back on the active list. There was just the possibility that it might be the chief. He hid behind the thickest tree he could see, and answered.

The voice in his ear sounded not a bit like Sir James Proud. It was American; East Coast, perhaps a trace of Massachusetts. 'Is that Bob Skinner?' it asked.

'Yes,' he answered, quietly, although there was no one to hear him. Everyone was still inside the hotel.

'This is Clyde Oakdale, Bob.'

Skinner frowned. Oakdale was the acting senior partner of Sarah's late father's law firm. He was handling, personally, the winding up of Leo and Susannah's joint estate, of which Skinner himself was co-executor. But there was something in the lawyer's voice that told him this call was not about an estate matter. At once, he saw the future stretching out before him. Legal separation, a property split, a custody battle unless he agreed to his children becoming in effect Americans, and if he did, years of shuttling across the Atlantic to visit them, until it all became too much trouble. 'Yes, Clyde,' he said wearily.

'Bob,' the lawyer continued heavily, 'I have some very disturbing news for you.'

'Let me guess. It's about Sarah.'

'Yes it is. How did you guess?'

'Call it intuition. I think maybe you should talk to my solicitor, rather than me.'

'Bob,' Oakdale exclaimed, testily, 'I don't know what you mean by that, but whatever it is, it seems we're not connecting up here. Now just shut up, will you. By making this call I am breaking a direct client instruction, but what the hell, you need to know, regardless. So please listen to me.

'Sarah has been arrested.'

'You what?' Skinner exploded, forgetting for the moment where he was.

'You heard me. She is being held by the detective division of the Erie County Sheriff's Department for questioning about the murder of Mr Ron Neidholm.'

'Ron Neidholm? That name rings a bell.' Bob frowned as he searched his memory. 'Yes, Babs Walker told me about him. Pro footballer; he and Sarah had a thing at college.'

'That's the man. Big Ron is quite a local hero, hence there's a real shit-storm about his killing. I've tried to speak to Brad Dekker, the sheriff, but he won't take my calls.'

'What happened?'

'At about nine yesterday evening, the police were called by neighbours to a disturbance in Mr Neidholm's house. They found him dead in the kitchen, with a knife in his chest, and Sarah standing over the body. When she calmed down she told them that she had found him like that, but they arrested her straight away and took her in.'

'And she's still there?'

'Yes. They're talking about charging her.'

'Where are you? You're with her, aren't you?'

'I'm a civil lawyer, Bob. I have John Vranic, our firm's top courtroom attorney, there with her.'

'Can't he get her released on bail? I mean . . . Oh, this is fucking nonsense!'

'The District Attorney's office is not being compliant on this one,' said Oakdale. 'The DA is a friend of mine, so he went a little further with me than they have with John. Her prints are on the knife, Bob, as clear as day.'

'You're kidding me.'

'I wish I was.' As the lawyer paused, Skinner heard the sound of a door opening across the lawn. He ignored it, instead he started marching back towards the road. 'Bob,' Oakdale went on, 'Sarah didn't want me to call you. I can't think why, but she said she didn't want you involved. But I had to call you, for the children's sake if nothing else. If necessary I can justify it ethically through your position as co-executor of her parents' will.'

'Fuck ethics,' the policeman snarled. 'If you hadn't I'd have killed you. Tell your man Vranic from me to get her out of there. Put the whole estate up as a bail bond if you have to, but get her released.' He came to the public road, and broke into a run towards the car. 'I'll be out there just as soon as I can, by tomorrow morning your time at the latest.

'You call Dekker, or Eddie Brady, his chief of detectives. You tell whichever of them you get that I am coming and that when I get there, I want to see every scrap of their case against my wife.'

181

'I'll do that,' said Oakdale, 'and I'll do everything I can to get her bail today, even if I have to put her before a judge to do it. You just try to stay calm.'

'Calm? Fuck calm, that's long gone. I'll work on staying merely angry, and you can tell Brad Dekker that too. See you.'

He unlocked the car and slid behind the wheel, just as the two Toyota Landcruisers pulled out of the Fir Park Lodge driveway. Skinner cast not a glance in their direction; he was fully occupied calling up a number on his phone.

A few seconds later, his call was answered. 'Neil,' he said urgently, 'this is Bob. I should call McGurk with this, but I don't know him well enough. Besides, it's more personal than business. Shit, it's all personal. I'm in Perthshire; I have to call in on Andy, then I'm back down the road, pronto. I want you to get on to the travel agent and book me on the first possible flight to New York, with onward connection to Buffalo; economy, business class, first, I don't care, just get me on it. If you can, get my keys from Alex . . . she's in her Edinburgh office . . . and go out to Gullane, pick up my passport, and pack me some clothes.'

Not even when his anger over the threat to his job was at its hottest, had Neil McIlhenney ever heard his friend so agitated. 'Okay, Bob, I'll do all that. But what is it? What's up?'

'I'll tell you when I see you, man. Right now, I don't have the time . . .' his voice shook with rage '. . . or the self-control. Better you don't know anyway; that way Alex can't bully it out of you. This is something I'll have to tell her in person too.'

37

'I appreciate the urgency of your enquiries, Superintendent,' said David Candela, 'but couldn't this have waited until close of business? Couldn't you have interviewed the chap at home?'

'I could also have sent my colleague Detective Sergeant Regan,' Maggie Rose answered. 'George would have marched straight up to your reception desk, flashed his warrant card, and demanded to see Mr Sheringham there and then. That's his style; I find him quite a useful blunt instrument when I'm dealing with an awkward customer. With you involved though, Mr Candela, I thought it would be more appropriate if I came along myself, with Inspector Steele, and asked you to arrange for us to speak to the man in private.'

The autocratic senior partner was mollified. 'Yes, of course,' he said at once. 'I appreciate your discretion. You say this is a purely routine interview?'

'It is. If it was otherwise we'd be seeing him on our premises, not yours.'

'I'm sure. Very well, let me show you to one of our conference rooms, then I'll fetch Eric.'

'Thanks. Since we're being discreet, before you do that, could you tell us something about him? For example, is he quiet or extrovert?'

'I don't really know a lot about him,' Candela confessed. He leaned back in his chair and put his hands behind his head. Steele glanced around his office, taking it in. There was a flat-screen computer terminal on a corner of the big desk, yet somehow it seemed to be balanced on the other side by a photo of a man in uniform, set in an ornate antique frame. The total effect was surprisingly traditional in a modern building, as if it had been designed to give the feel of two-hundred-year-old values in a twenty-first-century environment.

'Young Sheringham is one of our last round of graduate recruits. That means he'll be bright. You can assume that, because we rarely take lower than a first when we do our university trawl. The reason I don't know much about him is that we've put him in our family department, so I don't come across his work. I'm a corporate partner myself; as well as being top dog around here, that is. I may have been a late entrant to the firm, and there may be the family tradition, but I've got into this chair on merit.'

'You're still a full-service firm, then?' asked Steele.

'Apart from buying and selling houses. We got out of that line of work when we moved up here. Best left to the estate agents and those solicitor firms who are clinging on to traditional offices. Come on.' Suddenly Candela pushed himself to his feet. 'I'll install you and fetch the boy.'

He led them out of his office and along a corridor. Its walls were glazed, allowing them to see into a modern open-plan office with an imaginative layout, which meant that no employee was directly looking on to the desk of another. They could see across the floor and through the windows on the far side. On the other side of the Western Approach Road, Steele noticed that several windows on one floor of the block opposite were shattered. It was dark and deserted, although the floors above and below were bright and buzzing with action.

'What's that?' he asked casually.

'That's the scene of the other fire on Saturday,' the solicitor told him. 'Their bad luck that the Academy fire was first, and on a Saturday.'

Candela led them round a corner, then stopped at a beechwood door. 'In here,' he said, showing them into a small windowless room, with a round meeting table and six chairs, and two Peter Howson prints on the walls. 'Won't be a minute,' said the solicitor, closing the door behind him.

It re-opened a few minutes later and a young man came in, alone. Eric Sheringham was tall and fairhaired; he wore a white, short-sleeved shirt, and dark trousers that looked as if they were part of a suit. The detectives knew that as a graduate trainee he would be no more than in his early twenties, but he looked older. His eyes were pale blue and very vivid,

like Andy Martin's, Maggie thought, if another colour. She wondered if
he too wore contact lenses.

'Mr Candela said you wanted to see me?' he began. They looked for
signs of nervousness, but saw none.

'Yes, Mr Sheringham; please sit down.' She introduced herself, and
Steele.

'What can I do for you?' the would-be lawyer asked, politely.

Stevie Steele looked back at him, unsmiling. 'We're investigating the
arson attack that took place on Saturday at the opening of the art
exhibition that your firm is sponsoring.'

'Oh, that. Pretty spectacular, wasn't it.'

'And pretty criminal,' said Rose, sharply. 'Quite apart from the
potential danger to life, from panic as much as from the fire, that painting
was insured for half a million pounds.'

'Wow, that much?' Sheringham looked impressed, but not rattled.

'You don't care about it, then?' The Superintendent felt herself
approaching her annoyance threshold.

'Not much. I've seen better at the end-of-year exhibition at the
Lauriston art school.'

'I don't think Ms Rose was talking about its artistic merit,' said Steele,
with a half smile. 'I think she was talking more about the principle of
arson. Are you against that?'

The young man smiled back. 'I'm against arson in principle, but let's
just say I'd get more worked up about some fires than others. This one
rated pretty low on my personal scale of outrage . . . apart from the fact
that I was there, of course.'

'Yes, you were, weren't you. We noticed that from the list of interviewees. Your statement was pretty brief. You said you didn't see anything.'

'That's right. I was on reception. I had to stay at my post during the
ceremony, and Mr Candela's speech, to register any late-comers. All I
saw were people's backs.'

'Do you know a woman called Andrea Strachan?' Rose asked suddenly.

Eric Sheringham blinked; she thought she saw the first flicker of
uncertainty in his eyes. 'No,' he answered, quietly.

'You sure? You were at Edinburgh University at the same time. You
overlapped there for a couple of years.'

He paused. Rose knew that he was either searching his memory or covering his tracks. 'Yes,' he announced at last. 'Sorry, I did know an Andrea Strachan. She was a chemist, and she used to take part in union debates. She dressed like my mother's auntie, and she used to stand up and preach at everyone in a funny high voice. Yet she never spoke to anyone directly apart from then. We called her the Dormouse. Like in the Mad Hatter's tea party. You remember, the dormouse wakes up every so often, says something, then goes back to sleep. Is that the woman you mean?'

'That sounds like her. Did she speak to you on Saturday, at the opening ceremony?'

'I never saw her at the ceremony,' Sheringham shot back, quickly; maybe too quickly, Steele thought.

'So you didn't slip her into the thing, without an invitation?' he asked.

'No.' The reply was more considered, and firmer.

'That's funny,' said Steele, his voice hardening. 'Because she says you invited her.'

'Well she's a liar. I don't know her to speak to and I didn't invite her anywhere. I don't even know where she lives.'

'Do you have a telephone directory?'

'Yes, of course.'

'Well, she's in it. Miss Strachan says she had a phone call last Friday night inviting her to the Academy next day. Mr Sheringham, there's a floor full of lawyers here, and another above. Before we go any further, would you like one of them to join us?'

For the first time, he looked flustered. 'Not yet,' he replied. 'I'll know when, don't worry.'

'Okay. The thing is, sir, the call to Miss Strachan was made from your mobile.'

Panic and relief seemed to cross the man's face at the same time. 'Ah, so that's it,' he exclaimed. 'My mobile was stolen.'

'I've heard that one before somewhere,' said Steele, coldly. 'Haven't you, Superintendent?'

Rose nodded. 'So often that I did a check before we came along here. You haven't reported a stolen mobile.'

The relief was gone, leaving only the panic. 'I didn't bother,'

Sheringham protested. 'I didn't see the point. It was a pay-as-you-go phone, and I only had a couple of quid left in the voucher. I fancied a new one anyway.'

'Have you bought one yet?'

'No. I haven't got round to it.'

Rose leaned across the table. 'Mr Sheringham, are you telling me the truth?'

'Yes.'

'In that case, will you be kind enough to let Mr Steele search your desk right now? Or if you'd prefer it, I'll ask Mr Candela's secretary to do it, to avoid you any unnecessary embarrassment. Oh yes, and if we don't find it, would you be prepared let me have officers search your home? All of this is just to confirm your story, you understand. Would you agree to that?'

The trainee shook his head; his complexion had gone several shades paler than when he had entered the room. The look of panic in his eyes had given way to one of pure fright. 'No,' he whispered, then slid his right hand into his trouser pocket, took out a royal blue Ericsson cellphone and laid it on the table.

Steele picked it up; he saw that it was switched on and flipped it open. Quickly, he flicked through the menu and selected 'call list', then he stood and walked round the table. 'Let's have a look, shall we,' he said. He chose the first log entry; a name showed on the LCD read-out. Sonia. 'Who's that?'

'My girlfriend.' Steele moved on; another name. Hazza. 'My pal,' Sheringham whispered. He moved on. Sonia, once more.

There were six more calls to Sonia, two to Hazza, three others to friends called Bill, Marti and Brick, all logged by name, before the first number showed. It had an 0131 prefix and the call had been made on the previous Friday. 'Whose is that?' asked Steele.

'I don't know,' Sheringham replied. 'I can't remember.'

'Well I can,' said the inspector icily. 'It's Andrea Strachan's. Time for you to shut up, sir, and get that lawyer in here.' He turned to Rose. 'I'll go and speak to Mr Candela.'

He left the room and headed back down the corridor. After a few yards, he stopped, took out his own cellphone and re-called Adam

Broadley's number. 'Is Andrea still with you?' he asked, when the psychiatrist answered.

'Yes. She's fine. I'll probably release her tomorrow, if it's okay with you.'

'A hundred per cent okay. If you decide to discharge her tonight, I'll even pick her up, if she wants. Meantime, I've got some news for the two of you that you can explain however you like. It looks like we've found God.'

38

If Skinner had been less preoccupied, he would have noticed that Andy Martin's office in the Tayside police headquarters building was bigger than his own. Indeed his friend would probably have pointed this out to him. But both had other things on their minds.

Martin's forehead was ridged in a frown to match Skinner's own. 'Bob, I don't know what to say.'

'Neither do I, so I'm saying nothing else until I get to Buffalo. Then I'll be asking plenty.'

'Sure; just keep it level, that's all. Now, is there anything that I can do while you're away?'

Bob looked at him gratefully. 'Yes, there is. A couple of things; one you'll find easy, the other maybe not. First, I'd like you to keep in regular telephone touch with Alex. Just make sure that she's okay and all that. She'll be as frantic about this as the rest of us, and she's got no one to lean on at this moment.'

'Sure, I'll do that. I'll ask Karen to call her, once you've broken this to her and headed out of town; might be better.'

'As you see fit. Now the other thing. When I got Oakdale's call, I was in the middle of a bit of private enterprise, involving a man named Cecil Williamson, aka Skipper. He's a contemporary of Michael's. He's from Motherwell and he runs a country house hotel up near Birnam. It's called Fir Park Lodge.

'I was trying to get an up-to-date photo of him, without alarming the locals, to show to old Aidan. If he'd identified him, there's a guy on his payroll called d'Abo, who's done a bit of time. I was proposing to have a chat with him, before I squared up his boss.'

Skinner hesitated. 'Andy, I know the autopsy report knocked the suspicious death investigation on its head, but . . .'

Martin stood up from behind his desk, and walked to the window. 'That enquiry may be stood down, Bob, but we still have an interest in finding out how he wound up in the river. You've put a name in the frame, so I'll look into it. I won't be as subtle as you, either. I'll pull d'Abo in straight away.'

'Thanks, mate.' Skinner stood himself and looked across the room at his friend. 'Just in case it isn't this Skipper, it might do no harm to have a list of estate owners on your patch, especially those with salmon rivers running through them. My brother's last meal wasn't something he knocked up on a fire at the roadside. It was rich man's fare. If it wasn't Williamson, although he's a heavy favourite, I will find the man who fed it to him.'

'I'll get someone on it,' said Martin. 'Now try and forget it for now. You have, if I may say so, more important things to attend to.'

Bob shrugged his shoulders as he headed for the door. 'Maybe so, son,' he murmured, 'but I will attend to them both in time, mark me on that. Guilt is one of the strongest motivations there is, be it for covering things up, or for uncovering them. My private dread is that before I'm finished, I might have to do both.'

39

'This man,' exclaimed Andrea Strachan. 'You say he knows me?'

Stevie Steele nodded. 'He was at university at the same time as you.'

'What's his name?'

'I can't tell you that, I'm afraid.'

'Why? Because I might fall at his feet and worship him?'

Steele glanced across to the passenger seat, saw her smile, and laughed out loud.

'No. It wouldn't be like you to worship a false god. Idolatry's forbidden, remember.'

'Could I forget?' she exclaimed. 'That's one of the many things my father's drummed into me over the years.'

'How do you get on with your father?' Stevie asked.

Out of the corner of his eye, he saw her smile flicker again. 'What is this? Am I still being interrogated?'

'Nah,' he said, 'that's all over. It was an idle question, that's all. Well, almost idle. Here I am picking you up from hospital, and I'm taking you home, when I might be taking you to your parents.'

'Just in case I harmed myself, you mean?'

'No! Oh, Christ, Steele, shut up. Mouth open, foot straight in. I think just driving would be a good idea.'

'Maybe, but I'll let you off the hook. And I'll overlook the Name you just took in vain. After my crisis, I thought, and Adam agreed, that it would be better for me not to go back to that atmosphere. My father holds highly orthodox views, which he never ceases to proclaim, and we felt that given the nature of my illness, it would be easier if I wasn't exposed to them. It's worked out all right, too.'

He looked across at her again. Her hair was pulled back in a ponytail, and he saw that she was wearing lipstick and eye make-up. Yes, pretty;

191

very definitely attractive. 'Adam recommended that I wear make-up; to let my real personality out, he said. His diagnosis was that in my schizophrenia, my other side had taken me over completely.'

Her smile became dazzling. 'Of course, there is the possibility that this is the real nutter you're looking at now.'

'If it is, it suits me fine.' The words were out before he had time to consider them.

'Thank you, sir.'

He looked at the road ahead. 'Can I ask you something else, Andrea?'

'Within reason.'

'When we saw you on the video tapes, and when we began our talk yesterday, you looked . . . different. Why was that?'

She took a deep breath. 'Because I'd stopped taking my medication. When I got that call last Friday, it just did my head in. You know what I mean? I just screamed inside; I thought that it had all been a sham, that I wasn't cured, or under control at all, and that the medicine was all useless. So I stopped taking it. What you saw was what happened as a result.'

Andrea looked across at him. 'How does that make you feel, Steven?' she asked. 'It makes me feel like a bit of a cripple still.'

He felt himself frown. 'It makes me angry, Andrea, that's how it makes me feel. For the guy who called you did so knowing what it could do to you. That's one of the most evil things I've ever come across. He won't be doing it again. Not if I can help it.'

'Nor if I can. I'll try to make myself remember from now on; God does not use the phone.'

40

Walking back into his office in the Fettes headquarters building as a serving officer should have been one of the most satisfying moments of Bob Skinner's life, let alone his career. He had been faced with a threat and he had crushed it; normally he would have taken a moment to savour his triumph, but he had no moments to spare.

Instead he went straight to his desk and switched on his computer; he fidgeted impatiently in his seat as it booted up, but eventually he was able to log on using his private password . . . *Michael*. He opened the file on which he had stored a number of highly sensitive direct-line telephone numbers. When he had found the one for which he was looking, he picked up one of his telephones, a black, old-fashioned handset, and keyed it in.

A flat emotionless voice answered. 'Yes?'

'Adam, it's Bob.'

'Hello, mate, how the fook are you?' The man's tone had changed in an instant. 'I'd heard you were ill. Not that I believed it, mind.'

'I've never been better. Things get exaggerated along the way.'

'Must have been, or you wouldn't be calling me on this line. What can I do for you?'

'A small favour.' He paused. Major Adam Arrow was one of his most trusted friends, although the story of their relationship would never be written down. Arrow was a serving army officer, but he worked in the sector of the national security machine that the public do not see. He had served undercover in many trouble spots, and had seen and done things that would have turned a weaker man into a lifelong insomniac, yet he still slept well, every night, and had risen in the Ministry of Defence to a position so sensitive that he was responsible only to the Secretary of State himself, and in extreme circumstances, when things had to be politically deniable, not even to him.

'Remember,' Skinner continued, 'that time you looked into my father's MoD file?'

'Of course.'

'Well, there's another one I'd like you to look at, one that you'll find isn't nearly as distinguished as my dad's. He's my family secret, my brother.'

'Michael,' said Arrow, quietly.

As it had been with Alex, Bob's surprise was pure reflex. 'How did you know about him?'

A soft laugh came down the secure line. 'Are you forgetting who you're talking to, mate? Come to that, are you forgetting who you are? The first time you ever got involved with the security services, you were subjected to top level vetting. There's nothing about you that isn't known and on file; at my level I have instant access to all of it. This line you called me on has a clever little device, at my end at least; it's linked through my computer, and whenever there's an incoming call it identifies the person on the other end through the number and pops his file up on screen. I'm looking at it right now.'

'Is it up-to-date, though?'

'Pretty much. I know what you were doing in the States a couple of months back. I know that your brother was found dead at the weekend, and looking at the most recent entry, I can guess why you sound in a bit of a rush right now. Is that current enough for you?'

'It's so current that it's worrying.'

'You're top rated, mate.'

Skinner snorted, 'Uhh? Am I a threat then?'

'No. You're important, and you know things ordinary people don't. You're a national fookin' treasure, Robert. So we have to know everything about you.'

'Fuck. Don't tell me any more. Will you look into Michael's Ministry file for me?'

'Sure, not a problem. What do you want to know?'

'I want to know the truth about what happened in Honduras; the incident that led to him getting kicked out.'

'I'll see what it says. How soon?'

194

'The usual. Soon as you can.'

'When can I get back to you on this line?'

'I don't know. I'm off to the States; since you're that clued up, you'll understand why. I'd like you to courier a report to Neil McIlhenney in my Special Branch office, marked for my eyes only, on return. I don't want this going through my assistant. He's too new. I don't know him yet.'

'Okay,' said Arrow. 'Good luck in Buffalo.'

'Thanks, Adam.' Skinner gave a small shudder as he hung up the phone. He operated on the fringes of, and on occasion deeper inside, the secret society, but even he could still be surprised by the length of its arm. He checked his watch and stood up; he thought about stepping along the corridor to say hello to the chief, and to Jack McGurk, his new executive assistant, but that would have cost him time he did not have.

He was glad that the Special Branch outer office was empty when he stepped through the door. Normally he would have been happy to spend time with a bright young copper like Alice Cowan, but at that moment in his life, all he wanted to do was to pick up his bag and papers from Neil McIlhenney and catch his plane.

The big inspector was waiting for him in his office. There was a small suitcase, cabin-sized, standing beside his desk.

'Thanks, pal,' said Bob quietly. 'This is above and beyond the call of duty.'

'But not friendship. Don't sit down; you're on the five-fifteen shuttle connecting to the seven forty-five flight to New York. That gets you in about eleven, US time. You have an airport hotel reservation then an early morning flight to Buffalo. You'll be there for half-nine. The tickets are ready for collection at the airport.' He picked up the case, and an envelope from his desk. 'Come on, we're obscenely tight for time, so let's shift. You can tell me on the way what this is about.'

McIlhenney led the way out of his office and down the stairs to the car park behind the Fettes headquarters building. He drove quickly out on to Carrington Drive; a few turns later they were on Queensferry Road, heading for the Barnton Roundabout at substantially more than the permitted speed limit. 'Right,' he said, as they hit a stretch of straight road.

His face became more and more solemn, and more and more pale, as Skinner told him the story. He was a detective too; he knew the conclusion to which the bare facts pointed.

'Oh, man,' he whispered, as his friend finished. 'Oh, man. The dead man, Ron Neidholm, have you met him?'

'No. Until that little bitch Babs Walker rubbed my nose in his picture I'd never heard of him. I'm told I should have, but gridiron football's not my game. Does he mean anything to you?'

'Yes, he does. I follow it a bit on television. He's not Joe Montana, John Ellway or Dan Marino, but he's pretty close. He's outlasted all of them too.'

'Until now,' Skinner grunted.

'Mmm.' He paused. 'Our Spencer's a great American football fan; Neidholm's one of his favourites.'

'God knows how he's going to take it then, when he finds out that Auntie Sarah's topped his hero.'

'Bob, for fuck's sake,' McIlhenney shouted. 'You cannot afford even to think like that, far less say it out loud.'

Skinner flushed at the rebuke, and chewed his lip. 'I know, pal. I'm sorry. But . . . It's just that I've had a few hours to think about this now, and I'm going to have a few more until I shuffle into fucking Buffalo. And from what Oakdale told me, it looks pretty bleak.'

'Maybe it does, but plant this thought in your head and do not let it waver. No way could Sarah kill anybody. She is not capable of it.'

The big man's eyes dropped. 'I'll try, Neil, and it's nice of you to say that. But you and I both know, from professional and personal experience, that that isn't true. There are always circumstances, my friend, in which we can do things we never contemplated. You know that as well as I do.'

'Not Sarah,' McIlhenney insisted. 'I know you two have been alienated lately, but you're not going to tell me you doubt her in this?'

Bob shook his head. 'No, I'm not; and I won't, I promise you. I'm sorry I even expressed the thought. But man, this on top of everything else. We've all got our breaking point; maybe I'm getting close to mine.'

Neil laughed. 'Aye, sure. That'll come when they tighten the screws on your box, man. Even then you'll probably kick it open. You will get over there and you will get this sorted, or you'll fire up the local boys to sort it themselves.'

'You have faith in me, don't you?'

'We all do. And it's justified. Look at today, look at Councillor Maley, who was last seen bustling out of Fettes with her spiky tail between her legs. Sarah did not do this, and you'll get her clear.'

'And if I do? What then?'

'What do you mean?'

'I mean there are other questions.'

'Only if you choose to ask them.'

They drove on in silence, until McIlhenney sped round the approach road to the airport. 'Going back to Maley,' he said at last. 'I've got something on her.'

'Indeed? Will it keep till I get back?'

'Probably. He's in Shotts Prison. I just need to check out a few things more.'

'Go and see big Lenny, if you need to,' said Skinner. 'Tell him I sent you, and that I'd trust you with his life. He'll get the humour in that.'

The inspector nodded, as he drew to a halt on a double yellow line in front of the airport. Two uniformed traffic officers approached as they stepped out of the car. McIlhenney flashed his warrant card and frowned at them; they backed off.

Skinner took his flight bag from the back seat, and his passport from his friend's hand. 'Thanks, man,' he said sincerely, 'for everything you've done. But there's one more thing.'

'Name it.'

'Alex. I'd hoped to see her to tell her about this, but I just haven't had the time. It's a hell of a job, telling her that her stepmother's in the slammer for murder; there's only you and Andy that I'd ask to do it, and I'd rather it was done face-to-face. You'll find her at her office; she thinks she's waiting for me.'

'I'll do that.'

'And tell her I love her.'

McIlhenney grinned. 'She knows that, man.'

'Aye, but tell her anyway.'

41

'How did we do with Sheringham?' Maggie Rose asked briskly. Steele and Regan faced her across the desk in her small office.

'He either hides the incriminating evidence in mysterious ways, ma'am,' the inspector replied, 'or there ain't any. We went in there with our search warrant at seven o'clock, and we searched every inch of it, but we found nothing explosive or inflammatory apart from a can of hair-spray.'

'I thought he lived alone.'

'He does,' Steele replied, 'but us guys, these days, we're full of surprises.'

'The only hair-spray in our house is mine, but I'll take your word for it. Did you put a sniffer dog in?' She caught his frown. 'Sorry, I should have taken that for granted. It didn't react to anything, then?'

'There was a blown condom under the bed, but that was all that excited it.'

'She must have been in heat,' Regan muttered. Rose glared at him.

'There was nothing at all, absolutely nothing?'

'Well,' said Steele, 'there was an extra remote. The boy's a gadget freak. He's got a snazzy hi-fi, a big telly, DVD player, video, and all of them work off remotes. But there was an extra one.'

'Is that significant?'

'Long shot, but it could be. The technical boys say that it might be possible to trigger an incendiary with a telly remote, if you set it up right. But we'd need to have the detonator to know that, and it was pretty much melted in the fire.'

'Yes, damn it, so it was.' She looked at the two men. 'What you're telling me, then, is that we don't have any grounds for continuing to detain him?'

'Apart from being a little shite, no, we don't,' the inspector admitted. 'The phone call isn't enough, not nearly. Even last night, once he'd had a chance to think about it, he was claiming that someone could have taken his phone from his pocket, used it, then put it back. It was made at seven-thirty; there was a staff drinks party in the Candela and Finch offices last Friday evening, part of the bi-centenary celebrations.'

'So he could be telling the truth?'

'Yes, and if he is that gives us a list of about a hundred and fifty guys to work through. If he isn't, it makes no bloody difference; the phone call alone isn't enough.'

'He goes, then. I'll phone his solicitor; I'd better start making soothing noises as well. George, go down to the cells and get him.'

The sergeant nodded, and left the room.

'There's one thing worries me about turning him loose, Maggie,' said Steele as the door closed.

'I know. He's still the main suspect. Suppose he tries to scare Andrea again?'

'He needs the fear of Himself put in him then, just in case.'

'No, he needs me to advise him and his lawyer, politely, about the need to make no contact with Miss Strachan, while this enquiry is unresolved, and she remains a potential witness. Sheringham's well advised, Stevie. However personal you might find this thing becoming, he'll be more afraid of the Law Society than he is of you.' She smiled at him.

'But keep an eye on her, informally,' she offered, 'if you want. Someone made that call, and if it wasn't our man downstairs, he's still around, he knows about Andrea, and we don't know about him.'

Steele nodded. 'I agree. I'll keep her safe, don't worry.' He looked at Rose. 'I like her; that's all I'm saying, but there's something about her, Maggie. With her medication stable and her confidence back, she really is a completely different personality. She's attractive, and she's got a dry sense of humour about her that takes you by surprise.'

'But she's wounded, Steve. Don't forget that.'

'I know she is. She knows what's happened to her, and even though she's fine under treatment, she hasn't forgotten it. She can't hide her pain completely . . . any more than you can.'

Maggie started; she looked sharply at him, and for a moment he thought that he had said something that would destroy their easy relationship, until she turned her face away and looked out of the window.

'That obvious, huh?' she murmured.

'It is to me.'

'Is the whole force talking about me, then?' she asked. 'About me and my husband?'

'Not the whole force; only those who don't know any better, although that's about ninety per cent. Those who know you both, reckon that if you've got problems, you're strong enough to sort them out in time. While you're doing that, they don't change the people you are.'

She turned back to face him, leaning back against the edge of her desk. 'We don't have problems, Stevie,' she whispered. 'I do. Mario's sleeping with your ex-girlfriend . . . his own cousin . . . and I don't mind. I wish I did, but I don't. That's all part of it, you see. I don't and I can't.'

'Maggie, sorry,' he exclaimed. 'I shouldn't have said anything. I wasn't prying, honest.'

'I know you weren't. Somebody had to say something, eventually; I'd rather it was you than Dan Pringle, or George, or some other dipstick. You may have a reputation among women as a dangerous guy, Stevie, but as far as I'm concerned you're a nice bloke. You listen, and you care. So listen to this. The thing is, I'm glad that Paula and Mario are indulging themselves with each other. Because it takes a big weight off of me! Understand?'

He put his hands on her shoulders; to her inward surprise, she did not flinch, not pull away. 'I think so,' he replied. 'Now you understand this, Detective Superintendent Rose. I don't know what's happened to fuck up your head, and instinct tells me that I do not want to know, but whatever it is, however awful, it is not big enough to overcome your spirit. You are a very attractive woman, Maggie, but you're more than that. You're the strongest woman I've ever met, and I've admired you through all the time we've worked together. You may have given in to self-doubt, and persuaded yourself that you can never overcome this problem, and have let it dictate how you live your life. If you have, you are wrong. I don't believe there is anything that you can't face down, with what's in here . . .' he put a finger against her forehead '. . . and in here.' He tapped the same finger against her chest, between her breasts.

He took her hand in his, squeezed it and held it. 'Sorry to be a little informal, ma'am,' he murmured. 'But you're worth it.'

She looked solemnly up at him, and realised that for the first time in as long as she could remember, she felt no hint of revulsion at the touch of a man. She lifted his hand, in turn, to her face, and held it gently against her cheek for a few seconds, then let it go.

'Forgiven, inspector,' she murmured, full of confusion, but smiling. 'And thanks for caring. What if you're wrong, though?'

He raised an eyebrow. 'You're not going to tell me, are you, that you don't have the courage even to try?'

42

It had been years since Neil McIlhenney had seen Lenny Plenderleith. Bob Skinner had told him that the man had changed during the years of his imprisonment, and for the better, in many ways, but one thing remained. He was still as big as ever.

The giant laughed softly. 'So I can trust you with my life, can I,' he said. 'He hasn't lost his touch, has he. So you're his man, are you? What's happened that he can't come to see me himself? He always has before.'

McIlhenney was struck by Big Lenny's quiet confidence. He had changed indeed from his days as principal enforcer to the late and almost unlamented Tony Manson. The gang leader had been mourned only by his protégé, a fact which had proved unfortunate to his killers.

Skinner said, after Lenny's imprisonment for the murder, that the greatest mistake a man could make was to underestimate him. Some of those who had were no longer around to regret it.

'He's got problems; family things. He's in America at the moment, trying to sort them out.'

'He's got one in Scotland that I know about; tough luck about his brother winding up in that lady's basement. Do they know what it was yet? Did somebody do him?'

'He died of a heart attack . . . while he was salmon fishing maybe.'

Lenny Plenderleith leaned across the Shotts Prison visiting room table; they were alone, at McIlhenney's insistence. 'You and I will get on better, Mr McIlhenney, if you don't spin me any more fairytales. Nobody goes salmon fishing when a river's in full spate, and bursting its banks, especially not, as the *Scotsman* informed me, an alcoholic who's lived the last thirty years of his life in a Jesuit hostel. Maybe he did die of a heart attack, but how did he wind up in the Tay?'

'We don't know,' the inspector admitted. 'But he died of natural causes, so finding out is not at the top of Tayside CID's things-to-do list.'

'They'd better move it up then, or is Bob not coming back from the States?'

'He'll be back, all right, but I'm not sure when.'

Lenny frowned. 'So what's happened in America that's more important than his brother?'

'It's a family matter, that's all; it's got nothing to do with this visit, I promise you.'

'I'm curious, though. I read about his in-laws being killed a few months back; I even had a look at the *New York Times* website. The old man rated quite an obituary; he was a friend of the Kennedys and the Clintons, so it said.'

'You certainly keep yourself informed,' McIlhenney observed.

'I have to do something in here; I've done my Open University degree. I did ask if I could get day release from here to do a doctorate at Napier, but they wouldn't wear it. Bob said that after I'd done ten years I should ask again, and he might be able to help. In the meantime, I'm writing; I've done the obligatory reformed lifer's autobiography, a book about the career of Tony Manson, drug lord with a social conscience, etc., and another about his murder and what happened after it. I wanted to do one about Bob Skinner, too, but he won't play.'

'So what'll you do instead of that? Fiction?'

'Eventually maybe, but not yet; next I plan to do an academic study of the homicidal mind. It'll go on to look at people like West, Dahmer, Shipman, Sutcliffe and so on, and it'll try to give voice to their thoughts as they did what they did.'

'What about your own?'

Plenderleith looked sternly at his visitor. 'Please, spare me that. Although I have killed people, I don't have a homicidal mind in that sense. I am a sociopath; that's allowed me to do what I've done in the past. But I am also a clever sociopath; I know that I cannot continue to do those things and retain the possibility of ever breathing free air, and thanks to my inheritance from Tony I won't be under any pressure to do them when I'm released. No one has a problem being left alone with me; I'm probably the safest man in this place.' He grinned at McIlhenney.

'I do virtually all my research on the internet. When I'm logged on I read a selection of world newspapers, to keep up with current affairs. There's some interesting stuff out there.' Plenderleith paused and glanced across at the policeman. 'I even read about this actress,' he said, 'a year or so back, who chucked it all to marry some dumb copper in Edinburgh ... lucky bastard that he is.'

'Sure,' said the inspector, with sudden bitterness. 'So lucky that his first wife died in her prime and left him with two kids. But you know about widowhood, don't you, Lenny? You killed your wife.'

The giant drew a breath; for a while, Neil thought that the interview was at an end. But then he exhaled and glanced across to the window. 'Wrong subject for us, then,' he murmured. 'I'm sorry; I didn't know that.'

'You must have missed the *Scotsman* that day. My Olive had a fine obituary; Bob Skinner wrote it.'

'We all owe Bob, then,' said Lenny, 'me as much as anyone. He might be the guy who got me banged up in here, but he was only doing his job . . .' he laughed '. . . not that I made it easy for him. He wasn't just doing his job, though, when he put in a word to get me a standard lifer's tariff, when any other copper . . . you included . . . would have left me here to rot, doing a minimum thirty years. So how can I help him?'

McIlhenney leaned forward, elbows on the table. 'Apart from his family things, the boss has had another problem lately. There's this councillor, Agnes Maley; she's had it in for him for years. Just lately, she's really been getting above herself. It's time she was brought under control.'

Lenny shook his huge head, smiling. 'Black Agnes, eh.'

'You know her?'

'Oh yes, I know her. If I'd read that she had been fished out of a river the other day, rather than Bob's brother, it would have surprised me a lot less. But you'll need to be nifty on your feet to get anything on her.'

'Maybe we have been. I've been looking into her past, and at some of the people she's been associated with. About twelve years back, there was a nasty murder in Edinburgh. It involved a rent boy, called Paul Deary . . . yes, I know, an appropriate name. He was found, naked, in a

204

skip just along from the Elsie Inglis. Not just a murder; the way he was killed told us that the lad had been made an example of. His throat was cut and his balls were stuffed in his mouth.' The inspector gave an involuntary shudder.

'We leaned on a lot of people, and eventually we found out that he had worked in a male brothel right in the middle of the Old Town, under the control of a pimp called Jason Fargo. We raided the place mob-handed and lifted everyone; I was in on it myself. We found the usual selection of clients, but we let them go. One of them was a journalist, so we were fairly certain it would be covered up. Instead we concentrated on the boys who were working there; the Big Man led the investigation himself. He showed them all photographs of Deary, at the scene and in the mortuary. He asked them to imagine the boy's last moments. He asked them to consider how safe they would all be if the guy who did it wasn't caught. And then he locked them up and waited.

'It only took one night in the cells. Two of them started talking and eventually they all did. They told us that Jason Fargo had come in the night Paul was killed and taken him away. He'd pulled him out of there, screaming, by the hair. They told us about another kid who'd disappeared as well, about six months earlier. Both boys had been freelancing; they'd been working the pubs in Leith and keeping all their money. In Fargo's place, they got a third of what they earned, if they were lucky. They were slaves.

'We turned Jason's flat over, looking for forensic traces, but there was nothing; we were in trouble then, because we needed more for the Crown Office to proceed with a murder charge. Then one of the boys told us that he'd been with Jason once, and he'd stopped at a lock-up garage out off Causewayside. He'd gone in, come out with a stereo, locked it again and driven off. The lad had assumed, correctly, that it was used to store knock-off, and had thought no more about it.

'He took us there; we opened it under a warrant, and went in. Bingo; the kid's blood was up the walls, and his clothes were in a pile in the corner. There was stolen gear all over the place and Jason's prints were all over it. Fargo admitted it; it surprised us at the time, but he just folded. He even took us to the spot in the Queen's Park where he'd buried the first lad . . . poor kid, I can't even remember his name. He told us what we had guessed, that he had killed Paul like that to scare all the others off private enterprise.

'The Crown Office threw every possible charge at him; murder, forcing under-age boys into prostitution, keeping a disorderly house, the lot. The judge he drew was a well-known practising Catholic; he gave him a minimum twenty-five years.'

He stopped; Lenny Plenderleith applauded, silently. 'Well told, inspector. You had me right on the edge of my seat there. As a matter of fact, I remember the case very well. Tony was very pleased when Mr Fargo got stuffed. He did not approve of the wee boy business. Yes, I'll grant you, he was into saunas himself, but in Edinburgh, properly run, they can be positively therapeutic. Your friend McGuire should agree with that; Tony's estate, which I administer, sold a number of them to his very attractive cousin . . . kissing cousin, from what I hear . . . Ms Viareggio, although some of the purchase price was paid by a cheque signed by Mr McGuire's mother.'

The giant grinned as he watched McIlhenney fail to mask his surprise. 'There's a lot big Mario doesn't tell you, eh Neil,' he said. 'On the other hand, there's hardly anything that people don't tell me; nothing at all when I want to know. But I'm sorry. Go on with your tale.'

The inspector pulled himself together. Lenny had been right; the news about Christina McGuire helping to fund Paula's sauna purchase had come as a complete surprise. 'Right, and this is where Maley comes in. Fargo's place was in her council ward at the time, and she's like you. She knows everything that happens on her patch. We didn't pursue that angle at the time; it would have been pointless anyway. But the other day, I went round a few people who were involved in that case. One or two of the lads involved have made decent lives for themselves. I got a tip from one, who can remain nameless. He told me that he believed that Jason Fargo was only able to operate for as long as he did because he was paying backhanders to Agnes Maley.'

'Mmm.' Plenderleith murmured, almost impatiently. 'So?'

'So, Jason Fargo's in this very nick, Lenny; I would like to know from him if that is true. If it is, I'll need it in writing, signed. There'll be no comeback on him, I promise. I'll feed the information, personally, to contacts I have within the Labour Party. It'll be enough to put a stop to Maley's political career.'

A rumbling sound seemed to emanate from deep in the man's great chest. 'Ahh, Fate can be a bugger, eh. I'd have done that for Bob. Jason would not have refused me; I may be a smart sociopath with his future mapped out, but as far as the boys in here are concerned, I am still the man to whom you like to say "yes". But sadly, you're about a month too late.' He sighed.

'Mr Fargo is indeed in Shotts nick; the news is not generally known at this moment, in case some of the younger inmates get alarmed, but he's in the hospital wing, in isolation. The man has full-blown AIDS, inspector, and it has attacked him here.' He tapped the side of his head. 'He's fucking brain dead, Neil. The most I'd get out of him would be a drool.'

'Shit!' McIlhenney hissed; then he saw that Lenny was looking at him, in a strangely direct way. There was more to come.

'Going back to the criminal mind . . . a real criminal mind, I mean, not Mr Fargo's which was never up to much in the first place, even before it went into melt-down . . . the worst thing you guys can ever do is to underrate it. What I am going to tell you now will be of absolutely no use to you, or Bob, because I learned it at the time from Tony Manson, who's even deader than Fargo. So it's hearsay. Sure, I could write it down for you, but it could never be proved. If you tried to feed it to your sources, first they wouldn't believe it, and second they'd look at the signature: Lenny Plenderleith, mass murderer, casual observer of the Edinburgh scene at the time, and unlikely friend of Agnes Maley's enemy, DCC Bob Skinner. We'd all probably wind up in the civil courts, or worse.'

McIlhenney sighed. 'You're right, of course. So what is it that we can't use?'

'Just this; and remember that it came from Tony Manson, who knew everything and everyone on the criminal scene in Edinburgh. As the tabloids had to say, he was the Godfather of his time. The fact is that Jason Fargo did not pay, as you put it, backhanders, to Maley. He ran the place, paid the kids their pittance, took his own wages, and gave her what was left. Black Agnes was the boss, Neil. The set-up was his idea, and the flat was in Fargo's name, but it was bought with cash which she supplied.'

'Why didn't he shop her then?'

'Work it out; man. He knew he wouldn't have lived to stand trial. Think back to those days, and to the way it was in Edinburgh. There were three teams; there was ours, there was Jackie Charles and his lot, and there was a third one, not as big as us, but a grouping nonetheless. You knew about Jackie and us, but you could never get a handle on that third one. You were never even sure if it was organised, or whether it was just a load of villains picking the scraps off our table. Well it was, and Black Agnes was at its heart. Her boys did the stuff we wouldn't; protection, the wee boy business, smuggling cigarettes and all that.

'After Fargo got done, she realised that she was pushing her luck, so she packed everything up and concentrated on being a councillor. But when she was in business, nobody, not you, not even Bob Skinner himself, ever had a sniff of her, because her tracks were covered too well, and because all you could see was what a fucking pain she was as a councillor. But she was much more than that, Neil.

'Jason Fargo didn't kill those boys off his own bat, man. He did it on Agnes's orders.'

43

'You're quite sure I'm not going to hear from him?' Andrea asked. They had found a corner table in the bustling Brown's, only a few yards along from 121 George Street, and were waiting for the lunch they had ordered to be brought to them.

'As sure as I can be,' Stevie answered. 'Maggie . . . Superintendent Rose, spoke to him and his solicitor and advised him that the investigation's still open, that you're a witness and that he's still a suspect. He'd be spectacularly stupid to come anywhere near you after having his card marked as clearly as that, and I don't think he is.'

'Do you still think it was him who phoned me?'

'To be honest, Andrea, I'm not sure any more; his story now is that someone else must have used his phone to make that call.'

She frowned for a second. 'But if it wasn't him, that means . . .'

He nodded. 'I know what it means, but I really don't think you need to worry. It's our thinking that you were lured along to that exhibition as a fall . . .' he paused, and smiled '. . . girl. That hasn't worked. Fine. So what possible reason could the man have to try it on again?'

She looked at the table as she pondered what he had said. 'Yes. I see the logic in that. So you're telling me to forget it altogether, keep taking the tablets and get on with my life?'

'Exactly. As a bit of added security, I'll give you my phone numbers. If we're wrong and it does happen again, you should call me right away.'

'Okay.' She looked at him, coyly. 'Does that mean that there'll be no more surprise invitations to lunch?'

He grinned back at her. 'Not necessarily. I have got a life outside CID, you know. I'd like to be your friend, Andrea, instead of your investigating officer. I'd like to get to know you, in an ordinary situation.'

Her blue eyes flashed at him. 'What, both of me, you mean?'

'I prefer this model, but I'm game for anything.'

'I'll bet you are. You might find getting to know me a frustrating experience. I'm not really one of your modern girls. I'm a virgin, you know.' She frowned, severely.

'What?' he shot back. 'Both of you?'

A short, snorting laugh exploded from her. 'I may have two personalities, but that's as far as it goes. Sorry to sound so priggish; what I meant was that I've never had a proper relationship with a man before.'

'You mean an improper one?'

'God, I can't say a thing to you.' She put her hand to her mouth and gasped. 'Did you hear that? I just took His name in vain. Steven, you're having a bad influence on me already.'

'Sounds promising.'

'I'm promising nothing.'

'And I'm not asking for anything, other than to be your friend.'

'Okay, take me to the cinema, then.'

'What do you want to see?'

'*Lord of the Rings.*'

'Deal. When?'

'Tomorrow. Two dates in one day might be rushing things a bit.'

'I'll pick you up at seven.' He took a card from his pocket and handed it to her. 'There; Stevie Steele in your hands. That's every phone number I've got, office and private. The home ones are ex-directory, so don't leave it lying about.'

'I'll keep it in my Bible,' she said, casually, 'just to be safe.' He had to look closely at her, to be sure she was joking.

A sound at their side caught his attention; a waiter stood ready, with their lunch.

'Steven,' Andrea began as he picked up his cutlery. 'About the fire. Since it wasn't a convenient crazy like me, and since you're discounting the man who phoned the newspapers, have you any idea who burned the silly picture?'

'Not a clue.'

'So what will you do next?'

'We'll probably look at all the people who could have taken the lad's mobile and used it to make the call to you.'

'How many?'

'To be exact, one hundred and forty-two. A hundred and nineteen if we leave the partners out of it.'

'How long will that take?'

'That depends on a few things; on how many of them gave us statements on Saturday, on how many we have to re-interview, on how many officers we use to do it.'

'So I might be stood up tomorrow night?'

'Not a chance. Even detective inspectors get time off. Besides, there's another factor I didn't mention; that's how lucky we get. You never know, the first person we interview might confess.'

'Did you think you were lucky when you saw me on those tapes? That is, not me, her. Oh, you know what I mean.'

'I know, and did we ever think we'd got lucky! Especially when we found out who she was and what she'd done.'

'Are you sorry you weren't?'

He laid down his fork, reached across and took her hand. 'Who says I wasn't?'

A blush came to her cheeks. 'I know I was,' she whispered. 'The others would just have locked me up, wouldn't they? It was you who stood up for me, wasn't it?'

'Not alone. Maggie did too.'

'Then thank her for me.'

She started to explore her lentil salad, and Steele turned his attention to his tagliatelle de la casa. 'Can I ask you something else?' she exclaimed, when she was near the end.

'Could I stop you?' he countered.

'Why are you sure that burning the picture was a religious protest?'

'It's the only possible motive, Andrea. Can you suggest another?'

'No, I can't, but . . .' She paused, as if she had thought better of whatever it was she had been about to say.

'But what? Go on.'

'Och, it just seems to me that it was awful well planned, that's all. Someone who does something like that is a fanatic, right?'

'Right.'

'Do fanatics plan things that well? When I, she, no, I, did what I did, there was no planning involved at all. I made the device then wandered like a sore thumb into their service, and tried to plant it in what was supposed to be an unobtrusive manner. It was a nonsense from the start. I was simply driven by my voice telling me to do it. What happened in the Academy, on the other hand, was planned like clockwork and executed perfectly. If the person who did it is a schizophrenic like me, it would have been a shambles. You ask Adam Broadley if you don't believe me.'

'I might, but not because I don't believe you. Go on.'

'This was done by a clear-thinking methodical person with technical knowledge. That doesn't fit the fanatic theory, as I understand it. Fanatics are the sort of people who walk into places and blow themselves up. This person planted the device in secret, triggered it and got away scot free. Not only that, he set me up as, as you put it, a fall girl.

'So while you're interviewing all these people, why don't you ask yourselves at the same time, why else this might have been done?'

44

'Stop here,' Bob Skinner told the taxi-driver as he approached the drive that led up to the Grace mansion. He paid him in crisp new US currency, fresh from an ATM in John F Kennedy Airport, and stepped out into the street. It was still short of nine a.m., but the morning was hot nonetheless. His Scottish summer clothes felt suddenly very heavy. He stood at the foot of the path, out of sight of the house, and took a deep breath.

He had called his daughter from London, and had found her as shocked and disbelieving as he had known she would be. He had promised to keep her in touch with developments, and then he had tried his level best to block the nightmare from his mind.

All the way across the Atlantic he had fought against the urge to think of this moment, to anticipate it, to plan for it. He had played CDs on his Walkman all through the flight, and on the shuttle to Buffalo; Clapton and King, a Stones compilation, Counting Crows, a live Van Morrison double set, all bought at Heathrow and chosen because it was heavy stuff that would force him to listen. He had watched television all the way through a short, sleepless night in his hotel room, finding a channel that seemed to be devoted entirely to showing repeats of *The Sopranos*, wondering to himself how long the fictional Big Tony would have lasted in Edinburgh, as opposed to Lenny Plenderleith's late boss.

The moment had come, though; he braced himself and thought positively, of Mark, Jazz and Seonaid, and how pleased he would be to see them. He picked up his bag from the sidewalk, turned the corner and walked up the path. He thought the door might open as he approached the house, but no one could have been looking out. The garage door was open; only the Jaguar lay inside. He stepped up to the entrance and rang the bell.

He had assumed that it would be Trish who would answer. When the heavy door opened and he saw Sarah standing there, he was struck dumb . . . as was she. They stood staring at each other, neither moving, neither seeming to know what to say.

And then from the hall, there came a yell of 'Dad!' and James Andrew charged out past his mother, throwing himself up to be caught and hugged to his father's chest. Bob felt a sharp sensation as the child bumped his pacemaker, but he ignored it in the sheer relief of seeing him again.

Leaving his flight bag abandoned on the step, he carried him into the house. 'Hello, kid,' he whispered into his ear. 'How much mayhem have you been causing while I've been away then?'

Eventually he set his son back on his feet. 'Go and play,' he told him. 'I'll see you in a minute. I need to talk to your mum.'

Jazz ran off, towards the kitchen and, he guessed, to the yard. He turned back to face Sarah. She had recovered her composure; he fought for his. 'What are you doing here?' she asked, in a quiet, matter-of-fact voice.

'What the hell do you think I'm doing, honey?'

'So Clyde called you; I told him not to, yet he did.'

'Too bloody right he did,' Bob exclaimed, his voice starting to rise, before he calmed it. 'There are three kids here, and their mother was in jail. How could you expect him not to?' He walked into the kitchen. The trip was catching up with him fast; he needed coffee, badly, but fortunately there was a jug on the filter. He poured himself a mug, went to the fridge and added barely enough milk to turn it brown from black.

He turned back towards her. 'I guess your name hasn't been linked to the investigation yet,' he said. 'No media outside.'

'No,' she said. 'Sheriff Dekker and the DA made sure that I was kept completely incommunicado. They took me away from Ron's house very quickly and I was held in the DA's office, not at the police building. The press assumed I was there, so they camped outside. They were only told that a suspect was in custody; no name, no gender even.'

'A remarkable show of discretion in the States.'

She nodded. 'Yes, I admit that's puzzled me too.'

214

'I can guess the reason,' he grunted, darkly. 'When did they give you bail?'

'A judge granted it last night, in chambers; she set a million-dollar surety, but John Vranic assured her there was more than enough in the estate. It's temporary, though; if I'm indicted and arraigned, it'll be considered again then.'

'If?'

She winced and looked away. 'No,' she whispered. 'When. John told me to expect to be in open court this afternoon. Then the whole media thing will explode.'

'We'll see about that.'

'Bob, I'm lucky it hasn't happened before this.' She walked over to him. 'You look beat; do you want me to make you something to eat?'

'Wouldn't do any harm. Eggs, bacon, that sort of stuff; my cholesterol's fine, remember. So, you'll be glad to hear, is everything else.'

'You slew your dragon, then.'

'Let's just say she's wounded; slaying's a bad topic around here. I'm back in post, and that's the main thing.'

'I'm glad for you,' she said quietly as she opened the fridge, and took out a box of eggs and a pack of bacon.

'Thanks.' He turned his head and looked out of the window at James Andrew as he attacked a climbing frame that had not been there when he left. 'I'm sorry, Sarah. I got obsessed; I admit it, I went off at half cock and let it come between us. Now all this shit's come down on you, and I feel it's my fault. It's been my week for guilt and no mistake.'

She lit a gas ring, under a big frying pan. 'Bob . . .' she began, a catch in her voice. 'I have to . . .'

He put up a hand. 'Don't do that just yet, love, please. Just answer me something. When you found the guy, was the door of his house lying open?'

'No.'

'In that case, since he was dead, who opened it for you?'

'Nobody,' she whispered. 'I had a key.'

He felt his head swim, and for a moment thought that he might be having another attack, in spite of his pacemaker. But the thump of his heart in his chest told him that he was not. 'Okay,' he said, in a flat, emotionless voice that was a masterpiece of self-control. 'Just so as I know when I see the police.'

'You're seeing the police?'

'This very morning. I phoned Brad Dekker on my way here from the airport and told him to be ready for me, with Eddie Brady, at ten o'clock.'

'Bob, you can't get involved in this,' she exclaimed.

He smiled at her, for the first time since she had opened the door. 'Who can't?'

45

Angus d'Abo had known many an unexpected visit from the police, but he had never rated a detective chief superintendent before, so he was understandably rattled as he looked across the bar table at his visitor.

'How did ye ken to find me here?' he asked, nervously.

'You're a creature of habit, Mr d'Abo,' Rod Greatorix told him. 'Our local uniformed officers told me that you have your lunch here in the Cannon every day in life.' He looked at his plate. 'Do they do a decent bridie in here, by the way? I feel a bit peckish myself.'

'No' bad,' the man replied. 'The haggis is best though.'

'Why are you not having it then?'

'Ah couldna' have it every day.'

'You're a bloke who believes in a balanced diet, then?'

Angus d'Abo shrugged his shoulders. 'Ah like what ah like, ken. There's plenty tae eat up at the Lodge; ah hae the choice frae the kitchen at night. But it's a' salmon or game. The guests that come there dinna expect pie and chips, like.'

'Unless it's venison pie and game chips.'

'Aye, that's right.' He looked down at his plate; the baked beans were starting to congeal.

'Go on,' said Greatorix, 'get stuck in. I'm in no rush.'

He sipped his ginger ale and watched as the bald, nut-brown handyman bolted down his Forfar bridie. He knew from his file that d'Abo was fifty-two years old, and that his last conviction had been ten years earlier, but he noted that the man still looked fit enough to climb a drainpipe without difficulty. He waited, as d'Abo mopped up the last of his beans with the last of his chips. 'How long have you worked at Fir Park Lodge?' he asked, the moment he was finished.

217

'Three year; since Mr Williamson bought it. Ah've never been in ony bother, like,' he added, defensively.

'I'm not saying you have. Does your employer know all about you, though? Does he know you've been in prison?'

D'Abo blinked, nervously. 'He never asked,' he exclaimed. 'Has someone telt him? Are you goin' tae tell him?'

The detective shrugged his shoulders. 'If he's going to hire people without checking them out, it's not down to me to mark his card. Relax, Angus, this isn't about you.'

The handyman looked at him as if he required a lot more persuasion if he was going to believe him. 'I've asked about you, don't worry,' Greatorix continued. 'The local people vouched for you. They've got their ear to the ground; if you'd gone back to your old profession, they would know.'

'Well, what is it aboot?' D'Abo looked only a little less suspicious.

'We're making enquiries about a man whose body was found in Perth last Saturday.'

The man's defences went back up so quickly that Greatorix smiled. 'No, Angus, I'm not going to ask if you did it. This guy died of a heart attack, and fell into the river somewhere. All we're trying to find out is where he was. He wasn't reported missing, and he was only identified by chance. We think he might have been a guest at a big house along the riverbank.'

'Why no' ask Mr Williamson?'

'Because we're asking you. We don't know Mr Williamson. What's he like to work for, as a matter of interest?'

'He's a'right. He kens nothing aboot fishin' though, a lot less than most of the guests he has. Ah think he only bought the place because he fancied bein' a country squire.'

'Is there a Mrs Williamson?'

'Naw. There's folk think he's havin' it off wi' the hoosekeeper, but he's no.'

'What makes you so sure?'

D'Abo shot him a sudden lascivious grin.

'Ah, I see,' Greatorix chuckled. 'Tell me, is the Lodge busy?'

'It does a' right. It's fu' this week, but no' every week.'

'This man I'm looking for; he'd have been there about two weeks ago.'

D'Abo frowned. 'A fortnight since?' he muttered. 'Aye, we were quite fu' then. What would he look like, this man?'

'He'd have looked in his late fifties, grey, overweight, and poorly dressed.'

'Poorly dressed? He'll no have been at the Lodge, then. They're a' fuckin' bandboxes we get in there.'

Greatorix hesitated, and then took a decision. He reached into an inside pocket of his jacket and took out a photograph. It showed a man's head, viewed from above and in half profile. It was of Michael Skinner, and it had been taken in the mortuary, once he had been cleaned up. It was presentable, but in no way did it look as if he was merely asleep. He handed it to d'Abo. 'Are you sure?' he said. 'That was him.'

The handyman took the photograph and gulped, then gagged. For a second Greatorix thought that bridie, beans and chips were about to come flying his way, but the initial shock seemed to pass. The policeman studied d'Abo's face, as he studied the photograph.

'This man was never a guest at the Lodge; Ah'm sure o' that.' D'Abo frowned, and scratched his chin. 'And yet . . . Ah've got a feelin' Ah've seen him somewhere.' He picked up the remains of his shandy and took a drink, swilling it around his mouth before he swallowed, as if to wash away a bad taste. He looked at the photograph again, then across to the bar.

'Aye,' he exclaimed. 'That could have been him; Ah'm no certain, but it could have been. If it wis, Ah saw him the week before last, in here, yin lunchtime. He was wi' another bloke, aboot the same age as him.' His eyebrows went up, as if a light had been switched on in his head. 'Wednesday, it wis; Ah ken that because Ah had a bridie for ma lunch, like the day.'

'Did you know the other man?'

'Ah never seen him afore; never seen either o' them afore.' He tapped the photo. 'But this man here, he was awfy fond o' the drink. He wis only in here for less than an 'oor, but by the time he left he wis as fu' as a fiddler's bitch. The other bloke had tae help him oot the door.'

'Was Mr Williamson in here at the same time? Could he have known them?'

'Neither of them has ever been at the Lodge; Ah kin tell ye that. As for Mr Williamson, he couldna hae been here. He was at his place in Florida then; he wis awa' for three weeks, and Mae the hoosekeeper was runnin' the place. He only got back last Wednesday.'

46

'You believed him, did you?' asked Mario McGuire; then he nodded, to himself, rather than to McIlhenney. 'I suppose you must have, or you wouldn't have come bombing down to Galashiels to talk to me about it.'

He pulled open a drawer of his desk, took out a KitKat biscuit and tossed it across to his friend. 'Here, chew on that. You're looking unnaturally fit these days.'

'You, on the other hand,' said Neil cheerfully as he unwrapped the biscuit, broke off one finger and used it to stir his tea, 'are looking knackered. Are you not getting enough sleep?'

McGuire glowered at him. 'Just because you're my best pal, inspector, don't think you can push your luck.'

'Some would say that's what you're doing, Mario. But I won't be one of them. I've got to say something serious, though, as your best pal. You have to resolve your situation, and sooner rather than later. I know how things are with Mags, and I know she's given you the biggest pink ticket in history. But no one else in the force knows the real story, not even the Big Man. All they see is you living with your wife, and playing away games with Paula. The grapevine is talking of nothing else these days, and that's not good.'

'I might be inclined to say "fuck the grapevine",' Mario retorted.

'You might, but you can't, and you know why. It's not just you who's the subject of the station gossip; it's Maggie as well. It's one thing you being Jack the Lad; you're not the first copper in this situation. But you are the first one whose wife's a senior officer too. We all know there's talk of Mags leaving CID and going to chief super. What sort of command authority is she going to have among the uniforms if they're all whispering about her behind her back?'

His friend looked at him for a while, as if he was trying to form a reply. But when he spoke it was to ask a question. 'So what should I do, Neil?'

'You have to give one of them up, man. You either keep your relations with Paula business only, or you leave Maggie. Since you're giving up the wee boy, there's really no obstacle in the way of you doing that.'

McGuire's face twisted. 'I don't want to leave her!' he protested. 'She won't sleep with me, but there's more to us than that.'

'Then give up Paula.'

'And embrace the celibate life? Is that what you're saying?'

'I might say it, but I know you too well to see it happening,' he conceded. 'Listen, I care about you, and I care about Mags, but you have to sort this out.'

'Get it through your head, man. I don't want to.'

'No, you get it through yours; you have to. It's not about what you want; it's something you have to do for Maggie's sake, for her self-respect and for the good of her career.'

'I have to leave her for her self-respect?'

'Yes, and you have to tell everyone that she's chucked you out.'

'You don't ask much of a friend, do you?'

'I'll ask whatever I think it's going to take. Just talk to her, Mario, please. The pair of you have to realise that you are two bloody goldfish swimming about in a bowl with the whole bloody police force, or near as damn it, looking at you. And not just the force,' he added. 'Lenny dropped a big hint this morning that he's heard about it.'

'You're kidding!'

'No I ain't. Big Lenny's a remarkable man. He knows your mother's a silent partner in Paula's saunas, for a start.'

McGuire's jaw sagged. 'He does?'

'Yes, and it's more than I did, pal. Doesn't look too good, the head of Special Branch being taken by surprise by a lifer. They bought the things from Manson's estate, remember. Effectively that means from Lenny. Your mum didn't cover her tracks very well.'

'Obviously not. I wouldn't want it getting out either.'

'Don't worry. Lenny won't tell anyone. He regards information as currency, and he's not going to spend any without a purpose.'

'So he's got a hold over me?'

'Of a sort, but he won't use it. If he did, the boss would find out, and he wouldn't like it. For some reason, odd since he once tried to kill him, Lenny values big Bob's friendship more than anything else.'

'Mmm,' said McGuire. 'You have had an interesting morning. Especially the bit about Maley.'

'That's why I came down here. I wanted to talk to you about it. When you were in my job, did you ever take a look at her?'

'Of course I did. For much the same reason you are now, because the boss was pissed off at her. I couldn't help him though. I came up against blank walls everywhere I went. No one would tell me anything about her that I could use.' He smiled. 'The chief braced her once, mind you, in a meeting. He dropped a hint that he had a file on her.'

McIlhenney looked amazed. 'Proud Jimmy did?'

'Yup. It shut her up for a while too, until she realised that he was bluffing. In the light of what Lenny told you, she must also have realised that if he really had had a file on her, she'd have been up to her ears in it.'

'So, mate, what's your advice? Knowing what I know, what should I do next?'

Mario spun in his chair. 'That's a good one. All I can tell you is what I would do, and that is nothing. I don't think there's any chance of proving what Lenny told you. Unlike my dear mum, Maley must have covered her tracks completely, for we've never had a sniff of her being a real villain, from any of our intelligence sources.

'I think you have to watch and wait. The classic CID approach; watch everything she does from now on, and wait for her to do something that you can use to bring her down. You might not have too much time, though. If she gets this Holyrood seat she's after, we might all find that she's after us, with a vengeance.'

47

What did the barman say?' asked Andy Martin.

'Bar woman,' Greatorix replied. 'The guy behind the bar today wasn't on two weeks ago; he was sick and the licensee was away, so his . . . the licensee's . . . wife had to pull the pints as well as dish the grub. She remembered Michael Skinner, but only because he was pissed.'

'What about the man he was with?'

'The only thing she could say for certain was that he wasn't a regular, but she didn't think she'd ever seen him before. She was harassed that day, she said, but she struck me as the sort that finds everything too much trouble. Her description wasn't any better than d'Abo's, far as she could recall, probably because all her attention was on Mr Skinner getting himself skunked.'

'Did you show her the photograph?'

The head of CID smiled, with grim satisfaction. 'The licensee wasn't too happy with me afterwards, but I did. She wasn't a hundred per cent, but she pretty well confirmed the identification. She said that he looked much the same two weeks ago, when his friend huckled him out of her pub.'

'That's something, at least,' Martin exclaimed. 'In fact, apart from the identification, it's the first positive thing that's happened in this investigation. Bob's "Skipper" might have been a false lead, but we got a result out of it by accident.'

'Maybe, but how do we take it forward?'

'I've got someone compiling a list of estate owners on our patch. Maybe we can pick the people off that who might fit the vague description we have for Michael Skinner's companion, source their photographs and show them to d'Abo and your landlord. Maybe we'll even find one who answers to the name of Skipper.'

'As Mr Williamson doesn't, by the way,' Greatorix told him. 'My man d'Abo, and the local uniforms who know the man, had never heard of that nickname. He's known up there as Cecil, and that's it. He must have left Skipper behind in Motherwell.'

'But Andy, can we justify this?' The head of CID looked his deputy chief in the eye. 'I had a break-in to an office in Montrose last night; the safe was done and quite a bit of cash was taken. I've also got a drugs operation under way in Dundee. It's going to take manpower to pursue this Skinner thing, and for what? He died of natural causes. Maybe he had his heart attack as a result of falling in the river, after wandering off while he was drunk. If we do find his pal, and he did dispose of the body, that's probably what he's going to claim.

'I have to prioritise; that's the way it is here. You're new here, so maybe you don't understand that yet, not fully at any rate. But if the chief constable was sitting in on this discussion, I know what he would say.'

Martin sighed. He could have ordered Greatorix to proceed, and, if he had read a threat to take the matter to the chief, forbidden him to do so; but the last thing he wanted was an argument with a valued and experienced colleague . . . particularly when he knew the man was in the right.

'And so do I,' he admitted. 'Put it on the shelf, Rod, as far as CID is concerned. I'll brief the uniformed branch to ask around in the general area of Birnam and see if we can come up with other sightings of Michael and his mate, but that's as far as I'll take it.

'If Bob wants to crank it up when he gets back from the States, I'll won't stop him, but until then, let's just wind it down.'

48

For all that he was a politician rather than a policeman, Bob Skinner had learned to respect Bradford Dekker, the elected Sheriff of Erie County, the district of which Buffalo was the heart. He had no illusions that he was an investigator, and had never tried to represent himself as such to the Scot. He knew that his responsibility to the people was to maintain public order and safety by putting the right men and women in place to run an efficient force.

However, their earlier dealings, following the deaths of Sarah's parents, had never required him to take a view of that efficiency. He had met Eddie Brady, the chief of Erie detectives, but he had never before observed his department at work.

As the three men sat round a table in Dekker's office, Skinner looked at Brady, appraising him openly. He could sense hostility in the man, something that he had never encountered before. He felt impatience stir within him.

The sheriff read his mind. 'I'd better tell you, Bob,' he began, 'that Eddie is not completely onside with this meeting. He doesn't feel that it's appropriate for us to be sitting down with the husband of the only suspect in a big-profile homicide. Normally I'd be uncomfortable with it myself.'

The visitor turned his eyes towards him. The sheriff was in his mid-forties, as was Brady. But where the detective had a creased, rumpled look about him, he was immaculate, in a suit made of a sheer material that undoubtedly looked great on television. 'Sure, Brad,' Skinner acknowledged, steadily. 'I hear what you're saying. For my part, all I can tell you is that if I had Eddie's wife, or your wife for that matter, on remand in Edinburgh and I was about to charge her with nicking a pair of knickers from Marks and Spencer, never mind with an indictable offence, I'd invite you to meet with me as a sheer professional courtesy.

'But that apart, let's you and I get Eddie sorted on this. You've ordered him to meet me for the same reason you and the DA have gone to extraordinary lengths to keep Sarah's identity a secret up to now. You know that I still have access to her father's political friends, among whom, as you'd expect, I did some quick research before I came here. Brad, your term of office, and the DA's, run out next year. He's standing for re-election but you're looking to take the next step up the ladder, to the New York State senate. So you do not want any more political flak than you will encounter in the normal course of events, and especially you do not want me making trouble for you within your own party. There is also the fact that Leo Grace got you your start, and even though he's dead, you owe him.'

Bradford Dekker gave him a thin smile. 'Everything you say is true, Bob.'

Skinner turned to Brady. 'So let's cut the shit, Eddie. I'd like you to run through the evidence against my wife. Forget the politics; that's what got me through the door. What I'm after now is professional courtesy.'

The American frowned, then shrugged his shoulders. 'Okay,' he conceded, not quite amiably, but with no sign of any continuing grudge. 'You ain't going to like any of it, though.' A ring-bound folder lay on the table in front of him. He pushed it across towards the Scot. 'Those are the scene-of-crime and autopsy photographs.'

Skinner picked it up, and opened it, hoping that his distaste did not show. The first shot had been taken, he guessed, with the photographer on a chair. It looked down on the body from high above. Neidholm had been wearing a polo shirt when he died; it was yellow in colour apart from the dark stain across his chest. The footballer was staring up at nothing through dull eyes, and his mouth hung open in the manner of death, a look that no movie could ever mimic. The policeman looked at the face; if it had any expression left it was pure surprise. As he studied it, he realised that he felt nothing at all; no pity, but no antipathy, no anger, either. He could just make out the handle of the knife against the stain. The blade had been thrust at an upwards angle, and had sunk entirely into the victim's chest.

'There must have been a lot of force behind the blow,' he murmured, absently.

'The blade was razor-sharp,' Brady said. 'A woman, any woman, and not just a strong lady like your wife, could have shoved in it as far as that.'

Skinner flipped over to the next photograph; it showed the same scene from a different angle, as did the next, and the next, and several after that, so that the change of location and subject took him by surprise. At first he wondered what it was, until he realised that he was looking at a sheet. The photo was an extreme close-up, focused on a hair; it would appear simply fair to the casual observer, but Bob knew exactly what colour it was. There were other shots of Neidholm's bed, some showing more hairs, others from a greater distance away, recording faint stains.

He turned from page to page rapidly, until he came to the first of the autopsy shots. They had been put together in sequence, he knew, for the victim was intact, naked on a slab, with the knife still embedded in him. In life, Skinner mused, he surely had been a massive man, in every respect. Without warning, he closed the folder and put it back on the table. 'Autopsy report, please,' he snapped.

Brady picked up a slim document and passed it over. Bob took it and read through it, slowly and carefully. When he was finished he laid it beside the photographs.

'Okay,' he said dryly, 'so he's really dead. Talk me through it.'

'There's not much to tell, Bob,' Brady replied. 'We took a call from the neighbour, Mr Polanski, saying that he'd heard screaming from the Neidholm house and that he'd seen a lady at the back door in a distressed state.'

'Distressed?'

'Hysterical, even. There was a patrol car a block away; it was there literally in a minute. One officer went to the front door; the other went round the back and found your wife standing in the kitchen over the body, with a glass of water in her hand. Officer said she turned to him and asked, "What kept you?" He took the glass from her and cuffed her.'

'Did she protest her innocence?'

'No, she became violent; she struggled and started to yell.'

'What did she yell?'

'To be specific, she yelled, "What are you doing, you asshole?" That's what the officer said.'

'Hah,' Skinner barked. 'Doesn't that sound to you like a protestation of innocence?'

'It sounds to me like abusive language.'

'The DA will not challenge my interpretation, Eddie. Will he, Brad?'

The sheriff looked at him cautiously, but eventually shook his head. 'I don't think so for a minute, Bob. Carry on, Eddie.'

'Yessir. The patrol officers called for detectives. Fortunately, the first man on the scene, Sergeant Dick Madigan, is a capable and experienced guy. He knew your wife, and the victim, from high school. He called the sheriff directly and told him what had happened.'

'And I told him to take Sarah straight away to the DA's office and hold her there,' said Dekker. 'She was off the scene long before the first media got there.'

'Is Madigan a lieutenant yet?' Skinner asked, with the faintest of smiles.

'No, but he will be soon. Eddie.'

Brady nodded. 'After that, we put a forensic team in and gave the place a total going over. Here I get embarrassed,' he said, 'because I gotta be blunt, Bob. Your wife was all over that house. We printed the knife while it was still in the body. The victim's prints were on it, because it was his, one of a set of kitchen knives. Absolutely the only other traces on the handle were your wife's. Some were mixed in with Neidholm's but we were able to separate enough. She had a full grip of the knife . . .' he made a motion with his hand '. . . in exactly the same way as you'd hold it to stab someone like the victim was stabbed.'

'Has she given you an explanation for that?'

'She's made no statement yet, other than to declare her innocence. John Vranic reserved her position.'

'Quite right. Go on.'

'If you insist. Like I said we went over the whole place. We found forensic evidence of her presence in the house in several locations. There were fingerprints in the living room, the den, the main bathroom and the en-suite bathroom attached to the victim's bedroom. We found hair from her head on a chair in the drawing room, in a brush on Neidholm's dressing table and on the back of a pillow. We found her pubic hairs in the shower trap and in the victim's bed. We matched these against samples that she provided voluntarily. We also found . . .' Brady stopped. 'You want more?'

Skinner glared at him. 'Go on,' he hissed.

'We found stains on the bed-sheet; body fluids. Analysis so far shows two blood types; the victims and your wife's. We don't have full DNA test results yet, but . . .'

'But I know what they'll show,' the Scot conceded, with a grimace. 'Okay, Eddie. You've proved that my wife had sex with Ron Neidholm. You've proved that she found his body.' He paused, and rapped his knuckles on the table. 'But where have you proved that she killed him? Was his blood on her?'

'We found traces on her shoes.'

'From the kitchen floor; that means nothing. How about her clothes? Her shirt, slacks, whatever she was wearing? Were there blood splashes on them?'

'No, but the pathologist said that death was almost instantaneous. There didn't have to be any.'

'Come on, man! We're talking about a massive knife wound that ripped straight up under the sternum and into the heart. Of course there were blood splashes. Have you ever seen a fatal stabbing where there weren't?'

'Our guy says there needn't have been any.'

'And our guys, as many as we need to convince a jury, will say there must have been. Forget it. Can you prove that she was in the house for any longer than she says? Her story is that she let herself in with a key Neidholm had given her, went into the kitchen and found him there. Have you got a time of death?'

'He was still fresh when the scene-of-crime doc got there. He'd barely started to cool. But that's not an issue.'

'The length of time she was in the house could be. The autopsy report found no signs of intercourse on the body, so you can't argue that she had sex with him then.'

'No,' Brady admitted. 'Those stains were a couple of days old.'

'Exactly, so you have no physical evidence of her being there other than at or immediately after the time of death, and you have no physical evidence of her killing him.'

'Christ, Bob, we have her prints on the knife.'

'You also have his. Plus, you've proved that she was in the house days before the killing. She must have handled the knife then. That's all the prints prove; that she handled it. Evidentially the knife will support the proposition that Neidholm killed himself.'

'Why the hell would he do that!' the American protested. 'The guy's rich, he's a sporting hero, plus he's just got back together with the love of his life.'

'By that token, why the hell would Sarah want to kill him?' Skinner shot back. 'Show me a scrap of evidence that says she might.'

Chief Brady shifted in his chair. He glanced at Dekker, then back at Bob. Eventually he reached into a folder on the table and took out a sheet of paper, encased in a clear evidence envelope. Carefully, he passed it across. 'That was in her purse,' he said.

Skinner took Ron Neidholm's letter of proposal to his wife. His face was impassive as he read it, once, twice, three times. When he had finished studying the words, he held it closer and peered at the signature.

'It's his blood,' Brady told him. 'Remember, the autopsy report mentions a healing cut on his left thumb. The guy sliced himself open and signed it in blood. That's how serious he was about her.'

The big Scot shook his head. 'This might be evidence against me, Eddie, but not Sarah, surely. If I'd been in Buffalo and had found that, it might have made me think about fucking killing him.'

The chief of detectives drew himself up in his chair. 'It's our contention that your wife went to confront him about this letter. We reckon she went to turn him down, he got heavy about it, things turned nasty and she panicked and stabbed him. The only reason we ain't charged her yet is because the DA wants to talk to Vranic about taking a guilty plea to second degree homicide.'

'He'll also accept a plea to involuntary manslaughter, Bob,' said Sheriff Dekker. The chief shot him an exasperated look. 'She could get a pretty light sentence.'

'No way,' Skinner muttered.

'Think about it, please. Ron Neidholm was a local hero; if this case goes to a jury, any jury . . . Need I spell it out.'

'You heard me, Brad. No way. My wife did not kill this bastard.' He turned back to the detective. 'So far, Eddie, you've told me about the crime scene; that's all. Tell me about the rest of your investigation.'

'What investigation? We caught her in the act, or as good as.'

'You did no such fucking thing, because she didn't do it. Your guys got there before she had time to get herself together and call them herself, that's all. Are you actually telling me you don't have any supporting witnesses, to the relationship or anything else?'

'No, I'm not. We have two witnesses, friends of your wife, who have testified that she and Ron were intimate during their college days. They say that when he went off to play football Sarah dumped him, and went to New York, then Scotland, where she met you. He never married, or had any long-term relationships; when they met again recently, the witnesses say he was ecstatic.'

'How did they meet again?'

'At the home of one of the witnesses.'

'Babs bloody Walker!' Skinner exclaimed.

Brady looked alarmed. 'I can't tell you that.'

'You don't have to, man, I know her all too well. The little bitch put them together, and she did it with malice in her mind. Sarah never talked to me about Neidholm until Babs told me the whole story, embellished, I dare say. You put her on the stand and, under oath, I will have Vranic crucify her.'

'Who's your other witness?' he demanded.

'Again,' the chief protested, 'I can't give you her name. I will tell you that she drove past Neidholm's house last Saturday, and saw them get out of his car. She says that they appeared very affectionate towards each other. Later she drove past in the other direction, on her way home. She saw Sarah through a bedroom window; she was naked.'

'Did she tell anyone about this, apart from you?'

'She told the first witness.'

'Then you might as well give me her name, for you can bet that Babs Walker will have told Sarah she was seen, and by whom.'

Dekker nodded to his detective. 'Might as well, Ed.'

'If you say so. The woman's name is Alice Bierhoff.'

'So who else did dear Alice tell about my wife and big Ron the football stud?'

Brady blinked. 'I don't know.'

'You mean you didn't ask her?' Bob exclaimed.

'Hell no. How would it have been relevant?'

'If you can't fucking see that . . .' he retorted. 'It would introduce someone else who knew about the relationship. Another woman, say? Another woman who had designs on Neidholm herself?'

Sheriff Dekker held up a hand. 'Hold on, Bob. You're getting ahead of yourself.'

'Maybe so, Brad, but you get my point. This case has not been properly investigated. Eddie,' he snapped. 'Did your forensic team search for the presence of anyone else in the house?'

'There were no prints, other than those of Neidholm and your wife.'

'Killers often wipe them, man. But what they can't do is pick up every single body hair that might fall off them, or every single soil sample they might bring on to the scene on their shoes. Did you search for extraneous samples or did you simply settle for what was on the bed?'

'We saw no need to do more than we did.'

'Do you see it now?' Skinner fixed his eyes on Brady, hard, unblinking, intimidating. The man tried to look away, but found that he was unable to do so.

'If it'll satisfy you,' he replied, eventually. The words came out as a croak.

'Satisfy me? What sort of a fucking investigator are you? Eddie, every miscarriage of justice that I can think of came about because of coppers like you, people who went for the first obvious solution and, because the facts seemed to fit, didn't bother to look any further. A detective has a public duty to carry out a complete, exhaustive investigation of every case, whatever the circumstances. There is no such thing as enough evidence, especially when there is the slightest possibility that some of it might actually disprove the guilt of your obvious culprit.' He stabbed the air with his index finger, aiming it straight at Brady.

'So yes, you get your forensic team back on the job, if they haven't contaminated the whole damn scene, and get them looking for traces of someone else, the person who actually killed Ron Neidholm. And as for the Bierhoff woman, if you won't interview her properly, then I will.'

'Now wait a Goddamned minute,' Brady squealed. 'You cannot do that. I'll arrest you if you try.'

Skinner glared at him, until the man flinched, visibly. 'Bring help,' he murmured. 'Lots of it.'

'Now, gentlemen, please,' Dekker exclaimed. 'Let's cool our tempers here. Bob, you have made your point. There are things that need to be done in this investigation that haven't been. They will be, though, I'll see to that. However,' he continued, 'I have to say, as a lawyer as well as sheriff, that I still see a pretty good case against Sarah. On the basis of what we have now, we have to proceed. You mentioned politics a while back. Given the victim, if we just let her walk on this, the flak would be unbelievable. We're going to need more than alternative theories to keep this away from a jury. I'll go as far with you as I can, but . . .'

'Give me twenty-four hours,' Skinner asked, his voice calm once more, 'until you charge and arraign her, and keep her name secret till then. Plus, I want to go with Eddie as an observer when he re-interviews the Bierhoff woman . . . I've never met her; he doesn't have to tell her who I am . . . and I want her and Babs Walker warned that there will be consequences if they leak Sarah's name to the media before any charges have been laid.'

Dekker nodded. 'You can have all of that. The last part's already been done. The DA himself laid down the law to the wits about talking to the press.' He turned to the chief. 'Eddie, when will you see Bierhoff?'

'What's wrong with now?' Skinner rumbled. 'The clock's ticking already.'

49

'We've got to take a decision on this, Stevie.' There was a degree of impatience in George Regan's tone, but Steele tolerated it, partly because he liked the gruff detective sergeant, but mainly because this time he knew that he was right.

'Go on, then,' he conceded. 'Talk it through.'

'Okay. We've been through the Candela and Finch staff lists, concentrating on males, because whatever the Vargas woman might have put in her picture, the God who made that wind-up call to Andrea Strachan was definitely a man.

'We've still got Sheringham in the frame as a suspect, but without any supporting evidence that puts him in possession of the materials it took to make the incendiary device, that's all he'll ever be. Plus, though he accepts that the call to the girl was made from his phone, he maintains someone else nicked it and made it.'

'And that,' Steele interjected, 'could only have happened during the staff party.'

'Right; that gives us a list, if we leave in the partners, of one hundred and thirty-seven males, one hundred and nineteen, if we take them out. Take away Sheringham and we've got a hundred and eighteen.'

'But were they all there?'

'I've asked Mr Candela that; he checked and told me that eleven staff members were out of town on business last Friday evening. So we've got a hundred and seven men potentially in the frame. After the incident on Saturday we interviewed all the staff members who were there, and all eighteen partners. Of the staff people we spoke to, twenty-three of them were males, not counting Sheringham.'

'But can we rule out the possibility that the bomb was triggered from outside the building?'

'No, but if we take this further, we go there second. I'd say we must concentrate on the people who were actually inside the room. Even at that, though, Stevie, if we're going to be thorough and not rule out people on grounds of importance, we've got a list of forty-one. I've got all their statements sorted out for us to go through in detail, but I've had a quick shuftie through them, and nothing jumped out at me. None of them even mentioned Andrea, so how will anyone have spotted someone less noticeable?'

Steele nodded. 'I take your point. I don't expect to get anything from the statements either, but they're all we've got. We can't get search warrants for forty-one people, forty-one bloody lawyers at that. And we can't exactly ask all of them to talk to Andrea on a mobile phone and say "Hello, dear, this is God". It's a nice idea,' he chuckled, 'and it might even be good therapy for Andrea, but it's not on. No, George, I agree with you. We'll probably have to go through these statements again, and maybe even re-interview a few people, but it's all just to show the bosses that we haven't stopped trying. This investigation is stalled, stuck, stone cold.'

Regan sighed. 'Still, best get on with it, and keep Dan Pringle happy.' He reached for a pile of statements on his desk. 'Do you want to split these down the middle?' He glanced at the inspector, and saw that he was staring ahead at nothing, with a frown on his face. 'Stevie?'

'What? Oh sorry, George. I was away for a minute, thinking of something Andrea said to me at lunch, and what it might mean.' His eyes narrowed as he looked at his colleague. 'What if our getting bogged down in this was the whole idea?'

50

Bob Skinner had often wondered exactly what a soccer mom was. As he looked at Alice Bierhoff across her comfortable, well-furnished living room, he began to understand. She was a classically pretty woman, and had an outdoor look about her, well scrubbed and with an all-embracing enthusiasm shining from her eyes, and a smile permanently on her face.

There were pictures of her son Byron all over the room, in various stages of growth, from infancy to twelve; understanding moved a step closer for Skinner when he saw that the most recent showed him in his football kit . . . as is true of most Scots, soccer was an alien term to him. There were no photographs of Mr Bierhoff. They must have been removed, Bob guessed, after the stockbroker shocked the neighbourhood by moving in with a cheerleader from a college basketball team.

Eddie Brady was still seething quietly at his presence, but Dekker had stood firm. Skinner had been included on the interview, with Brady and Sergeant Madigan; he had been introduced simply as a colleague from another agency. Bizarrely, Alice Bierhoff's bland nod and smile at the description had made the image of Johnny Rotten flash before his eyes, as he looked at her, the chorus of the Sex Pistols' 'Pretty Vacant' ran through his brain.

He stood by the window as she served tea to the two Erie detectives. He had declined; he had drunk enough American tea in his time.

'So you're chief of detectives, Mr Brady?' Alice twinkled as she sat opposite them. 'I guess I'm honoured. What can I do for you?'

Brady sipped his tea, and gave a short, spluttering cough. 'Sergeant Madigan and I,' he began, when he had recovered, 'would like to go over a couple of points in the statement you gave our colleagues, after Mr Neidholm's death.'

'His murder, you mean?' she exclaimed.

'I suppose, although technically we haven't yet ruled out suicide.'

'Ron?' she exclaimed. 'Kill himself? You have to be kidding.'

'Like I said, it's a theoretical possibility, that's all.'

'I should think so,' Alice chuckled. 'But what about my deposition? It was all true, every word of it. I saw Sarah Grace and Ron necking at his front door, and later when I drove past I saw her through his window. She was smiling, like in a, you know, contented . . . to be polite . . . way, and she was putting on her bra, although she didn't seem to be in too much of a hurry about it.'

'You must have driven past pretty slowly,' said Madigan, with an apparently amiable smile.

Mrs Bierhoff missed the point. 'I always do. I never exceed the speed limit in the neighbourhood . . . or anywhere, for that matter,' she added hurriedly. 'But of course, having seen what I saw earlier, I was naturally curious when I drove back.'

'Are you sure Dr Grace didn't see you?' asked Brady.

'Absolutely. From the look on her face she was only seeing one thing. Poor Ron,' she sighed, a finger going to her eyelashes, wiping away a non-existent tear. 'He was a bit of a legend at school and at college, you know. All the girls were jealous of Sarah, when she landed him, and we were so surprised when she dumped him.'

'Are they still jealous?' asked Madigan.

'We've all moved on since then,' said Alice, in a tone that was almost matronly. 'It's Sarah's husband I feel sorry for, having been in the same position myself. I was out of town when it happened, but I heard about him collapsing at the funeral. Next thing, almost as soon as the poor man's recovered and gone back to his job in Scotland, she's making whoopee with her old boyfriend. The poor man.' She paused, and gasped, as a thought came to her. 'Hey, you don't think it could have been him killed Ron, do you?'

I wish, thought Skinner, by the window.

'Absolutely not,' said Brady. 'Chief Skinner was in Scotland when it happened. To get back to your deposition, Mrs Bierhoff,' he continued, hurriedly, 'we'd like to add to it by asking you who you might have told about what you saw?'

'But that was in my statement. I told Babs Walker; I mean I felt that I had to. She's Sarah's best friend, and always has been. I thought that she might be able to talk some sense into her, or at least, to tell her to be more discreet. When you get down to it, I suppose, you can hardly blame her. Ron is such a stud, and Sarah's husband's quite a bit older than she is, but still . . . poor man.'

Watching Brady, Skinner could see that the back of his neck had gone red. 'I suppose Babs maybe told Ian,' Alice went on, 'although that might have been awkward.'

'Why?' asked Madigan.

'Because he was there before Ron of course,' she said. 'Ian and Sarah were close all through school, and then when they got to college . . . before he ever took up with Babs, of course . . . they got even closer, as close as you can get in fact. Sarah left Ian for Ron. He put a brave face on it at the time, but I could tell the poor boy was hurting. So maybe it wouldn't have been the kindest thing for Babs to tell him they were back together again.'

Skinner stood, impassive, listening; he wanted to ask the next question, but he knew that he could not let her hear his accent. Even Alice would make four out of that.

'But apart from Mrs Walker,' Madigan went on. 'Did you tell anyone else?'

Alice frowned; the wrinkling of her forehead seemed to age her five years in an instant. 'No, I don't think so.' She paused. 'I told Mary Maggs, my cleaning lady, but she doesn't know anyone around here, plus she's seventy-one years old. And I told Candy Brew at the library, but Candy's discretion personified. And that's it; honest injun.'

Brady nodded, put his hands on his knees and pushed himself to his feet. Madigan took the cue and rose also. 'In that case,' said the chief, 'we won't occupy any more of your time.'

'A pleasure,' Alice answered, vacuously. She glanced at her watch. 'My, it's almost time for me to go pick up Byron.' She showed them to the door, smiling briefly at Skinner on the way out. He gave her a blank, expressionless stare in return. Her eyes flickered uncertainly, but she said nothing, holding the door open for them and waving a quick goodbye as she closed it on them.

'Well?' Bob asked as they walked down the drive to Brady's car.

'Walker? I don't think so for a minute.'

'There you go assuming again, Eddie,' the Scot snapped. 'It's a new line of enquiry. Will you follow it up, or will I?'

'Okay, okay. We'll look at it.'

'And what about this Candy Brew? Did Neidholm have any history with her?'

Both detectives laughed. 'You can forget that, sir,' said Madigan. 'Candy is short for Candrace. He's a guy.'

51

Maggie glanced at her watch as the living-room door opened and he came in; it showed a minute or two after seven-thirty. 'Straight home or via Leith?' she asked.

He frowned. 'I thought you weren't going to ask questions like that any more.'

'Yes, I know you did, but the thing is, in spite of everything I'm still a woman. And you know us girlies, Mario. We can be fickle.'

'As it happens, straight home,' he told her, brusquely. 'I had a late briefing with the team.'

'You mean you took them for a pint?'

'Something like that. I had an unexpected visitor earlier on; that knocked my schedule for the rest of the day.'

'Poor you. Well, now you're here, grab yourself a beer and sit down. I've got something to tell you.'

He looked at her, his curiosity aroused; almost for the first time, he noticed that she was wearing her pale blue silk dressing gown and that the hair at the back of her neck was wet from the shower. He threw his jacket across a chair and headed for the kitchen, only to pause at the door. 'Can I get you something?' he asked.

She picked up an empty glass from the floor and held it out for him. 'You can get me another g and t, if you like. And remember, no lemon.'

'I know you don't take lemon.'

Maggie smiled cheerfully. 'Sorry. I said it just in case you got me confused with someone else.' The thought crossed his mind that she might be having more than her second drink, but he took the heavy tumbler from her without comment.

He was back in less than a minute, a tin of Stella Artois in one hand and his wife's gin and tonic in the other. He handed it to her and settled on to the couch beside her. 'Okay,' he said. 'What have you got to tell me?'

'A few things, but first things first. I had a call late this afternoon from our very efficient solicitor. The deal is done with the Chamberlains. We've agreed to surrender custody, and they've agreed without prompting that Rufus can spend four weeks out of every year, outside the school terms of course, with his big sister and brother-in-law.'

In spite of himself, Mario let the pang of regret that shot through him show on his face. 'That was quick,' he muttered.

'No point in hanging about; it wouldn't have been fair to keep the child in limbo.'

'When?'

'They're driving up on Saturday. They'll come to pick him up on Sunday morning and go straight back to Hampshire. That means you can still take him out this weekend.'

'No,' he countered, 'it means we can. We'll both take him somewhere; give him a treat.'

'Work permitting.'

'Fuck work. Some things are more important.'

Maggie drained a third of her gin and tonic. 'Bloody hell!' she exclaimed. 'Was that Mario McGuire who just said that? The next head of CID?'

'What's got into you, tonight?' he asked, smiling for the first time since he had come in. 'Apart from half a bottle of gin, that is. Hope you put the wee fella to bed the right way up.'

Maggie chuckled. 'He's fine, don't you worry. Sound asleep.'

'So I guess I'm making the dinner.'

Somehow, without him noticing, the distance between them on the couch had closed. What he did notice was that her robe had loosened, and that her right breast had slipped loose. 'Maybe I've got other plans,' she whispered. Holding her glass steady she stood up; the sash of her dressing gown untangled and the garment fell open. 'Someone I like very much gave me a pep-talk today; and some very sound advice too. I've decided to follow it.'

'And have you got to get drunk to do it?' he asked, as he looked up at her.

242

'If that's what it takes, won't it be worth it? Come on.' She turned and walked, steadily and purposefully, towards the door. Mario rose and followed her.

When he reached what had become her bedroom, the silk gown was on the floor, and the glass was on the bedside cabinet, empty. She stood there naked, as full-bodied and surprisingly provocative as ever she had been. As he gazed at her, she moved towards him and began to unbutton his shirt. He saw that her hand was trembling; the drink had not dulled her fear of what they were about to do. He held it and stilled it, then ripped off his tie with one hand.

And then their eyes met.

'You don't really want this, do you?' she asked, with the hint of a sob in her voice.

He shook his head. 'No. And neither do you. Even if the thing itself was nothing to you, you wouldn't really want to; not with me. Isn't that true?'

She nodded. 'It is,' she exclaimed, with a great sadness. 'It's got nothing to do with Paula, either. It's you, Mario. It's in your eyes when you look at me. You know all there is to know about me, and what happened to me, and because of it, you can't keep distaste from showing in your eyes. You'll try if I really ask you, because you care for me and you're a good man, but it'll always be there, and you'll never be able to help it. I'm not the same person I was to you before, and I never can be again.'

He looked at her, saying nothing, but admitting with his eyes the truth of what she said.

'But it's me too,' she went on, 'for exactly the same reason. Because you know, you can't ever be the same person to me again either.'

'No,' he muttered at last. 'I can't. We're done, Mags.'

He stepped over to what had been their bed, and sat on it, heavily. 'I had a pep-talk myself today,' he said. 'Neil was the unexpected visitor I mentioned. He came to see me about something he's working on, but then he got ripped into me, about the way I've been behaving, about the way people have seen me treat you. He made me realise that I was fooling myself, thinking we could go on as we were.'

'Not you alone,' she told him, 'but us. I thought I'd be fine with the way it was. I was even going to send Paula flowers and a thank you note.'

'Hah! She'd have loved that. No, Mags, if I was a bit short when I came in tonight, it was because I'd worked myself up to tell you that I'm leaving, as soon as Rufus goes. For a moment there, I thought there was a glimmer, but you're right; it's gone too far for us both. What I really wanted you to believe, though, and I still do, is that I'm doing it for the reason Neil more or less battered into me; I'm doing it for your sake, and for the sake of your career.'

She sat beside him, and took his hand. 'I do believe you,' she whispered. 'Like I said, you're a good guy.' She paused. 'Will you go to Paula?'

He shook his head at once. 'No. That would be as wrong as if I stayed. I'm not being seen to leave you and move in with another woman.'

'Will you keep seeing her?'

'Would it bother you?'

'Not a bit. And why should it, if it hasn't up to now?'

'Then to be honest with myself as well as you, I probably will. It might fizzle out, or it might go on for thirty years. Who knows? But I don't think we'll ever live together. I don't know if I ever told you, but the family trust owns Uncle Beppe's place. Auntie Sophia's going to live with Nana Viareggio for good, so it's going begging. I'll move in there, and you can stay on in this house, if you want to.'

'Don't you want your share of it?'

He grinned, and shook his head. 'I don't need it, honey. Anyway, you'll have this and more coming in a property split.'

'No!' Her vehemence surprised him. 'You give me this house and that'll do me. I don't want any more. I owe you, Mario. I owe you my life, and I'll never forget it. I'm not going to stay here for long, though.'

'I can understand that. That's a deal then. I'll clear off what's left of the mortgage and you can sell it.' He paused. 'Of course, maybe if we both moved somewhere else, together . . .'

She squeezed his hand, and gave him a sad smile. 'You don't really believe that, any more than I do. You said it earlier; we're done. It wasn't all bad, though, was it?'

'No, it was not. In fact, I have to tell you that if you were, like you say, faking it all along, you had your act honed to perfection.'

'You gave me plenty of practice.' She was suddenly aware of her nakedness. She picked up the silk robe and put it on. 'So, you want to go and get a take-away?' she asked, matter-of-fact. 'You must be starving.'

He stood up from the bed, and retrieved his tie. 'Yeah, okay. Pizza, kebab, or curry?'

'Fish and chips.'

He laughed. 'Trust you to be difficult.' He put his hand on the door knob, then stopped. 'Mags, tell me something. When did it all go down the pan?'

She took a quick breath. 'When I told you about myself, all about myself. I think we were done from then on. If I'd done it at the very start, maybe we'd never have got married, and then we'd have been spared the grief.'

'In that case,' he replied, 'I'm glad you didn't. For the good times we had, the grief's been well worth it.'

52

'Bob, you have to head Brady off before he embarrasses himself,' Sarah protested. 'He can't possibly imagine that Ian Walker could have had anything to do with Ron's death.'

'How the hell could I do that, even if I wanted to?' Bob retorted. 'I kick-started this bloody investigation, when he was happy to send you straight down the river. I can't turn around and tell him to rein it in. Besides, he needs to be checked out, after your loose-tongued friend Mrs Bierhoff stuck him well in the frame.'

'No friend of mine!'

'Thank Christ you see that. If only you'd seen the same about dear Babs.'

'I've always known what Babs was like, but in spite of everything she's always been my friend. I can't help it.'

'We'll see if that survives her old man being interviewed by the police.'

'But why?' she exclaimed. 'What possible reason could Ian have had to harm Ron?'

'They're looking at the possibility that he might have held a grudge against him for a long time. Over you, in fact. Alice told them that you chucked him for Ron when you were in college. Is that true?'

'No, it isn't! Ian and I were more friends than anything else. We had a relationship, sure, but we never made a commitment to each other. It wasn't a case of me chucking him at all.'

'Alice suggested that Ian might have seen it that way.'

'Well, the bitch is wrong,' said Sarah, angrily.

'You sure about that? Did you ever talk it through with him?'

'No, but . . . Bob, this is ancient history.'

246

'That may be, but there's been a new chapter written lately. What if Ian heard about it and didn't like it?'

'Not a chance. I just don't believe it.'

Skinner shrugged his shoulders. 'For what it's worth, neither do I, but Bierhoff made the suggestion and the police have to look into it.'

'Well let's hope they do it discreetly.'

'Brady will, don't worry.'

Sarah frowned. 'It's your discretion that's worrying me.'

'What do you mean?'

'I mean that you haven't said a word about Ron and me,' she exclaimed, her voice rising. 'I keep waiting for you to explode, but it's not happening. All I see is icy calm. Or is it just indifference? Is our marriage already over as far as you're concerned?'

He looked at her, unsmiling. 'My only purpose at this minute,' he answered, 'is to prove that you didn't kill Neidholm. I don't actually care who did, but given the circumstantial evidence against you the only way I can clear you is by finding that person. Once I've done that, you and I will deal with us.'

She bit her lip, and sat forward in the big drawing-room chair, tugging nervously at her hair. As Bob stared at her, he noticed for the first time the dark circles under her eyes, and the lines around them that seemed not to have been there before. 'That's something, I suppose,' she conceded. 'It would be easy for you simply to let me go to jail.'

'Easy?' he retorted. 'Do you think I want my kids visiting their mother in the slammer?'

She frowned. 'In other words, "don't make any assumptions, Sarah".'

'If you like.'

'Don't you feel anything?'

Finally he allowed himself a smile, but it was not one that she enjoyed. 'Sure,' he said. 'I feel bloody pleased that your lover's dead. It takes a great weight off my shoulders and a great temptation away from me. He looked good on the slab, though; it was obvious what you saw in him.'

'No it wasn't,' she answered, quietly. 'For one thing, he was here for me.'

The barb got to him, and he winced. 'Touché. No, let's not get into this now. Let's just concentrate on the job at hand. Does the name Candrace Brew mean anything to you?'

'No. Should it?'

'Not necessarily; but he's heard of you all right. He was on Alice's gossip list; she told him all about you and Ron.'

Sarah shuddered. 'Ugh! It makes me feel soiled, knowing that cow's been telling the town about me. Who is this person Brew?'

'He's the librarian.'

'The librarian! My God, our library's always been an information exchange. It'll be all over town.'

'Honey,' said Bob, quietly, 'if Brady's investigation doesn't get a result by this time tomorrow, it'll be all over Good Morning bloody America.'

'Don't remind me, please. I'm scared enough as it is.' The truth of that showed in her eyes.

He sighed; it was the first sign of tenderness he had shown towards her since his arrival. 'You must be. I'm sorry, I shouldn't have said that.' He smiled at her again, but more kindly this time. 'Let's do something about it, then. I want you to think back, to the time when you arrived at Neidholm's house. Then I want you to describe what you saw.'

She leaned back in her chair, frowning. 'I can't remember, Bob,' she whispered, after a few seconds. 'All I can see in my mind's eye is Ron, lying there dead on the floor.'

'Of course you can remember. Just close your eyes and concentrate. Tell me what you saw.'

She did as he said. He watched her as she concentrated. 'There was a man walking a dog,' she said at last. 'An old black man, walking an old black dog.'

'Did you recognise him?'

'No, but I would if I saw him again.'

'Good. Now, what about cars; did you see any cars?'

She hesitated. 'There was one; a blue Dodge people-carrier. The driver was a woman; she was collecting a kid.'

'From where?'

'From a party; in the house across the street from Ron's.'

'How did you know it was a party?'

'There were balloons tied to a tree in the yard; and there were still a couple of children playing outside, even though it was nearly dark.'

'Good. Anything else?'

'No. After that I pulled into Ron's driveway.' She opened her eyes. 'Does any of that help?'

'No, in that you didn't see the real killer driving away,' he said. 'But maybe the old man with the dog did. Or maybe the woman in the Dodge van did. The police can find them and ask them. If they'd done a proper job from the start they'd have traced them by now.'

He frowned. 'A party, eh,' he mused. 'What do you do at a party these days?'

'Play, if you're a kid. Drink beer if you're you. What else?'

'You take photographs.'

Sarah sat upright, suddenly. 'Or you film it!' she exclaimed, showing her first sign of excitement. 'Bob, there was a lady filming the kids when I drove up. It was nearly dark, but that's no problem to a modern movie camera.'

Instantly, Skinner was as excited as his wife. 'In that case, let's hope she took plenty of footage.' He jumped to his feet. 'Come on. Tell Trish to pick up Mark from school when it's time. You and I are going out.'

'Why? Are we going to see Brady?'

'Bugger him,' he laughed. 'We're going to find the woman with the camera.'

53

The young Steven Steele had been brought up in Dunfermline, and it had gone against the grain with his police superintendent father when he had applied to join the force across the river rather than his own Fife constabulary.

He had dug his heels in nevertheless, refusing to consider a move that would have led to comparisons between them for years ahead. In Edinburgh, Stevie had never felt himself to be involved in a race to match his dad's progress up the promotion ladder, and indeed that of his father, before him; in Fife that is exactly how his career would have been seen.

As it happened, he had made inspector at thirty-two, five years faster than Steele senior. He believed that his success owed a lot to the understanding of the police culture that had been built into him in the family home; it had made him less in awe of senior officers than other young coppers, made it easier for him to relate to them, and consequently for them to notice him. Just as he had never paced himself against Superintendent Steele in Fife, neither had he picked any of his fellow officers in Edinburgh as a benchmark. However, he had on occasion looked at Maggie Rose as an example; she had taken longer than him to break out of the mass of constables with potential, but as far as he knew there was no police tradition in her family. Once she had, though, her ability had been recognised with a series of promotions.

Steele knew that he and Maggie worked well together because they brought the same skills to the job, and because, intellectually, they were well matched. Okay, he was a couple of rungs below her on the ladder, but time would take care of that. He had wondered on occasion about her family; she never spoke of anyone, other than Mario. His speculation was that she had been an orphan; perhaps she had lost her parents in an accident, for there was an unexplained hurt within her that he could see. Their exchange the day before had been the first time they had ever spoken of personal matters; until then it had always been work, or the occasional piece of social nonsense over an after-hours drink with other colleagues. There had been a spark between them; it had been very faint, no more than a firefly on a cold night, yet he had felt it. He had the sense to know, though, that she was territory beyond his limits, not just because of the formidable, dangerous Mario McGuire, but because he sensed that there were depths to her that no one would ever reach, or be allowed anywhere near.

As he stood on the stone landing outside the Albany Terrace flat, it occurred to him that Margaret Rose and Andrea Strachan had two things in common. They were both troubled women, and maybe, he suspected, Maggie's problems ran deeper than Andrea's; also, neither of them seemed to have any grasp of how attractive they were to a normal, healthy male like Detective Inspector Steven Steele, copper-about-town.

As he pondered them both, thoughts of a third woman came to him; someone with whom, a few months before, he had shared a bottle of Pesquera, in sombre mood, in a dark wine-bar, after a post-mortem examination which he had witnessed, and which she had carried out. Sarah Skinner had her troubles too; she had not spoken of them, but they had been there to see, and he had known lonely women before. Unlike Maggie and Andrea, however, the deputy chief constable's wife knew exactly how attractive she was, and was in no way afraid of herself. He still was not sure what had made him kiss her, or whether it was she who had kissed him. He only knew that it had happened, and that for her, as for him, it had been the opening of a door. It had only been pure, abject cowardice that had made him close it again, without stepping through, by offering her the excuse of coffee at his place. He wondered whether, if they ever had the opportunity to play the same scene again, he would be braver.

He frowned and put the thought out of his mind as he pressed Andrea's doorbell. He heard her footfall, lightly on the other side of the door; grinning, he put his eye to the spyglass for a moment, then stepped back, so that she could see who he was.

251

She was smiling when she opened the door, and he felt his heart lift; he had seen the woman who lived on the other side of this Andrea. For a moment he wondered if he would have the same feeling every time they met. She seemed smaller than before, and he realised that she was barefoot, wearing jeans that were frayed at the hems and a university sweatshirt that he was sure did not date back to her dowdy student days. Her brown hair was tied back from her face in a ponytail.

'Have I missed something here?' she asked, glancing at her watch. 'Did we decide to make it tonight for the pictures?'

'No,' said Stevie, brightly. 'I've been thinking about what you said at lunch. We've hit the wall with our investigation and I wanted to talk to you some more about it.'

He sensed her tense a little. 'You're not coming back to me as a suspect, are you?' She was still smiling, but some of the light seemed to have gone out of her eyes.

'Absolutely not,' he said at once. 'If we were, it wouldn't be me who came to see you.'

'Why not?'

He grinned at her. 'Work it out.'

'Ahh,' she exclaimed. 'So the police are a bit like doctors; not allowed to get personal with the clients. You'll have to forgive me, Stevie; I really am naïve in these areas.'

'You sure are. When are you going to invite me in?'

She started, with a tiny jump, and put a hand to her mouth. 'Oh, I'm sorry,' she laughed, and threw the door open wide. 'Straight through there.'

He followed her pointing finger and stepped from the tiny hall into a square living room, with two big windows that reached almost from ceiling to floor. They were uncurtained, but still had their original wooden shutters, a popular feature with the Georgian and Victorian architects who designed the New Town. Andrea's flat faced north-west, and the room was bathed in the warm light of the evening summer sun.

He looked around as she closed the door and joined him. The room was a strange mix of austerity and colour. The two armchairs were upholstered in stiff, old-fashioned, imitation leather, with brass studs on their facings, and the sideboard and occasional tables were dark, dull things. In contrast there were bright, primary-coloured cushions scattered around, and vivid landscapes on the walls, with not a hint of Van Gogh about them. A vase of fresh cut flowers stood on the sideboard and alongside it a compact Sony hi-fi was playing something breezy by Jools Holland.

'Get rid of the furniture,' he murmured, as she came to stand behind him.

'I know what you mean,' she confessed, 'but it was my granny's.'

'Then donate it to Age Concern and get some new stuff. She won't mind.'

'You didn't know my granny. "Waste not, want not", that was her motto. Actually it should just have been "waste not"; she believed that wanting was a sin. Granny Strachan was firmly on the zealot side of my family.'

'What about Grandpa? Where was he?'

'Well out of it, in a cemetery on the Isle of Lewis; he died about fifty years ago.'

In the background, Jools ended with a flourish, and the CD changer switched to a surprising piece of blue-grass by someone who sounded to Steele like Dolly Parton, with a voice as clear and sharp as her chest was rounded.

'So what is it, inspector, that you want to talk to me about?' asked Andrea. 'Sit down,' she insisted, pushing him towards one of the uncomfortable chairs. 'Let me get you a drink. Would orange juice or cola be all right? I don't have anything alcoholic.'

'Anything.'

She opened a door to his left; he followed her with his eyes into a small kitchen. A fridge door swung open and he heard can-opening sounds; she reappeared with a tin of red cola in each hand. 'Will it do like this?' she asked. 'All my glasses are in the dishwasher.'

He grinned as he took it from her, letting his hand brush hers for a second longer than necessary, and noting that, like Maggie Rose the day before, she did not flinch from his touch. 'You're getting more decadent by the day, Andrea,' he chuckled.

'Good,' she said, firmly, and folded herself into the other chair, tucking her feet under her and managing somehow to make the thing look comfortable. 'Now what is it, or were you just looking for an excuse to see me again?'

'I probably was,' he admitted, 'but I wanted to speak to a chemist, and you're the only one I know. I've had some daft thoughts running about in my head, and some questions I need answering.'

'About what?'

'Bombs. Specifically, incendiary devices that wouldn't leave a trace after they'd done what they were meant to do.'

'And you think I'm a specialist, do you?' She gave him what he hoped was a mock frown.

'No, not at all; like I said, you're a chemist.'

'With special experience,' she added, dryly, with a raised eyebrow.

'Chuck it. I'll go if you like.'

She smiled, like a rainbow through a shower. 'No, I like you being here; you're the first man to come through that door who hasn't been a relation or a doctor. Okay, this bomb of yours; how would you set it off?'

'Remotely; with either a device triggered by a radio signal or a simple timer.'

'I don't see how you could do it, then. You'd have to use combustible materials to start your fire. Their reaction wouldn't make their elements disappear; I'd expect there still to be a residue, an oxidisation, that could be traced afterwards.'

'What if you used a material that would be natural at the scene, like oil in a garage, or paper in an office? Any traces that were found wouldn't seem unusual.'

'No,' Andrea agreed, 'but what about your trigger device? That wouldn't disappear into thin air either. Suppose you simply lit a blue touch paper and retired, that would leave a trace of what it had been before it was consumed.' She laughed. 'You can't do it, Stevie; you'd be talking spontaneous combustion, and that's not a very efficient way of starting a fire, at least not the sort you're talking about.'

'What sort might it work on?' he asked, casually.

She smiled again; pure rainbow this time, no shower in sight. 'Strictly speaking this is physics, not chemistry, so I'm just guessing, you understand. But maybe there's me, for a start. By the nature of the phenomenon, though, you'll have to stick around till it happens . . . if you're interested that is.' She stretched her hand out towards him, and he took it.

'Oh, I'm interested, all right,' he murmured, grinning back at her. 'What do I do if you show signs of bursting into flames?'

'As I told you,' she replied, 'it's never happened before, but I'd guess you throw a blanket over us and do what you have to, to keep them from getting out of control. I have been told, though, that it might be more interesting if you just let me burn.'

She unwound herself from her chair and stood up. 'It could take some time, though; a few weeks, months even. So while we're waiting, I'll just make us a nice salad.'

54

'That's the house,' said Sarah. He drew the Jag to a halt and looked across the street to where she was pointing. A single deflated balloon still hung from a tree in the yard.

'Okay,' he muttered. 'Let's see if the lady's at home.' He opened the car door and swung it open.

'Do you want me to come?' she asked.

Bob paused. 'Better not,' he replied, after a couple of seconds of thought. 'I'm pushing my luck with Brady as it is. Let me talk to her. If there's anything I think you need to hear or see, I'll come back and get you.'

He stepped out on to the road and started to walk the fifty yards towards the house. As he neared it, he looked to his right. The sheriff's department's crime scene tape was still stretched across Ron Neidholm's front door. It spoiled the look of the place. Skinner could see personality in houses; without the tape this one would have looked friendly and welcoming. Sometimes he thought he could see their history also. He looked at an upstairs window and pictured Sarah, framed in it, with a dreamy look in her eye as she dressed. He snapped his gaze away and turned in to the driveway of the house across the street.

He had always been struck by the size of the plots on which even the most modest of American houses are built. 'This is a big-ass country, my man,' his poor, dead friend Joe Doherty had said to him once. 'We ain't stingy with our land like you Brits.' He guessed that the acreage on which he stood was around the same as that of his own home in Gullane, and wondered how much less it had cost.

The front door opened before he reached it. A straw-haired woman appeared, leaning against the frame and frowning at him as he approached; she looked to be in her early thirties, around Sarah's age, and was dressed much as his wife did at home, in jeans, tee-shirt and trainers.

'Can I help you?' she asked.

Skinner smiled at her; her expression softened a little, but suspicion remained in her eyes. 'I hope so,' he replied. He took out his warrant card and held it up for her to see; at home or abroad, he never went anywhere without it. 'I'm a police officer. I'm not from around here, but I've been working with the Erie County sheriff in the investigation of Ron Neidholm's death. There are a couple of things I'd like to ask you.'

The woman gasped, involuntarily. 'Oh yeah,' she exclaimed. 'Poor Ron; how awful! He was such a nice man, for all that he was a big sports star; he was so ordinary, and so pleasant. I just can't imagine him being killed like they said. Right in the middle of my little boy's birthday party too; why I spoke to him that very afternoon. He came across to say hello.'

She paused, and gave him an appraising look; Skinner found himself reminded of Alex, when he had taken her to Edinburgh Zoo as an eight-year-old. She had peered at the pygmy hippos in exactly the same way. 'You're Scottish, aren't you?' she asked.

'I am indeed,' he replied. 'From Lanarkshire originally, but now from Edinburgh.'

'How interesting. I'm Scottish too,' she tittered, 'not that you'd know it to listen to me. Actually, I'm Canadian, but my parents emigrated from Scotland to Toronto about forty years ago. They came from Bellshill. That's in Lanarkshire, isn't it?'

'It sure is. My mother was brought up there.'

'Hey, small world. Won't you come in? My name's Elaine, by the way; Elaine Aitchison. My husband's Scottish too; well, Scottish from Hamilton, Ontario. His job moved us down here.'

'Nice to meet you,' he replied. 'My name's Bob Skinner, if you couldn't read it on my card.'

She led the way into a house that would have seemed large in Scotland, but which by American standards was modest in size. He followed her through into a reception room that was furnished as traditionally as anything he had ever seen; three-piece, fabric-upholstered suite, set facing a big fireplace with a console television beside it. The room had

257

windows to the front and back; in the yard he could see a playpen, in which a child was kicking a ball, on unsteady legs.

'That's Ally, my younger son,' said Mrs Aitchison. 'He's just two. Ryan, my older boy, turned seven on Monday; it was his birthday party we were having when poor Ron was killed.'

'You said you spoke to him just before he died.'

'Yeah. He saw the party balloons, and once the kids had arrived he came across to wish Ryan happy birthday. He brought him a football, and he'd signed it, too.'

'Did you know him very well?' asked Skinner.

'Well enough. Francis, my husband, thought it was great having a football star for a neighbour, but Ron might as well have been a shoe salesman by the way he acted.'

'Did you talk to him for long on Monday?'

'Not really; I was in the middle of the party. But he stayed long enough to organise a touch football game for the boys and we spoke then. I asked him about his girlfriend. I'd seen him with her at the weekend. She was new; actually I don't recall seeing him with a girl on any of his visits before.'

'What did he say about her?'

Mrs Aitchison sighed. 'He lit up like a Christmas tree, the poor man. He said she was someone he'd met up with again after a long time, someone he'd never stopped loving. He told me that she'd just split with her husband, and that he hoped she'd settle down with him, since he'd decided to quit football for good.'

'Was he expecting company on Monday?'

'I think he was expecting her. He said he had to go, because he thought he'd be having a visitor that evening, and he wanted to get ready. He said he didn't know when, but he was pretty sure she'd come. When I think about it again, it could only have been her he was talking about.'

'Did you see her arrive?'

'No. I saw the police take her away, then drive her car away, that was all.'

'Did you see anyone else come to the house before that?'

'No; but then I wasn't looking, I was feeding eighteen kids and getting them all to the bathroom and such.'

258

Skinner frowned. 'Elaine,' he asked, 'did anyone from the sheriff's detective bureau speak to you on Monday?'

The woman shook her head. 'No.'

'Has anyone since then?'

'Not at all; you're the first.' She looked at him. 'How exactly are you involved with them, Mr Skinner?'

'You could say I'm running a quality control check on their investigative techniques.'

'How are they doing?'

'Badly,' he said, grimly. 'So no one's approached you at all about Monday?'

'A television reporter did, but I didn't like her so I told her I'd seen nothing, and to get her crew the hell out of my driveway.'

Skinner grinned. 'Good for you; I can't stand it either when they get intrusive.' He paused. 'Can you remember,' he continued, 'whether anyone did any filming during the party?'

'Sure,' she answered, at once. 'I did. It wasn't what you'd call filming though; I have a digital camera that takes still shots, and very short video clips.'

'Do you still have the pictures you took?'

'Sure. They're on a memory stick. Would you like to look at them?'

'Yes please.'

'Come through to the kitchen, then. I'll connect the camera through my laptop, and you'll see the images bigger.'

'Fine.' He followed her out of the living room. The kitchen was much brighter; he could see why she kept her computer there, even though it was a Toshiba portable. He waited while she linked the camera, a small Sony, through a port in the back of the laptop case, then booted it up. While the machine readied itself she poured two mugs of coffee from a jug and handed one to him. He took it automatically, without even thinking about it.

'Okay,' she announced as the images on the screen became fixed, 'let's go.' She clicked an icon and waited for a new window to open, then clicked again. A photographic image appeared. It showed a small boy, with freckles and a gap-toothed smile, standing beside the playpen in the

259

back yard, leaning on it. He was wearing black trousers and a Buffalo Bills replica shirt.

Elaine Aitchison stood aside. 'You drive if you like,' she offered. 'Just click the button below the track-pad to advance the pictures.'

'Thanks.' He stood in from of the Toshiba and found the button, then began to click. Another shot of Ryan appeared, and another, then one of him with his younger brother. A dozen photographs into the stick, Bob stopped. There was a man in the image on the screen, hefting Ryan up to his shoulder; the boy held a brown football with NFL markings, and gaped wide-eyed at the camera as if he could not quite believe what was happening.

'That's Ron,' his mother murmured. 'And just think, a couple of hours later . . .' Her voice tailed off into a shiver. 'Ryan's heartbroken, you know; I think every little boy in Buffalo must be. If his girlfriend did it, like they're saying, then God help her.'

'She didn't do it,' said Skinner, quietly.

'You know this?' asked Elaine. 'For sure?'

'For sure.'

He clicked his way on through the photos on the memory stick, quickly, losing count, as all of them seemed to have been taken around the barbecue in the back yard, and out of sight of Neidholm's drive. But at last, the scene changed; he reached an image of Ryan and four other boys, in the front of the house. Ryan had thrown his football, in Ron Neidholm style, and his friends were jumping to catch it. The background was wrong, though; it showed only the garden, and nothing on the other side of the street. He clicked again, and again, and again, and again, and . . . stopped.

He was looking at a photograph of Ryan running down the yard to retrieve the brown ball. Ron Neidholm's driveway was in the background, and in it there were two cars parked, a red sporty job, a Camaro or a TransAm, he guessed, and before it, blocking it in, a white saloon.

'Wow!' he whispered.

'You got something?' Mrs Aitchison asked.

'I think so.' He moved on to the next image. Ryan had recovered the ball and the car was still there. In the next shot, he was throwing it again. His body blocked out the white vehicle, but in the further distance, in

Neidholm's doorway, he thought that he could see a tiny figure, back to camera, either entering or leaving the house.

He glanced to the side. 'Elaine,' he asked, 'can you zoom in on these images? To be specific, on that doorway?'

'Sure,' she replied. 'Let me show you.' She picked up the camera, made an adjustment and pressed a button. The figure in the doorway grew larger, but as it did it lost all clarity, and became no more than a black blur.

'Take me back to the last image, please,' Skinner murmured, 'and see if you can focus in on the number plate on that white car.'

She did as he requested. Together they looked at the screen as the car grew larger; as they watched, letters became clear and legible.

Bob's grin widened, until eventually it was as if it stretched from ear to ear. As he looked at the licence plate, he felt almost consumed by a huge feeling of relief. 'Jesus,' he laughed, 'talk about signing your name everywhere you go!'

55

'So that's it,' Paula exclaimed, 'you've actually moved out?'

He nodded. 'I'm in the process of, yes.'

'You're not giving yourself time for second thoughts? You're not just giving yourself a bit of breathing space?'

'No; neither of us needs any breathing space. We both know it's over.'

'But why has this happened all of a sudden, Mario? You told me what your problems were, but you said you were handling them, and that you and Maggie were content to go on the way you were. God, I never felt like a whore before, but I do now!'

She turned away from him, but he put his hands on her shoulders and brought her back to face him once more. 'You can stop that right now,' he said, firmly. 'This has got nothing to do with you.'

'You can say that, but the rest of bloody Edinburgh won't see it that way. I suppose I'm a bit late to be thinking of that now.'

'The rest of bloody Edinburgh can think what it will, but I can tell you this; they won't hear it from Maggie, and they sure as hell won't say it in my hearing. Paulie, the things that killed our marriage have nothing to do with you and me. They were covered up for too long; now they've got out of the box and we can't handle them. Losing custody of Rufus might have been the catalyst for this, but in a way it's been a blessing too.'

'But you were so fond of that wee guy.'

'Yeah, I know, but he's going to be much better off with his uncle's family.' He wrinkled his nose. 'Hell, I can always get a puppy.'

'And what's Maggie going to do on her own?'

'She's going to do her job; get on with her career. As for being on her own, she's been that way since she was a kid. Even when we were married, there was a part of her that I could never get near.'

'There's a part of me you'll never get near, too; I hope you realise that.'

262

He grinned. 'Hell. I wouldn't want to get any where near her. She's a dangerous woman.'

'You'd better believe it,' she said, in mock warning. 'But this part of me isn't.' She slid her arms around his waist and pressed herself against him, burying her face in his chest. 'This part's just a selfish bitch; she's glad that you're out of it. And if it's been wrong all along, I suppose I should be glad for Maggie too. You never know; maybe she'll find the right man, in time.'

'Maybe she will, but it sure as hell ain't me.'

When Paula looked up at him, she was frowning. 'That should worry me, you know,' she whispered. 'Maybe you'll find the right woman.'

'Maybe I've found her,' he replied. 'Maybe she's been there all along. Maybe this is the way it should be; me in your mum and dad's old place, you here, living our lives and getting together when we feel like it.'

'And maybe you should stop trying to see the future. Look at your friend Neil; you could never have guessed what would happen to him, after his wife died.'

'That's true, but there aren't too many women like Lou around. Anyway, you have to be looking to land one.'

'And was Neil?'

He frowned. 'No,' he said slowly.

'There you are then. Don't you tell me that you don't know a single woman that you fancy a bit.'

He ran his fingers through her silver hair. 'I will tell you that I don't know a single woman . . . or a married one for that matter . . . that I fancy as much as you.'

'Aye,' Paula murmured, doubtfully. 'Let's see if it stays that way.

'Speaking of Neil,' she continued, 'how's he going to take you and Maggie splitting up? He's close to her as well as you, isn't he?'

'Neil was more or less the detonator that set off the explosion,' he told her. 'He sat me down and talked to me and made me see the whole thing the way it really was. Your ex, Stevie, did something similar for Maggie, at around the same time.'

'Stevie, eh,' she mused. 'He's a deep one, that. You think I'm secretive? He's a kind bloke, though; too gentle for me in the end, but those big soft eyes of his . . . Oh they have an effect, I can tell you.'

'He needs to watch who he looks at then,' Mario muttered, darkly.

'What do you mean?'

'Remember Alice Cowan, the girl who worked for me in SB?'

'Yeah, she shops in my deli. What about her?'

'She saw Stevie in a wine bar with someone he definitely should not have been with; a married lady.'

'Knowing him, it was probably perfectly innocent; he was probably counselling her.'

'Not the way Alice told it.'

Paula's eyes widened; she smiled. 'Oh dear,' she said. 'It's not like Stevie-boy to be indiscreet. Did you talk to him about it?'

'No danger. I'm not getting into that. If he wants to shaft his career, he can get on with it. No, I filed it away mentally, and I told Alice to forget what she had seen, for ever.'

'And will she?'

'For sure.'

'Won't she tell Neil, now she's working for him?'

'God, no. Anyone but Neil.'

Paula's eyes widened even further. 'It wasn't his wife, was it?'

'Of course not; I'd have fucking killed Stevie myself if it had been.'

'I'm intrigued.'

'Don't be. I'm telling you no more. I shouldn't have let that much slip.'

'In that case it's forgotten already, honest. But speaking of Neil and his wife, now that we're sort of legit., will I get to meet her?'

'Probably. I'll let the smoke clear, then maybe invite them to dinner at the new place. By that time Neil may have solved his problem.'

'What problem?'

'A woman called Agnes Maley.'

'Black Agnes? What's she been up to? I thought she'd cut her links with the shady side of Edinburgh.'

He threw his arms wide in a dramatic gesture, and his head back. 'Jesus,' he laughed, 'you know about that too! Police intelligence; a contradiction, like they say.'

'I'm from Leith, Mario,' Paula reminded him. 'And I'm in the sauna business. So what about Agnes?'

'She's been making trouble for the boss, that's all. Now it looks as if she's about to get a Holyrood seat. Neil wants to fix her wagon before that happens.'

'He's going to have trouble then; Agnes covers her tracks, plus she's got a lot of friends.'

'How does a female scumbag like her have friends?'

'She helps people. They remember it, not least because Agnes never lets them forget. I heard a story about her the other day, as it happens.' She paused.

'Let's have it then,' he said, impatiently.

'Okay, hold your horses. Do you know a woman called Joanne Virtue?'

Mario laughed. 'Joanne Virtue? The Big Easy? Every copper in Edinburgh knows her; one or two have known her intimately as well, so they say.'

'True enough; your colleague Superintendent Jay for one, from what I hear. Joanne was on the game for years, but she was an honest worker; no drugs, no clap. A couple of years ago, she hung up her G-string and got a job as manager of a sauna at the bottom end of the New Town. A few weeks back, the neighbours started giving her trouble; it's in a half-posh district and there were one or two noisy incidents. They sent a petition to the council asking for the licence to be withdrawn. This would not have been happy news for the owner, and might have had consequences for Joanne, so she was really worried.'

'I'm not surprised. What did she do?'

'She went to see Agnes. The place isn't in her ward or anywhere near it, and the local Labour councillor had even signed the petition, so you'd have thought that would have been that. But no; Agnes said "leave it with me". A few days later, the petition came up before the committee, and the Labour members voted against it, *en masse*. Agnes had taken it to the group and told them she wasn't having the girls who work there forced on to the street.'

Mario stared at her. 'But why would she do that? It's not that long since Agnes had a sauna in her own ward closed on just those grounds.'

'Don't ask me. That's as much of the story as I was told. If you or Neil want to hear the rest, you'd better ask Joanne.'

56

'So you've got bugger all,' Detective Chief Superintendent Dan Pringle pronounced. 'That's the sum total of what you're telling me, is it, Maggie? You're almost a week into this investigation, and you've got no suspects and no positive lines of enquiry.'

'I wouldn't quite . . .' a voice from his left intervened.

It was still short of ten a.m., and the head of CID was not in one of his sunnier morning moods; he glowered at Stevie Steele. 'You shut up, inspector. I was talking to your divisional commander, not you.' He turned his hostile gaze back on Rose. 'Well?'

'I wouldn't quite say that, sir,' she snapped back. 'We've been pursuing this investigation diligently since the incident happened. We identified a potential suspect almost immediately, someone who had access to the picture and who was a schizophrenic with a history of religious freakery.'

'Aye, you said. So why isn't she still in the frame?'

'Because she was eliminated at an early stage; she was set up. Whoever booby-trapped the *Trinity* lured her along there so she could take the blame.'

'How do you know that?'

'She told us she had a phone call, a voice telling her to go as God's witness. We established that she did have a call at the time she said, but from a mobile belonging to someone in Candela and Finch's office.'

'So what about him? Why isn't he banged up?'

'He was,' said Rose, impatiently, 'but we had to release him. He denied making the call, and said that someone must have borrowed his phone without his knowledge.'

'Did you dust it?'

'Of course we did.'

'And did you find any prints other than the suspect's?'

'No.'

'Was the girl known to the suspect?'

'They were at university at the same time.'

'Well?'

'It's not enough.'

'Who else have you got?'

'No one.' Rose sighed, exasperated, and glared at Pringle. 'Dan, what's got up your shirt? We're doing our bloody best here.'

'You're trying too bloody hard then! You've got clear evidence that this schizo girl was enticed along so she'd be there on a plate for you. You've got a suspect with knowledge of her condition . . .'

'No, there's no evidence that he knew her history.'

'Or that he didn't.'

'And what's his motive, Dan? Why should this trainee bloody lawyer whose interests don't seem to run beyond the local winebar decide to fire-bomb a work of art?'

'Maybe he was paid.'

'Oh, come on!'

'Maybe he was; but what does it matter? You've got a case against this guy . . . What's his name?'

'Sheringham.'

'. . . Sheringham. That's all that need concern you for now. Send it to the fiscal.'

'What?'

'You heard. Clear your tray. Send the papers on Mr Sheringham to the procurator fiscal and let Crown Office take the decision on whether to prosecute. I don't see the difficulty in that.' He seemed to soften a little. 'Look Maggie, I know that you and Mario are on the rocks, and I'm sorry about it, but maybe your private life's been dulling your professional eye, so to speak.' She gasped in outraged protest, but he held up a hand to cut her off. 'To answer your slightly impudent question, ACC Haggerty has been getting up my shirt, not big-time yet, but it's heading that way. The big fella could be back at any minute and Willie's going to want him to find a clean desk. So you clean it for him. Savvy? You send a report on Sheringham to the PF, pronto, so that I can tell him we've got a result. That's not a suggestion, it's an order, so get on with it.'

267

'I'll look like an idiot!' Rose snapped.

'No, the fiscal will if he doesn't prosecute. Do it.' The head of CID pushed himself up from his perch on the corner of Rose's desk and headed for the door. He was almost there when Stevie Steele stepped across and blocked his way.

'I'm sorry, sir,' he said quietly, 'but I'm not wearing that.'

'You're not wearing what, son?' Pringle boomed. 'You'll be wearing a fucking uniform if you're insubordinate with me.'

'Don't threaten me, sir.' The inspector's voice was steady and icy calm. 'And don't ever shout at me again, or tell me to shut up. I'll be on this force long after you've gone, and don't you forget it. Maggie's my boss, and you're not going to come in here and walk on her like that. You owe her two apologies, one for doubting her judgement and the other for even thinking that it might be affected by what's happening at home. And you ain't leaving this room till she has them.'

'Stevie,' Rose interposed, 'let it drop.'

'Aye, son,' Pringle rumbled, 'you do that.'

'No way,' he answered, evenly. 'I've been making the running on this investigation. It's mine more than Superintendent Rose's, and I am telling you that we cannot report Sheringham for prosecution.'

The chief superintendent seemed to back off, fractionally. 'Why not?'

'Because I've been into his background and his movements in the period; he doesn't have the ability to make the sort of device that destroyed the picture, and he hasn't been in contact with anyone who might have. If the fiscal asked me whether I could give evidence under oath as to this lad's guilt, my answer would have to be a great big no. I'll grant you that there's a chance that he might be guilty of making a stupid call to a vulnerable girl that triggered a renewed episode of schizophrenia, but as far as I know, being a mean-minded little arsehole is not an offence punishable under Scots criminal law!'

For the first time since he had come into Rose's office, the belligerence started to fade from Dan Pringle's eyes. 'If you're feeling Mr Haggerty's hot breath on your neck, sir,' Steele continued, 'send him along here and let him talk to us. But don't tell us to do something that's eminently fucking stupid, just to placate him. Instead, can we have a sensible discussion about the future of this investigation, rather than just a shouting match?'

The two men stood facing each other, Pringle's agitation contrasting with the inspector's calm. Finally, the head of CID turned and resumed his seat on Rose's desk. He glanced at her. 'You've got two apologies, Maggie.'

'Accepted,' she replied.

He looked back at Steele. 'And you, son, have probably earned a place in my bad books for the rest of my career . . . or for the rest of the week at least. Let's have this sensible discussion.'

The inspector nodded, and sat back down on his hard wooden chair. 'Very good, sir. I've been doing some private brainstorming, and I've reached a conclusion about this investigation. We're not going to get a result here, not until we clear up another enquiry.'

'Which enquiry?' asked Rose, puzzled.

'One that we don't even know about yet. I was on my way to talk to you about this, Maggie,' he explained, 'when Mr Pringle arrived.' He looked at the two senior officers. 'Let's consider this for a minute. Why would anybody really want to blow up a two-bit work of art?'

'For the reason we thought Andrea wanted to,' the superintendent replied. 'Misplaced religious zeal.'

'And cover it up? You don't really believe that, do you? I don't, not any more. Look at the precedents; zealots don't mind being caught. The September the Eleventh hijackers all thought they were going to paradise in a blaze of glory; there was no attempt at concealment after the event. I've done some research closer to home too; leaving aside the sectarian vandalism that happens occasionally in Scotland, the most famous incident here was back in the fifties, when a man attacked Dali's *Christ of St John on the Cross* in the Kelvingrove Art Gallery in Glasgow. There was nothing subtle about that; he just walked up to it and started ripping it up with a blade.'

'Aye, and look at the Venus de Milo,' muttered Pringle, his normal humour returning. 'Someone knocked the arms right off that.'

'He was never caught,' Steele shot back. 'Let's stay serious, though; last Saturday's incident was carefully planned. To the extent that we were even provided with a dead cert suspect that we could grab without

269

question, one who wouldn't even be prosecuted, but shipped back to the funny farm, case closed. All that just to burn a dodgy picture and get away with it? I don't think so.'

'An insurance job, then,' Pringle muttered.

'Who'd benefit? Only the owner, and that's the Guggenheim in Bilbao, so you can forget that. In this case there wouldn't be a benefit anyway, since I'm told that the painting would almost certainly have fetched more at auction than its insured value, which relates to the original purchase price. No, I've got another question. Instead of asking what the benefit of the crime might be, let's ask ourselves, what was its effect?'

He looked at Rose and saw a smile cross her face. 'What was it, then?' asked the head of CID.

Steele looked up at him. 'It tied up just about every fire appliance in Edinburgh, when the roads were at their busiest. So when there was a second outbreak in the city centre, very shortly after the Academy incident, the fire services were unable to turn out in sufficient strength to prevent major damage being done to the building.'

'But that wasn't a suspicious fire,' Maggie countered. 'If it had been, the brigade would have alerted us right away.'

'How many major fires are there in Edinburgh city centre in the course of the year? Half a dozen in a bad year, that's the answer. Yet last Saturday, we had two, the one at the RSA, and a second, in an empty office building in the Exchange, no more than half an hour later. If that's not suspicious, I don't know what is.'

'Have you spoken to Matt Grogan?' asked Pringle.

Steele nodded. 'This morning. He told me that it was an electrical fire, probably starting in a piece of equipment that had been left on, and spreading rapidly through the wiring of the computer network. There were sprinklers but they were ineffective because of the type of fire it was. There was also an automatic alarm system that alerted the security staff right away. Normally the Fountainbridge Station would have responded inside three minutes, and the fire would have been contained, but all their appliances, and those from Macdonald Road, had been despatched to the relatively small fire at the Academy. It took them twenty minutes to turn out, given the traffic situation. By that time all they could do was stop it spreading up or down. The floor where it started was melted.'

The head of CID tugged at his moustache. 'But you said it was empty?'

'Not unoccupied, though; it's the head office of Tubau Gordon, a major investment manager. And here's something else that's interesting; normally there would have been people in on a Saturday, Far East traders following up on Hong Kong deals. Last weekend, though, there was a general holiday in China, so there was no one there.' The inspector looked at Pringle. 'What does that tell you, sir?'

The ageing, crumpled detective grunted. 'That I was a fucking idiot for telling you to shut up. Apart from that, it tells me you'd better look into that firm right away, to see if you can find a connection between them and the exhibition fire.'

'I have done, sir. Their chief executive was on the invitation list, signed in, too. When the picture went up in flames, he was right there.'

'Better go and see him, then.'

'I plan to, sir.'

'Just be careful, then, Stevie. If there's anything in this, then, unlike me, he's a right clever bugger.'

57

Neil McIlhenney smiled at the woman as she led him through to what passed for her office in the New Town basement. 'I never thought of you as a businesswoman, Joanne,' he said.

'What are you talking about, man?' she retorted. 'I've been in this business for years.'

'Maybe,' he agreed, 'but on the shop floor, not in management. What happened?'

She shrugged her broad shoulders; she looked much different from the last time he had seen her, when she was working the streets and had picked up the wrong customer. Joanne Virtue was still a striking woman, but the blonde dye and heavy make-up had gone. Her hair was back to what he had guessed was its natural brown, and her face was scrubbed and fresh. He had wondered on occasion about her age; now, without the cosmetic cover-up, he could see that she was in her early forties, a little younger than he had imagined.

'Too many close calls,' she admitted. 'I can take care of myself, but every night you go out on the game, you push your luck a bit. I'd been at it too long, and I was getting nervous. A guy said the wrong thing to me once, and I had a knife at his throat in a second. He nearly pissed himself, then he started raising bloody hell. I wound up having to give him money to stop him calling the polis.'

'Would he not have settled for a freebie?'

'What would he have used?' Joanne asked, dryly. 'Ah'd scared all the lead out of his pencil.'

McIlhenney grinned. 'So how did you get this job? Or do you own this place?'

'Christ, no. I manage it for an ex-client, a bloke called Kenny Bass, from Falkirk. Officially he's in the scrap metal business, but he's got

272

other things too, like this place, and another one in Broxburn. He's a nice enough guy, Kenny, but . . .'

'Sure, he can get a bit severe if he's crossed.' The inspector nodded. 'I know Kenny Bass. I know what he owns and I know how close to the edge he comes. But he's nothing. If he ever gives you any bother, Joanne, just you tell me.'

'Thanks, Mr McIlhenney; I'll bear that in mind. Not that I've got any problems with him, though. For a while I thought I might have, but I got it sorted.' She reached to her left and pulled open the top drawer of a metal filing cabinet. 'Do you want a whisky?' she asked.

His eyebrows shot up. 'Hell no! It's not even midday yet.'

She glanced at her watch. 'It's only a minute or two short. Anyway, that never stopped you before.'

'Times have changed.'

'And mountains have moved, eh. So what did you want to talk to me about?'

'About your recent bit of bother, but first I want to ask you about something else. I've fallen by some information that you might have had, shall we say, professional dealings in the past with a colleague of mine, Detective Superintendent Jay. Is that true, Jo?'

'You don't really want to know that, do you?'

'Too damn right I do,' said McIlhenney. 'I've got a new job now, one that means I want to know everything.'

'Ah,' she exclaimed, 'you have, have you? I heard big Mario'd been moved, right enough. Some boy, him; his uncle's barely deid, and he starts ridin' his cousin. Not that I've got anything against Paula, mind; she's got a touch of the saint about her, has that girl.'

'Never mind that; they're only business partners, anyway. So what about Jay?'

Joanne nodded, once, briefly. 'Yes,' she whispered. 'He was only an inspector then, though. He used to call by when I was working, and if there was no one about we'd do a bit of business.'

'You mean he paid you?'

'Don't be daft.'

'You mean he accepted sexual favours? In exchange for what?'

'Nothing, Neil; he never asked for anything, and I was never stupid

273

enough to ask him for money. I never had any police bother around that time though, so I put it down to expenses, so to speak.'

'Do you still hear from him?'

'No, not since he got his big job down in Leith.' She looked at him nervously. 'What are you going to do with that?' she asked.

'Nothing at all,' he told her, 'unless I need to.'

'Why would you need to?'

'If there was ever any thought that he might be promoted again; I couldn't have that.'

'Just keep my name out of it, then.'

'No worries on that score. Now, this other business; the angry residents versus the White Rabbit sauna . . . some name that, by the way.'

'Better than a sign of the zodiac, like most of them.'

He laughed. 'I understand', he went on, 'that the local petition got knocked back by the council, against the run of play, so they said.'

'I don't know about that; as I understand it the committee just told them tae wind their necks in. It's no' that bad here, Neil,' she protested. 'I run this place properly. The guys that were making the trouble came from the pub on the corner, no' here. My customers are as quiet as mice when they leave here; the last thing any of them want is to draw attention to themselves.'

'I'll accept that,' McIlhenney conceded, 'but you've left out a bit of the story, haven't you; the bit about you asking Agnes Maley for help.'

Joanne Virtue flushed. 'I never did,' she exclaimed.

The inspector frowned. 'Have you just been bitten by the stupidity fly or something?' he asked. 'Because that's what lying to me would be; downright bloody stupid. I'm not suggesting that you went to Agnes; I know that you did. What I want you to tell me is, why. This place isn't even in her council ward, yet she laid down the law in the Labour group to have it kept open, when she's had other places shut on her own patch. So please don't piss me about; I don't have time for that. Just tell me the story,' he said, 'the whole bloody story. Why Agnes?'

She took a bottle of Bell's and a glass from the filing cabinet drawer, poured herself a double and knocked it back. 'Because she's a customer,' she replied.

'What, you mean she comes here for a sauna?'

Joanne looked at him scornfully. 'I think that fly's bitten you now,' she chuckled. 'She's a lesbian, a dyke, a daddy dyke at that, to be fairly polite about it. She's discreet though; keeps it well away from home. There's one girl working here who's prepared to . . . entertain her. I don't like it, but I put up with it, because if I didn't, I'd be shut down in a minute, and that would piss off Kenny.'

McIlhenney did not even try to stop the grin from spreading across his face. 'Is she a regular visitor?'

'Monday evenings and Thursday evenings, regular as clockwork.'

'Couldn't be better,' said the detective. 'What time do your girls start to arrive?'

'About four o'clock.'

'Fine, that gives us time to set up.'

'To set up what?'

'A hidden camera.'

'What!' she shrieked, fear showing instantly on her face. 'You can't do that. I won't let you.'

'I'll bet you will.'

'But she'll kill me! Or she'll go to Kenny, and he really will.'

'None of these things will happen.'

'I won't. I'm telling you I won't.'

The grin vanished in a flash. McIlhenney reached out a massive hand, and seized the woman by the chin, twisting her face round until she was looking into his eyes; there was none of his usual amiability in them, only a look that went right into her bones. 'I want you to think about something, Jo,' he whispered. 'Who scares you the most? Agnes Maley, or Kenny Bass . . . or me?'

58

'Are you going to tell me now, Bob?' Bradford Dekker asked. 'Why are we here?'

Skinner was smiling as he twisted round in the front passenger seat of Richard Madigan's car, to look at the Erie County sheriff in the back. The sergeant sat stiffly behind the wheel, almost at attention, with his boss as a passenger.

'Because I want to show you something, Brad,' he replied, 'quite a few things, in fact. And thanks for agreeing to do this, and give me the chance.'

'I must admit that it's against my better judgement, in a way,' said Dekker. 'I don't feel comfortable without Eddie Brady here.'

'If Brady's doing what you told him to do, he's serving this investigation . . . and a damn sight better than he has in the past. For example, look at that.' He took a folder from his lap, and took out a sheet of A4 paper, which he handed across to the sheriff.

He looked at it for a few seconds, frowning.

'That's a blow-up from a photograph taken by the woman who lives across the road from Ron Neidholm's house. You'll see that it's timed and dated; it was taken less than half an hour before your officers found my wife in Ron Neidholm's kitchen, in a state of shock after discovering her lover's body. That shot is crucial evidence, Brad; it's always been available to you, but it took me to find it, because the guy in charge of your investigation was so fucking sure of himself that he didn't bother to order his detectives to interview potential witnesses who might just have seen something else.'

The sheriff took a quick, deep breath, and exhaled, but said nothing. Skinner reached across and tapped the paper in his hands. 'As you'll see, the photo shows a car licence plate, Empire State type. The vehicle was

276

parked in Ron Neidholm's driveway.' He took another photograph from his folder and handed it across. 'As that wider shot proves. The number on the plate is a vanity registration forming the word 'LIBRIS'. Did you study Latin at school, Brad?'

Dekker shook his head. 'No, but I know roughly what it means; "books", isn't it?'

'Near enough.' He produced a document and gave it to Dekker. 'That's the registration document; it names the owner of the vehicle as Mr Candrace Brew, of 1216 Oregon Way, Buffalo. Mr Brew is employed by Buffalo and Erie County public library service as librarian in Waterside branch library, five-zero-two Wanaganda Street. Mr Brew was also named by the witness Alice Bierhoff as one of the three people she told about seeing my wife in an intimate situation through the open window of Ron Neidholm's bedroom.'

Skinner took the last item from his folder and handed it over. 'That's a photograph of Mr Brew; Sergeant Madigan obtained it from the library service's human resources department. I've shown it to my wife; she recognised Mr Brew at once. She and Neidholm were having dinner last week in a lakeside restaurant called the Lazy Lobster, or some such, when he approached their table and asked him for his autograph. She described the man as effusive, embarrassingly so for someone of his age, and just a little bit spooky. She also recalled that he appeared to be suffering from a skin condition; she could see a symptomatic rash on his wrist and he was wearing white surgical gloves. Those things don't leave prints on knife handles, Brad.'

Skinner smiled again. 'Are you feeling the buzz, yet, sheriff?' he asked. 'I've got nothing against elected police chiefs. If the system runs counter to my culture, fair enough. It's worked in your country for a long time. But I've often wondered whether guys like you don't get envious of the real policemen they command, whether they don't itch to get out there on the street with them. At home, in my rank, I'm finding it harder and harder to do that, and there are times when it does my head in. So I guess you must feel it a bit too.'

Dekker nodded, and gave a small grin as he leaned back in his seat. 'Yes, you're right; I've always been envious of guys like Richard, here.

I've always been a political realist, though; if I did that and an investigation went sour, I'd be gone at the next election.'

'In that case, I'm going to make your day,' said Skinner. He nodded in the direction of a building across the leafy street. 'He's in there, in Waterside Library, just waiting for you. See that white car over there, in the park at the side? That's his. It's your big moment, Bradford. Elected or not, you're an officer of the law; so get across there, you and your sergeant, and make the arrest in person. You'll be a bloody hero, man; you could run for Governor of New York and get elected.'

Dekker looked doubtful. 'Have we got enough to do that?' he asked.

Skinner nodded. 'You've got some t's to cross, but you've got him. Richard's been working with the technicos since they were sent back in to do a proper job, haven't you, son?'

The sergeant turned in his seat. 'Yessir. The scene-of-crime team identified dirt samples through the hall, and in the kitchen, that do not belong on that site. They also found on the kitchen floor, materials, specifically hairs from a human head and minute flakes of what appear to be dried, dead skin, that were neither from the victim, nor from Dr Grace. Identical hairs were adhering to the hygienic plaster on the victim's left thumb. The scientists now hypothesise that when he was stabbed, Mr Neidholm snatched at his assailant in a reflex gesture, and detached them at that point.'

'You take a hair sample from Brew,' said Skinner, 'as soon as you get him back to headquarters, and your case will be closed; trust me on that.'

The American looked at him from the back seat. 'This investigation has indeed been flawed from the outset, hasn't it, Bob? I'm sorry for the embarrassment it caused your wife.'

'Don't be,' he replied, grimly. 'She put herself in the situation.'

'Nevertheless. What am I going to do about Brady?'

'If he was mine I'd retire him, quietly. You've got a relatively small detective department, Brad. To get the best out of it, its leadership has to be exceptional, not just adequate . . . even if that means going down the ranks to identify someone like Richard here, then hauling him up the ladder, fast.'

He grinned. 'That's tomorrow's problem, though.' He opened the passenger door, and put his right foot out on to the sidewalk. 'I'm going to walk home from here; much as I'd like to, I can't be in on the action. It's your big moment, sheriff; get on in there and get your man.'

59

'Where does the name come from?' asked Stevie Steele. The man behind the desk looked across at him, as if his attention had been wandering before their conversation had even begun.

'Eh? Sorry, you took me by surprise,' said Francis Dolan; he was a trim man, with sharp blue eyes and sun-bleached hair and could have been aged anywhere between fifty and sixty. 'The company was originally a Scottish-Spanish partnership; it was set up twelve years ago and those are the names of the founders. We're no longer a partnership, though. Three years ago we incorporated and floated on the Stock Exchange; at that stage I went from partner to chief executive.'

'Are the founders still involved in the business?'

'Sir Allan Gordon's still the chairman, but Alfonso Tubau cashed in his stake soon after the flotation, and retired to make wine on his farm near Sitges. Actually the incorporation was a neat way of divesting ourselves of the Spanish end; it never did very well. Since the closure of the Madrid office, our share price has risen steadily; we're doing so nicely that we've become a take-over target for an American firm.'

'Welcome?'

'Not very. There have been feelers, but so far the board do not regard the price quoted as being acceptable.'

'What if they raised it?'

'If they raised it by enough, and wrote in some safeguards for existing investors, the directors would have a duty to recommend acceptance. All that's academic, though.'

'Because of the fire?'

Dolan pursed his lips. 'Not quite. Because of the consequences, would be a more accurate summation.' He frowned at Steele. 'Tell me, inspector, are you prescient, or do you have insider knowledge?'

The detective stared back; it was his turn to be taken by surprise. 'Neither. Why?'

'Because when you called me and asked for this meeting, I was on the point of telephoning Sir James Proud and asking him to send a senior officer to see me.'

'Am I senior enough then?'

'For the moment you are. You can decide whether to refer what I'm going to tell you up your chain of command. But first, maybe you'd like to tell me why you wanted to see me.'

'Certainly,' Steele replied. 'I'm investigating the outbreak of fire at the Royal Scottish Academy on Saturday. It's being treated as a case of arson.'

'As a witness,' Dolan exclaimed, 'I have to tell you that that was self-evident at the time.'

'Can you describe what happened?'

'I described it to one of your officers in the aftermath.'

'I know, but I'd be grateful if you'd do it again; it's not uncommon for things to be recalled that might have been overlooked in the panic after the outbreak.'

The lean, tanned businessman shrugged, swinging to and fro in his swivel chair. 'Very well, but there's still not much to tell. David Candela was halfway through his speech when there was a whoosh, and the picture burst into flames.'

'What happened next?'

Dolan smiled. 'I suppose you might call it David's finest hour. For all his army background, I've always thought of him as a dry, lackadaisical character, but he took command on the spot and ordered everyone out of the building. "Clear the gallery," I remember him shouting. "Clear the gallery. No time for heroes." We did clear it too, damn quick. David ordered his staff to gather us together at the side of the building and hold us there until the fire engines arrived and the blaze was under control.'

'Did it seem out of control?'

'Not at that point, but David was concerned that there might have been more than one device.'

Steele nodded. 'You can't argue with that thinking,' he conceded. 'Who called the fire brigade?'

'I'm not certain. It could have been the curator, it could have been David, it could have been anyone; I was legging it out of there by that time. We weren't outside for all that long. The fire was contained pretty quickly, from what I gathered, and the firefighters checked everything else. After that we were allowed back in for the champagne and what-nots, and to be interviewed by your people. Now that I think about it, I remember seeing you there.'

'And that's it? Specifically, you don't remember seeing anyone doing anything out of the ordinary at the time the picture went up in flames?'

'No, not a soul. That really is all I can tell you.'

'Fair enough. It doesn't take us any further, but to be honest, I doubt if we're going to get any further. So what about your fire, and your problems? At least you're still able to operate, from what I can see.'

'On these two floors, yes we are,' Dolan agreed. 'One thing they get right in modern buildings is the integrity of each level in extreme conditions.'

'How has your business been affected?' asked the detective.

'Before I answer that,' the other man replied, 'let me explain a little of what we do, and of our structure. We are investment trust managers, pure and simple . . . more or less. We don't get involved in the unit trust end of the business; never have, never will. We offer services to high net-worth individuals, for whom we believe that ITs are a far more reliable and efficient vehicle. Unit trusts have their place; they're okay for smaller investors, but that's not our market. I have a friend who runs a restaurant, which he describes as strictly for fat people. That's us in a way; we're the fat cats' fund manager.

'Investment trusts are companies which exist purely to make money. The only business they have is buying and selling shares in other companies. As an investor in an investment trust, you're a shareholder in that company, and your shares will rise or fall in value as the investments held by the trust rise or fall. Their beauty as a vehicle is that they allow you to spread risk by holding a very wide portfolio without the hassle of monitoring and trading them all individually. Their management charges are lower than units, and these days they're tax-effective because you can invest in them through Investment Savings Accounts.

'Tubau Gordon invests in three sectors; the UK, for proven, steady performance, European markets, which are developing rapidly, and the Far East, which may have lost some of its sparkle, but which remains pretty sexy in the long term, if a little riskier than it was. Each of those sectors operates as a separate business within a business. Each has its own staff, its own analysts and its own decision-makers, reporting back to a responsible director, who reports in turn to the main board, of which he or she is a member, and to me. Each business is . . . or was located on one of our three floors. The fifth floor, where we're sitting now, accommodates Tubau Gordon Europe, and the executive offices. The seventh floor houses our UK business. The sixth floor, which no longer exists, was where our Far East trusts were located.' Dolan stopped and looked at Steele. 'With me so far?'

The detective nodded. 'Yes. I've got some shares in ITs; even though I might not be that fat a cat.'

The fund manager smiled. 'Good choice, as long as you're not with Tubau Gordon Oriental.' He pulled his chair closer to his desk. 'In the financial world, confidentiality is everything. We take that to extremes here. We have no cross-over between the staff in each of our divisions. Each operates completely separately, with no interchange of information to avoid the temptation of insider dealing. To ensure this, each division has a completely separate information technology set-up. There's no way you can cut into seventh floor data from this level, and there's no way that I, as a corporate manager, can access any of it directly.'

'I'm beginning to guess the consequences of the fire,' said Steele.

'I'm sure you are. The damage upstairs was total. The entire IT system of Tubau Gordon Oriental has been destroyed, and with it all of our computer records for its current financial year, which has been running since January the first.'

'Don't you back up?'

'We back up on to a separate mainframe, outside the network, but that was also located on the sixth floor. It's gone too.'

'Paper records?'

'Yes, and all reduced to muddy ashes. The only paper that survived the fire was in rolls in the staff toilets.'

'So what have you lost?'

'As I said, we've lost everything; the current investment position of every one of the clients of Tubau Gordon Oriental. We'd have to go back as best we can and rebuild every transaction to the beginning of the calendar year. That would take God knows how long and even then we'd only have an approximation. We will have to ask every company in which we're invested to issue duplicate share certificates, but with the settlement system we'll never know what was in the pipeline, since we do our own trading. It's impossible; in practice, all that we can do is credit everyone with everything they had at the time of the last audit and take it from there. It's a disaster of unthinkable proportions.'

'What about previous years? Has all that gone too?'

Dolan looked up to the ceiling. 'No, thank God. Once our audits are all completed we archive the records of each year in a secure data warehouse. On top of that we archive our computer records on a six-monthly basis. Had it not been for the fire, that would have happened on Tuesday.'

Steele felt a flutter in the pit of his stomach, but kept it to himself. 'How many Far East trusts were there?' he asked.

'Three public; Japanese, Chinese, and new markets.'

'Three public, you said?'

'Yes. There was also one private trust located upstairs, and managed under our corporate umbrella. It's a family trust; not a unique situation. This one belongs to the Candela family.'

'As in . . .?'

'Yes, it's David's. It used to be managed within Candela and Finch, but he switched it here a few years back, because he liked our security systems and our in-house trading facility. Ironic, is it not?'

'It sure is,' Steele conceded, impassively. 'When you began,' he continued, 'you said that investment trusts were more or less all you did. What else is there?'

'We have a currency section,' said the chief executive, 'speculating on the global money markets. That was on the sixth floor; it's gone too. Never rains, eh.'

'That's what we find.' The policeman waited until he felt that he had all of Dolan's attention once more. 'So why were you about to pick up the phone?' The silence continued, for several seconds.

'Because,' came the reply at last, 'I have just finished a reconciliation of our total assets; investments and cash in the bank and in transit. It's difficult, given the missing Oriental portfolios, but by my calculation, we're thirty million out . . . on the downside.'

'Bloody hell,' Steele exclaimed.

'That's an understatement.'

'Will it finish you?'

'No, it won't, but it will send our share price floor-wards and make us a snip for any predators that are out there.' Dolan stood up and walked to the window of his office; he gazed along the Western Approach Road, at nothing in particular.

'So, inspector,' he asked, 'are you going to call in the cavalry?'

'I'm going to call in the fire brigade, first off.'

'I have done already. And I've called in independent experts. I did that on Sunday. They both agree that the fire started in a computer terminal that was left on over the weekend to receive incoming faxes . . . a normal procedure, and that there is no evidence of it being deliberate. Someone seems to have been dead lucky, Mr Steele.'

'So far,' the policeman retorted. 'I'm going to need a list of every person employed on the sixth floor with the skill to make thirty million disappear without being caught. Obviously, that will include the manager of the Candela family trust.'

'I wouldn't bother with that, inspector. David manages it personally. It's another of his many skills.'

60

'How'd you like to stay in Buffalo and be my chief of detectives?' asked Bradford Dekker.

'No offence, sheriff,' Skinner replied, 'but if I stayed here, I'd be after your job. Elected people trying to manage policemen are the bane of my life back home; if I lived here the only way I could handle it would be to become one myself.'

'If the voters of Erie County knew all that's happened over the last couple of days you could run as the Taleban candidate and still get elected.'

Bob pulled over a kitchen stool and sat on it, glancing out of the window. With the phone to his ear, he could see Jazz playing in the garden, with Trish watching over him. 'So it's over, is it?' he asked.

'Yes. Poor old Candy Brew is downstairs right now in conference with his attorney, that's if the woman can get him to stop sobbing for long enough to listen to what she's got to tell him. When Madigan and I walked into his office he looked at us and burst into tears, and he's been like that most of the time since.'

Dekker sounded elated, understandably. 'The hair and skin samples matched his,' he continued, 'like you said they would, but we didn't need to throw that at him. We didn't need to throw anything at him, in fact. He told us the whole story as soon as we sat him down in the interview room. Hero worship can be a deadly thing, Bob, when it goes to extremes. Mr Brew had more than a crush on Ron Neidholm; he was downright in love with him. His house is like a shrine, an absolute shrine. He's from Chicago, originally, but he volunteered to us that he took a job in Buffalo because it was Ron's home town. His obsession was no secret either. It was a standing joke among the staff in Waterside Library, and among some of the borrowers as well. We've re-interviewed the Bierhoff woman;

she admitted that she didn't just happen to mention Sarah and Ron to him, she did it to wind him up.'

'Bitch,' Skinner snarled.

'And how. She drove Brew right off the rails; he admitted to us that he went to Neidholm's house to ask him if it was true and if it meant that he wouldn't play football any more. The victim invited him in and took him through to the kitchen, because he said he was about to start fixing a salad. He said that he was expecting company. Candy's story is that when he confronted him, asked him straight out, Ron was evasive at first, suggested very politely that it was none of his damn business. But he persisted, and finally the big guy lost his cool. He told him that he had had a lifetime of guys like him, who thought that football was the only thing in the world, and that finally he had had enough. He wanted a normal life, among real people with a wife and kids, and no more freaks like Brew.' Dekker was excited, now, in full flow; at last he paused for breath.

'While he was yelling this, according to Candy, he reached out and grabbed him by the hair with his left hand. That ties in with the samples that were found on the sticking plaster. The guy thought he was going to slug him with the other one, and he got terrified. The knife was lying on the counter beside him. He says he doesn't remember picking it up . . .'

'None of them ever remember,' said Skinner, quietly.

'I'll bow to your experience on that. Anyway, he says there was this blank moment, and next thing he knew, Ron was on the floor at his feet with the knife in his chest. He just ran for it then, out of the house, got in his car and drove home. He sat there for two days, doing nothing, waiting for us to come for him, only we didn't. After a while he plucked up the courage to switch on television, and he saw a report. It said that we had a prime suspect, a woman, and that charges were expected imminently. He knew they must have meant Sarah and he began to relax.'

'He was going to let her take the blame?'

'Without a second thought; he believed, in fact he still does, that she deserved it. In his mind, if it hadn't been for her throwing herself at Neidholm, as he put it, life would just have gone on as it was. That's why he approached him in the restaurant. He'd never had the nerve to do that before, or to write to him, or anything else; he only worshipped him from as close as he could get. Neidholm never had a public relationship, you see. Half of America thought he was gay; as for Candy, he just assumed it. So when he saw him there with Sarah, he experienced a flash of pure terror. He could tell how easy they were with each other, and he had this sense that everything was going to change, that all his fantasies were going to be taken from him, by this woman, whoever she was.

'He fretted about it from that point on, until Alice Bierhoff told him her story, and the poor guy just went nuts.'

'Will he go for an insanity plea?'

'I don't know yet. The DA's offered him a plea deal to second degree homicide; that's what his attorney's trying to talk to him about. If he takes it, then Sarah won't have to testify. If he doesn't, I'm not so sure.'

'You might try telling him from me that if he puts my wife on the witness stand and makes her admit to an affair in public he really will be fucking crazy.'

'He's never met you,' Dekker chuckled, 'so he wouldn't understand, but I'll do what I can to keep that from happening.'

'So what's our position now?' asked Skinner.

'Sarah has her passport back. She can leave Buffalo any time she likes.'

'When's this going to hit the fan?'

'Brew's attorney won't go public while we're still negotiating, but I can't hold it beyond tomorrow midday. If he hasn't accepted the DA's deal by then he'll be arraigned on a charge of first degree murder.'

'Punishable by?'

'In theory, death, but we won't go for that.'

'If you did, Bierhoff should be on a table alongside him.'

'I agree, but there's nothing she can be charged with. I've already made sure that she'll live from now on with the knowledge that her tongue got a man killed. If this does go to trial the whole of America will know it.'

He heard Dekker draw a breath. 'Bob, I want to thank you again for this.'

'Don't, please. In a way, I'm to blame for it all; if I hadn't gone charging back to Scotland it would never have happened. Neidholm and

288

FALLEN GODS

Sarah, I mean; sure, Brew might have gone off the rails eventually, but probably not.'
'Can you say that for certain?'
Skinner blinked at Dekker's quiet question, then thought about it. 'Can I say that my wife wouldn't have had a fling with the guy even if I had been here?' he murmured into the phone. 'Maybe I don't want to know the answer to that, Brad.'
'No. Maybe you don't.' He paused. 'So what are you going to do now?'
'I'm going to shuffle out of fucking Buffalo, that's what I'm going to do. If I can I'll get us on a plane to New York tonight, then back home tomorrow. I'll call Clyde Oakdale and ask his office to put everything in place.'
'Good luck to you then, sir. Should Sarah be required to testify, I'll contact you directly.'
'You may not have to. See you, Brad. Gook luck in the elections . . . not that you'll need it now.'
He hung up, then called Oakdale at his law firm, and gave him brief, terse instructions. When he was finished, he walked upstairs. Sarah was in the nursery, playing with Seonaid. She looked at him over her shoulder as he came into the room. She tried to read his expression, but failed. 'Well?' she asked. 'Who was that?'
'The county sheriff,' he told her. 'You're in the clear.'
She turned and handed their daughter to him, then gave a huge sigh of unfettered relief. 'Thank you,' she whispered, her eyes moistening. 'Thank you so much.'
'Maybe you should thank her,' he said, kissing Seonaid on the forehead, 'and the boys.'
'No. I'll thank you; no one else could have done it.'
'Eddie Brady should have done it,' he replied.
Sarah rubbed a tear from her cheek. 'So that little man actually killed Ron.'
'Stone fucking dead, honey. You know what they say; the harder they come, the bigger they fall, or something like that.' He looked her in the eye. 'But it's not over. Now you have something else to face. I'm taking the kids back to Scotland; we're leaving as soon as Clyde can get us on

289

a flight. I won't have them here to be filmed and photographed when this thing breaks in the media.'

'And what about me?' she asked, quietly.

'That's your choice, love. I've told Oakdale to book a seat for you too; it's up to you whether you're in it when the plane takes off.'

'What do you want?'

He laid the wriggling Seonaid on the floor and let her crawl towards a toy. 'If I was going to kick you out I'd hardly have got you that seat, would I? Listen, Sarah; when I went back home to defend my job, I rejected you, and not for the first time, either. When you coupled with Neidholm, you were rejecting me. All I have to say to you is that I regret what I did now. I didn't consider what effect it might have had on you, and I apologise for that. As for what you did, I'm not going to ask whether you regret that, and I'm not going to make it a precondition of coming home. It's your life, and your decision, but when you make it, be in no doubt that I want you to come.' He reached out a hand and touched her face, for the first time since his return. 'I've taken you for granted; I'm sorry for it.' He smiled, faintly. 'I can't promise that it won't happen again, but if it does, I'll be sorry then too.'

Sarah took hold of his fingers, and held them to her cheek for a second or two, then twined her own with them. 'Whether you believe this is up to you, but when I went to see Ron at his place, when I found him, I went there to tell him that I was turning him down and going back to you. I'd made my choice then, and it's the same one I make now. I'm coming home.'

'Good,' he murmured. He looked at her solemnly. 'There's something I know I'll ask you sooner or later, so it might as well be now. If the Bierhoff creature hadn't seen you with your tits out, if Candy Brew had never existed, and Neidholm was still alive, would you have told me about what happened?'

Sarah looked back at him, unblinking. 'I don't know, and that's the truth. As for regret, I don't know about that yet either. I'll always feel guilt that what happened between us led to his death, but not too much, because if it hadn't been me, it could just as well have been someone else. But regret? Ron was here, you had rejected me, like you said. He was kind, he was good, he was gentle, he was old familiar ground, and I

290

found myself wanting him. So I can't work out whether there's anything there to regret. As for things not happening again, if you can't promise, I won't either, not if the same circumstances arose, but I certainly don't plan on it.'

He nodded. 'Fair enough. Let's pack, and get the kids ready. With luck we can pick up Mark from school and head straight for the airport.'

He turned to leave, but she caught his arm. 'Hey, I almost forgot something. When you were out, Alex called, to see how things were. We talked for a while, and during our conversation she said something really weird, about your brother.' A puzzled look crossed her face. 'What brother?'

'It's a long story; I'll tell you all about it over the Atlantic. How was Alex with you, incidentally?' he asked her.

'She's been friendlier, I have to say, but at least she didn't call me a two-timing tart, or any other choice descriptions.'

'She wouldn't. She told me some truths about me, though.'

For a moment all his hurt showed in his face, and she felt his pain within her. 'Bob,' she said, breaking the silence. 'So we're not the golden couple the world thinks we are . . . and when this comes out in court the world's going to know it too . . . but we're still pretty formidable, and we've still got more going for us than at least eight out of another ten. Remember that, and remember this too. There's one thing more than anything other . . . more than the kids, even . . . that's taking me back to Scotland, and that's the fact that I love you.'

He looked at her, and gave a long slow smile, one that she had not seen, she realised, since the day that Seonaid had been born. 'And for the avoidance of doubt, honey,' he told her, 'I love you too.'

'I never had any doubt,' Sarah whispered. 'Come on, let's get ready.'

'Yes.' He bent to scoop up the baby in his arms. 'By the way, do you want to phone friend Babs before we leave?'

Sarah looked at him and snorted. 'Like hell I do!'

61

'This must be an unusual experience for you,' said Andrea.

'What do you mean?'

'Saying goodnight to your date on her doorstep, and not being invited in.'

Stevie gave her a wounded look. 'Having a date's an unusual experience for me these days.'

'That'll be right; I'm not so innocent I'll believe that. Are you disappointed that the evening ends here?'

'No. Honestly. You set the pace; I told you that and I meant it.'

'In that case, let me tell you something. The pace might hot up, quite significantly, when I stop feeling that the policeman in you is still interviewing me about that damn fire. All night, charming as you've been, I've had the feeling that there are still questions you want to ask me, but don't like to, since this evening's meant to be just about us and nothing else. You've also, if I may say so, looked remarkably smug, as if you've just done something very clever, and can't wait to tell me.'

Steele leaned against the wall beside her front door and smiled at her. 'There's not much subtlety about me, is there? You've got two out of three right; where you're wrong about is that I can't tell you, not yet at any rate.'

'Two out of three's not bad,' Andrea conceded. 'So what is it that you want to ask me?'

'I don't need to at all, actually; I could find out from other sources, but it would be quicker if I got it from you.'

'Go ahead then.'

'Okay, if you're happy. When you were in trouble, for trying to burn down the Baptists, and you appeared in court, who acted for you?'

'A woman called Davina Chapin, of Candela and Finch; they're our family's lawyers.'

'Mmm,' Steele muttered, trying to sound matter-of-fact, and succeeding. 'Thanks.'

'You mean that's it?' she exclaimed. 'That's all?'

'Yup,' he assured her. 'I promise that's the last question I will ever ask you about this investigation. In the event that we do need to talk to you about it again, it'll be Maggie Rose who does it. I'll be nowhere near.'

'Promise?'

'Promise. I'll declare a personal interest.'

Andrea took his hand and tugged him gently off the wall. 'In that case,' she said, 'I'd best make an honest copper of you. Would you like to come in? Just for a coffee, you understand.'

62

'I hope you're grateful,' said Neil McIlhenney, as he pushed a video cassette across Bob Skinner's rosewood desk. 'I took Thursday night off the football to get that for you. I had to frighten Joanne Virtue to do it as well; I wasn't very happy about that.'

'You must have been impressive if you could scare big Jo. What's on the tape?'

'A virtuoso performance, signifying the end of the career of Black Agnes Maley. You can watch it if you like, but I wouldn't recommend it. I'd like it back afterwards if you do; it belongs in my safe.'

'Just tell me then. What have we got on her?'

'Improper use of influence in return for sexual favours,' McIlhenney replied. 'That sums it up as politely as I can.'

'And Joanne Virtue helped? The Big Easy herself?'

'Yup.'

'Good for her; as of now she's on the list of those to whom we owe favours. Can we prosecute Maley?'

'Not for what's on the video. What they're doing isn't against the law, no money's seen to change hands, and all three of them are of age. In theory there's corruption, but we'd never make it stick. Anyway we don't need to.'

Skinner tapped the cassette box. 'I take it there's another copy.'

'Yes. It's in the possession of the First Minister's security adviser.'

'Jock Govan? He's laced up as tight as they come.'

McIlhenney nodded and laughed. 'He was just about sick when he saw it. I don't know whether he showed it to his boss or not, but it's had its effect. Maley's off the list for Holyrood and her resignation as a councillor will be tendered formally to the Lord Provost this morning. She's gone for good, and we've got a criminal intelligence file on her as well.'

'Big Jo is safe, is she?'

'Maley's been warned off, don't worry.'

The DCC beamed. 'Happy Mondays, then. Thanks a million, Neil; I never expected a result like this when I set you on the woman.' The smile vanished, abruptly. 'I never thought you'd have to get your hands so dirty either. I know it can't have been pleasant. I won't forget it.'

'You do exactly that, boss; forget it. When it comes to favours exchanged between you and me you're still well in credit.' He picked up the tape. 'I'll take this, if you don't want to see it.'

'Do that.'

McIlhenney nodded, then held out a big padded envelope, which had been tucked under his left arm. 'This was delivered to me on Friday morning,' he said, 'from your sinister pal Arrow.'

Skinner took it from him. 'There's nothing sinister about Adam,' he chuckled. 'What you see is what gets you. Thanks again.'

'No problem.' The big inspector looked down at his friend, back in his accustomed chair. 'Good to see you there at last,' he said. 'You got a result in the States, then?'

'The man was in court while we were still on the runway at JFK on Friday. He'll plead to manslaughter; there'll be no trial . . . for which I am profoundly grateful.'

'And you and Sarah? Did you get a result there too?'

'She came back with me; let that speak for itself. I've learned a lot, Neil, about her and about me. I'll change, or at least I'll do my best. You've helped in that too, mate; whatever you say, if there was ever an account between you and me it's tilted well back to you.'

'You'll be at the football in North Berwick on Thursday, then?' asked McIlhenney.

'Count on it.'

'About bloody time too; we've been a man light for weeks now.' He turned and walked out of the DCC's office. As soon as the door had closed, Skinner picked up the package on his desk, ripped it open, and tipped out the contents. Three documents fell on to the desk; one of them, he saw immediately, was a note from Adam Arrow.

He had just picked it up, when his internal telephone buzzed. He picked it up. 'Jack,' he said, knowing that his exec would be on the line.

'Sir,' said Detective Sergeant McGurk, briskly. 'The head of CID's been on; he's got Superintendent Rose and Inspector Steele in his office, and he'd like to bring them along. He wants to brief you on an investigation they've had running in your absence.'

'Tell Dan to hold on for a bit, please, Jack. There's something I have to read up on first; I'll call them when I'm ready.'

He hung up and turned back to the contents of Adam Arrow's package. He read through them slowly and carefully; once or twice he raised an eyebrow, but for most of the time his expression remained impassive. Finally, he finished the last of the three documents, returned them to the Jiffy bag in which they had been delivered, and stored it in a deep drawer in his desk. When he was finished, he picked up the phone once more and called McGurk. 'Okay, Jack,' he announced, 'I'm ready. Wheel them in; you come in too; most things I hear you can hear as well.'

'Very good, sir. Will you need coffee?'

'If anyone's desperate I've got a filter machine here that's rarely empty; I'm not running a cafeteria, though.'

Two minutes later, his door opened and Detective Superintendent Rose stepped in, followed by Steele, Pringle and McGurk. Maggie had been the DCC's exec, on her way up the ladder. He knew her well, and gave her an appraising look as she sat on one of the sofas that he used for informal meetings. He was pleased to see that the tension she had been showing the last time they had met seemed to have gone; she looked purposeful and relaxed. In contrast, Pringle looked gloomy and preoccupied. He wondered whether it was just another of Dan's famous Monday mornings, or if there was something more.

'Good to see you all,' Skinner began, once everyone was settled comfortably, or in McGurk's case as comfortably as anyone of his height could on the low furniture. 'It's bloody good to be back, I don't mind telling you. Now, what have you lot been up to while I've been away? You're going to need to start from scratch, I'm afraid. A few things have happened to me lately; I feel more out of touch than I've ever been in my life.'

He saw Rose glance at Pringle; he caught the head of CID's brief nod for her to proceed. 'This has all built up in the last week, sir,' she said. 'It began last Saturday, with a fire at an exhibition of religious art in the Royal Scottish Academy. A picture went up, in the middle of the opening speech by the chief sponsor, Mr David Candela.'

'Who?' asked Skinner.

'David Candela; he's senior partner of Candela and Finch, the lawyers.'

'Mmm. Okay.'

'It was clear from the start that an incendiary device had been planted. The building was cleared, the fire services turned out *en masse*, the fire was extinguished, the rest of the exhibition was checked out and cleared, and the guests were allowed back in.'

'A storm in a champagne flute,' the DCC murmured.

Rose smiled. 'That's what we thought. We attended, we interviewed everyone present and we conducted a thorough investigation. This led us to a suspect, a young woman who was present at the opening, even though she hadn't been invited, and who'd had access to the picture before the event. This person was an obvious suspect; last year she was involved in an incident of attempted religious fire-raising and underwent psychiatric treatment as a result.'

'The girl Strachan?' Skinner interrupted. 'Yes, I remember hearing about the case. The treatment didn't work, then?'

'That's just the point, sir. It did. We were fed the girl; she was meant to take the blame. Someone made a malicious call to her, told her that God was calling her again, and that she should go to the exhibition. Given her recent history, she just flipped.'

'You pulled her in, though?'

'Yes, of course. We might have bought her as the culprit, too, but for Stevie.' She glanced at Steele and he saw a trace of a smile cross her face. 'He thought to check her phone records, and he traced the mobile from which the call had been made.'

'Good, but standard procedure nonetheless. So you had another suspect?'

'Yes, a trainee lawyer employed by Candela and Finch. But he denied making the call. He claimed that someone could have borrowed his phone and used it, during an office party. We had no way of disproving that, so we had to release him.'

'Did he know the girl?'

297

'They were at university at the same time, but there's no evidence of an acquaintanceship. However, when she appeared in court last year she was represented by Dav Chapin, of Candela and Finch, so anyone in the firm could have known of her.'

'Okay, so your investigation was rubbered. Or did you have a way forward?'

'No sir,' said Rose, 'sideways. Stevie took a broader look at the whole situation, and came up with a completely different scenario. As a result we believe that the fire at the Academy had nothing to do with protests or religion. We believe it was staged deliberately, to engage the fire services. They were barely there before there was a second outbreak, in the empty office of Tubau Gordon plc, a fund manager up in the Exchange district. By the time the firemen got up there, a whole floor had been completely destroyed.'

'And was this fire deliberately started?'

'There's no evidence of that, sir. But an entire division of the company was wiped out; its records all the way back to January were totally destroyed. When the chief executive of the company did a financial reconciliation, he discovered a loss of thirty million pounds.'

'So it was deliberately started?'

Rose smiled. 'As I said, there's no evidence of that. The fire service, and independent people, conducted a complete investigation. Everyone's agreed that it was an electrical fire caused by overheating in a computer, which was routinely left switched on. The experts say that as far as they can see it was an accident.'

Skinner grinned. 'But we're not as bloody stupid as them, are we? We don't ignore the obvious.'

Rose returned his smile. 'No, boss, we do not.' She turned to Steele. 'Stevie, would you like to take this up?'

The inspector nodded. 'Yes, ma'am. The obvious, sir, is that these two fires were both spontaneous outbreaks, but there was evidence of detonation in one and not in the other. The experts' view is that if there's no forensic evidence of fire-raising, there's no case. But what if the computer where the fire started was the timer? What if it was rigged to set it off itself at a specific time? There would be no forensic evidence, would there? None you could see, that's for sure. So we're down to circumstances. Let's consider the loss. Tubau Gordon is an investment trust manager, and a good one; there's no way even a bad investment manager could blow thirty mil within an IT without it starting to showing up to his colleagues from the start. So as I see it, the loss must have been generated in the company's secondary business.'

'Which is?'

'Currency speculation,' Steele replied. 'And guess what? The computer where the blaze began was the one used for that activity.'

'But why go to all the trouble of holding up the fire brigade? Even with an automatic callout system, the computer would be gone by the time the fire-fighters got there.'

'Because the back-up computer and all the paper records had to be destroyed as well. And it had to be done that weekend. Three days later those records would have been archived off-site.'

Skinner smiled, and punched the air in a mock gesture. 'Clever boy, Stevie. So who's the link?'

'David Candela. His family has a private investment trust which uses the dealing services of Tubau Gordon. It's located on the Oriental floor, where the currency division was also housed. Mr Candela manages his trust himself; all the instructions to the brokers come from him. He enjoys round-the-clock access to the building and he's a regular attender at weekends; the security log shows that.

'Further investigation over the weekend has revealed that Mr Candela was a regular client of the Maybury Casino. He's a heavy gambler, and frequently complains about the house limit, even when he's losing.

'To sum up, sir, my belief is that Mr Candela has extended his gambling by dealing privately on the currency markets, but he hasn't been using his own assets, he's been using those of Tubau Gordon. He's been getting into the currency department and running a private account, protected, no doubt by a code word known only to him, and one that no one could enter by accident. A bank audit over the weekend shows that the loss has been run up over the last couple of months. It would have been spotted this week; that's why the lot had to go up in flames last Saturday.'

Skinner nodded; he glanced at the lugubrious Pringle, then back at

Steele. 'So why aren't you turning cartwheels, Stevie? Why do I sense that there's a big "but" coming?'

'Because we can't prove a bloody thing, boss,' exclaimed the inspector, tersely. 'All the solid evidence there might have been is melted. Any one of seventy people could have had access to that computer, and could have run up the loss. The only thing we have to link in Candela is that phoney fire in the Academy, which for sure he triggered himself at the exact moment he planned . . . and we have no way of proving either that he planted the device or triggered it.'

Skinner pushed himself up from the sofa, walked over to his window and gazed out on to Fettes Avenue. After a minute he turned and looked back at his colleagues. 'So what you're telling me, boys and girl,' he said, 'is that we've got some clever fucking lawyer in Edinburgh who's committed the perfect crime.'

'That's about it, sir,' said Rose. 'We know it's him, but there's no way we'll ever touch him for it. It looks as if he's done just that.'

The deputy chief constable stretched his arms above his head. A wave of jet-lag caught up with him; he stifled a yawn. He grinned; a smile that they were all used to and that some of them had thought they would never see in that room again.

'No, Mags,' he said. 'He only thinks he has.'

63

The place was understated, if anything. It was a very plain house, conservative in its design, without the ramparts and turrets found all too often in folly dwellings of its age, built from locally quarried stone, and smaller than might have been expected in such extensive grounds. And yet, there was something about it that reeked of money, and old money at that, maybe two hundred years old. Andy Martin's staff had established that it had been in the same family's ownership since they had built it in the late nineteenth century.

Bob Skinner stopped his BMW just where the driveway opened out into a wide garden area in front of the mansion. He was blocking the narrow road, but that did not worry him; in fact it suited his purpose. It was well into the evening, but the day had been fine, and the summer sun was still bright.

As he looked around the grounds, they reminded him of Fir Park Lodge, but these were kept better. He could see the stripes on the close mown lawn, and appreciate the neatness of the flower beds, and the careful way in which the shrubs and bushes had been trimmed. Off to the back and to the left, he saw outbuildings; stables once upon a time no doubt, but now garaging for a russet-coloured Range Rover, which stood gleaming outside. He stood for a moment and listened; from somewhere not far away came the splashes of a river running. Even though the spate was over, it still sounded full and fast.

A small sign on the lawn asked him to 'Keep off the grass', but he ignored it and marched straight across, towards the grey granite house.

He was several yards short of the heavy brown front door when it opened. A tall thin man appeared; he was wearing grey corduroy trousers from an age when fashion meant nothing, a green pullover with suede patches on the shoulders and elbows, and he was glaring at his visitor.

'Can't you read, man?' he barked, as Skinner approached. 'And look where you've parked your car.'

'Sure I can read,' the policeman answered, 'English, Spanish and French, in fact. But sometimes I like to ignore rules, if I think they're stupid. There's a bit of a rebel in me, you see. As for my car, I left it there because I didn't want it to disfigure your charming house.' He walked on, unbidden, through the wide doorway and into a panelled hall; he stopped and looked around. 'Very nice,' he said, amiably.

'Get to hell out of there!' the other man exploded. 'Just who the hell are you and what do you think you're doing here?'

Skinner beamed at him. 'Just imagine that I'm Michael Aspel, that this Jiffy bag I've got under my arm is a big red book, and I'm saying, "David Candela, This is Your Life". Let's start off there.'

Candela made a furious, exasperated sound. 'You're a lunatic,' he exclaimed, 'a well-dressed lunatic, but a lunatic nonetheless. I'm calling the police.'

Suddenly, Skinner seemed a little less amiable. 'I wouldn't do that. I am the police.'

'In that case I'll complain to your inspector.'

'You'd be several ranks too low if you did that.'

Candela blinked, then stepped into the hall himself, heading for a small silver box on the wall, beside a grandfather clock. 'Don't do that either,' his visitor advised. 'I know what that is; it's a panic button linked to your alarm system. It would only be an inconvenience to your monitoring station if you activated it. There wouldn't be a response.'

The lawyer stopped. 'Very well,' he said. A little uncertainty had crept into his voice, but he was still in control of himself and showing no sign of alarm. 'If this is an official visit, you'd better come through to the drawing room. I've seen a few of you people over the last ten days or so; I have to say they were all a damn sight more polite than you.'

Skinner smiled at him, cheerily. 'This is me being polite, Mr Candela,' he exclaimed. 'I'm nowhere near being rude, not yet, and rude's only a step along the way to nasty.'

'Bloody lunatic,' Candela muttered as he led the way into a long room, oak-panelled like the hall. It was furnished with big soft armchairs in flowery fabrics; a refectory table stood near the door, and three portraits, each carefully lit from above, were suspended from a rail along one wall. Windows looked out and down towards the river, and a double patio door opened out on to the grounds.

'Nice place,' the policeman commented; a sincere compliment. 'I suppose it's been in your family since the nineteenth century?'

'Yes, we built it,' the lawyer snapped impatiently. 'Look, do I know you?'

'You should; if you were serious about your precious firm and not just a fucking dilettante, you'd know me all right. You know my family, though; Candela and Finch has represented it for about thirty years. And of course you have a personal connection with us.'

Candela frowned. 'Would you like to explain that?'

'I'll explain it by asking you something. How did my brother Michael die?'

The colour drained from the thin man's face in an instant. He looked towards the patio door as if he was about to run for it; Skinner forestalled any attempt by taking a step to his right, blocking the way. 'You're . . .' he gasped.

'I'm Bob Skinner,' said the policeman. 'I'm pretty well known in Edinburgh, but you're not really interested in the city, are you? You're interested in the casino and in playing up here. For all you pretend, your position as senior partner is written into your firm's constitution. You don't actually manage it, one of the other guys does that.'

He took the padded envelope from under his arm. 'It really is all in here, you know, your whole exciting life.'

Candela had gathered his thoughts. 'I know nothing about your brother!' he exclaimed. 'I read about his death in the newspapers, but that's all.'

'Oh, don't be fucking silly,' Skinner retorted. 'I wouldn't have brought it up if I didn't know for certain. Before I came here, I spoke to a man called Angus d'Abo, in Birnam. I showed him your photograph . . .' he tapped the envelope '. . . and he identified you right away as the man who came into his local with Michael a few days before he died. Mike got completely trousered and you carted him off. Before I spoke to d'Abo I faxed the same photo to Brother Aidan at Oak Lodge. He clocked you too, old as he is. He identified you as the man my brother called

Skipper, the man who took him away from his home and never brought him back.' The DCC grinned; he was taking a deadly enjoyment from the account.

'Skipper was your nickname in the army, Mr Candela,' he said, then saw the man's eyes narrow. 'Yes, I've got your service file in here too; I had it sent up to me by secure fax this morning. I've got Michael's as well, of course. They tell me that the two of you served together in Honduras; you were a company commander in the Scots Guards, and he was a lieutenant in the Sappers. When you went out on patrol, he and his guys would often go with you, in case something needed blowing up.'

The policeman paused; a corner of his mouth flicked upwards, a strange gesture. When he spoke again there was a catch in his voice. 'There was so much I never knew about my brother, Candela, because I never asked. I did as my father wanted and I left him to live out the rest of his life away from me; at first because I couldn't trust myself near him, then eventually because I didn't see the point of reminding him of the old hatred between us. Rodney Windows . . . in case you don't know him either, he's one of your partners in Candela and Finch . . . sent me reports on him every year, but that was all I ever knew about him.

'When I read his army file this morning, though, I found out a hell of a lot. For example, he was some sort of a fucking genius at demolition. You guys were on special ops down there, weren't you? He wasn't there just to clear fallen palm trees in the jungle. You were setting traps for the insurgents, booby-trapping their supply dumps, setting remote devices in their villages, all sorts of brutal stuff that never got reported anywhere. Mike was so good at it that for a while your CO and his turned a blind eye to his drinking. Until the fire-fight incident, that is.'

Skinner held up the Jiffy bag and took a single step towards the other man. 'It really is all in here, Candela; everything, including the answer to something that's always niggled me. When my father eventually told me about Michael's discharge from the army; he said that he was spared prosecution for manslaughter because of my dad's own military record. If he told me that, then that's what he believed, but as a policeman I always doubted it. And I was right. The two guys who were killed were shot by his weapon, all right, but there was no evidence of him actually firing it. More than that, some of his guys, the other Royal Engineer lads with the unit, testified that when you ambushed those rebels and the fire-fight happened he was so cross-eyed drunk that he couldn't have fired anything. They said that he wasn't even there; he was flat on his back at your camp in the jungle.'

The policeman took another step towards Candela. 'Then there's this; the two guys who were killed had duties with the quartermaster's unit. There had been major stock discrepancies from that unit in the days leading up to the incident. You had orders to arrest those two guys and hold them for military police questioning as soon as you got back from that mission. And those orders were confidential; only you knew about them. No one could prove anything about you either, of course. The engagement happened in the dark, and friendly fire incidents do happen. But still . . .'

He paused. 'So you resigned your commission, revived the law degree you'd put on ice, and went into the family firm, a year ahead of schedule. Mike resigned his too, and came back to Motherwell to become a piss-artist, until finally he got out of control, I tried to batter his brains out, and he had to be put away.

'And you knew about that, of course. My father set up the trust that looked after him through your firm, rather than use his own. He did it for the sake of confidentiality, but it backfired on him. You found out, and naturally, you didn't forget.'

He tossed the envelope on to a chair. 'All information is useful, isn't it, Candela? It's my stock in trade; I take pieces of information and use them to build models; of events, scenes, crimes. My officers down in Edinburgh, and one in particular, has done a bloody good job on you over the last week. He worked out that the fire in the Academy was a scam, and from there it was a short step to Tubau Gordon. Once he got in there, and he looked at the circumstances of that fire, at where and when it was started, your name jumped out at him. When he was told about the thirty-million-pound loss that's been uncovered since, your motive, and your guilt, became self-evident.'

Skinner smiled. 'That's as far as he could go, though, poor lad; that's all the information he had, so the model he could build with it only shows how fucking clever you've been. Giving us the girl might have been risky, only it wasn't, because of the way you set her up. It's funny, setting up Andrea was much the same as you did in the jungle . . . when you used someone else's weapon and left him to take the blame.'

For a moment Candela relaxed, but only until Skinner took another step towards him. 'Ah, but I've got more knowledge, though. I can build the model a bit higher. Looking at the timings involved, I know that when you realised that you had lost the biggest and most exciting gamble of your life, and that you were about to be exposed, arrested, disgraced and all that stuff, you thought of my poor brother. After all these years, maybe he'd prove useful again. So you checked that he was still in Oak Lodge, and you got in touch with him.

'I can almost hear the conversation, you know. At some point you established that Mike still had his skills . . . I knew that myself from something Aidan told me . . . and then you invited him to your place in the country. Once he was here, you told him what you wanted him to do.'

Skinner sighed. 'I hope he didn't agree just like that; I'd prefer to believe that he didn't. So how did you force him, I wonder? Did you really beat him with a hammer? Was it you who put those marks on his body, not some drunken fall? Or did you torture him by filling him full of drink and then depriving him of it, until he did what you wanted, and built you a device to trigger the fire in the painting, and another one for the computer, undetectable because everyone, even the experts, would think it was part of it?'

He saw Candela's eyes narrow, very slightly. 'Yes, that was it, wasn't it.' He nodded. 'Know what I think Mike did? I reckon he made a device that would blow out the fuses of the computer and cause a big power surge that would start a massive electrical fire, then he showed you where to install it within the computer, and how to set it as a timer. The security records show that you went into Tubau Gordon on Thursday evening, less than two days before the fire. I suppose you did it then. It worked, too; I've seen the reports. The heat was so intense that there was nothing identifiable left; a nuclear explosion couldn't have done more. Score one for Michael.'

He stared at Candela; his pretence of amiability was gone. 'So?' he hissed. 'How did my brother die?'

'He had a heart attack,' said the lawyer, 'simple as that. We had dinner here, he got drunk as usual, and he fell down dead. Naturally, I didn't

want him found here, so I gave him to the river, at the foot of the garden.'
He gave the policeman a look of pure contempt.

'And that's all I'm telling you.'

'You don't have to tell me any more. I know everything now.'

'And much good may it do you, Mr Skinner. You still don't have a case you can take to court. There's no forensic evidence, Michael's dead, and you cannot prove, nor will you ever, that I was responsible for one penny of that loss.'

'You're really not much of a fucking lawyer, are you,' said the DCC. 'Superintendent Rose and Inspector Steele of my staff are, even as I stand here, working overtime putting together a report for the Crown Office. Tomorrow morning they will present it to the Lord Advocate, in person. It's touch and go, but you're a betting man, Mr Candela. Knowing how the LA feels about bent lawyers, would you lay a tenner against him taking you before a jury?'

'He'd never get a conviction.'

'No?'

'Not one that would stand up at appeal.'

'Does that matter? As soon as they get a warrant for your arrest, Maggie Rose and Steven Steele will pick you up, either here or in Edinburgh. I'd like it if they were able to huckle you out of your office, actually. That would be nice.'

'I'd still be acquitted though.'

'You'll be ruined too.'

'Don't you believe it.'

The policeman let out an explosive, brutal laugh. 'You don't get it, do you, Candela? This is personal. Whether you killed him or not, you took Michael away from somewhere he was happy, and you forced him back into his past, to do your will. You used him one last time, and then you just threw him away. Listen, I'm under no illusions. My brother was little short of a beast as a young man; he was a drunken, sadistic thug. But somewhere along the line, with help from the good Brother Aidan, he found the good within him, and he lived a contented, if unfulfilled life.

'Then you came along and took him away from it. And you did worse; you treated him like a dog, before and after he was dead.'

307

Skinner's eyes were chilling as he looked at the lawyer. Finally, fear showed on Candela's face. 'Suppose you do walk away from your so-called perfect crime, you're still going to account for it in public and for the rest of a life which I hope, if you have any sense, will be very short.

'You're going to be a pariah, Candela, a social outcast. If necessary, our report to the fiscal will be, regrettably, leaked to the media. You think no one will use it? Ultimately, we might not have enough for a criminal conviction, but a civil jury would be pretty certain to find against you, should you choose to sue for defamation . . . especially as you couldn't offer any defence, since you're guilty as fucking sin.' He picked up the envelope. 'If you don't believe me, ask my daughter, like I did; she's a bloody sight better lawyer than you ever have been, or ever will be.'

'But leaking that report would end your own career,' the man whispered.

'Don't be stupid. It would never be traced back to me. Don't you have any idea of what I can do?'

He started for the door. 'Think about it, Candela. There's about a twenty per cent chance you're going to prison. But there's a one hundred per cent certainty you'll be disgraced. Plus, you'll have me on your back for the rest of your life.'

He glanced around the distinguished room. 'This place must have a library. And, gun control or not, you've probably got a pearl-handled revolver lying about somewhere.

'Ask yourself this,' said Bob Skinner, as he left. 'What's expected of a real gentleman in your situation?'

64

He glanced around his drawing room. 'Did you ever fancy oak panelling in here?' he asked.

'Certainly not!' Sarah replied. 'Much too old-fashioned. What brought that on?'

'Ah, nothing,' said Bob. 'You're right; that sort of stuff belongs to another era.'

'I should think so.' She turned back to the *Scotsman*, and to the front page story. 'Will this man Candela be convicted?'

'There's a chance. He's remanded on bail, so we have as long as we like, within reason, to complete a case. We've got a search warrant for his place in Perthshire and his flat in Edinburgh. We might just find some supporting evidence; even if it's only wire that matches the material used on the Academy fire-bomb, it could turn a possibility into a probability.

'I'm still hoping for another outcome, though.'

'A guilty plea, do you mean?'

'Yeah, something like that.' He pressed the button of the television remote, and turned on *A Question of Sport*.

'Do you know yet when Michael's funeral will be?' she asked.

'I'll hear from the undertaker tomorrow, but I think it'll be next Tuesday. He'll be cremated in Gourock; Brother Aidan will take the service. That'll suit all his friends through there. Afterwards, his ashes will be interred beside my mother and father, in the cemetery in Motherwell.'

'That's good. Appropriate. Will you go?'

'Of course. And you, if you want.'

'That's good too. Of course I'll come.' She paused. 'Speaking of funerals,' she continued. 'I had a call from Babs today, the bitch that she

309

is. She said that Ron's mother's arrived in Buffalo, and that she's planning to hold his service on Saturday week, once the DA's office has released his body.'

He looked at her, frowned, and shook his head. 'Don't even think about it,' he said.